SICK

Jay R. Bonansinga

WARNER BOOKS

A Time Warner Company

NOTE

This is a work of fiction. The names, characters, places, details, and incidents are either the product of the author's imagination or are actual facts that are used in a completely fictitious context.

WARNER BOOKS EDITION

Copyright © 1995 by Jay R. Bonansinga
All rights reserved.

Cover design by Diane Luger and Tony Greco
Cover photograph by David McGlynn

Warner Books, Inc
1271 Avenue of the Americas
New York, NY 10020

 A Time Warner Company

Printed in the United States of America

First Printing: September, 1995

10 9 8 7 6 5 4 3 2 1

HE SHOOK OFF THE SHOCK . . .

♦♦♦

Frank caught his breath and struggled back to his feet. He was in a world of death now, death as black as ink. A world of twisted bundles of flesh, and whimpering sounds of traumatized little boys, and a shadowy figure shrinking up into the ceiling. A world where cops forgot they were cops, and bad guys were magic, and the whole damn thing unraveled in explosions of blood red thread. . . .

YOU'LL LOVE *SICK*

♦♦♦

"*SICK* IS ENDLESSLY INVENTIVE, WITH A STUNNINGLY ORIGINAL PREMISE, and secrets upon secrets that keep unfolding like the petals of a black rose."
—**Brian Hodge, author of *Nightlife* and *The Darker Saints***

♦

"WHAT A RIDE! *SICK* IS A DARK AND COMPELLING STORY, BRILLIANTLY TOLD, that explores new depths of psychological terror and suspense. Hold on to your seats, folks. This one is going to take you to places you've never been to—or imagined." —**Rick Hautala, author of *Winter Wakes* and *Shades of Night***

♦

"A ROLLER COASTER OF A SUSPENSE NOVEL! The terror and excitement build relentlessly from the very first page [of] this nerve-wracking thriller."
—**Matthew Costello, author of *See How She Runs***

♦

"A HARD-EDGE TALE OF SUSPENSE AND OBSESSION. This novel dazzles and disturbs with its sharp images and in-your-face plot." —**Thomas F. Monteleone, author of *The Resurrectionist***

Also By Jay R. Bonansinga

The Black Mariah

Published by
WARNER BOOKS

Dedicated to Roger Bardwell (1925-1994) :
Teacher, Friend, Hero

AUTHOR'S ACKNOWLEDGMENT

Lots of love and gratitude for invaluable assistance, wisdom, and friendship: Treva Bachand, Jeanne M. Bonansinga, Peter Miller, Jennifer Robinson, the folks at PMA Film and Literary Management, Hank Jenkins, Harry Jaffe M.D., John Delmerico, David A. Johnson, Tina Jens, Ben Adams, Bob and Phyllis Weinberg, Anthony Schneider, Alice Bently and the Stars Our Destination, Paul Rubenstein, Brad and Angie Throop, Michael Stein, Ted Okuda, Bruce Ingram, Benjamin Adams, Airyanne Ward, Norman Pokorny, Peggy Nadramia, Peter Grunwald, George and Chris Romero, Mary Curry, Shunta Curry, Ruth Greenthal Ph.D., Erik Stein, Jimmy Franco, Bob Garcia, Tod Bonansinga, Jeb Bonansinga, Sully Bonansinga, and Diane Bonansinga. A special thank-you to the following authors for their unique bodies of work that both informed and inspired this tale: Karen Osney-Brownstein, Thomas Harris, Josh and Marcia Friedman, H. P. Lovecraft, David Simon, Harlan Ellison, Jeanne Achterberg, William Goldman, Raymond Fitzsimons, and Candice Pert. And last but not least, a very special thank-you to my god-like editor, Mauro DiPreta; keep on pushing me, my man, it works!

PART I

The Box

The mouse of Thought infests my head,
He knows my cupboard and the crumb.
Vermin! I despise vermin.

—E. B. White
"Vermin"

Word begets image and image is virus.

—William Burroughs
Naked Lunch

People can die of mere imagination.

—Chaucer
The Miller's Tale

1

Pin-Up Girl

I

"Let's get down to business, shall we?" The HMO specialist smiled as he took a seat behind his massive desk. His name was Calloway. Tanned, fit, head full of Kennedyesque blow-dried hair, he sat forward on his swivel with the relentless sincerity of a camp counselor. "What makes you think you need a neurologist?"

"Been having dizzy spells," Sarah replied, feeling exceedingly claustrophobic inside the airless little office. "And headaches, too—migraines." She thought about it for a moment. "Really nasty ones."

The neurosurgeon nodded. "That's no fun. That's no fun at all." He glanced down at Sarah's file for a moment.

Sarah waited.

They were huddled in a corner room with mini-blinds drawn over the windows to shut out the institutional feel of the hospital courtyard outside. The neurologist's desk was center stage. The surrounding walls were covered with an assortment of framed certificates and innocuous landscape paintings. A little too innocuous, Sarah thought wryly: The place reminded her of a brand-new Howard Johnson.

Sarah Brandis was sitting in a somber little chair canted off one corner of the desk. Hands folded in her lap, expression fixed, she appeared to be carrying all of her forty-one years. She wore a conservative wrap-front skirt, cowboy boots, and a baggy aubergine cardigan. Negligible makeup accented her deeply lined eyes. Her dark hair, which was veined with iron gray, was pulled back into a French braid. Everything was purposefully modest. Muted. She didn't want anything to distract from the grim proceedings. Nevertheless, a careful eye could still discern an exceptional form beneath the demure garb.

The one word that best described Sarah's statuesque figure—the same word, in fact, that several of her friends had adopted over the years in describing Sarah's own disposition—was *generous*. Sarah had generous hips. Roomy thighs. Even her face was physically generous, round, with the wide plush lips and aquiline nose of her late French-Canadian mother. But the true fulcrum of Sarah's physique was her bosom. Inherited from her grandmother Nina, straining the girth of her sweater like twin hillocks, Sarah's breasts were emblems of her soul. As though her charitable heart had literally expanded out through her chest.

These assets had taken their toll. From the moment she had sprouted into womanhood during the summer of 1966, she had thought of her breasts as hideous deformities. By the eighth grade, they had swollen into full C-cups. This wreaked havoc with her ballet lines. Her pliés and arabesques were for-shit. Running and climbing trees and playing Red Rover quickly became problematic, if not impossible. By the time she was a senior in high school, she'd been tagged a slut. For no good reason other than her zaftig figure. But, over time, Sarah had learned to exploit the attribute, like the character actor who learns to use a physical impediment as dramatic texture.

"Says here you've been taking antidepressants," Calloway said without looking up from the file.

"Yes." Sarah didn't blink, just kept gazing evenly at the well-dressed medico.

"Currently taking them?"

"Yeah," she replied quickly, not wanting to get into her troubled past, her bouts with depression, her occasional forays into the mental health system, or her current tenuous hold on reality. She was starting to get a bad feeling about where this interview was headed, and she wanted to cut to the chase before the fear ate her alive. "I'm taking four hundred milligrams of Desyrel per day," she added. "Have been for several years."

"Any side effects?"

"Uh . . . other than a little drowsiness and a dry mouth . . . not really."

"So you've had no other symptoms?"

"No," Sarah replied, and clasped her hands as though she were praying.

"Nausea? Vomiting?"

"No."

"Blurred vision?"

"Nope."

"Fainting?"

"No."

"Loss of balance?"

"Like I told you, it's just the dizzy spells and the headaches, which, at first, I figured must be due to the Desyrel, but then my regular doctor—"

"Steve Mulder?"

"—yeah, Dr. Mulder, he did an EEG and took some X rays and thought I should come see you."

"All right, fair enough." Calloway paused to write something in his file. He looked up and smiled. "I understand you're a dancer?"

"Not really . . . I mean . . . it's more like performance art. . . ." She was stammering now, taken by surprise. It was another personal detail toward which she preferred discretion. Not that she was ashamed of being an exotic dancer; on the contrary, the art of stripping had grown on her. Her dreams of being a prima ballerina long ago compromised, she had learned to appreciate the power of being up there on the runway in front of an audience of lonely men. The attention. The control. The nourishing glare of all those hungry eyes. At the moment, however, the subject seemed a little complicated. "It's . . . a long story," she said finally. "I guess I'm just anxious to get your thoughts on the headaches and whatnot."

"That's what we're here for." The doctor rose and came around the desk. "Whattya say we have a look."

For the next fifteen minutes, Calloway conducted a series of tests known in the medical biz as a complete manual neurological exam. To the uninitiated, it would probably seem as though the doctor were an overzealous state trooper checking Sarah's sobriety. He made her walk heel-to-toe without looking at her feet, and then made her touch her nose with the third finger of her left hand. He tickled the base of her feet. He drew a Q-Tip across her closed eyelids. And finally he pulled an ophthalmoscope from his bag and looked very closely into each eye.

It was at this point in the proceedings that the neurologist suddenly paused and made a clicking sound in the base of his throat.

"What is it?" Sarah blinked and felt her stomach fill with ice water.

The doctor put his instrument away and walked around behind his desk. He motioned at Sarah's chair. "You can sit down now," he said.

Sarah sat down and didn't breathe.

"You have major papilledema," he announced, stroking his lovely Hugo Boss floral print tie. "Which means you have a swelling around both optic nerves."

Goose bumps crawled up the backs of her legs. "Which means?"

"Which means there's a pesky little something in your head that shouldn't oughta be in there."

Sarah could barely make her mouth work. "You mean . . . like a tumor?"

The doctor nodded. "That's certainly a possibility. I'd put my money on it. Of course, we can't tell for sure until we get you in here to run a full battery of tests." He pulled a scheduling book from his desk drawer. "I'd like to get you going as soon as possible on a series of arteriograms and MRIs . . . possibly some exploratory surgery. How does Friday sound?"

Sarah stared at the man as though he were speaking a foreign language.

II

New York has its boroughs and bridges and galleries. Los Angeles has its movie studios and palm trees and drive-bys. But Chicago, home of the worst team in baseball and the best pizza in culinary history, has its own inimitable kind of weight, its own brand of thereness, like a great big crescent-shaped barnacle ripening in the cleavage of the Great Lakes. It's the City of Big Shoulders. Hog butcher to the world. It's the Second City, a greasy, teeming enclave of eight million working stiffs just trying to keep Polish sausages on their formica. It's the Windy City—named for the blowhard politicians rather than the actual wind. But alas, during Chicago's nine months of winter, the Hawk does indeed play its keening wail across Lake Shore Drive and Oak Street Beach. Especially in October. The wind is omnivorous in October, licking up your pants, sucking the juice out of your engine, chewing at the flagpoles, the treetops, and the high wires.

On her way to work, the night after her fateful exam, it was this very same October wind that snapped Sarah out of her grief.

She was tooling down Clark Street in her rustbucket Toyota. The tears had started around North Avenue, tracking down her cheeks and dabbing the torn vinyl. By Wells

Street, she was sobbing. Shoulders trembling, lips curled back in a sloppy wail, white knuckles Vise-Gripping the wheel, she had blubbered all the way down to Division. The radio was turned up, sizzling with a symphony of static and country-western, drowning the sound of her own weeping in her ears. All at once, the wind buffeted the roof of the Toyota and Sarah swerved. The car lurched and nearly clipped a garbage can. Sarah sucked in her tears immediately. And she drove the rest of the way in drained silence.

She arrived at Dante's at about quarter to ten and parked in the lot across the street.

Dante's Inferno was unique among strip clubs in Chicago: Somebody had actually put some thought, albeit strange thought, into its design. In fact, the original designer must have been in the latter stages of some syphilitic fever dream because the place was bizarre. The front entrance was framed by a pair of enormous Mick Jagger–like fiberglass lips along the roof and the sidewalk. The mouth seemed especially famished this evening. A pair of small arc lights flanked the lower jaw and shone up into the roof of the mouth, accented by tiny electric blowers fringed with plastic cutout flames. The enormous upper lip was peeling, chips of hot pink paint falling every now and then. The massive fiberglass teeth were the color of wallpaper paste, weathered by years of pollution and carbon. Recessed inside the mouth was a huge black scrim, reinforced by chicken wire.

The door was embedded in this scrim.

Inside, the motif continued. Bisected by a huge island running down its middle, serving as both runway for the dancers and service bar for the gawkers, the place was a scale model of a gigantic, drooling mouth. Side tables were molded and spray-painted to look like huge molars. And the pièce de résistance was the runway itself. Sculpted in pink fiberglass, the twenty-foot-long platform was a colossal tongue.

Sarah strode through the crowded bar. Through the veils of blue smoke. Through a beaded doorway. Down a narrow hallway, and into her dressing room.

She took off her clothes, threw on a tattered kimono, and started putting herself together. She refused to buckle under to the fear. The show must go on, she kept thinking. Isn't that what Judy Garland would say? Sarah started with a Cover Girl soft focus around her tired eyes. Rosewood tan. Nothing more. Her skin tone was so dark she didn't even need a base. Next came the liner. She preferred Deep Black Diamond from Quintessence. Under the lights it looked great, and the company didn't test on animals, which was always a big plus. Her lashes were next. Tonight she was using Stay-Put Riviera cocktail lashes. Finally she painted her lips with Artmatic Liquid Plus in fuchsia fire, ignoring the delicate little wrinkles around the corners of her mouth—*God, she hated those wrinkles*. She leaned back and regarded her image in the mirror.

"Close enough for summer stock," she murmured.

She stood up, removed her robe, and threw it over the back of the chair. In the harsh light her olive skin looked bruised and rashed. Her cellulite was spreading, across the expanding rolls of her tummy, along the fleshy underside of her thighs. *Saddlebags,* she thought *goddamn saddlebags*. The tattoos only served to heighten the world-weary quality. The first one dated back to her eighteenth birthday. A friend had taken her to a little parlor down on the South Side. She had gotten a tiny scorpion on her right thigh. Others followed, marking various passages in her life. The sacred hearts on both sides of her buttocks marked her long delayed breakup with one of her early boyfriends. The tiny moon and stars on her left shoulder marked her first public performance.

She went over to the battered metal armoire and selected her costume. Tonight was Josef von Sternberg Night. She drug out the whole shebang—the garter belt, black seamed stockings, tux jacket, top hat, and cane. *The Blue Angel* was one of Sarah's favorite movies. She had first seen it heavily edited on TV years ago; but later, after viewing the film on cassette, Sarah fell in love with the dreamy eroticism, Dietrich's dominatrix-chic, and the surreal design. Sarah adored musicals, especially golden-age Hollywood musicals. The Technicolor escape of her childhood was etched indelibly in her subconscious, every flickering moment, every sumptuous Vincente Minnelli dance number, every twist of Fred and Ginger's feet.

Across the room came a soft knocking. "Sweetheart? You almost ready?"

Sarah turned toward the door. "Come in, Duff."

A barrel-chested troll in a polyester blazer named Duff Sellars stuck his head in the room. "Stage is set," he told her. "Ready when you are."

A sixtyish man with a stocky neck and a bald head shaped like a missile, Duff was the manager. He'd been working at the club for as long as Sarah had been dancing there. Nearly twelve years now. His superiors were a shadowy little consortium of sleazoid entrepreneurs with vague connections to the Sabatini crime family. But Duff Sellars wasn't part of that world. Duff was pure show people. Weaned as an advance man for Ringling Brothers Circus, he treated stripping as though it were still some noble form of vaudeville. Duff had become a Dutch uncle to Sarah, worrying over her health, her failed relationships, even her vitamin intake. Fact was, Duff loved the big-boned gal.

"On my way," she said, securing her hat with a bobby pin and starting toward the door.

Duff followed her into the hallway. "Uh . . . listen, sweetheart . . . we gotta talk."

"Yeah? Okay—shoot." Sarah was heading through the dim light toward the stage doors. She hadn't told Duff about her health problems and wasn't about to get into it now. The sound of the band was vibrating fuzzily through the floor. They were playing an acid house vamp. She heard the thump of a bass line, the scratch of the turntables, the buzz of the tube amps, and muffled voices. The little boys were getting restless and her migraine was returning.

"Had a meeting with the firm last night," Duff said as they

approached the stage steps. The *firm* referred to the owners and their oily little legal practice. Duff always hated such meetings. Always bad news.

"And?" Sarah looked at him.

"They're coming down on me about the squirt guns."

Sarah rolled her eyes. "Drunken Teamsters shooting Kool-Aid at me through plastic Uzis is not my idea of entertainment."

"I hear ya, kiddo, I agree, but what am I gonna do? It's a sign of the times, I dunno. But it's just the beginning."

"What are you saying, Duff?"

"What I'm saying is, there's a whole slew of changes coming down from the top."

"Changes."

"That's correct, and I don't want to see you get caught in the crossfire."

"What kind of changes, Duff?"

Duff shrugged. "You know how it is."

There was a long silence, and Sarah stood in front of the iron stage doors, listening to the muffled thudding of her theme song, gathering her bearings. The pain was in her head again. It was a rusty bottle opener under the ridge of her brow, yanking upward in fits and jerks. It popped electric blue in her mind, and made her nose and eyes water. It was like someone trying to open her skull. "You don't think," Sarah started to say, "they would . . . ?"

Duff looked deeply into her eyes. "Think about the squirt guns, sweetheart. Will ya do that for me?"

Sarah kissed his forehead, walked up the steps, pushed open the stage doors, and walked onstage.

The wall of sound was waiting. The synth bass drum machine was rattling the foundation. Crackling turntables ripped through the smoke. The follow spots converged on her, light exploding in her face, changing colors to the thunder beat of the music. Red *beat* orange *beat* yellow *beat* blue. Sarah sauntered across the runway in her best Dietrich stride.

The accountant was waiting for her at one end of the bar.

The one she called Mister Peepers. Perched on a stool, thick glasses upturned and gleaming, the skinny little man was a regular. He worshiped Sarah and always managed to scrape together an extra twenty bucks on Tuesday nights just to have Sarah come to his table and kibitz about annuities and treasury bills. A few years ago, Sarah learned that Mister Peepers had once been a seminary student and was drummed out of the church on a trumped-up morals charge. Something about a young altar boy. But Sarah didn't mind; Mister Peepers was like all the other regulars—deep down, just a frightened little boy, terrified yet entranced by a woman's sexuality.

Catcalls washed over the stage like a wave.

Sarah found a tiny fountain chair waiting for her and propped her left spike heel on it. The flash of her crotch coaxed another wave of hyena hollers from the boys. Sarah played with herself to the beat of the music. Samples of Dietrich's voice gusted through the grunge. *Falling in love again! Fah-fah-fah-falling in looooove again!* Sarah tossed off her hat, threw it out to sea, peeled off her coat. The revelation of her majestic cleavage goosed the crowd into a frenzy. Dozens of hungry eyes, wide as wet marbles.

Sarah danced. Sashayed. Waltzed. Spun. Imagined scenes from Busby Berkeley wonders. Imagined chorus lines from Esther Williams movies. But it was difficult tonight, difficult as hell. The pain was a palpable thing now. A worm in her forehead, writhing in rhythm with the grind, wriggling through her brain, throbbing behind her eyes, making her sweat, throbbing, throbbing unmercifully.

Sarah unsnapped her bra and freed her breasts.

In the darkness the little boys clamored.

They were out in full force tonight, gathered at round tables behind Mister Peepers. The Twins were there: two enormous, bearded bikers with identical bellies and chain-mail vests. The Straw-Sucker sat nearby, a spindly blond college kid who perpetually nursed a rum and Coke during Sarah's routines. On the other side of the runway stood Mumbles, a fidgety, balding businessman who constantly whispered God knows what under his breath while he watched. And the others, nameless fraternity kids, greasy-fingered mechanics, and jittery drifters. Little boys all. Frightened, lonely, needy little boys.

Sarah navigated the runway. Bathed in blue light, glistening, she ran fingertips up and down her thighs. She unsnapped her garter belt and tore it away. The sad little hyenas answered. Sarah kept dancing, imagining Gene Kelly hopping over tiny little sailor boys. Tom and Jerry dressed in navy whites. Darling little choreographed steps. Spinning in a sea of magenta fire, reveling in the waves of attention and love and desire . . . .

Something was wrong.

At first, it was just a subtle little glitch. A minor twitch during a particularly elegant twirl. But before Sarah knew what was happening, she had broken stride. It occurred with a suddenness that was almost jarring. She had stumbled. And it was all because of the look in their eyes.

They were watching in such an unusual way tonight, their eyes fixed on—of all things—Sarah's face. And heading back toward the curtain for her big finish, Sarah wondered what the hell was going on. Music thrumming and thundering climactically, feedback crashing in her ears, she snapped off her G-string and tossed it overboard.

The hungry eyes soaked her up.

And then it was over, and Sarah was halfway back to her dressing room, passing a cracked mirror, before she realized just exactly what they were staring at. They were staring at her runny mascara.

The dirty tears in the corners of her eyes.

III

Somebody was buzzing.

"Hold your horses, I'm coming," Sarah muttered on her way across her cluttered living room. It was nearly noon on

Thursday, the day before she was due to check into the hospital for her tests, and she was still in her robe. She sidestepped Gypsy, her obese cat, and padded across the hardwood landing to the front door. "Hello?" she said into the intercom.

"Where the hell you been?" The voice crackled through the plastic speaker, shrill and funky. It was Maxine. Fellow stripper, Hispanic-black and proud of it, repository of half the silicone in the Western world. Maxine was Sarah's best buddy; and best buddies weren't easy to come by in a world full of transient friends and false promises.

"Maxie?" Sarah winced.

"Well, it ain't Aunt Jemima."

"What are you doing here?"

"That's a fine way to treat a friend. . . . You can just eat shit and die yourself."

Sarah smiled wearily and pressed the IN button. "C'mon up."

A moment later, Maxine was standing on the threshold. A rail-thin woman with caramel skin, enhanced bust, and magnificent dreadlocks, she wore a black leather jacket over torn leopard leotards. Every conceivable extremity of her sleek body was pierced. There were dozens of gold rings in each ear, studs in her nose, a loop in her lower lip, and even a silver safety pin through the webbing of her left hand. It was common knowledge to most patrons of Dante's that Maxine was pierced in many of her private areas as well.

As a fellow dancer, Maxine had hit it off with Sarah immediately, especially after learning of Sarah's background in ballet. Raised in the Detroit ghetto, Maxine had worked her way out of poverty as a cosmetologist. For years, she had toiled in night school, studying theatrical makeup and dreaming of being a big-time makeup artist. Hard times and an unexpected pregnancy had put the temporary kibosh on Maxine's career; but she hadn't lost her dreams.

Sarah had long ago grown accustomed to the high levels of education among exotic dancers. These weren't the stereotypical bimbettes with as much plastic in their brains as their implants; many of these women were fringe bohemian types with useless degrees or frustrated family lives. In fact, this made the whole skin trade all the more interesting.

Sarah kissed Maxine on the nose. "I'm sort of under the weather today."

"Girl, you been under the weather all week."

"I know," Sarah rubbed her eyes. She was tired of crying, tired of hurting. She was, to put it mildly, plumb tuckered out. But fear was the world's most potent amphetamine. "Come on in," she said, turning back toward the kitchen. "I'll get you a cup of mud."

"No, thanks, just passing through." Maxine glanced around the messy flat. "On my way down to Grant Park. Gonna kick it with some folks at the Blues Fest, thought you might come along."

Sarah sighed. "I don't think so, not today."

"What is going down with you, girl?"

"Nothing—what do you mean?"

Maxine gestured at the room. "Hiding out in this sad-ass apartment. Can't even answer the phone. Living like some sort of motherfuckin' hermit all of a sudden."

Sarah glanced across the living room.

The apartment was a typical Chicago crackerbox. A narrow rectangle of moldering plaster, stained hardwood, and secondhand furniture. Every available inch of wall was covered with lobby cards and movie posters. *Guys and Dolls* hung over a cheap particle-board bookshelf. *Singing in the Rain* and *On the Town* were mounted above the rusty kitchen sink. *Ice Capades, 42nd Street,* and *Pin-Up Girl* were arranged along the back of the broken-down sofa. And dozens of old, campy glamour photos bordered the east windows: Judy Garland, Bert Lahr, Ginger Rogers, Ann Miller, Gene Kelly, and Cyd Charisse.

Sarah went over to the window and gazed out at the overcast morning. "Guess I got a little bit of the blues myself," she murmured.

Maxine came over and put a hand on Sarah's shoulder. "You need somebody to talk to?"

Sarah turned and faced her friend. "Go do your thing, Maxie—I wouldn't be any fun today anyway."

"You sure you want to be alone?"

Sarah gazed back out the window, the sudden uncomfortable silence a reminder of her tumultuous past. Maxine knew a little bit about Sarah's days in the psych ward down at Cook County, her severe bouts of depression, the suicide attempt in her late twenties. At one point, Sarah had even revealed to her friend the long vertical scar on the inside of her wrist, and the one she kept disguised with pancake makeup. But nobody—absolutely nobody—knew about Sarah's work with Henry Decker.

Or the imaginary box.

It had started in the winter of 1980. With both of her parents dead and gone, and no job, Sarah had been picked up in a drunken stupor near Buckingham Fountain, still dressed in her soiled Danskins after a disastrous audition. She was placed in a group home on the northwest side. And it was there, at the Shales House, that Sarah had met a progressive young therapist and Ph.D. candidate named Henry Decker. Henry was a casual man, big and robust, a former all-American center for the University of Illinois. He took an instant liking to Sarah. And the feeling had been mutual. They would work for hours on Sarah's pain, her thinly veiled rage at her abusive mother, and her mysterious, repressed guilt—guilt for some nameless act, so corrosive that it was literally devouring Sarah from the inside out. The solution was a very simple mental device to deal with all the angst and pain.

A box.

Henry had first encountered the technique of visualization after reading a fascinating paper on self-hypnosis. He had described the process to Sarah, and Sarah had instantly responded to the idea, latching on to the visual angle like a fish taking a hook. Sarah started imagining a tiny little box in her head. Like a jewelry box, only sturdier, with a strong lock.

And into this box Sarah locked up all her pain and rage and guilt. All the malignant, crippling, venomous crap. Locked it up tight. Forever and ever. Sealed in that little box.

The device had worked liked a charm. Sarah had instantly improved, and within a month she was well enough to move out of the Shales House and get a job and start her life over again. She kept in touch with Henry Decker for several years, and to this day, she still received an occasional birthday note or Christmas card from the man.

Of course, the box was still inside her somewhere, sealed up like some forgotten bank vault.

"I'm fine, Maxie—really," Sarah finally said after whirling away from the window. "You go and do."

"You sure?"

"Absolutely."

"Okay . . . but don't say I didn't try." Maxine shrugged and turned to leave, then paused in the doorway. "Girl, if you got any need to call and talk about anything—I'm a push button away. You hear what I'm saying?"

Sarah nodded.

Maxine took a deep breath and then walked out.

IV

It was in his face.

Sarah could tell the moment that Calloway greeted her and ushered her into his office, sitting next to her on the corner divan: Bad news was on the way. It was written all over his face. In the sheepish way he offered her coffee without fully making eye contact. In the way he picked lint from his Hartmarx slacks before getting to the point. And mostly in the way he looked at her.

Like Christ gazing at a leper.

"We've got some things to talk about," he said in a measured tone.

Sarah could only utter, "All right."

"Before I get into specifics," he began, "I'd just like to assure you that we've left no stone unturned here. Over the last week and a half, you've been through the most comprehensive series of neurological and diagnostic tests available anywhere. Our technology here at Northwestern is state-of-the-art. And although we encourage second opinions, we stand by our record of unprecedented consistency."

It sounded rehearsed, and it was also a pitifully insufficient description of the tortures to which Sarah had been subjected over the last ten days.

First, there had been the sadistic series of scans in the basement labs. The MRI and the CAT scan, and still more EEGs. But they were nothing compared to the final torment: They called it an arteriogram. Sarah referred to it as the worst pain inflicted by one person upon another in the history of the known universe.

It had happened three days ago. Due to the MRI being inconclusive, Sarah was forced to spend the night at Northwestern for this last-resort test. And more than anything else it had focused all her fears like rays of sunlight refracted through a magnifying glass into one single pinpoint of white-hot pain. In a sterile dungeon under the neurology ward, they had unceremoniously razored her hairline back a couple of centimeters, shaved her pubic hair bald as an infant's cheek, and rolled her under an X-ray arm. Then they shoved a needle catheter up her femoral artery just above her groin and started threading—upward, upward, upward—through her heart, through her jugular, and up into her brain. It wasn't exactly painful. Painful is the wrong word. *Violated* is how Sarah felt.

Then they injected the dye. She had instinctively opened her mouth to scream, but no sound had come out. Only tears. Only spontaneous tears flowing down her face into the fabric of her hospital gown. Sarah had thought for sure—no, scratch that, she had known beyond all doubt—that she was going to die right then and there. The pressure had been enormous, gargantuan. It had felt as though a land mine had exploded behind her eyes. Midway through the test, however, she had mercifully passed out.

"Listen, I appreciate your confidence," Sarah finally managed to say, interrupting the flow of Calloway's infomercial. "But I've been through the mill with these tests, and it's about time I got some answers."

The doctor nodded dutifully, stood up, and went over to the door. Evidently he had left it ajar when he arrived, probably out of habit, and now he seemed to prefer a modicum of privacy. He carefully pulled it shut until it latched.

This all frightened the hell out of Sarah. It wasn't exactly the dread of hearing the inevitable bad news. It wasn't even the gravity of her situation. It was the waiting. The *not-knowing*. And in the last couple of days, it had gotten so bad that Sarah had started to imagine the box again. That ornate little box in which she had locked away her fears and her pain. It was amazing how crystalline this imaginary box had remained in her memory. She could still see its shape, its weight, and its color, with vivid clarity. It was roughly the size of a cinder block, walnut brown, its impermeable wooden sides and brass fittings tarnished with a patina of age. And the ancient Yale lock clasping its lid was congealed with rust.

Secure as a tree trunk.

And now she had a whole new load of pain to put in it.

"So, whattya say, Doc?" she finally said. "Am I dead meat or what?"

After a heartbeat of silence, Calloway looked her square in the eye and said, "Yes, Sarah, you have a growth."

Silence.

Hearing the verdict wasn't the shocker Sarah thought it would be. She expected a stabbing pain in the heart, a loss of breath, a faintness, maybe even nausea. She had visions of puking all over the neurologist's brushed suede Pierre Cardin loafers. She thought it would be hellish. But in fact, it was actually somewhere between hellish and a relief. As though she were finally turning a page in her life and starting a new chapter. For better or for worse, the clockwork had turned. And after a moment's thought, she looked at him and said, "A growth?"

"A level-four tumor rooted in the occipital lobe."

"Hmm."

Sarah didn't know whether to scream or cry or pound her hands on the armrests, the neurologist's manner was so measured, so goddamned stoic. All at once Sarah found herself wondering whether this whole thing was her fault after all. All her childhood fears, her phobias, her superstitions, all the drug-induced ruminations throughout her twenties and thirties—they all came flooding back on one great nauseous wave. It was a primal fear that there was something different about her, something about her brain. The way she could make herself sick just by thinking about it. The way her nightmares used to cause outbreaks of acne, and rashes, and new oddly shaped moles on her body. The way her moods had always coalesced into weird pains, or strange injuries, or birthmarks she never knew she had. She had locked all those fears safely away in the box. But what if . . .

She glanced up and noticed Dr. Calloway was rubbing his mouth uneasily, as though he were trying to verbalize something.

"What is it?" Sarah asked. "What's wrong?"

Calloway looked over at her file for a moment. "Ordinarily, we would recommend immediate surgery for a growth this substantial," he said, his eyes averted. "Unfortunately, due to the anomalous shape and the . . . *rootedness* of the tumor . . . our best course of treatment would be cobalt radiation therapy."

The room started to go all milky and unfocused for Sarah. She swallowed broken glass and said, "What do you mean, the anomalous shape?"

"The tumor is buried deep in the ganglia, and it has a distinctive shape."

"What do you mean by distinctive?"

"It's a shape we haven't seen before."

She blinked. "Meaning what?"

"It's . . . well . . . here, let me show you one of the scans."

He got up and walked around behind his desk. He found a thick, salmon-colored Pendaflex file brimming with X rays. He rifled through the X rays and found the one he liked. Then he returned to the divan and showed it to Sarah.

"I assume this is my brain." Sarah stared at the milky image.

"That's right." The doctor pointed his manicured pinky nail at a large white blemish in the heart of the X ray. "See this? This is your occipital lobe."

Sarah began to get goose bumps. "Yeah?"

"This mark here is the tumor, the occipitaloma rooted in the core of the lobe."

Sarah's heart turned to stone.

"As you can see, it's quite large and has an unusual shape, and the problem is, the tumor is so engaged with the rest of your occipital lobe that if we attempted a craniotomy, even with our sophisticated lasers, we would damage too much of the surrounding ganglia, thus risking loss of visual functions and possibly other sensory apparatus. . . ."

His voice was beginning to drone, melting into incomprehensible babble.

Sarah wasn't listening anymore; she was too busy staring at the scan, the Day-Glo swirls and filigrees, and the large white blemish in the center of the picture. The tumor was anything but strange to her.

Its shape was horridly familiar.

2

Not in Kansas Anymore

I

One of the oldest communities on the north shore of Lake Michigan—Evanston, Illinois—was an enigma. Two parts suburb to one part city. Amid enclaves of ancient trees, manicured lawns, and stately Victorian homes, the noisy elevated train cut a five-mile swath through the town like a greasy tattoo. Upscale restaurants and L. L. Bean distributors competed with funky corner newsstands and pawnshops. The national headquarters of the Women's Christian Temperance Union was located here. As were several violent factions of local street gangs. On any given autumn afternoon, platoons of bohemian street musicians competed with flocks of hormonal Northwestern students out cruising for boobs and beer. It was all part of the community's weird rich pageant.

On the east side of town, there was a quiet, tree-lined boulevard bordered by rows of nineteenth-century gaslights and stone park benches. The choppy waters of Lake Michigan were less than a hundred yards away, but a natural rampart of mammoth oak trees kept the street tranquil and sun-dappled. At the far end of the boulevard, where the pavement terminated into a wrought-iron gateway, the Mind-Body Institute stood high and stubborn against the crisp autumn sky.

At the moment, there was a large man in the backyard wrestling with a garbage bag.

"C'mon, you sumbitch," Henry Decker growled at the black plastic bag, his legs ankle-deep in dead leaves. He had just conducted the last session of the day, and now he had the rest of the afternoon to do his chores. A mountainous man, well over six-five, with shoulders like the Deerborn Bridge, he was dressed in old flannel and well-worn logger boots. His once luxuriant mane of sienna hair was flecked with gray, pulled back in a ponytail. His tan, chiseled face was weathering like the bottom of a red clay riverbed.

Henry was approaching his fiftieth birthday and was none too happy about it. Once upon a time, he was the Incredible Hulk. Arguably the greatest center who ever snapped a ball for the Fighting Illini. During the 1964–65 season, he helped carry the team to the Rose Bowl, was named All Big Ten, and was largely responsible for an unprecedented record-setting season of zero sacks and zero losses of yardage. It was an achievement that had yet to be matched, and in typical form, Henry Decker received no credit. The center was the unheralded backbone of the offense, football's equivalent to the straight man. But now, with the glory days long behind him, Henry's body had settled and softened like an old plow horse. His knees were shot. Arthritis had settled into his back. And his playing weight of 260 had risen embarrassingly close to 300. His Olympian arms were hamhocks now, and his belly had become thick as redwood.

"Having trouble, Henry?" The voice came drifting across the east fence. It was Lillian Kemp, sad, brittle divorcee who lived next door and rarely had the strength to change out of her robe. Lillian had been wrestling with a Valium addiction for as long as Henry could remember. Henry liked her and was determined to get her into therapy.

"Hi, Lillian—you caught me with my leaves down."

Henry could see her peering over the knotty pine. She had curlers in her hair and a Virginia Slim between her fingers.

"Whattya say you do mine when you're finished with yours?" She smirked and took a quick drag off the cigarette.

"You couldn't afford me."

"Is that a fact?" Another quick drag, another smirk. "I hear you work cheap."

"No, what you probably heard was that I *am* cheap."

"Just the way I like 'em—cheap and superficial."

Henry grinned. "Behave yourself, Lillian."

"So, when are you gonna let me cook you some of my special Hungarian goulash?"

"That sounds like a—"

Henry stopped abruptly; somebody was ringing the institute's doorbell.

"To be continued," Henry said, tossing the bag aside. "Excuse me, Lillian."

He marched up the flagstone walk.

The building was an immense Victorian house rising up three stories, topped by giant dormers and corner bay windows. A carpet of ivy clung to the rear. Tarnished green awnings shaded the side windows and portico. Tangles of grapevines and daylilies bordered the wraparound porch. It was a structure from another era, as anachronistic as it was stately, and Henry had poured his heart and soul into it. He'd done most of the renovations himself. The masonry, the tile work, even the unique little curved window that lay between the two chimneys, a window that had become the building's trademark.

It was known as an "eyebrow" window, mostly because of its peculiar arched shape, not to mention the fact that the slate roof curved over it like the ridge of a giant's brow. Henry had sent away to Lancaster, Pennsylvania, for the perfect reproduction of its original glass. The pane had arrived three weeks later, mummified in bubble wrap; and it had taken Henry a full two days of meticulous soldering to get the half-moon of glass just right. The result was well worth it. The eyebrow window, embedded dead center in the attic slate, gave the house a mythic, cyclopean quality, like a structure straight out of a Grimm's fairy tale.

The institute was Henry's baby. A dream he'd been harboring ever since he'd gotten his doctorate: a self-supporting center for the practice and study of inner healing. The institute was the nexus of all that Henry had learned and believed regarding the future of humankind. And after sixteen years alternating between hardcore social services work and psych counseling at Cook County Hospital, Henry had mucho thoughts on humankind. He'd agonized over every detail of his institute. The layout. The decor. The hours of operation. The advertising. The affiliations. Even the name: the Mind-Body Institute. Warm and friendly enough for New Agers. Focused enough for the frontier science establishment. But after four years of growth and many individual success stories, Henry was still lacking the one thing for which he'd always strived: the respect of his peers.

The medical establishment had always been a tad slow to accept new thinking, even when many of these healing techniques had been widely used for centuries in the East. For Henry, acceptance had always been, and continued to be, an uphill battle. He was always struggling for grants. He'd been laughed off the stage at numerous conferences. And he was persona non grata at the American Psychological Association. He sensed a sort of intellectual backlash directed at him, as thought he were some sort of clinical Benedict Arnold who had forsaken all that he had learned about hard science.

Henry longed to show those suckers what's what.

"Keep your socks on," he murmured as he strode through the back door, across the kitchen, and down the front hall to the rhythm of incessant ringing.

When he finally reached the door and opened it, Henry did a double-take.

"Sarah?"

II

"So, anyway . . . that's my sad story in a nutshell." Sarah felt an odd ache in her heart after explaining her recent diagnosis and her charter membership in the inoperable tumor club. She was sitting on a wicker fountain chair on the threshold of the greenhouse, and the Indian summer heat was hammering down on the leaded glass above her, making the back of her neck sweat. She had worn her favorite denim jumper, the one with the spaghetti straps and the matching denim hat. She wasn't exactly sure why, but she had felt compelled to look as fabulous as possible for her former head shrinker.

"I can't imagine how devastating this must be for you," Henry uttered softly. He hadn't said more than a couple of words since they had sat down. Midway through Sarah's tale, his face had become drawn, and he had started slowly shaking his head. Hound dog eyes all droopy, dirty hands rubbing against his flannel, he looked like a big dumb lumberjack who'd stumbled into a charm school.

"There's more," Sarah said. "You remember the box?"

Henry cocked his head and gave her a funny look all of a sudden. "The box?"

Sarah reminded Henry about all the work they had done together back in the early eighties. All the unfocused rage and guilt and shame she had dredged up for him. And the relaxation exercises Henry had devised. But mostly she reminded him about the box, the little imaginary container into which she had locked up all the shit and the pain.

"I vaguely remember the box," Henry said after a few moments' consideration. "I remember, at the time, it was the only thing that seemed to work for you."

"Yeah, well . . . I think it worked a little too well." Sarah rubbed her eyes.

"I'm not following," Henry said.

Sarah looked up at him, her eyes wet now. Her skull was throbbing. Felt like a bonfire raging behind her forehead. She had taken two tabs of codeine before she had left her apartment that day, but the pain was back like a banshee. "The neurologist showed me an MRI of my brain," she said flatly. "Showed me why they couldn't remove it surgically, how it was buried and tangled up in the rest of my brain. But there was something else about it, something unusual—the shape."

"The shape?" Henry wrung his hands.

"It was *square*, Henry. Like a perfect cube. And . . . and the minute I saw it . . . I knew . . . I knew what it was."

"Okay, slow down for a second."

"It's the box, Henry." She scooted out to the edge of her chair and bored her gaze into him. "The box is in my head. And it's killing me."

"Whoa, there!" Henry raised his hands and stood up; and for a moment, he looked like a referee at a Big Ten bowl game who had just noticed illegal motion in the backfield. "Hold it right there," he said, and came over and gently laid a beefy hand on her shoulder. "You're getting way ahead of yourself, kiddo. Now, I want you to slow down, take a deep breath, and let's deal with this thing in a logical fashion. Take things one step at a time."

Sarah didn't take a breath, but instead looked up at him with tears welling in her eyes. "I'm scared, Henry—they want me to start radiation treatments next week."

There was a long stretch of silence.

Finally Henry looked down at her and said, "What would you say to a fried-egg sandwich?"

Sarah gawked at him for a moment, stunned by the goofy non sequitur.

"I was about to fix a couple for myself," Henry said. "Will you join me?"

Sarah began to smile through her tears and all at once she remembered what it was about Henry Decker that she had always liked. "I hate fried-egg sandwiches," she said at last. "But I wouldn't say no to a BLT."

Henry nodded, went over to the counter, and grabbed his apron.

They ate on the patio.

Henry turned out to be an excellent cook. Sarah couldn't remember ever having a BLT with avocado and salsa before, but it was delicious. They also had healthy dollops of Henry's homemade sour cream potato salad and fresh-brewed mint ice tea. They small-talked about each other's lives. Yes, Henry had been married briefly in the late-eighties to a grad student, but the marriage had fallen apart after a year. According to the woman, Henry already had a spouse—*his work*. No, Sarah had never married, and yes, she was still dancing *in that burlesque place,* to borrow Henry's phrase. They laughed about the old days in the Shales House, and before they knew it, nearly an hour had passed, and the tension had eased significantly.

At length Henry broached the subject of Sarah's illness.

"Number one thing to remember," he began, "is that it's *your* body we're talking about. Cobalt radiation is certainly a valid choice—"

"Not for me," she corrected.

"I hear what you're saying." Henry pushed his plate away and rolled up his sleeves. "You're looking for an alternative. That's valid as well. As it just so happens, the work we did years ago—the biofeedback and the relaxation techniques—it's all become standard fare in the field of holistic medicine. See, in the last decade we've learned a lot about health and the human psyche. We know there's a direct relationship between health and emotions. And we also know that emotional states can affect the outcome of a disease."

Sarah looked at him. "Sounds good to me. Where do I sign up?"

"Not so fast, kiddo. I want you to understand exactly what we're talking about here. What I'm saying is, the process that conjured up this hated box in your head will be the very same process we tap into in order to heal the cancer."

"I'm not too sure I want to revisit that box ever again," Sarah said.

"Sarah, listen—it's like the firewalkers. Those folks in

Trinidad and India who walk across the hot coals. Nobody feels any pain. Nobody's blistered. It's all because of their imagination. They form a mental image. The cool moss, they call it. A patch of cool moss in their heads. And it doesn't work unless they really taste it in their minds, the texture, the spongy feel, the odor." Henry paused for emphasis, crossing his big arms against his chest. "Then they just sashay as pretty as you please through the hot coals."

Sarah nodded sheepishly.

"See, we've known for years that the brain releases chemicals like endorphins and hormones," Henry went on. "But just recently we've discovered these nifty little things called neuropeptides. Hundreds of different kinds. Secreted by nerve cells in your brain. They're the chemicals of emotion, Sarah. Believe it or not, each individual neuropeptide corresponds to individual receptors throughout your body. Like tiny little keys. Unlocking potentials, altering structures."

Sarah nodded and slugged down the last few fingers of her iced tea. It was dawning on her just exactly where the therapist was heading, but something about the whole conversation was beginning to bother Sarah. "I think I see what you're getting at," she said, gazing into Henry's eyes. "You're doing the same thing with cancer patients right here, aren't you?"

"Yeah, exactly. Through imagery and forms of deep meditation, we try to get people's minds to convince their bodies that there's hope."

"I get it." Sarah glanced across the patio and thought for a moment. The afternoon sun was beginning to set, and shafts of light were filtering through an overgrown trellis of grapevines and sweet peas. The season had yet to turn, and Chicago was still waiting to see its first hard frost of the autumn.

Sarah whispered, "The cool moss, huh?"

III

There were several films from the golden age of the Hollywood musical, which fell between the early 1930s and the early 1950s, that had always been perennial favorites of Sarah's.

Top Hat was one of them. The first of the seminal Astaire-Rogers team-ups, shot in glorious black and white in 1935, *Top Hat* was a frothy little farce of mistaken identity; a hundred and one purely sublime minutes of sophisticated mating ritual choreographed by the great Hermes Pan. Pan and Astaire would go on to devise many outstanding number in many outstanding films, but *Top Hat* was their greatest achievement. It included one of Sarah's sentimental favorites, "Cheek to Cheek."

An American in Paris was another one. Directed by the legendary craftsman Vincente Minnelli, the movie had created quite a stir when it was first released in 1951, and rightly so. The story of a lonely American painter, played by Gene Kelly, searching for love in the City of Light, *An American in Paris* was the most visually beautiful musical ever filmed. Sumptuous. Almost psychedelic in its use of color and impressionistic design. It won an Academy Award for best picture, and Sarah would always remember the way she felt the first time she saw Gene Kelly's delicious choreography during the final ballet sequence: completely touched by some aesthetic god she would never understand.

But Sarah's all-time favorite had always been, and would continue to be, *The Wizard of Oz*. Much had been written about this 1939 chestnut. Adapted from the popular kids' book by L. Frank Baum, the movie became an instant classic when it was first released and has survived the generations as a television staple. The images have been burned into our collective movie memory: Margaret Hamilton's malevolent, pointy-hatted sneer; a seventeen-year-old Judy Garland singing "Over the Rainbow"; Ray Bolger's spindly-legged break-dance as the scarecrow; and, of course, the march of the Munchkins. The choreographer was a fellow named Bobby Connely, another artist whom Sarah had read about and studied. But oddly enough, what stuck with Sarah over the years from *The Wizard of Oz* was the horrific Freudian darkness that lurked just underneath the surface. The leprous, psychotic apple trees, the shriveling witch's feet, and the terrible winged monkeys.

These were the cultural icons that Sarah would never be able to shake.

And perhaps this was why—three nights after her reunion with Henry—Sarah found herself sitting in her dressing room at Dante's, alone, her mind casting back to these familiar images. Her kimono was pulled tight across her naked body. Her chest was rising and falling with studied regularity. Her eyes were closed tight. She was imagining:

Herself. In black and white. Standing in a modest little bedroom in the rear of a Depression-era farmhouse. Pine dresser, old-fashioned bed, and oak door.

There's a stillness, as if a great storm has just passed. Sarah goes to the door and pauses, as if contemplating her next move. She does this deliberately, as though acting out a part she has played over and over again. Finally, she takes a deep breath and begins opening the door. . . .

Sarah opened her eyes.

Henry had explained the process thoroughly. Proper breathing was essential. Sarah found that the best technique for her was to close her eyes and take a quick breath inward and a long breath outward, repeating it over and over again for about five minutes. Then came the most important part: utilizing the right image.

"We know the box is significant," Henry had said. "But we want to get rid of it now. We want to blow it away. In order to do that, you've got to choose a setting that has resonance for you."

"What do you mean by resonance?"

"Something you can access easily, something you've seen or fantasized about that has always relaxed you."

Sarah had thought about that one for a moment and then informed him. "I don't get relaxed that often."

"Maybe it's the rain," Henry had offered. "Some people love to visualize a warm spring shower, washing away their tumor. Other folks choose personal metaphors. For instance, I had this older guy who was a retired teacher. He sent his cancer into remission by seeing the spots on his lungs as mistakes on a blackboard. He saw himself erasing the spots. Wiping away all the mistakes."

It hadn't taken Sarah long to choose an image.

That was three days ago, and she'd been practicing religiously ever since. Every spare moment she could get. She'd been practicing in the shower. She'd been practicing in her car on the way to work or the grocery store. She even located a quiet corner in the waiting room outside Dr. Calloway's office to practice a little imagery before going in and telling him to take his radiation treatments and shove them where the sun don't shine. Sarah had jumped on the imagery bandwagon with a vengeance, and by now she was getting pretty good at accessing this new virtual reality in her head.

She closed her eyes again and took another series of measured breaths.

Visualizing:

The door, coming open, revealing the world in three-strip Technicolor. Saturated lemon yellows, deep forest greens, and Easter-bunny purples. It's a magical fairyland, and Sarah cautiously moves into this land one step at a time. She knows for a fact that she's not in Kansas anymore . . .

A sound. A spurt of faint little giggles coming from within the forest. Sarah spins toward the noise. She sees

*the Munchkins. A row of tiny heads bursting from the
undergrowth. Male and female, young and old, they're
all grinning.* "Welcome back to Munchkinland, Sarah!"
*The Munchkins joyously cry in unison. Little chipmunk
voices in harmony. Some wear lederhosen, others have
ballerina costumes and rosy cheeks and whimsical hair-
styles.* "We'll help you get rid of that wicked old brain
tumor!"

She blinked.
The image was spreading through her like warm honey.
Slowing her heart rate. Relaxing her tense muscles. Calming
her like a salve on her soul. It was her favorite sequence
from her favorite musical.
She kept breathing steadily, imagining a world in Technicolor.

*The Munchkins are behind her. In front of her. Beside
her. Taking her hands and cheerfully leading her across
the yellow brick road to the town square. Sarah takes a
seat on a big soft toadstool.*

*"I'll get the tumor, fa-la-la," burps the little Munchkin
engineer from behind her, and he reaches up to the top
of Sarah's head and opens her skull. He pulls out an
object the size of a cinder block. Square. Moldering
with age. It's the color of earthworms.*

The tumor.

*The Munchkin engineer hands the blocky tumor to the
Munchkin scientist. "I'll melt it with my handy-dandy
magnifying glass," the scientist says, and pulls out his
ornate little glass from his pocket. He focuses the beam
of sunlight on the tumor.*

The object begins to heat up.

"Melt it away!" sing the tiny gals from the Lullaby League. *"Melt it away, fa-la-la—la-la-la!"* The voices rise. *"Melt it away—!"*

Sarah stopped.

The sound of knocking threw cold water on her reverie. Pulling her tie-string across her waist, slipping on her thongs, she turned to the door and said, "That you, Duff?"

"Yes, sweetie," came the muffled reply. "You decent?"

"As decent as I'll ever be."

Duff came in with his tail between his legs. Hands in his pockets, jaw set in a grim expression, he looked like he had just been force-fed a steaming plate of shit. His big fat polyester tie was loosened around his neck. His face was flushed. "How's it going, kid?"

"It's going, Duff, you know how it is."

"Same old story?"

" 'A fight for love and glory,' " Sarah said in a singsong voice. This was his cue.

"How's that thing go . . . ?" Duff rubbed his knuckles against his chin. It was a game that they played on a regular basis. Quoting old songs. Loser buys a round. Duff was never really any good at it, but he still liked to play. "A case of do or die!" he suddenly said, snapping his pudgy little fingers.

"Give the man a stuffed poodle!"

"You know something?" Duff was fidgeting nervously. Something was eating at him.

"What's that?"

"Bogart never said, 'Play it again, Sam.' Ain't that a kick in the head? He said, 'Play it.' Just 'Play it.' " Duff looked down at his wingtips.

Sarah grinned, and then glanced at her watch. "Jesus, I didn't realize how late it was getting."

She sprang to her feet and went behind an oriental divider. Slipping off her kimono, she quickly started climbing into her G-string and black push-up job. Her breasts barely fit into the Fredericks décolleté bra, but she didn't mind too much. Less than a minute into her routine, it would be coming off. Tonight she was Vampira, Mistress of Darkness, complete with campy music, batwing mask, and mile-high stiletto heels. She'd purchased most of the getup at Taboo Taboo, but had to go down to a scary little S&M place on South Halsted for the bustier.

Over the last couple of days, Sarah had immersed herself in her work. Planning the Vampira routine. Exercising. Trying to eat well. It had taken her mind off the illness. Off the pain. And between her imagery with Henry and her rekindled enthusiasm at work, it was as if her life had taken on a new purpose. A new direction. She was going to get well. And even though she was a long way from winning a spot with the Paul Taylor Dance Group—in fact, one might even say she was nothing more than a lowly, aging stripper shaking her tits for a bunch of frustrated alcoholics—by God, she was going to be the *best* lowly aging stripper in the business.

"Just had another meeting with the owners," Duff's voice came drifting over the divider.

"I didn't know that, Duff."

"Yeah, yeah, and you remember I was talking about all the changes."

"I seem to recall something along those lines, yeah." Sarah laced up the bustier, making her D-cups runneth over with pale flesh. She slipped a cape around her shoulders and emerged from behind the divider.

"Well, what I mean to say is, Mr. Sabitini has asked me—holy Christ, kid, that's a swell getup—but anyway, like I said, the Sabitinis have asked me, well, actually, they told me—"

"Spit it out, Duff," Sarah said, sitting down at the makeup mirror, digging out her black Lee press-on nails. "What are you trying to say?"

There was a moment of agonizing silence, then Duff's voice.

"You're fired, kid."

Sarah froze.

It was amazing that s͏ hadn't seen it coming, with all the complaints coming do from the pricks at the firm. The snide comments about Sarah's performance. Always something wrong with her costumes or her attitude or her music. The real problem was Sarah's age. Her weight. Her softness. Welcome to the end of the twentieth century—the bulimic, stick-thin, Prozac-fueled, thinly veiled misogyny that ruled the glamour pages.

"Kid, I feel terrible about this, those bastards sittin' down there in their friggin' LaSalle Street ivory towers." Duff was reaching into his back pocket. Pulling out his wallet. Thumbing through bills. "I want you to take this, and if you need anything, a place to stay, whatever, you call me."

He tried to hand Sarah a couple of fifty-dollar bills.

She stood up and pushed the bills away. "Keep your money," she said, and then she kissed his bald head. "It's not your fault, Duff. I'll be fine. Now if you'll excuse me, I've got one last show to do."

Duff stared.

Sarah sat back down and put on the rest of her nails and her Wicked Witch eyeliner. Then she stood up, regarded her reflection for a moment, and walked out.

Duff followed her into the hallway. "Kid, listen, you don't understand—"

Sarah paused by the stage steps, the sound of her heart beating in her ears. The muffled thud of music was vibrating the stairs. Sarah swallowed back the rage. Swallowed back the urge to scream. Her blood felt as though it were boiling in her veins, about to explode through her ears. But instead of crying out, instead of letting the tears come, Sarah turned and took one good, long look at Duff Sellars.

The look must have worked, because all Duff could do was nod sadly.

Sarah walked up the remaining steps and pushed the stage door open.

The inferno of light and sound greeted her, as always, and

made her eyes throb. She swam through the fire. Spinning, spinning, spinning one last time to the sound of the Challengers doing the theme from *The Twilight Zone*. Sarah tore away her bustier and tossed it out into the darkness.

It landed on the floor.

She kept blindly bumping and grinding to the beat-box grunge, her eyes adjusting to the dark glare. She blinked. She did her little Bela Lugosi move, swinging the cape around in front of her face and slipping off her bra. But when she pulled the cape away and revealed her bosoms, there was hardly a ripple out in the lounge.

Her eyes were finally adjusting, and as she scanned the shadows, she saw just how empty the place was. Only the most die-hard regulars had come in tonight. The Twins were in back by the pinball machine, nursing brown bottles. And Mumbles was over by the door, loaded to the gills, trying to stand erect in his wrinkled suit. Sarah flung her cape out at the dead silence with a flourish, and then she noticed the corner of the runway, an empty chair backlit by the green glare of tungsten.

Even Mister Peepers was gone.

IV

During the years that Sarah was a resident of the Shales group home—before Henry Decker had arrived—Sarah had been carrying around a busload of anger. Anger in all its forms. Anger directed at her late mother, anger directed back on herself, anger directed at other people in general, even anger without any focus or direction at all. Just low-down, ugly, debilitating, spit-spewing anger. And up until the day Henry had walked in the door, Sarah had developed several weird behavior patterns through which she channeled her rage.

She used to sneak out after hours, steal the administrator's Buick, and make her way across town to the Kennedy Expressway. Once on the highway, she would speed westward, pedal pinned to the floor, and see how fast she could go before chickening out and releasing the accelerator. On other occasions she would hide in the home's basement and try to tunnel under the rotting brick wall using only a tablespoon, scraping feverishly, like she was in some old B-grade prison movie. Once in a while, she would even lock herself in her bedroom closet and punch the wall until her fists were raw and bloody. She had always been a big girl, and had been able to wreak a significant amount of damage on the house's cheap drywall before the administrator got wise.

Of course, much of this venting had cooled down once Henry Decker started working with her.

But every once in a while . . .

"Let's just not get our panties in a pinch," Sarah whispered tersely to her cat, who was curled up and slumbering loudly in Sarah's lap. Sarah was sitting on the ottoman by the window. "Things are going to get better. . . . "

Sarah was trying to get a handle on her emotions, remembering all the old destructive behaviors. She had just returned from her swan song at Dante's and she felt like screaming. Like ripping her carpet up with her teeth. Like tearing her hair out by the graying roots. But Gypsy just kept slumbering blithely through it all, purring noisily, oblivious to the fact that Sarah's world was coming apart at the seams.

The cat had been Sarah's only roommate and confidante for nearly seven years now, ever since Sarah had rescued the animal from the Humane Society. Early on, the cat had been an emaciated skeleton of a creature, with matted gray fur and one bad eye that seemed to wander fitfully. Sarah had nurtured the animal back to health, and within a year or so, the cat had filled out nicely. She had become Sarah's shadow, following the woman from room to room, sleeping with her, sitting on her lap whenever possible. Over the years, the cat had grown into a roly-poly ball of gray fur, a fixture in Sarah's life.

Gypsy wasn't the only object of Sarah's maternal impulses over the years. She had tried to adopt a baby numerous times, but was not surprised to learn that the Illinois Department of Children and Family Services didn't take too kindly to a mother with past mental instability, as well as a somewhat indelicate career in the adult entertainment industry. Sarah was forced to become a professional den mother, baby-sitting the children of other strippers, looking after Duff's grandkids, or taking cookies and secondhand toys down to the Harrison Street Orphanage during the holidays. But the lack of her own kids—not to mention a life void of serious relationships—had taken its toll on Sarah over the years.

Now it was about to blow up in her face.

"Things are going to get better," Sarah whispered to Gypsy. "God knows they can't get any worse."

She didn't want to think about her shitty life anymore. Her anger was like a brushfire sometimes. You start fanning it, the wind starts blowing, and look out. The whole damn place goes up. No, that was not a good idea. No punching out drywall tonight. She started taking deep breaths. She lifted Gypsy off her lap and set the dazed cat on the windowsill.

Then Sarah leaned forward, face in her hands, eyes pressed shut.

Imagining:

The Technicolor world buzzing with frenzied activity.

Dozens of Munchkins, all shapes and sizes, are gathered around the blocky mass of cancerous tumor. They are kicking it, smashing it with little Munchkin hammers. Some of them are even trying to burn it with little gas torches. The tumor is impervious, impenetrable. Like a great slab of wet gray marble.

Opening her eyes, Sarah felt her flesh crawl, her scalp prickle.

Perhaps it was merely the anger and frustration at losing

her job. Or the unflagging stress of the tumor, ruminating over whether or not to have the cobalt treatments or keep on searching for alternatives. Or the constant pain, the pain in the morning when she got out of bed, the pain like a horrible party in her head, pulsing with subsonic throbs, wearing her down until the codeine didn't work anymore and all she could do to squelch the agony was put her head under the cold shower and wail for endless minutes. But whatever the reason, it had been goi␣ ␣n like this for over a week now. No matter what she visualized, no matter how hard she tried, she kept imagining the box to be indestructible.

"Okay, just take it easy and take a breath," she murmured, "just relax and breathe and see the damn thing going away."

She closed her eyes again.

The Munchkins are swarming.

The mayor of Munchkin City is perched on a crooked tree above the tumor, snapping his little whip down on the workers. "Melt it!" he cries. "Burn it away—fa-la-la! Get rid of that nasty tumor, get rid of it—fa-la-la!"

Below him, scores of little people are trying to destroy the obscene gray cancerous block. Ballerinas are pouring acid on it to no avail. Green-faced midgets are slamming sledgehammers against one side. Lollipop Leaguers are launching little explosive mortars into the other side. But the tumor is implacable.

Sarah dug her fingernails into the side of the ottoman and then sprang to her feet.

"This is ridiculous!"

She went into the kitchen, rifled through the cabinet above the fridge, and found a bottle of Bombay Sapphire. She filled a jelly jar and drank the gin down in a single gulp. It felt like a machete twisting in her gut. She refilled her glass, drank it down, refilled it again, killed it. The gin ran out on the fourth glass.

"I'm afraid that's the last of the good stuff for a while," Sarah said to the cat, who had padded into the kitchen and was rubbing against Sarah's ankle.

Sarah retired to her bedroom. Before calling it a night, she swallowed a handful of medication. Another two capsules of Rheumatrex, an anti-inflammatory usually prescribed for arthritis. More codeine, about sixty milligrams worth. And her nightly antidepressant. She knew she was flirting with disaster, taking all the drugs on top of the Bombay Sapphire, but she was in no shape to care anymore.

Lying in bed, head buzzing in the dark, she waited for a sleep to come like a soldier bracing for a sneak attack.

She closed her eyes.

Bam! Munchkins are slamming battering rams into the tumorous block. Foooosshhhh! Flamethrowers. Kabooooooommmmm! Dynamite. Nothing works, nothing.

The tears came then.

Sarah brought her hand to her mouth and bit hard into the meat of her palm. Her chest tightened and hitched, and tears streamed down her temples, saturating her pillow. She convulsed silently for several minutes, letting the emotions toss her: an angry storm tossing a life raft at sea. The crying jag lasted for several minutes, and it drained her thoroughly.

At length, the drugs and booze began to smother her. She turned away from the window. Pale blue neon from the outside was seeping into the room, striping the wall, blinking. Sarah began counting the blinks. Before long she was sinking into oblivion.

The fever dream started shortly thereafter.

V

She opened her eyes and realized at once, with sudden dread, that her bed was moving.

Sarah tried to sit up, but she was too woozy. Her eyes were unfocused, dazed, and the damn bed kept pitching and yawing and spinning. Was she drunk? Where was Gypsy? Was it morning already? She managed to turn her head sideways. Daylight streamed urgently into the room, objects swimming in and out of focus. And the noise, like a freight train rushing right outside her window. She struggled to sit up, and suddenly, with great horror, she realized that it wasn't the bed that was moving at all.

Her entire building was spinning.

She managed to pull herself up into a sitting position against the headboard. The G-force kept her pinned to the wood, but she was able to see the rest of the room. All of it in blurry black and white. The pine dresser sliding across the hardwood. The needlepoint sampler vibrating against the wall. The little colonial table skittering about the floor near the window. And through the window, framed like a proscenium, the violent swirling eddy of a cyclone.

"My God," she uttered, ripping away the blankets and scooting out to the edge of the bed. "We must be in the middle of a twister!"

She stumbled across the room, nearly tripping over Gypsy, who was cowering near the foot of the bed. She scooped up the cat and held the animal tightly, then spun toward a noise behind her.

A shape was floating by the window, levitated by the wind. It was Dr. Calloway, sitting in a rocking chair, covered with blood. He was decapitated. He cradled his own head in his lap as though holding a pet that had gone to sleep.

The severed head opened its eyes and began to speak. "The tumor has a distinctive shape," the voice announced cheerfully. "It's buried too deep in the ganglia to surgically remove, but I wouldn't advise opening it, not this box of worms."

The doctor smiled and earthworms suddenly wriggled from his mouth like delicate gray ribbons flagging in the wind.

Sarah screamed.

The entire room pitched to the left, tossing Sarah to the floor. She dropped Gypsy and nearly tagged her head on the corner of the bed. The noise rose. An angry locomotive. Sarah struggled to get back on her feet. Pulling herself up by the bedpost, she gazed back at the window.

The doctor was gone.

A new figure was drifting into view, rising up from the ether, soaring along the currents. A black-clad crone on an old-fashioned broomstick. Pointy hat. Flowing cape. Very familiar. Looked a lot like Margaret Hamilton, the actress who played the Wicked Witch of the West, but it wasn't Margaret Hamilton. It was a different woman, maybe a little younger. Big-boned, deeply lined eyes, long gray hair, and a mean smirk.

Sarah's mother.

"Don't you know what's wrong?" Jessie Brandis hissed as she floated past the window. "Use your brain, child— don't you have any idea what's happening to you?"

Sarah staggered backward. Away from the window. Away from the horrible ghost. Shielding her eyes, gasping for breath, Sarah cowered in the corner. Sliding down to a crouch. Mouth filled with metallic ice shavings of panic. Her heart was racing now. It couldn't be, it was impossible, her late mother was gone, dead and buried.

The house lurched again.

Sarah careened across the floor, landing hard against the wall. The sudden pitch in gravity knocked the breath out of her lungs. And she gasped and fought back to her feet. The house was falling now, spinning wildly, the gravity sucking the air out of it. Sarah felt buoyant as she tumbled around *the floor on her hands and knees. The house fell faster and faster. Sarah shrieked. The wind thundered.*

Finally the house landed.

The impact was like an elephant sitting on her. Everything went black as Sarah slammed hard against the opposite wall, her teeth rattling. She collapsed to the floor and was covered with dust and debris. She sucked in a breath. She clawed at the floor, madly searching for her cat, her back exploding with pain. A moment later the dust settled.

Silence returned.

Gypsy was under the bed, mewling loudly. Sarah went over to the bed and rooted the cat out of the shadows. Gypsy was okay, scared to death, tiny heart palpitating, but generally okay. Sarah stood up and took a deep breath. There was a strange kind of hush in the airless room, as dust motes sparkled in the new sunlight. Sarah took a few steps toward the door and then hesitated. The silence had deepened, as though the very air had frozen in anticipation of Sarah's next move. Sarah didn't like this; she didn't like this one little bit. She squeezed Gypsy tightly and took one last breath.

Then she opened the door.

The Technicolor world sang out at her like a wordless opera. Sarah froze. It was so beautiful, so vivid and familiar and heart-wrenching, she could barely breathe. The house had evidently landed in some lost paradise. There were exotic byzantine trees and purple flowers. Vermilion vines snaking up around ornate columns that terminated in the sky. Wisteria twined around everything, along the lower branches of banyan trees and oddly trimmed hedgerows.

"Hello?" Sarah called out as she took a step across the porch.

There was no answer except for the pained silence. Sarah strode down the porch steps and into the alien world. There was a narrow road twisting off to the left. Gleaming yellow bricks. The herringbone pattern sparkled in the sun. Sarah followed it. "Hello! Anybody here?" Sarah called out as she walked, holding Gypsy tightly.

There was something unsettling about the stillness of the place. Almost as if some horrible event had taken place here just moments ago—perhaps the cyclone itself—and now the entire living population had skittered away to tend to the injured and the dying.

"Hello! Is there any—" Sarah froze in her tracks. Out of the corner of her eye, something had moved. She whirled. Fifty feet behind her, where the farmhouse had landed, there was a tiny shriveled object near the foundation. Sarah walked cautiously over to it and knelt down to take a closer look.

Her heart jumped into her mouth.

It was a tiny human arm poking out from under the house. Blackened and emaciated, it looked almost petrified. It was barely alive, trembling slightly, its hand curled into a tight little fist. Sarah reached down to comfort it, but before she could touch it, the fist opened suddenly. Sarah jerked back, stunned. Then she noticed an object in the little palm.

A key.

Sarah picked it up and looked at it. It was an old-fashioned skeleton key, tarnished with age. A hissing sound drew Sarah's attention back to the arm. The arm was shrinking away, contracting back into the ground beneath the house in a puff of noxious smoke. Sarah stood up and looked at the key.

There was a murmur. Tiny voices. Quivering, frightened voices rising around her. Sarah glanced over her shoulder.

"What in God's name—?"

An object had materialized in the middle of the path about twenty feet away. As if by magic, it now sat just as big as life on the yellow bricks. The tumor. A big filthy cube of dark matter about the size of a cinder block. It had transformed slightly since Sarah had seen it last. It now had old rusty hinges and an ancient brass lock plate on it.

The box.

Sarah took a few steps toward it, and the voices rose around her, warning voices, like little quivering strings.

Sarah walked the remaining few paces, and then knelt down by the box. She looked at the key. The voices swelled, wailing, DANGER, stop, DON'T DO IT!

Sarah put the key in the lock and turned it.

The box burst open with volcanic suddenness.

Devouring the universe.

3

Flesh and Blood

I

Not much at first. Just a scintilla of light zipping up the fabric of darkness, but soon the spark is joined by other sparks, and before long, there are flames. Ribbons of yellow brilliance slashing the shadows. Bringing sensations. Heat. Sharp pain. The odors of ammonia, thick and acrid. Rotting meat. Cinders and rust.

"OHMYGOD—!!"

Sarah whiplashed forward, lungs heaving. It felt as though she had been underwater. Holding her breath until the very last moment of oxygenation. Then she had suddenly emerged into the light and air. But she wasn't in the water; she wasn't outdoors at all. She was in her bedroom, and her bedroom was on fire.

Wait!

Something was desperately wrong. As her eyes adjusted to the dark, she realized that she must have fallen out of bed. Nightmares, more nightmares. She must have rolled off the edge because she was on the floor. No, that wasn't right, either. The floor was cold and rough. Gravelly. She was on a cinder floor, and the ceiling was gone, replaced by dripping stalactites of broken fluorescent tubing, torn asbestos, and tar paper.

Sarah rose to her feet, heart racing.

She was in a strange abandoned building, and the building was on fire. How? How the hell did she get here? Flames dotted the floor, dappling the walls and windows. Alkaline odors hung thick in the smoke. The room was huge, warehouselike, with hulking objects covered with Visqueen. She started toward an oblong shadow, a doorway, but after a couple of steps she collapsed. Her legs were burning, scraped and bruised, as though they'd been over an obstacle course. She looked at her hands. Her fingers were covered with soot and grime, and something else, dark and sticky. She was dressed in torn dungarees and a filthy Chicago Bulls T-shirt.

Sarah began to cry.

As a little girl she'd been a sleepwalker. It had started around the time she had entered kindergarten, and at first it was merely nocturnal movements. She would kick the covers off, wriggle out of her bed, and end up across the room. *Noctambulation,* the pediatrician had called it. But over the next decade, it had worsened. Sarah would scare the bejesus out of her mother, bumping into the woman's bed in the middle of the night. Or she would wake up in the gully out behind the Brandis home, her hands caked with mud and her clothing torn to bits by brambles. It usually occurred during times of stress, before a big test at school or after a particularly ugly episode with Jessie. But the worst part was the waking up. The disorientation. As though a horrible wish had come true, as though Sarah had been banished by her wicked mother to a far-off place.

Sirens echoed in the distance.

Sarah glanced across the cavernous room to the far windows, the sudden fear cutting off her tears. She could see the adjacent streets through shattered, grimy glass. Desolate storefronts and boarded windows. A lone vapor light. Where the hell was she? The sirens rose. Sarah could feel the heat on the back of her neck. And that hideous smell. Fetid, ripe, like rotting garbage, only worse.

She limped toward the exit, wading through trash, empty bottles, and tins of butane. Heart slamming hard in her chest, throat stinging, she paused in the doorway and glanced back at the shadows.

At first, she merely blinked, and didn't fully register the way the flames were organized. The filigree of fire looping across the floor. Tendrils of butane glowing in the shadows like heavenly hieroglyphics. Then she realized somebody had written in flame the word ALIVE.

Dizziness poured over Sarah as she turned and stumbled out the exit.

II

"Settle down," she muttered as she crept up the stone steps of her building.

The cab idled impatiently behind her.

She was worried that somebody might see her limping along in this filthy getup, and the questions would be unanswerable. *Hi, Sarah. What's the matter? Doing some midnight jogging? Just out starting some fires?*

The trip back home had been discreet enough. Sarah had fled the mystery building down a side alley and had emerged on North Avenue, a street that she was vaguely familiar with, thank God. Since she didn't have a dime in her pockets, the train had been out of the question, so she put her head down and started walking east. She was dazed, shivering and terrified. If any street punk had come along at that point, Sarah would have been easy pickings. But something deep inside her had driven her onward. Call it survival instinct. Call it stubbornness. But Sarah wasn't about to fall apart tonight. She had been down that road, thank you very much, and she wasn't ready to take a trip back down it.

It had taken her nearly an hour to reach Wells Street.

Thankfully, near the corner of Wells and North, Sarah had stumbled upon a cab driver who was willing to take her back to her building and wait outside for his fare. During the ride home, Sarah had sat in stunned silence in back, staring at the beaded seat covers, taking deep breaths, and rubbing her stained hands on her shirt. She was racking her brain for explanations. Was it the tumor? Calloway had told her there might be severe symptoms tied to the occipitaloma. Tastes, odors, hallucinations, seizures, loss of memory, blackouts, the whole range of neurological snafus. *Artifacts,* Calloway called them. And Sarah had a feeling tonight's incident could have very well be a harbinger of many more artifacts to come.

"Just settle down and stay calm," she repeated to herself, alone on the porch.

She opened the foyer door and went inside.

There was a fifty-fifty chance that Sarah would get lucky and find the inner door unlocked. The two other tenants in the aging three-flat were extremely lackadaisical when it came to security. Mrs. Garcia, the portly old matron on the first floor, usually left the inner door wide open after checking her mail each afternoon. And the schoolteacher and his wife, the Hastingses, they remembered to lock it about half the time. Sarah took a deep breath, walked over to the inner door, and turned the knob.

The door creaked open.

Thank God.

Sarah started up the stairs.

The feeling came to her halfway up the staircase. It started in the pit of her stomach, a sick, weak sensation, as though she were on the verge of falling. Then the tiny hairs on the back of her neck stiffened, flesh prickling up and down her arms. It was the smell, mostly. The sharp, coppery stench. It rose as she approached the second-floor landing. Sarah took the last four steps two at a time and then rushed across the landing to her door, which was standing a couple of inches ajar.

She pushed the door open and stepped inside her apartment.

The blood trumpeted.

It was everywhere, dark red Zebra strokes on the walls, hand prints all over the floor, even starbursts on the ceiling. Sarah covered her mouth with both hands, holding in a scream. The place had been devastated. The couch was slashed and bleeding tufts of cotton. The lamps and chairs were overturned. Every glass surface had been shattered, the windows, the glossies, the lobby cards, and the movie posters.

Sarah moved slowly through the living room, hands over her mouth, barely containing the scream.

There was a horrible precision to the havoc, as though the perpetrator had followed some compulsive blueprint. The dining table was washed with blood and then dotted with carpet fibers and hair in geometrically spaced little clumps. In the kitchen everything was upside down: the chairs, the pots and pans, the table, the appliances. Even the stove and refrigerator had been ripped from their gas lines and moorings and then stacked neatly upside down on the Rorschach-spattered tile. But it was the blood that finally drove Sarah over the brink.

It was the crowning touch on everything. Stippled over the furniture. Stenciled across the baseboards. Smeared on the carpet. Smudged all over the trim and doors and wainscoting. And mostly *written*. The same word, endlessly duplicated in script, in block letters, in hasty scrawl.

ALIVE—alive-alive-alive—ALIVE!

All at once it struck Sarah like a lightning bolt to her heart. Where was Gypsy? Her sweet old fat cat. Where was she? Hands riveted to her mouth, trembling fingers still cupped over her scream, Sarah rushed across the living room to the bedroom, which was lying in similar disarray. Eyes scanning frantically. Landing on a dark object nestled in the blood-sodden bedsheets.

The matted, shriveled corpse of a cat.

Sarah's hands finally flew away from her mouth, and the scream, and the hurricane of emotion that followed it, escaped into the empty apartment.

III

Frank Moon was staring at a dead body when the sound of a beat cop's voice broke his concentration.

"Detective?"

Frank looked up and said nothing.

"Detective, something just came over the horn." The young patrolman was toddling up to Frank all bright-eyed and bushy-tailed, like a dog with a newspaper. Frank had seen a million kids like this kid. Babies in blue, Frank called them. Six months out of the academy, still wet behind the ears, and all charged up to serve and protect. Fix the world. Frank guessed it would take the street another six months to beat it out of this kid.

"Talk to me, Officer," Frank said softly.

"Call just came in from dispatch, got ten-thirty-three over on Lincoln. Possible witness."

Frank looked at him. "Witness?"

"Yessir. Woman said she was here earlier tonight."

"Who caught the thing? Binelli?"

"Pardon me?" the patrolman looked confused.

"Which detective," Frank enunciated carefully, "is over at the Lincoln address with the woman?"

"Oh, it's, uh, Detective Jones."

"Tell Becky I'll be there in fifteen."

"Right." The patrolman nodded and walked out, returning to his cruiser, which sat at an angle just outside the exit of the abandoned building. The blue bubble-light was strobing in through the doorway, throwing haphazard lines and silhouettes across the dark, cinder-strewn interior. Yellow cordon tape was stretched across the broken windows. The fires had been extinguished. The photographs taken. The prints dusted.

Frank turned back to the stiff and continued writing in his notebook, his hand encased in a rubber glove. *Victim—wht. Cauc. Female. Late 30's. No ID. Pro'bly hooker.* Frank stared down at the body for another moment, and then wrote: *Cause of death—appnt. Suffocatn.—interesting pckg—ligature marks around forehd.—post mortem dressings, wrapping tape—see ME's report.* Frank sighed and put the notebook back in the breast pocket of his Italian sharkskin jacket. He was thankful the stiff was fresh. Over the years he'd encountered bodies in every conceivable state of decomposition. Some of them had been so ripe they literally popped open when touched by the meat wagon boys. The poppers were the worst. The odor would stay in your clothes and your nostrils for days afterward.

A rail-thin man with angular features and close-cropped blond hair, Frank Moon, at thirty-seven years old, was the youngest detective sergeant in the Chicago Police Department, not to mention the head honcho of Area Thirteen's graveyard squad. Five other homicide detectives answered to Frank Moon. Above Frank, there were only the shift commander, the captain, the Chicago Police Department commissioner, and God. But Frank didn't believe in God, and he wasn't too crazy about his superiors, either. Frank was a prodigy; everybody in the system understood this. He came from old money, East Coast society money. Got a bachelor's in English from Duke, Master's in psychology from NYU. Graduated with honors in the early eighties from West Point. Did a stint in Europe for the National Security Agency and got his honorable discharge in '85. Became the highest ranking cadet in the history of the Police Academy and snagged his detective's badge before his thirtieth birthday.

Frank was a legend.

He worked alone, and he worked quietly. Methodically. His cases usually went down—cop parlance for *solved*—so nobody bothered him much. He also lived alone. Dated spo-

radically. Never had enough spare time to latch on to anybody, but he still loved the ladies, and he was occasionally
seen with high-profile women, media personalities, beauty
queens, and the like. All this was common knowledge. But
what was not common knowledge among his peers or anyone else, for that matter, was the music in Frank's head. Jazz,
mostly. It formed a distinctive and different sound track for
each case. Mob hits were big band swing, usually. Artie
Shaw. Kenton. Domestics were Basie. Suicides were Thelonius Monk. Gang drive-bys were Miles Davis. It allowed
Frank to tap into the rhythm of a case, to access his intuition.

He didn't have the music for tonight's case yet.

It would come.

Frank peeled off his glove and walked out of the building.
His Lexus was waiting for him under the lone vapor light.
Before getting into the car, he glanced across the street,
where the young patrolman was holding back a group of
gawkers. Frank pointed at the building and then at the meat
wagon, signaling that it was time for the ME boys to take the
body away.

The patrolman waved.

Frank got in his car and drove away.

It took him less than ten minutes to get up to Lincoln Avenue and find the address given to him over the cellular. The
three-flat was in a working-class neighborhood. Woman by
the name of Sarah Brandis. Claimed she was sleepwalking
and woke up at the scene. Claimed her place was ransacked,
her cat killed, blah-blah-blah. Frank didn't know what to
make of this lady.

Yet.

He pulled up to the curb in front of the place, parked,
showed his badge to the black and white out front. He hurried up the stairs and knocked softly on the door to the second-floor apartment. Detective Becky Jones answered the
door. An ashy-complected fiftyish woman who had been a
homicide detective in the Thirteenth for decades, Jones ushered Frank into the disaster area that was Sarah's apartment.

Frank got his notebook out.

"She's in the bedroom," Jones said softly into Frank's ear as Frank scanned the bloodstained living room.

"Who is she?" Frank murmured.

Jones told Frank all about Sarah, Dante's Inferno, the sleepwalking, the brain tumor.

"Looks like somebody's trying to make a statement here," Frank said, motioning at the bloody scrawl.

"It's the cat's blood."

"What cat?"

"The dancer's cat."

Frank rubbed his mouth. "Make sure forensics gets a bunch of snapshots of this stuff."

Jones nodded.

"And I want you and Binelli to run interference for me on this one." Frank looked around the room another moment, and then put his notebook away. "I want to talk to the woman."

Jones led Frank into the bedroom, where an evidence technician was stuffing bloody bedsheets into a clear plastic bag. Across the room, Sarah sat on the windowsill, watching, a blanket wrapped around her and a cup of Lipton cradled in her trembling hands. Her eyes were raw and watery.

Frank came over, pulled the bureau chair next to her, and sat down on it. "Miss Brandis, I'm Frank Moon," he said gently. "Detective sergeant with Chicago Homicide."

Sarah looked up at him. "Homicide?"

"That's right. There was a body found in an abandoned building at Hamlin and North. Stuffed into a garbage drum, wrapped in tape and rope and locked up tight. A woman. More than likely a prostitute. We think the killer tried to start a fire to cover the evidence."

Sarah looked confused.

"There were markings on the body," Frank continued. "Similar to the markings here. Now . . . I understand you were in the vicinity of Hamlin and North tonight?"

Sarah swallowed some tea. "There were markings on the body?"

"That's right," Frank said. "Miss Brandis—are you all right?"

"What?"

"Are you all right?" Frank regarded the woman for another moment. She looked pale as a ghost all of a sudden. Obviously terrified. Perhaps a little sick.

In Frank's mind, the jury was still out regarding this gal's involvement. The sad truth was, in most homicide cases, the guilty party was pretty easy to find. Usually a neighbor, a customer, a lover, a co-worker, or a friend. Frank couldn't even count the number of cases in which he had stumbled upon the actual murderer in a crowd right at the scene. People were dumb. And murderers were even dumber. But this Sarah Brandis person, she was jammed up in a way that Frank had yet to put his finger on. Of course, a person would have to be pretty sick to be a stripper. Nasty profession, stripping.

All at once, Frank found his gaze straying from her face. The lady had curves, that was certainly true. Dangerous curves. Frank caught himself eyeing the terrain under Sarah's blanket, and he silently cursed his libido.

"I'm . . . a little under the weather," Sarah finally said, brushing a wisp of graying hair from her eye. "You said markings on the prostitute?"

Frank nodded.

Sarah's eyelids fluttered for a moment. "What kind of . . . markings?""

"Are you feeling all right?"

"No—I mean, yeah—I'm . . . fine," Sarah swallowed hard. "What kind of markings are you talking about?"

"Markings similar to the ones here," Frank replied.

"The ones . . . *here?*" Her eyelids fluttered again, and her head nodded slightly, as though she were a toy winding down.

"Yeah," Frank said softly. "Somebody carved the word

alive across the woman's forehead. At least we think that's what it says; we won't know until—"

Frank abruptly stopped.

Sarah was slipping off the ledge, body folding up like an old suit of clothes, eyes rolling back in her head. Frank reached out to catch her, but it was too late. Sarah had already collapsed to the floor in a dead faint.

IV

Running, running for all she was worth, running down the yellow brick road. The angry black wind is on her back, hot and noxious. She hears the sounds behind her, the terrible sounds. Like a bubbling cauldron of insane, drooling, cackling old ladies. Suddenly . . .

Her toe catches a tree root, and she stumbles to the bricks. Her breath is knocked clean out of her. She gasps. And she crawls, looking back over her shoulder. And she sees it there in the middle of the road.

The tumor. The strange, black, glistening box. Its lid is gaping open, and scores of black-winged objects are pouring out of it. Black-winged monkeys and

"Sarah?"

the monkeys fill the sky like storm clouds. Like cancer. Chirping and squealing and cackling obscenely. Pouring out of the tumor box. "NO!" Sarah struggles to her feet and tries to flee. But the monkeys are swarming above her, cackling and squalling, blocking out the sun and

"Sarah—can you hear me?"

*now the wings are in her hair as she runs, little bony
black wings in her hair, clawing at her, spreading poison*

"Sarah!"

Her eyes leaped open.

At first, all Sarah saw was whiteness. White-on-white objects swimming in and out of focus. Soon, the objects coalesced into figures.

"It's okay, honey, you're safe."

It was the voice of the day nurse at Northwestern, a
plump, matronly woman named Mary Bergquist. The nurse
had gotten to know Sarah during her scans last week.

Sarah squinted through the haze and saw the woman's
face above her. The rest of the room came into focus then. It
was a private room in ICU. Mustard-yellow walls, hideous
orange padded chairs and clattering radiator. A television
was mounted near the ceiling in one corner, and the air
smelled of disinfectant and raspberry Jell-O. Swallowing
dryly, Sarah said, "What . . . happened?"

"You're in the hospital, sweetheart."

"That's right, Sarah," another voice spoke up. It was Dr.
Calloway. He stood at the foot of the bed, fidgeting in his
wool three-piece, a clipboard under his arm. His thick hair
was greased back smartly today, a real Marcello Mastroianni
look. His eyes were watery with nerves. "You had a little
fainting spell last night, but you seem to check out fine this
morning."

"Last night?" Sarah tried to move, but her arms and legs
were glued to the bed with narcotics. "What did you give
me?"

"Librium," Calloway told her. "You were tossing around
pretty good there for a while."

"Oh boy," Sarah muttered, and tried to sit up. Her body
felt like wet cement. She gazed around the room through
sleep-crusty eyes. She remembered bits and pieces of the

previous night, the blackout, and her poor cat Gypsy. "I assume you folks heard about last night."

"Yes," Calloway said. "Talked to the police this morning. Told them it wasn't unusual for a person in your condition to have, well . . . *episodes*."

The nurse shuddered. "That's just awful, what happened to your apartment."

"Yeah . . . yeah, it is." Sarah took a deep breath and rubbed her eyes. She missed her cat, but she couldn't cry anymore. It was as though her grief had run out.

"I hope they catch the son of a bitch who did it," the nurse said.

"You and me both," Sarah said.

Calloway tentatively approached the bed. He checked Sarah's pulse, looked in her eyes, and made a couple of notes. It was obvious the doctor was deeply shaken. He exchanged an awkward glance with the nurse and then looked back at Sarah. "Everything looks fine, Sarah. Other than a few bumps and bruises, everything seems A-okay." The neurosurgeon stepped back, swallowing hard and glancing at his notebook.

With great effort Sarah sat up against the headboard. "What's going on, Doc?"

"Pardon me?"

"The blackout, the memory loss. Is it the tumor? You can give it to me straight. Believe me, it couldn't get any worse."

Calloway turned to the nurse. "Mary, could you give us a few moments?"

"Certainly," the nurse said, and walked out.

The silence seemed to weigh the room down. Calloway took a step toward the bed and said, "I was able to dig up some of your old medical records this morning."

"Yeah?"

"Do you remember having a lot of skin problems as a kid? A lot of changes in your skin?"

"Slightly," Sarah said with a weary smile. "I was always having moles removed. Acne. You name it."

It was true. Back in elementary school, the kids used to call her "Pizza Face." In fact, for most of her life, Sarah's complexion had been a battlefield. Through her teens, she had completely shunned chocolate, french fries, anything that might have exacerbated her acne. But it wasn't only zits. The chronic outbreaks were often accompanied by rashes, eczema, flaky areas, even cysts. The whole disgusting gamut of skin lesions. They'd be there one week and be gone the next. Her mother had simply chalked it up to nerves. *Got the marks of Job again, child,* Jessie had said every time Sarah had suffered an outbreak. *Gotta stop being such a Nervous Nelly.* But Sarah had always feared it was more than simple childhood acne, more than mere hypochondria.

It was the engine in her skull, the Great and Powerful Oz: her fucked-up brain.

"But it changed a lot," the neurologist said, after another moment's hesitation, "your skin, that is?"

"Yeah, sure, it was something new every week. Still happens to this day. Why?"

Calloway pursed his lips for a moment, then dismissed it with a wave of his hand. "I don't know, it's not important. There's something much more important to talk about."

"Oh, yeah?"

Calloway sat down on the edge of the bed. His hip pressed against the IV tubes. "Sarah, listen to me. There's some news. While you were under, we took the liberty of running another MRI on your brain."

"You did what?"

"We took an MRI, a scan. I know you've been doing some imagery work, and I think that's fantastic." Calloway tried to smile; but it came out like a wince. "The fact is, you're occipital tumor is . . . it's in complete remission."

"Excuse me?"

"Spontaneous remission," the doctor told her.

Sarah gazed at the clipboard.

"It's pretty remarkable," the doctor deadpanned. "Observed it only three times in my career. Once while I was an intern at the Mayo Clinic. Once over at Cook County in the late seventies. And now you. But with you it's happened in a strange . . . well . . . let's say it's happened with unprecedented speed. Less than a week. See for yourself—" Calloway pulled a dark gray transparency from his clipboard and showed her a series of day-glo, postage-stamp-sized scans taken earlier that morning. "The tumor's completely debulked," Calloway enthused. "Which means, essentially, it's gone."

Sarah swallowed air. "Gone?"

The doctor nodded fervidly. "It's almost as if your brain simply absorbed it."

Sarah tried to focus on the scan. The milky block was gone. Now only the faintest little smudge lay buried in the occipital fissure.

Like magic . . .

"Less than a week?" Sarah swallowed and tried get her bearings. She felt like a butterfly tacked to a cork board. Her thoughts were swimming.

. . . as if your brain simply absorbed it . . .

"You made yourself well, Sarah," Calloway said.

Sarah nodded, closed her eyes, and let the words sink in. She couldn't be happy. She couldn't feel any joy. She wanted to be home. She wanted Gypsy back. She wanted her job back. All at once, she felt tears seeping through the cracks of her lids. It was time to weep. It was time to let the emotion wrap around her and shake her. She turned her face away from the neurologist, pressed her cheek into the pillow, and sobbed.

The doctor respectfully turned away.

A moment later, Sarah uttered, "Dr. Calloway, can you help me get out of bed?"

"I think you should probably rest now," Calloway told her.

"Please." She looked up at him. "Just for a few seconds."

The neurologist shrugged, came over, lowered the railing, and helped Sarah off the bed and onto her feet. She was dressed in a hospital gown that was open in back, showing

God and the world her butt tattoos, but Calloway didn't even seem to notice. He kept his eyes glued to the tiles. Sarah turned and crept slowly over to the window, her head throbbing. Looking out at the overcast light of the courtyard, she said, "I don't know how to feel—I don't—"

Sarah stopped herself.

Something on her arm caught her attention. In the glare of the window, her left forearm was pasty white, the tiny angel hairs glistening like filaments of spun glass. Underneath her wrist, where the tattoo of two snakes wrapped around a long narrow femur bone, there were two new marks.

Sarah stared at them for a quite long time, before uttering, "Jesus—what's—happening to me?"

V

The twilight was like a serpent, weaving around the periphery of the forest, squeezing in on them, choking the light out of the day. The air had turned heavy and dank, laden with the odors of the harvest. And their irregular breathing and nervous words came out in puffs of white vapor, syncopated to the rhythmic crunch of their boot steps.

"How do you feel right now?" Henry asked, hands in his pockets, walking steadily alongside her. He wore a bright red CPO jacket over his faded chambray shirt and denims. He felt like a big old circus bear, stomping merrily along, completely out of place on the trail.

"I'm cold," Sarah announced softly.

Henry slipped out of his coat and draped it over her sweater. Sarah shivered. They had been hiking for nearly an hour in Harms Woods, a forest preserve northwest of Evanston. They had started in the late afternoon, after parking near a picnic shelter. And they had planned on walking for just a few seconds, but the seconds had stretched into minutes, and the minutes into an hour. There was much to talk about. Sarah had spilled her guts. Told Henry everything. The nightmare and the key. Waking up in the burning building. Coming home and finding the carnage. The flying monkeys haunting her, tormenting her. Henry didn't know what to make of it all.

"What did Calloway say?" Henry finally asked, after walking along silently for a while.

"That's really why I came to see you today," Sarah said, pulling the CPO tighter around her neck. They were heading into a heavy canopy of elm trees, and the temperature was plummeting. The path narrowed slightly. "See . . . while I was out this morning, they took some MRIs of my brain."

"And . . ."

"And I'm cured."

Henry stopped. "*What?*"

Sarah stopped as well, and then looked at him. "The tumor is gone, Henry. Completely gone."

"Gone? I don't under—"

"Spontaneous remission, Henry." Sarah shivered again, grimacing at the wind. Her face was haunted, drained, her eyes ravaged. "It's that miracle we were hoping for."

There was an awkward moment as the words sank in. Henry just couldn't believe what he was hearing. A woman who was on the verge of the abyss less than a week ago, desperate, clinging to any alternative available to her. And now, all of a sudden, wham! Her tumor goes into remission. And all she can do is stand there, looking like it's the end of the world. Henry didn't get it. Sure, the business with the sleepwalking and the blood and the dead cat was scary as hell. But, Jesus! The fates had given this woman a second chance.

"My God, Sarah!" Henry finally took her by the shoulders. "You did it!"

"Yeah," she said softly, gazing at the ground.

"You're a walking miracle."

"Am I?"

"Sarah, what's the matter? Don't you see the implications? You healed yourself just by thinking about it. Spontaneous remission, kiddo, for God's sake!"

Sarah pulled away and strode down the path, into the tunnel of undergrowth.

Henry hurried after his, a million contradictory thoughts swirling around his head. What was wrong with her? Why the sullen routine? Perhaps it was the emotional roller coaster. The intensity of all the changes had taken its toll. Henry couldn't imagine how difficult it must be to deal with all this. Then again, maybe the significance of what she had gone through hadn't dawned on her yet. Sarah had always been a repressive personality, a sort of psychological Scarlett O'Hara, and Henry had always tried to take things slow with her.

Catching up to her, Henry laid a comforting hand on her back and said, "Sarah, listen, I know it's been a nightmare for you, but it's over now, and you've got to—"

Henry stopped. The daylight had dwindled to the point that, beneath the arbor of elms, it was almost completely dark, and the primeval shadows curled around them. The air was as still and cool as a tollbooth at midnight. But even in the gloom, Henry could see the tears glimmering in Sarah's eyes.

Pausing by an ancient oak, Sarah looked up at him. "I'm scared, Henry."

"Talk to me, what's going on?"

"My tattoos—they're growing."

"What?"

"I noticed it this morning—look." She pushed her left sleeve up and showed Henry the snakes on the inside of her arm. Even in darkness, Henry could see the two slashes of jailhouse green streaking off the bottom of the tattoo, like an inverted V.

Henry frowned, staring at the ghostly marks. "Those aren't veins?"

"They're all over me, Henry," Sarah said, closing her eyes as though blocking out some horrible inevitability. "They're on my legs, my tummy, wherever there's another tattoo, like letters, like ghost writing . . ."

"Automatic writing," Henry murmured, absently scratching his cheek.

Somewhere, either in some archaic text or some New Age paperback, Henry Kemp had read about the phenomenon. It was similar to a process known as automatic writing, where a psychic would channel a spirit onto paper, feverishly scratching out indistinct words and phrases from the other side. But in this new phenomenon, the human body was the medium. The entity would communicate through stigma wrought across human flesh. To Henry, it was absurd and fascinating in equal measure. But he never thought he would encounter it in real life.

"What do you mean?" Sarah seemed vexed. "Automatic what?"

"Writing, automatic writing," Henry was saying, snapping his fingers.

The realization was rising in him like an inexorable tide. What if? What if—at this very moment—he happened to be walking beside the flesh-and-blood incarnate of the very subject he had been seeking for most of his professional life? A real, honest-to-goodness *autokinetic?*

For years it had been a pet theory of Henry's. Something he occasionally talked about at symposia and conferences, usually getting laughed off the podium by the rank and file. The logical extreme of Mind-Body theory. The possibility that a mutated strain of brain cells exists in infinitesimally small percentages of the population which enables the possessor to willfully alter his or her own physiognomy. Over the years, Henry had pretty much given up on finding empirical evidence—most of his success stories at the institute were people who had simply overcome illness. But now, with the revelation of Sarah Brandis's gift, Henry's juices began to flow again.

They continued walking.

"Were you thinking about the tattoos when they grew?" Henry was trying to play it cool at first; he didn't want to come on too strong. "What I mean is, did they play a role in the Munchkin imagery?"

"I dunno . . ." Sarah was walking long with her arms around herself as though she were holding in her guts.

"You think you could make them grow again—purposefully, I mean?"

"I don't think so. What are you getting at?"

Henry scratched his chin. "Just wondered, you know. I assume there's a pretty good MRI record at Northwestern."

"I dunno, why?"

"No reason." After another few paces: "You know if they did a BEAM test?"

"BEAM what?"

"Stands for Brain Electric Activity Map."

"I don't know, Henry—I just want my life back."

"I'm also wondering about galvanic skin response tests, wide-spectrum EEGs, maybe some evoked potential tracings. You have access to your files, right?"

"I suppose so." She gazed uneasily into his eyes. "Why are you so interested in all this stuff all of a sudden?"

Henry shrugged. "I'm your therapist."

Sarah licked her lips. "It just seems strange."

"Let me ask you something," Henry said. "Would you be willing to participate in a controlled experiment? Let me run some tests? Videotape some of our sessions?"

"What?" Sarah stopped abruptly.

"I just want to help you to understand—"

"Wait a minute!" Sarah shot her hand up, cutting off his words. "If you're looking for a guinea pig, Henry, I'm sorry. I've been poked and prodded and tested until my brains have leaked out my ears. I can't do it anymore"

"No, no, Sarah, please, you don't understand what I'm—"

"You said it yourself, Henry," she interrupted, her eyes shimmering now. In the darkness, a single tear tracked down her cheek and dripped onto the rise of her bosom. "It's *my* body. I've been showing it to men for years, shoving it in people's faces, and right now, I just want to keep it to myself."

"Sarah, I didn't mean any disrespect."

She peeled off the CPO coat and handed it back to him. "I gotta go."

"Sarah, wait—where are you going to do?"

She was already backing away, backing toward the mouth of the tunnel. "I just need to be alone for a while."

"Let me drive you home."

"No." She raised her hand again as she backed out of sight. "I just need to be alone."

"Sarah, please—" But before Henry could say another word, Sarah Brandis had vanished.

Henry started after her, but then paused. It was hopeless. He could hear the snap of her footsteps echoing off into the distance, melding in with the restless autumn breeze. And soon Henry was alone, alone in the darkness, alone with the wind and the skittering leaves and his silent regrets.

He turned and kicked a log. Hard. The impact sent pinpricks of pain up his leg. He wanted so desperately to chase after Sarah, to pull her back and grab her by the shoulders and tell her the truth. The truth about the powerful emotions stirring in Henry after all these years. Emotions toward a patient, for God's sake—emotions that were keeping him awake most nights, imagining the touch of Sarah's bare collarbone on his lips, the curve of her breast on his fingertips, the whisper of her hair on his neck. But these emotions were tempered by Henry's obsessive ambition to make a name for himself in the scientific community, to solve the riddle of Sarah Brandis. And that was the most painful part of all: that Henry's ambition was interfering with his heart.

But instead of following his heroic impulse to chase after her and confess everything, Henry turned, and as he had many times before, swallowed all the pain, and walked away.

VI

An old Yale burglar alarm, the kind with the big Klaxon bell and brass hammer, had a distinctive sound. It would clamor noisily, relentlessly shrill, feeling to a passerby as though it might almost crack a person's skull. In the old days, the days of bathtub gin and Walter Winchell, a Yale alarm would do a bang-up job of protecting country banks, pawnshops, and drugstores, scaring away the nasty villains like smoking termites out of a stump. But these weren't the old days anymore; these were the days of grade-school kids with 9mm semiautomatics, five hundred channels of cathode crap in every home, and an obnoxious car alarm going off every five minutes.

An old Yaley bell didn't have the impact it once had.

At the moment, in fact, there was one ringing with very little import at the corner of North and Western.

The FilmFax Costume and Novelty Shop was being invaded and nobody seemed to care. The sleepy row of storefronts on either side of the shop sat impassively still in a cloud of yellow vapor light. Across the street, an all-night Laundromat played host to a couple of somber black matrons dressed in sweatshirts, snapping their gum, staring into middle space while their secondhand clothes turned in front of them. They hardly even looked up when the alarm went off.

Inside the novelty shop, things were hopping.

A shadowy figure squeezed through the jagged breech of broken display glass and entered the dark shop. He moved with a kind of jaunty precision. Like a cat with more than nine lives. Although the darkness obscured his countenance, it was easy to see the kind of body on this man. Compact yet muscular. Barely five feet seven, yet tightly coiled and charged with a kind of latent vigor. The kind of psychotic strength developed over years of lunatic repetition.

The figure thought of himself as the Escape Artist.

He reached the end of the main aisle. On either side were rows of period costumes, Napoleonic sabers, Nazi brownshirts, Civil War muskets hanging off wooden hooks. The Escape Artist ran his fingertips across the range of fabrics. Past the eighteenth-century twills, the fifties gabardines, the turn-of-the-century wools. The odors of ancient, musty uniforms filled his nostrils and made him dizzy, intoxicated. Now that he was free, the excitement was almost unbearable. His sinewy hand finally landed on the perfect ensemble. He ripped it from the hanger and quickly slipped into it. He made a fist like a battering ram and drove it through a display case.

The glass shattered on impact.

From the case he uprooted more goodies. Accoutrements of his secret trade. He tried them on, adjusting them, snicking and clipping various items into vintage pockets. Snick-snick-snick—snap! He started toward the rear, but paused by the manager's desk. The cluttered desk was a treasure trove of wrapping materials, tape and twine and rope. The tools of his trade. He pocketed as much as he could carry.

The distant sound of a siren raised his hackles.

It was time to make another quick exit. All in a night's work for the Escape Artist. He whirled toward the rear door, a battered metal panel crossed with caging and padlocked securely. A splash of red light shone down from the EXIT sign. *Ladies and Gentlemen, prepare to witness another amazing feat of evasion; the Escape Artist is impervious to locks of any kind; he can extricate himself from trunks, handcuffs, chains, or bonds of any sort.*

He lowered himself to the floor, pantherlike, and shimmied across the tile to the base of the door. Pressing against the bottom of the door, he forced it open just a couple of inches, just enough. He filled the gap with the edge of his shoulder, part of his arm and the point of his hip. Then he started to breathe, tensing, then relaxing, tensing, then relaxing, tensing, the—*Eureka!*

He was out.

Free again, free to roam the night. He moved silently across the lot. Then down a side street. Navigating the shadows. Moving among the buildings and the alleys and the fire ladders and the roof tops.

He had a destination in his mind like a seed. He wasn't sure how it had gotten there; but it was sprouting nonetheless, the tendrils spreading through his brain, tiny tributaries, maplike, leading him on another mission. Other than these inchoate desires, his mind was a tabula rasa, completely blank, unformed, as empty as a black hole in his skull. He had no memories. No morals. No fears. Only his strange identity, and the need to bring pain to the one named Sarah. All of it coalescing inside him like stardust sprayed across the cold night sky.

It took him about an hour to reach the alley behind Dante's Inferno.

Forty-five minutes later, around two-thirty in the morning, two figures emerged from the nightclub's rear exit.

"Listen, Maxie, it's not something I'm particularly thrilled about myself," Duff Sellars was muttering as he held the door open and waited.

Maxine appeared in the doorway. "Duff, honey, things are going to shit around here, and you know it." She was cupping her hands around a match, sparking a Marlboro Light. The glow bloomed against her ebony face, revealing thick eyeshadow. Peroxide curls. Weary brown eyes. Dressed in bright purple spandex and a black leather jacket, Maxine had danced a double shift tonight in the wake of Sarah's departure, and she was bone tired. Her mild chocolate cleavage had a strange artificial sheen in the harsh glow of vapor light.

"Whattya want me to do about it?" Duff said, pulling on his cheap J. C. Penney's overcoat.

"I dunno, fight the motherfuckers."

"You want me to end up in a trunk?"

"C'mon, Duff, those motherfuckers aren't gonna kill your ass."

"That's not true," Duff insisted, thrusting his hands in the side pockets of his coat. "That's how they work, those mob guys—you look at them the wrong way and they put a bullet in the back of your head."

"That's bullshit—" Maxine froze and glanced across the lot. "Did you hear that?"

"What?"

"I dunno, like a whizzing noise, like a *whhhssshh?*"

Duff shrugged. "You want me to walk ya to your car?"

"Yeah," Maxine said, gazing uneasily at the dark rooftops across the lot. "Maybe you oughta do that."

They started down the alley.

The pavement cut between two blocks of buildings. The nightclub was on one side, an old armory and converted warehouse on the other. A single streetlight smoldered sickly yellow at the far end of the alley. Along parallel rooftops, frayed utility lines connected the buildings like gargantuan spider webs. Soot-covered exhaust fans were planted here and there in tar. And something was dripping loudly, the sound of filthy liquid on tin echoing through the gloom. An abundance of hiding places, and plenty of razor-thin shadows crisscrossing the path.

As she walked, Maxine kept her eyes peeled upward, murmuring. "There it is again."

Duff looked up. "What? What is?"

"That sound—that whirr—"

Sudden movement.

"What the fuh—"

The attack was so quick, so savage, so impossibly out of context, that Maxine could only comprehend in sudden flashframe glimpses the great black sail unfurling above them, strobe-fast in the vapor light, swooping down off the high-tension wire, jackknifing toward them, black fabric blossoming, glint of metal in their faces, and then the arterial spray like a fine warm vintage misting in Maxine's face.

The collision threw Maxine backward onto the pavement.

She rose to a sitting position and sucked in a gasp, paralyzed for a moment, trying to get her bearings, trying to absorb what she had just witnessed. The nameless assailant had landed nearby and was now rising to his feet, brushing himself off, wiping blood off his length of thick chain. He was a stocky young man dressed in strange, old-fashioned garb. Woolen suit, bowler hat, and black evening cape from the 1920s. Maxine couldn't quite make out his face. Duff Sellars was a few feet away, rising to his knees, eyes gaping as though he'd been hit by a car. His neck was ruptured. Blood streamed from his torn carotid like a fountain. A moment passed, and Duff tried to speak, but instead collapsed in a pool of his own blood.

The assailant came toward Maxine.

"No!" The word burst from her lungs as she scooted backward on her ass, waving him away in absurd childlike panic. Then she managed to twist around toward the mouth of the alley and struggle to her feet.

She ran like hell.

The assailant came after her, and Maxine could hear his surefooted pursuit echoing through the shadows, coming closer and closer as she reached the end of the alley and clamored across Derleth Street. At this time of night the neighborhood was deserted and dark, and Maxine stumbled over the opposite curb like a drunkard running a marathon. She was trying to think as she ran, think, think of a way out, think of a reason why this deranged dude in old theater clothes was coming after her, think of how the fuck she could be talking shop with Duff one moment and covered with his blood the next, think, *think-think-think-THINK*.

Careening around the corner of North and Derleth, she headed east. She was hoping for a cop, a passerby, a car, anything.

She didn't see the coat hanger.

The metal wire tangled around her feet and sent her sprawling to the cement. The impact knocked her silly for a moment, lungs heaving, clawing at the filthy pavement. A muscular hand suddenly fell upon her foot and dragged her backward. Maxine screamed. A thick metal cable whiplashed around her ankles, tightened, and pulled her back toward a shadowy vestibule, a place where her screams would go unheard, a place where her final hellish moments would unfold in privacy, but she wriggled and fought and cursed this motherfucker with her last ounces of proud Afro-Spanish courage until the final blow of the metal linkage to her temple knocked the wind from her sails.

She twisted around in a daze and gazed up. And she got one last look at the Escape Artist.

He was a dandy, somewhere in his mid-twenties with light brown hair and a cherubic face. The bowler hat was pushed back at a jaunty angle, and his muscled torso was encased in Roaring Twenties finery. Metal chain-link was crisscrossed over his chest like a bandoleer, draped with padlocks, loops of wire, and rope. In the silvery streetlight his skin looked pale, almost translucent. But there was a toughness about him, like a handsome little gangster in some surreal vaudeville show. There was also a strange, tormented gleam in his dark eyes.

This tormented gleam was the last thing Maxine would see before mercifully passing out.

The Escape Artist did his work quickly and quietly, wrapping the rope around her throat and then sliding the intricately carved bone-handled knife underneath the rope. He tightened the noose with a twist. Maxine came awake with a start, eyes bugging. Another twist. Maxine shrieked a soundless shriek. *Twist.* Maxine was twitching now, her tendons and muscles shivering, spittle forming at the corners of her mouth. *Twist.* Eyes going white, cheeks turning the color of eggplant, tongue swelling. A final *TWIST,* and the sound of her trachea snapping like a celery stalk, her throat collapsing, the blood bubbling out of her mouth, frothing pink from her sinuses.

The Escape Artist released his grip and watched the knife spin as the tension loosened.

Maxine sagged like a balloon deflating, her ebony skin marbled with blood, and the Escape Artist gazed at her for a moment. The sad fact was, the Escape Artist didn't relish this part of the job; it was simply a necessary evil. Especially the suffocating part. It was never pretty, watching someone suffocate, but he assumed that *that* was precisely the point.

Reaching down, he quickly scooped up Maxine's flaccid corpse and carried her all the way back down the sidewalk to the alley behind Dante's. It was a miracle that no one saw this macabre drama unfolding. But the Escape Artist didn't worry too much about such things; he didn't worry about being caught. He had much more important things to do.

He reached the place where Duff Sellars lay in a deep red Jackson Pollock pattern on the pavement.

He dragged Maxine over next to Duff and lay her head in the sticky mess. Then he knelt and started the wrapping. The wrapping and the sealing were the most important parts. They required all the Escape Artist's strength and concentration. Binding their feet and torsos together with duct tape was relatively easy. Wrapping them with chains of iron and rust metal cable was a little more involved. Padlocking all the chains together was time-consuming. And winding the bodies with another layer of rope was a chore, to say the least.

The Escape Artist was covering the bodies with plastic when the distant sirens started approaching.

He finished his task quickly, sealing the bodies with more tape. Then he dragged his load across the alley to a large, empty metal drum. He hefted the bodies over the edge and dropped them inside. Their legs protruded out the top almost comically, but the Escape Artist didn't miss a beat. He carefully bent both sets of legs at the joints and then folded them inside like sardines in a can.

He was padlocking the lid in place as the sirens and flashing lights were coming down North Avenue. Some Good Samaritan must have called the cops.

The Escape Artist didn't panic. He calmly brushed himself off and strode toward the opposite end of the alley. Toward the west exit. Toward freedom. He worried not one iota about getting apprehended.

After all, he was the Escape Artist, and he had much work to do.

PART II

The Other

What do I care about my shadow! Let it chase after me! I run away and I escape from it . . . but when I looked in the mirror I gave a cry and my heart shook; for it was not myself I saw but the grimacing face of a demon.

—Nietzsche
Also Sprach Zarathustra

Said the Caterpillar sternly, "Explain yourself!"
   "I can't explain *myself*, I'm afraid sir," said Alice, "because I'm not myself, you see."

—Lewis Carroll
Alice's Adventures in Wonderland

PART II

The Other

A Prodigy Is Born

She opened the antique volume, and the crackle of its binding echoed like a smoldering ember in the silent room. She took a breath. She nodded at the listener, an enigmatic nod, and then she gazed down at the text.

"He was born in Budapest, Hungary," she began, her voice low and steady, "on March 24th, 1874. But for some reason he always celebrated his birthday on the 6th of April. He did a lot of things for reasons known only to him. In fact, from the very moment he was born, he was an enigma. A mystery. His mother, Cecilia, had always been bemused by the fact that he never cried as a baby. And he slept very little. In the middle of the night, Cecilia would go into his nursery and find him awake in his crib, staring up at her with his blue-green eyes as though he were waiting for some kind of a sign.

"His father was a rabbi named Samuel. When the boy was barely a year old, Samuel packed up the family and sailed to America. They arrived in New York in 1875 and took a lake steamer inland to the town of Appleton, Wisconsin, where

79

they settled and started a new life for themselves. But tough times were ahead. Because of his broken English, and old world ways, Samuel found it difficult to adapt. He was eventually fired from the local temple, and subsequently became deeply depressed, withdrawing into his rabbinical studies."

The reader paused, wetting her lips. She reached for a Styrofoam cup of tea cooling on the end table beside her. She took a sip, took a breath, and then continued.

"This unfortunate series of events might have spelled disaster for any ordinary family, but fortunately, the boy had developed into a responsible young man. He took over as the wage earner for the family, doing odd jobs and keeping his brothers in line. By the time he was fourteen, he had landed a steady job as a necktie lining cutter. And through the next few years, he became especially close to his mother. Nothing made the boy happier than to come home and throw his weekly earnings into Cecilia's outstretched apron, eliciting a big warm smile.

"Little did Cecilia know the fire that was smoldering deep in her son's belly.

"The glimmer was first revealed in the spring of 1889. The boy was working at H. Richter and Sons, cutting ties, when a fellow employee named Jacob Hyman showed him a card trick. It was nothing special. Just a simple hide-and-reveal, but the impact it had on the boy was galvanizing. The boy fell in love with magic. He immersed himself in the art, the craft of magic. He traded tricks with Jacob. And he went to magic shows whenever he was able to scrape together enough pennies from his meager wage. He came to idolize a popular practitioner of the day named Carl Herrmann. Known as Carl the Great, Herrmann was considered one of the best in the world.

"Of course, at the time, nobody realized just exactly what the boy was about to accomplish himself. . . ."

4
Silent Stone Lips

I

Jimi Hendrix sliced through the haze, a velvet reaper, disemboweling the shadows. The sound had a shape, an impossibly long, liquid shape, like a razor, gleaming neon-bright. And the pain, radiating from it, pulsing, surging. And the scream just underneath it, the human scream, uncontrollable, a woman, her piercing wave form flirting with the feedback.

Sarah managed to lift her eyelids and realized all at once she was slumped in the corner of a strange room.

At first, the objects coalesced around her like a dream. The dark, the cluttered space, the lamp shades draped in old chiffon, the incense and crack pipes smoldering, tattered couches at odd angles, and pornographic glossies on the wall. It smelled like a mixture of perfume and urine. Figures were standing over her. Sarah blinked and rose to a sitting position, her bare spine pressed against the cheap paneling. There was an enormous black woman with relaxed curls and platform shoes staring down at her. Her purple suede dress was down around her ankles, mammoth breasts hanging free, her pubic region gleaming with oil.

81

"Muthafuck!" the black woman uttered, staring down at Sarah as though witnessing the Immaculate Conception.

"Where . . . am I?" Sarah gazed up at Miss Purple Suede and then down at herself through teary eyes. Sarah was completely naked, her tattooed thighs and fleshy belly covered with a sheen of perspiration. Her heart started fluttering, her head throbbing feverishly. *Another blackout,* she thought to herself, *another goddamned blackout.* Her mouth was so dry she could hardly yell the words, *"Please tell me where I am!"*

The Purple Suede Lady was too stunned to speak.

Sarah gazed around the room.

It was formerly a subway station; Sarah could see through plate glass, the ancient tile walls, the tunnel, the old dripping fixtures. At one time, the room was probably an office, but now this quasi-whorehouse/opium den had squatted garishly into the heart of the station like some kind of architectural parasite. Clothes were strewn about the room, and another hooker stood in the opposite corner, screaming to wake the dead. Screaming bloody murder. Dressed in dirty pink spandex and leather, she was a portly little white woman, with wild strands of inky-black hair, stocky arms, and a derriere squeezed into her dress like a sausage. Her piercing cry carried all the power and thrust of an overzealous opera singer.

This lady was spooked.

Sarah struggled to a standing position. Her bare feet were bleeding, and her arms and legs were scraped and bruised. Her knees buckled for a moment, then held, and she staggered toward the exit. Scooping up a stray piece of clothing, she held her breasts with one arm and staggered through a beaded doorway into the underground. *Getting too old for this nonsense, lady,* her mind shrieked at herself as she rushed across cold cement. *getting much too damn old.*

"MUTHAFUCK!" The voice of the Purple Suede Lady rang out behind her, rising over the music and the screaming.

Sarah didn't look back. She just kept on limping across the filthy concrete toward the far exit, pulling the fake fur overcoat around herself, feet slipping and sliding on their own blood, soles numbed by the pain, goddamned boobs jiggling painfully with every stride, but she kept moving, moving toward the stairs at the end of the depot.

"Hold up!"

The sounds of platform soles were cobbling after her now, and Sarah started running. Running for all she was worth. Across the cracked bricks and cement, over the threshold of the steps, and up the staircase, breasts flopping, mind swirling with fear and confusion, legs and torso panging sharply, the pain like a tether, holding her down.

She reached ground level.

The gray autumn rain shrieked in her face, and it was bracing, and she scanned the streets. It was near dawn, and the half-light illuminated a *Tribune* truck across the street and a couple of paperboys gathering their wares. A half a block away, two cop cars sat in conference together, the vapor from their exhaust forming a cloud around them.

Sarah started toward the opposite end of the street.

Within moments, she was gone.

II

"I'll be there in thirty minutes," Frank said, slamming the receiver down on the bedside extension. The call had come a few minutes past six, waking Frank from a dreamless sleep. It had been dispatch. Somebody had caught two dead bodies across town with MOs very similar to the warehouse whore.

By the time Frank hung up the phone, he was wide awake.

He got out of bed and quickly ran through his morning regimen. Sixty pull-ups on the stainless steel Weider bar. Sixty push-ups. A bracing shower in his stark black bathroom, the onyx tile walls gleaming. A quick towel-off, and back into his carefully organized closet to choose one of the crisp Ralph Lauren shirts, an Armani wool jacket, peg bottom slacks, and a pair of Lagerfeld loafers from his impeccably ordered closet floor. His many shoes were lined up on a cedar rack according to their seasonal, practical, and stylistic attributes. The more formal toward the left side of the continuum, the more work-oriented shoes toward the right. This configuration never changed.

A five-minute breakfast in the immaculate kitchen. Nonfat yogurt, organic carrot juice, and tea. No time to read the paper. He could hear the heater cycling on and off as he ate. The apartment was arrayed like Frank's intellect, no useless decor, zero clutter. The furniture was Bauhaus angular, steel and glass. Walls were bare, expect for a four-by-eight blowup of a Leni Riefenstahl photo in a chrome frame: an art deco statue of an eagle on a pedestal that had always seemed vaguely fascist to Frank. The picture had been a gift from a former girlfriend, an aerobics instructor whom Frank had always suspected of Nazi leanings.

Frank left at precisely six-thirty.

He took LaSalle Street, a bustling promenade of merchants and upper-class apartment blocks teeming with early rush-hour activity. It seemed every schmo with a storefront window had the Halloween doodads out, the black cats and the witches and paper jack-o'-lanterns.

Frank Moon had always hated Halloween. All the little sugar-buzzed brats with their Bart Simpson masks, toothless smiles, and sticky fingers, ringing the doorbell again and again and again, gimme gimme gimme—it made Frank ill. Always standing close behind the little nippers were the incessantly smug suburbanite parents, dressed in their L. L. Bean finery, all smiles, trick or treat, ha ha ha. To Frank, Halloween was a pathetic, watered-down, Hallmark card version of some ancient Druid blood orgy. And Frank Moon had seen enough blood to last him a lifetime, thank you very much. He had seen horrors up close. Last spring, for instance, Frank had entered a room in a local tenement where some poor soul had ventilated his skull with a pump-action job, and Frank had felt something dripping on his arm. Figured it was a leaky pipe and didn't even bother to look up, just kept gazing around the crime scene, analyzing the evidence. But when he finally looked up to locate the source of the leak, he realized it wasn't a leak at all; it wasn't even water. It was brain matter dripping from the ceiling. An ear, a clump of curly black hair, and a portion of a left eye socket were stuck up there like a butterfly pinned to a cork board.

Yes, Frank had seen his share of horrors—real horrors—so many that the cardboard vampires and cutout monsters of the storybook and screen had faded in his mind to mere folk art, charmingly naive cartoons, macabre marionettes. Real evil was banal. Real evil was the mob hit man who stuffs dry ice into the cavities of a recent victim, then stores the corpse in a basement refrigerator amid the rib roasts and chocolate ice cream in order to throw off the medical examiner's time-of-death findings. Real evil was the north side rapist who methodically severs the head, hands, and feet of his latest victim to avoid identification. Real evil was the irate wife who shoots her husband with the family hunting rifle and then stages it as a suicide, forcing honey-pie's stiff, rigored finger behind the trigger guard with all the realism of a Marshall Field's mannequin. Frank Moon knew all this and more about evil: It didn't snarl, grow fangs, turn into a bat, or come from outer space. It was the guy next door, the guy who attended just enough junior college chemistry classes to know that a single drop of laboratory-grade cyanide on a person's skin would kill that person within two minutes.

After a while, repeated encounters with this kind of evil does something to a man—especially a homicide detective. Unlike uniformed officers, or vice cops, or narcs, or tactical men, or any other unit of the Violent Crimes Division, the homicide dick never encounters the heat of the crime. Never pulls his gun. Never roars after the bad guys in a Steve-McQueen-movie-moment-high-speed pursuit. Homicide detectives are note takers. Thinkers. They're the archeologists of the police department, picking through the aftermath. Always the aftermath. Learning secrets from the silent stone lips of the dead. And because of this, the homicide dick is passive-aggressive. He learns to sublimate his rage, his angst, his repulsion. For some, it's gallows humor. Sick jokes. For others, it's thinking of the crime as a game, a goofy board game. Some guys even view the job as one big comic book; and they're the gallant dark knights, out to avenge the victims.

Not Frank Moon.

The way Detective Moon dealt with all the horror was by concentrating. Frank's level of concentration was almost zenlike. The other detectives even joked about it. Called him Swami. The Guru. But it didn't bother Frank. He used his powers of concentration as a tool, a natural resource. He would see things at a crime scene that other cops would usually miss. He would uncover some minuscule bit of evidence through sheer intuition. He would snag a confession through dogged, stoic repetition. He would control his revulsion through a system of mnemonics, little rhymes and formulas and memory devices. And he would use the music. The jazz in his head.

At the present moment, in fact, Frank was on the verge of finding the perfect music for his latest case.

He pulled the Lexus around the corner of Division and Derleth and headed south. It was edging toward 7 A.M. Frank had been thinking about the bodies behind Dante's Inferno from the moment he had awakened, and he had his fingers crossed that (A) the MO matched the abandoned building murder and (B) the scene was still fresh. The Lexus skimmed across Huron Street, swimming through dead leaves matted to the pavement by a fine gray drizzle. Frank turned the wipers on. Outside, the early morning noises were muffled by the car's hermetically sealed windows. Jackhammers buzzed softly. Garbage trucks murmured. Some goof with a bullhorn was moaning something about Jesus. Frank ignored it all and loaded a compact disc.

Jay McShann's honky-tonk piano riff suddenly leaped out of the speakers. Kansas City blues filled the car. A walking bass line thumping like hot sex, cymbals sizzling, and McShann's whorehouse riff like the pump of sweaty hips. Frank loved the blues, listened to it often. But right now, it was all wrong. Too straightforward for a whodunit. Too sweaty. Frank pressed the EJECT button and the player spit out the silver wafer.

Frank chose another.

A moment later, a freight train filled the interior of the Lexus. Thunder and clatter to a 3/4 beat, a fire-breathing dragon of a drummer. Frank turned it up and felt the backs of his ears tingling. It was Gene Krupa, the legendary swing-era bandleader and one of Frank's favorites for years. Gene Krupa had revolutionized big band percussion. His jungle-beat toms and lightning bolt rim shots drove big bands from Benny Goodman to Lionel Hampton. But it was during the killer solos, the flights of fancy, that Krupa really took off. It was no longer the *shoop-shoop-shoop* rhythm of the ball-room bands, daddy, dig, this cat was BADOOM-BADOOM—BADDA-BOOMMM-BADDA-BOOMMM-BADDA-BOOMMM—BADOOM-BADOOM—BADDA-BOOMMM—BADDABOOMMMMM!

Frank arrived at the mouth of the Derleth Street alley in the perfect frame of mind.

He parked near the yellow tape and got out of the Lexus. He slipped on his rubber gloves. Flipped open his notepad. Put his lightweight Walkman headphones on. Snapped his shield around his pocket and limboed under the cordons, nodding at the two uniforms standing guard near the ambo and the meatwagon. There was a small phalanx of gawkers behind the cordons, neighborhood kids, a couple of sauce heads, some local street skells rubbernecking. Frank blocked them out of his mind. Completely. The next few moments were the most crucial in any investigation, those precious seconds when the scene was still fresh and the physical evidence was at its prime.

Frank walked up to a tall, lanky uniformed officer pacing near a large metal drum. The officer held a crowbar in his left hand and was tapping it on his leg. The drum had a broken padlock sitting on its lid and seemed to be soaking wet, probably from the morning mist.

"You first-on-the-scene?" Frank asked the lanky cop.

"Yeah, we answered the ten-thirty-three last night. Got here after the fact."

"Who opened it?"

The lanky cop looked exceedingly nervous. "I did. Pried it open. Saw the eye."

"The eye?"

The cop nodded. "Saw two large objects covered with tape and plastic and whatnot. Except there was an eye peeking out of one of the lumps of plastic. I saw the eye and I called an ambulance. The medic pronounced both victims right on the spot."

"Victims?"

"Male and female," the officer said. "Positive IDs on both. Daniel Sellars, sixty-three, manager of the strip bar behind us. The girl is Maxine Morrisey, a dancer at the bar. The cleanup crew said they left the bar at two-thirty and that's the last anybody saw of 'em."

"Witnesses?"

"Negative."

Frank nodded. "Okay, thanks a lot. I'll just need a few more minutes and then the ME guys can take over."

The cop walked away.

Frank reached down to the Walkman, pressed PLAY, and let Krupa's "Disk Jockey Jump" thunder in his ears.

The notebook came first, and at the top of the first page, he began recording the salient points: *730 hrs—Dispatch #42—2 bodies found—similar MO to abnd. building.* He recorded the incident number, the city ambulance number, and the medic who made the pronouncement. Gene Krupa thundered on. Next came the scene. Frank never went to the bodies first; he always started with the perimeter, walking a twenty- to thirty-foot circle around the remains, looking for fibers, prints, shells, fragments, blood, anything, anything at all. Spiraling down toward the body. Unfortunately, the rain had ruined the pavement for this one. *No vsbl. blood trails—no trks.—pave clean.* Krupa kept pounding away.

Frank went over to the bodies.

The lid came off easy. The padlock clattered off the edge and fell to the ground. Frank flinched at the smell for a moment, then set the lid down and looked into the drum. It was a grisly Picasso. Eyes gaped up through ragged holes in the black shrouds. Feet curled inward. A gleaming yellow death rictus peeked out. Fingers protruded through the chains. Blood spackled everything like raspberry jelly, and flies were buzzing angrily around the faces.

Krupa's cymbals crashed and sizzled majestically.

Frank made notes. *Sellars—W. male—60s—jagged linear laceration across neck—cause of death: massive blood loss.* Krupa wailed on the toms, sounding like an antiaircraft gun. *Morrisey.—B. Female—cause of death: strangulation.—note edema around neck and collarbone, discoloration, lividity in tongue and face.* Frank leaned over the edge, carefully peeled away a layer of tape and plastic, and pressed his rubber-coated finger against Maxine's shoulder. It had the consistency of a ripe avocado. Frank wrote: *Mild rigor setting in—guess six hours, see ME for better time-of-death estimate.*

Turning away from the flies and the black smell, Frank took a deep breath and cleared his head.

The drizzle had almost completely lifted, and now the bright overcast sky bolstered Frank's thought process. He had already concluded several things about the scene. The MO was very similar to the abandoned building/prostitute case. Very possibly a serial murder situation, although he wouldn't breathe a word of that to the shift commander. The press would be all over it like the flies on these bodies. And although there were still no witnesses in either crime, there was a thread of logic weaving through Frank's mind like a musical leitmotif.

Motive.

BADDABOOM-BADOOMMMM-BADDADDADDA-BOOMMMM!

The dancer—what's her name—Brandis, Sarah Brandis. The sleepwalker. Frank had read the night before in a surveillance memo that she'd been fired from Dante's. Disgruntled employees were always up for a huge percentage of kills in Metro Chicago. Frank had seen it many times before. Best motive in the world. But to pull off a goof trick like this—with the wrapping tape and the rope and the padlocks—a girl would have to be a nut case of the first order.

BADOOMMM—BADDABADDA-BOOOMMMM!

Frank reached down and goosed the volume. Krupa thundered. The man's cymbal work was the best in two decades of swing orchestras. Put Zildjian on the map. Frank started toward his car, stuffing the notebook back inside the inner breast pocket of his Armani jacket. He had a motive now, and he had the music, and he had much to do. He wasn't going to pop this one right away, no sir, this was going to go down right and true. There was a certain rhythm Frank wanted to establish with the DA and Intelligence and Tactical, a certain tempo with Surveillance.

DADDOOM-BADOOOMMM!

The lanky uniform was coming across the cordons toward Frank, moving his mouth.

"Pardon?" Frank lifted the sponge headphone off one ear.

"We all set?"

"Yeah, you can call in the crime lab sniffers now," Frank told him. "I want good shots of the whole shebang. Good ones, this time. Color. Everything dusted. Dust like crazy. And I want your CID report on my desk end-of-day."

"Anything else?"

"Yeah," Frank smiled. "Have a nice day."

And with these final words, Frank put the headphones back on and strode across the cordons to his Lexus.

BADDOOOOMMMM!

III

Sarah was on the floor by the refrigerator. The fridge door was wide open, the light and cool air seemed to calm her somewhat, the smell of old pickle relish and congealed mustard reminding her that life went on, and the world still turned, and food still spoiled in the crowded door shelves of her Amana.

She was wearing a long terry-cloth robe, a bandanna cinched pirate-style over her hair. She wore no makeup, and her face was scrubbed raw. She had taken a shower a couple of hours ago, after stumbling through the door in her pilfered fur coat. She had sobbed like a baby through most of the shower, scrubbing her arms and legs with a dish rag as though trying to scrape off radioactive paint.

The tattoos had appeared at some point last night, during her blank hours, the sleepwalking and God-knew-what-else. Jailhouse-green vertical slashes, growing, materializing like photographs in a chemical bath. The inverted v transformed into the letter A. Then an L. Then an I. Then: ALIVE, along the inside of her thigh. ALIVE, under her left forearm. ALIVE, above her belly button. ALIVE! And now the phantom tattoos stung to the touch like papery thin burns, pinpricks of pain radiating outward from their centers, the skin red and rashed.

What in God's name was happening to her?

"All right, let's get it together," she said, and looked down at her hand, where a leftover piece of barbecued chicken was nestled in her right palm, leaving a sticky ring of sauce around her finger and the webbing of her thumb. She took another bite and washed it down with the last ounces of Chardonnay that she had discovered lurking behind a carton of buttermilk. She tossed the drumstick across the kitchen.

It tasted rancid.

Her world was coming apart at the seams and all she could think about was food. She wanted a greasy hamburger, french fries, onion rings, coconut cream pie, macaroon cookies. Her head was a blur of fear and confusion, but the thought of eating seemed to steady her, anchor her to some partial foundation of normalcy. She felt the chills again, raking across the backs of her arms and feathering down her legs. She was exhausted, and her resistance was down, and she felt a cold—

The door buzzer made her start.

She rose to her feet, tightening the robe around her midriff. She took a deep breath and shook off a surge of dizziness. Then she turned and walked through the kitchen, across the living room, and over to the intercom. "Who is it?" she said, thumbing the call switch.

"It's Henry," the voice crackled.

Sarah exhaled a breath of relief. "C'mon up, Henry," she said, and released the lock.

Within seconds, the big man was standing outside Sarah's half-ajar door. "I wanted to check on you," he said, fidgeting in the doorway. "I was . . . worried."

He was wearing a bulky Shetland fisherman's sweater, the kind with the big wooden buttons, and worn khakis. His hair, which looked freshly washed, cascaded down around his broad shoulders. His expression was knitted with concern. He looked as solid as an oak, standing there on the landing, and Sarah felt a wave of emotion wash over her that almost made her blush. She was thankful for this big man, whatever his motivations might be. "Come in," she said with a jagged edge of exhaustion in her voice. "I was just about to heat something up for dinner."

"If this is a bad time, I can—"

She pulled him inside and shut the door.

Henry gazed around the apartment. "Looks like you've gotten the worst of the mess cleaned up," he said.

"Yeah," Sarah said, "I guess."

The living room was put back together as completely as possible. Most of the framed posters were missing their glass. Some of the lobby cards were taped back together. And most of the blood had been washed off the walls, although dark patches and pinkish areas still remained, with

ghostlike remnants of the word ALIVE peeking through here
and there. The furniture was back in place, some of it being
held together with duct tape. And the broken windows had
cardboard taped over them. Sarah had buried Gypsy in the
vacant lot out behind the alley, marking the gravesite with a
crude cross and one of the cat's favorite toys.

Sarah went over and sat on the edge of the dining table.
"But then again," she added, "it's not like the place was ever
going to win any awards from *Architectural Digest*."

"I like this place," Henry said, taking a seat next to her, his
massive weight making the table creak. "I think it's cozy."

Sarah smiled wearily. "Why did you come here tonight,
Henry? I know it wasn't to compliment my interior decorat-
ing."

"I wanted to apologize."

"You don't need to apologize for anything."

Henry raised his hand. "This is something I need to say. You
were spilling your guts to me yesterday and I came on way too
strong. You trusted me, and I betrayed that trust . . . and I'm
sorry."

Sarah nodded and then looked down at her bare feet. She
had Band-Aids on three of her toes. "Henry, I gotta tell ya—
I'm in a bizarre way right now. Something is happening to
me, and I can't stop it, and I swear to God it started with the
imagery. The box. The box opening up."

"All right, we'll deal with it."

"I wish I had your confidence."

"One step at a time, Sarah."

Sarah shot him a look. "I don't think you understand what
I'm telling you. I woke up in a *whorehouse* today—some
kind of blasted-out underground brothel—and I have no idea
how I got there."

"Did you see Callaway afterward?"

"No, no, I don't think the good doctor has any idea how to
deal with this anymore." Sarah sighed, feeling old all of a
sudden, very old. She took a breath and looked at the stocky
therapist. "Henry, let me ask you something. You were

quizzing me last night about the tattoos, how they were growing, and if it had anything to do with the imagery?"

"I remember."

"What were you getting at? What did you think you would find with all the tests?"

Henry licked his lips and gazed off at the ghosts of bloodstains on the wall for a moment. He looked to Sarah as though he were turning something over in his mind. "There are legends," he began, tentatively, as though testing the water. "All the way back to ancient Greece. Eastern cultures have 'em. Bedouin folklore. The Native Americans. They all have their own versions of the same archetype—people who can heal themselves, even willfully transform their own bodies. Now, in the last few years, the scientific community has been taking it on faith that we all have this potential. This potential to transform our bodies. But I think there may be people among us, exceptional people, who can do this in spades. In other words, I believe the legends are based on reality. Call them anomalies."

"Anomalies?"

"I'm talking about people with obscure mutations in their brain cells. People with an extra thymine molecule somewhere. Or maybe an extra DNA strand. Something that acts as a sort of generator, and it not only enables the brain cells to repair and manipulate themselves, but it allows them to repair and manipulate other parts of the body."

Sarah felt light-headed. She pushed herself away from the table and paced across the room. Then she turned and faced Henry. "You think this is me?"

Henry stood up. "I don't know, Sarah. I'm not sure there's enough to go on."

"Really?" She was trembling now, her hands gripping the belt of her robe. "Is that a fact? Not enough evidence? Let me show you something—" She reached down and pulled the robe away from her thigh.

"Jesus . . ." Henry stared at it for a moment, then came over for a closer look.

"Is that enough evidence?" Sarah asked him, her eyes shimmering with tears.

The phantom tattoo had spread down the inside of her right thigh like a green flame. Letters slashing the skin, almost childish scrawl, ALIVE. Henry swallowed hard as he looked at it. Then Sarah rolled her left sleeve up and showed him the marking on her arm.

"See . . ." she said, her voice wavering, a single tear tracking down her cheek. "They're . . . all over me . . . everywhere." Her entire body was trembling now, shuddering as she ran her fingertips up and down the strange insignias. "Look." She untied the robe and displayed her soft belly, the rolls of flesh like warm curdled cream, lined with faint stretch marks. She was wearing cotton panties and a well-worn Playtex underwire—*an old-lady bra,* Sarah called it— and her semi-nude, trembling body seemed especially vulnerable. "It's like somebody's writing goddamn graffiti on my skin."

She closed her eyes, and she fought the tears.

Henry came over and gently closed the robe. "All right, take it easy," he whispered, and cradled his arm around her back. Sarah buried her face in the side of his neck, and she smelled his smell, and she started losing her composure. "It's okay," Henry whispered.

Sarah began to weep, and she wept hard. She wept all the pain and fear into that bulky fisherman's sweater. And soon she was drinking in Henry's grassy, earthy smell, that smell of sweat and soap and old wood, and it filled her senses. And suddenly she pulled away, almost as though she'd touched a hot steam pipe. Her heart was racing.

"What is it?" he said, stunned.

"It's nothing—*nothing,*" she said, wiping her tears, turning and striding across the living room, feeling flushed and confused and embarrassed, like a pathetic little schoolgirl, infatuated with her counselor. She went into the kitchen and snapped on the lights. The tile felt cool on her bare feet, and she took deep breaths, and soon she had things nominally

under control. "Lemme get you something to eat, Henry,"
she called out to him, and opened the refrigerator door. She
scanned the empty shelves, the old Tupperware containers
filled with moldy remainders. "And I hope you're feeling
brave tonight," she added, "because the pickings are slim."

Henry appeared in the doorway.

Sarah continued rifling through the leftovers, babbling,
"Before you came I was sitting here trying to figure out what
to eat, and boy-oh-boy, we're talking major science project
in here, I mean, I hope you like penicillin because a lot of
this stuff has seen better days—"

She looked up.

Henry was standing over her, licking his lips, hands in his
pockets. He looked pained, and trapped, and maybe even a
little ashamed. "Sarah—" he said, swallowing hard, "I've
been a therapist for a good fifteen years, and I gotta tell ya, it
gets complicated. What I mean is, if you wanted to find
somebody else, I wouldn't blame you."

Sarah rose to her feet and looked at him. The fridge door
separated them, a strange cold barrier that shone bare white
light up into Henry's eyes. Sarah looked at him another moment. "What's the matter, Henry?"

Henry put his big callused hands on the fridge door. "The
thing of it is . . . I don't think I should continue being your
therapist without disclosing the truth."

"The truth?"

He swallowed hard. "Yeah, it's kind of a professional
courtesy, actually—you know, full disclosure . . . I guess you
could say I'm falling madly in love with you."

Dead silence.

Henry stared at his hands at though they belonged to
someone else. "Isn't that the stupidest thing you ever heard?"

Sarah was speechless for another moment. It felt as though
her feet were glued to the parquet floor and her bones and
tendons were liquid, hot liquid, flowing down through the
vessel of her flesh. She swallowed air. Then she looked
down at his hands on the door, and she gently touched his

knuckles with her fingertips. "I don't think it's stupid at all," she said.

Henry looked up, and their eyes met, and all of Sarah's pain seemed to flow into him.

"Maybe it's not so stupid," Henry whispered finally, as though it were a secret spoken in a confessional booth.

"It's not," Sarah murmured, and she leaned over the fridge door and kissed him softly on the lips.

Henry's hands rose to Sarah's cheekbones, gently cradling her face. And they kissed again, their passion rising like the heat in Sarah's loins. All at once, the surprises began to flow over Sarah like a salt wave, the tenderness with which Henry kissed, the tip of his tongue brushing her lower lip—*surprise*. The urgent and sudden hunger which vibrated Sarah's nerve endings, making her wet as she tasted the salty tang of his breath, his tongue, his rough whiskered chin on her neck—*surprise*. And the rush of electricity between her legs, the feathery current bolting up her tendons, stealing her breath, flushing her face and swirling through her brain—SURPRISE!

"Make love to me," Sarah whispered, her husky-velvet voice dropping about thirty-seven octaves.

Henry lifted her easily, hefting her soft ass over to the formica island in the center of the kitchen, easing her onto the counter, and then peeling away her robe. Sarah worked the sweater over his head, her heart thumping in her ears as she got Henry's shirt off and felt his thickly muscled pectorals, his big sweet belly, and his cock hardening under his khakis. Henry's hands were all over her at once, gentle-firm on her thighs and her tummy, caressing her heavy breasts through the fabric of her bra. Her nipples were tightening under the ribbon-weave like hard little bullets, tingling, singing up her nerve endings. She shoved him away for a moment, reaching around to unsnap her bra.

When her breasts fell free, Henry gaped.

"Get over here, Henry," Sarah whispered suddenly, unaware that she had even said anything, her brain buzzing now, buzzing. "*Please* get over here."

She reached out for him, and Henry slipped out of his pants in a flash and then slipped into her arms. Sarah plummeted into the waves of his scent, his heat, his strength, their salty wet kisses tender at first, tongues jousting softly, then pressing harder, more desperately. Henry's hands poured down her spine, his hungry fingers stroking the small of her back, reaching up, threading through her hair, tracing her ears, cupping her boobs, and then down to her ass.

When he entered her, Sarah's mind swirled with colors and light.

They made love like it was the last request of two condemned prisoners, all teeth and saliva and sweat. Sarah moaned and murmured and mewled, her voice a hoarse blur in her own ears, *give it to mama, good boy, yes,* his mouth everywhere at once, his lips melding with hers, *good boy, yes, Henry, Henry, Henry,* his warm breath, even the sharp edges of his front teeth were like warm rain drops on her collarbone, her nipples, her neck, and he was such a good boy, *good boy,* giving it all to mama, he was everything, everything Sarah had hungered for, he was fettucini with mussels marinara, he was marinated medallions of beef, he was Black Forest cake, he was New England crab cakes, and he was shrimp dejonge and Cajun jambalaya and homemade bread pudding with rum and raisins and light cream sauce, and oh God, oh my God, how he made her vibrate, like bubbles, like champagne bubbles, like root beer floats with French vanilla ice cream, and more than anything else, for one brief moment, one fleeting instant, Henry Decker did the impossible.

He made her forget the fear.

IV

An hour later they lay in a heap on the sofa out in the living room, the slanted blinds above them covering shattered glass, filtering out the fragmented beams of streetlight from outside. The living room was dark. They lay there for quite some time, listening to the radiators sputtering and cycling, their naked limbs intertwined and a cotton blanket draped across their midsections. Their wheels were turning. Processing the emotional tumult of the past few days. Trying to figure out where to go from here.

It was Sarah who spoke first.

"You mentioned an experiment."

"What?" Henry was staring at the slatted bands of light across the carpet, ruminating silently.

"The experiment you were talking about last night," Sarah said. "The tests."

"Yeah?"

"Where would you do something like that?"

"Friend of mine, David Johnson—he works at Northwestern. They've got this facility on campus—a co-op, really—where they run all sorts of programs. Psych 101 students earning extra credit, that sort of thing."

There was a stretch of silence.

"What are you thinking about?" Henry said.

Sarah started biting her fingernail, staring up at the ceiling. "Nothing, really."

Henry pondered her for a moment. Sarah's head was nestled in the crook of his arm—her sweet, lovely, gifted head—and Henry could smell the rich bouquet of her hair. He was spent, his legs felt like hollow papier-mâché, his cock like a bird that had gone to sleep in the nest of his pubic hair. Nevertheless, Henry felt galvanized. Transformed by the intimacy. For the first time in years—maybe in his whole life—he was happy, disgustingly happy. He had opened the door and walked right into a dream, and he never wanted to wake up. But beneath the tranquil surface, there was a vague dread, like a shark circling.

Henry knew there were a million kinds of trouble involved in patient-therapist affairs. Forget about it being highly unethical, it was downright dangerous. Not only could Henry lose his license, but he could also lose Sarah. The protocol gets all screwed up when a patient sleeps with her shrink; any level of objectivity   ᵈ therapeutic distance completely dissolves, and the therapist becomes just another piece of cargo in the overall emotional baggage. The last thing that Henry wanted to do was hurt Sarah. In fact, at the moment, with her dark curls flowing across his bare chest and her moist breasts pressing up against his belly, he was thinking that he might just want to spend the rest of his life with her.

"You know," he began to say in earnest, "you can always find another therapist."

"What?" Sarah shot a glance up into his eyes.

"Yeah, you know, if you're feeling uncomfortable . . . you know, with the arrangement."

Sarah's eyes got wet. "Are you crazy? You're the best thing that ever happened to me, Henry." She reached up, palming his whiskered cheek and kissing him.

Henry felt the emotion welling in his chest, his stomach tightening. Over the years, he had forgotten how lonely he'd become, living up in the drafty Victorian near the lake, obsessed with his work, giving his heart and soul to every sad sack who walked in his door. Now he was letting his feelings break down the dam and flood his world. Fuck professionalism, fuck ethics, fuck the American Psychiatric Board; Henry Decker was in a better place now.

Henry Decker was in love.

"I think you're pretty neat, too," he murmured, and stroked her hair.

In the other room, the phone started to ring.

"You want me to get it?" Henry asked.

"No, let it ring, it's been ringing all night, I just don't want to hear any more bad news."

Henry nodded.

Sarah looked at him. "Henry?"

"Yeah?"

"I want to do the experiment."

Henry blinked. "You what?"

Sarah sat up on the edge of the sofa and gazed down at him, a grave expression on her face. "I'll be your guinea pig."

Henry regarded her for moment, and then said, "You're sure you know what you're getting into?"

"Yeah, absolutely," she said. And then her voice lowered imperceptibly, her tone growing a fraction darker. "The question is, do you?"

5

The Netherworld

I

Northwestern University was the closest thing to the Ivy League that the Big Ten would ever have. Located in the northeast quadrant of Evanston along a mile's worth of prime Lake Michigan coastline, the school was a sprawling network of ancient brick and mortar. In the autumn, right around the beginning of the school year, if the sunset was just right and the wind off the lake wasn't too angry, the place looked positively haunted. Like some kind of gothic prep school straight out of a Charlotte Brontë novel.

The psychology building was especially prominent, although no less brooding. Rising up against the gunmetal sky, its scarred brick garrets cresting above twisted oaks, it looked more like a stoic old man than a building, hunched in perpetual grief. The south side was carpeted in ivy, and beneath a frieze of crumbling, sculpted letters, a large portal surrounded a series of stone steps. Flanked by pilasters, these steps led up into the shadows of the only door accessible to students and the general public.

Around noon, the day after their unexpected union, Henry and Sarah found themselves waiting outside this door.

"You okay?" Henry asked her, stomping his feet to stay warm, his breath visible in the chill.

Sarah nodded.

"Remember," he said, "I want this to be your decision. The instant you feel uncomfortable, we'll shut right down."

Sarah told him that was fine, and she said she was okay, and she asked him to stop worrying.

It was a Saturday, and the football team was away, so the campus was relatively deserted. Sarah lifted the collar of her tweed duster and gazed around the adjacent yards. It was cold. Bone-chilling cold. And the calico leaves fluttering across serpentine bike paths only added to her feelings of displacement. She was wearing a torn sweatshirt, black leotards, and Doc Martens under her coat. Although she had no idea what to wear to a psychometric experiment, she figured she would at least be comfortable.

"There he is!" Henry said, whirling toward the stone steps, his baggy parka swishing.

A gangly, bearded man had appeared in the shadows of the portal. Dressed in a gaudy cowboy shirt, black slacks, and broken-down pointy boots, David Johnson came down the steps looking like an academic idiot savant. A rustic egghead with no conception of the world outside his own little think tank.

And Sarah was about to learn just what kind of bizarre tank it was.

"Hey, this is going to be fun," the gangly man enthused as he came up to Henry.

"Dave, hi, this is Sarah."

"Hi," said the cowboy man, and Sarah couldn't help feeling as though she were being welcomed into a secret club.

"Dave and I go way back," Henry said, "all the way back to undergraduate hell at Michigan State."

"Henry was a fascist back then," Dave informed Sarah.

"Eat shit, Dave," Henry said genially, still a tad nervous. "You all set for our little powwow?"

"Yeah," David replied, rubbing his hands together, "we got some really neat stuff down there. Some great gadgets to work with today."

"You got the baby PET scanner down there?"

"You bet; we got the little one, we got the BEAM monitor, we got the EEG, we got the full snake apparatus, and—get this—we got a *hood*."

"You got a *hood* dow. ere?" Henry asked incredulously.

The man in the cowboy shirt nodded.

Henry turned to Sarah and said, "The MEG hood is an unbelievable tool for reading brain activity, stands for Magnetic-something-or-other—"

"Magneto-encephalograph," Dave corrected.

"Oh," Sarah said, shivering in her boots. It wasn't just the chill in the air, or the incessant fear in the back of her mind like an abscessed tooth, or even the talk of all this bizarre technology. It was the continuing reference to *down there*. Sarah was starting to wonder whether she really wanted to find out where *down there* was.

"Shall we go?" Dave said, turning on his bootheels and leading them back up the stairs and through the ancient door.

They followed the cowboy down the main hallway of the psych building, past empty classrooms and locked offices. The smell of the place—that stuffy, pencil lead and old varnish smell—reminded Sarah of her year and a half studying dance at the Art Institute. She had never really taken to academia, except for the movie screenings. She had loved seeing those pristine restored prints of her favorite old musicals. But after two long years of professors hitting on her and dance teachers discouraging her because of her "unfortunate figure," both her patience and her student loan had run out.

Dave led them around a turn at the end of the corridor, through a door marked STAFF ONLY, and down a rickety set of iron stairs.

They reached the bottom of the stairs and found themselves in a boiler room that smelled like fuel oil and old rubber. Sarah gazed around at the cement floor, the hulking furnace, the octopus of heating ducts and conduits. Everything had a layer of ashy filth.

"This way," Dave said, creeping down a narrow path between the furnace and a shelf cluttered with storage cans.

"Wait a minute," Sarah said, finally stopping in the shadows at the end of the shelf. "Where the hell are we going, Henry?"

Henry turned and smiled reassuringly. "Don't worry, it gets better. We're almost there."

"Almost where?"

"The sleep lab," Dave called over his shoulder, as he paused in front of another locked metal door, fishing for the right key. "You're gonna love it."

He opened the door.

"Welcome to the netherworld," the cowboy said with a mischievous grin, then ushered them inside.

At first, Sarah thought it was a joke.

The room looked like a cross between a country club prison and the Pirates of the Caribbean ride at Disneyland. It was carved out of the subterranean sediment of granite and shale, and its furnishings and equipment were embedded in the side of the earth like a prehistoric diorama. There was a living space, presumably for the sleep-pattern subjects, complete with kitchenette, bunk beds, video games, and white fiberboard organizers brimming with books and tapes and magazines. The opposite side of the room was crowded with high-tech machinery, computer monitors, and spaghetti knots of wires and cables hanging like stalactites. It smelled of disinfectant and recycled air. On top of one of the EEG machines in the corner was a plastic model of a human head, the phrenological markings sectoring the brain. Someone had stuck a cigarette in each of the skull's nostrils.

"Whoa," Sarah exclaimed, gazing around the lab, her voice swallowed by the dead ambience.

"Pretty cool, huh?" Dave said, taking a seat on one of the

swivel chairs in the corner. "The Psych Department uses it once in a while, chronobiology experiments, stuff like that."

"Sleep deprivation?" Sarah asked, taking off her coat. It was a moist room-temperature in the lab, and she was starting to perspire under the tweed.

"Sleep patterns, mostly," Dave said.

"Why don't you get comfortable over here, Sarah." Henry motioned at the living area and pulled a padded chair out from behind a desk. "We'll start with the simple galvanic skin response stuff, nothing too rigorous."

"Whatever you say, Doc," Sarah said, throwing her coat on the bunk bed and taking a seat.

Henry knelt down by Sarah's chair and looked deep into her eyes. "You sure you're okay with this? Just give me the word and we'll call it off."

"I'm fine, Henry," she said softly. "I want to know what's happening to me."

"You sure?"

"Totally."

"Okay." Henry rose to his feet. "You should probably pull your hair back in a ponytail for the contacts."

Sarah did as she was told.

They started with the hood. Sarah was positioned against a small, heavy-duty iron table. Racks of wave amplifiers were stacked on the table, and a huge styrene bonnet rose behind it like a sinister hair dryer. Henry peeled adhesive off the ends of electrodes and stuck them to Sarah's temples. They smelled like spermicide. Then Henry lowered the hood over Sarah's cranium. It came down to eye level, looking like some kind of alien beehive hairdo. Finally, Henry stuck several strips of litmus paper and galvanic sensors across her arms and palms and fingers. When they were all set, Henry went across the room and sat next to Dave at the Macintosh terminal.

"Okay," Henry said, "Let's start with the GSR readings—I want you to lower the surface temperature of your body, and I want you to do it by—"

"—thinking cold thoughts," Sarah finished his sentence. "Exactly."

Sarah nodded, lowered her head, and tried to ignore the silent tide of fear rising in her, fear of slipping over the edge into that nameless abyss. Instead of dwelling on it, she closed her eyes and started breathing deeply and thinking of her favorite movie musical.

The image materialized in her mind's eye.

She is standing at the mouth of the forest. The Tin Man and the Cowardly Lion and the Scarecrow are beside her, and they gaze out at the lush pink poppy field. The Emerald City is in the distance. They start toward it.

It begins to snow. Lovely, cottony snow falls on the poppy petals all around them. "Look!" cries the Scarecrow, "There's snow in your hair, and on your skin!" Sarah looks down and sees her ruby slippers frosted with snow. It's dusting her legs, her gingham dress, her arms, her face. Delicate snowflakes are clinging to her eyelashes. "Golly, it's cold," says the Cowardly Lion.

Sarah could feel the cold spreading through her, chilling her bones. She heard the buzz of a computer printer, fingers madly typing keypad entries.

She looked up.

Across the room, Henry and Dave were immersed in their monitors. "Oh, my God," Dave said, glancing up at the readings. The room was filled with the click-and-whirr-and-click of computers at work. Something was happening, something extraordinary; it was written across his straggly-bearded face. "Oh, my God—my God—*mygodmygodmygod,*" he muttered.

"I see it," Henry said, pulling out a printout tape from the GSR machine. "How you doing, Sarah?"

"Fine," she replied, feeling her skin tingling. She looked

down and saw the papery layer of frost on her forearm. Her hands were numb with the cold.

"Keep going!" Dave urged.

II

"Wait a minute!" Henry raised his hand, his eyes narrowing with tension. He wadded up the GSR printout and tossed it aside. "Let's take it one step at a time."

He wanted to say, *Let's call it off, kids, I'm sorry I thought of this insane stunt in the first place, let's pack up the gear and call it a day and come back when we know what we're dealing with.* He wanted to say, *Forget the medical establishment, and forget being a big shot, and forget proving the existence of autokineticism.* But it was too late. The curtain had risen, and now all Henry could do was try to direct this show as well as possible. He loved this woman so much it made his heart ache, and he would rather die than allow her to be hurt.

The instruments were going crazy, needles jumping, galvanic skin response already going berserk. The most amazing thing was how responsive her body was to the visual cues. Her skin temperature was already down around zero Celsius. Impossible, fucking impossible, but there it was. In another minute or two, she'd be succumbing to frostbite. Glancing up at the CRT, Henry saw the contour map of Sarah's brain. The magnetic fields were soaring across the screen. Glowing day-Glo blue, bright strawberry red, and lemon lime. They revealed a powerhouse of a brain. A nuclear reactor. Henry swallowed needles and said, "Okay, let's slow down, all right?"

The panic was stealing Henry's breath. He watched the displays flickering and the needles bobbing, and he felt as though he had just stumbled into the lair of a wild animal. Big mistake, this psychometric charade. *Big* mistake. "Let's try something else," Henry muttered, making fists.

"What are you talking about, Henry?" Dave protested, tapping his CRT. "Look at the MEG contours, this is *in-fucking-credible.*"

"*I'm not going to fuck with her head!*" Henry's sudden cry shattered the stillness.

"Take it easy, Kemosabe." Dave raised his hands in mock surrender.

Henry turned to Sarah. "Sorry, sorry about that—just nervous, I guess. Listen, Sarah, why don't you try to reverse the temperature. Think warm now. Try to get the surface temperature up."

Across the room, Sarah nodded.

"And listen," Henry said evenly, "don't for a second think you've got to continue if you feel uncomfortable. We can stop this nonsense at any time. Do you understand? We can pull the plug and regroup. You understand what I'm saying?"

Sarah told him that she understood and that she wanted to continue.

"Okay, when you're ready," Henry said.

III

Sarah took a deep breath and looked down at her hands for a moment.

They were shaking.

The contrary emotions were churning inside her, making her intestines burn and her bowels simmer. And all at once it occurred to her that she needn't worry about being some kind of upscale circus freak; she was already there. She was already in the dime museum, performing her feats of disgust and revulsion. She took another steadying breath, clenching and unclenching her hands, trying to get some warmth back into them. Her body felt like a tuning fork that was out of tune, the surges of overloading electric current singing through it. But she fought to stay focused, stay cool.

In some ways, she felt oddly emboldened in this little hideous lab with no windows. All because of Henry. The truth was, if it weren't for Henry, Sarah would be in a lunatic asylum somewhere at this very moment. But instead, she was sitting here in this macabre mausoleum with a high-tech hair dryer on her head, pushing her freakish brain to perform on cue. She was desperate to learn, to fight this thing. And as long as Henry was by her side, she would march right into Hell.

She closed her eyes and imagined a new twist on the poppy field.

"Look!" The Tin Man cries, pointing at the sky. Rays of sunlight are peeking through the puffy clouds. Droplets forming on the poppy leaves. The snow melts, and the air grows warm and humid as a greenhouse. Sarah starts to wipe her brow. The Scarecrow starts fanning himself. Then . . . something unexpected happens.

A glacial shadow slides across the sun, blocking out the warming rays. Sarah and the others glance up at the sky.

"No!" Sarah brought her hands up to her face, pressing her fingers against her eyes.

"What is it? What's wrong?" Henry was on his feet, shoving the clipboard aside, his gaze blazing with panic.

"I dunno." Sarah waved him off. It felt as though a damn had burst inside her, and spurts of radioactive water were flooding her bloodstream.

"Holy ssshhhhhh——" Dave murmured, looking at the MEG monitor. It was swimming with color, fiercely heating up. He tried to say something else, but couldn't even get the words out. The machinery was crackling.

"Sarah, what's wrong?" Henry demanded.

Sarah was stricken mute by the odd sensations, and she found herself remembering a variation of something her psychotic Christian mother used to harp about. *If your mind's eye offends thee, girl, pluck it out.* But Sarah couldn't do that, she couldn't pluck out her brain, nor could she understand why the sinister images kept popping into her head like some flicker-strip nickelodeon. The way they warped and distorted without warning—even amid all the fear and the pain and the illness, it just didn't make sense.

None of it made any sense.

"I'm just . . . I'm a little messed up," she said, and lowered her head.

A face appears in the sky, a leathery, wizened, warty old face superimposing itself across the clouds. It's the Wicked Witch. She waves her malevolent wand, and cackles, and says, "You can't hide from me! I'm alive now, and I'm gonna make you pay! MAKE YOU PAY!"

Sarah sprang to her feet, ripping the base of the bonnet from the machine.

"Jesus, look out—" Dave lunged across the table.

A smoke detector started chirping.

"—the machine!"

Sarah lurched, and sparks fountained from the torn amplifier behind her, puffs of black smoke curling out the back. The hood landed on the floor and cracked down the middle. Sarah tried to speak, but now the current was surging through her; another switch had been thrown. "I gotta—get—I can't—I can't do this!"

She started toward the exit.

IV

"*Sarah?*"

Henry came around the desk, reaching for her, then diving at her. He barely caught her legs. Sarah stumbled to the floor, the electrodes still connected to her head and arms.

She landed hard. The wind burst from her lungs, and she gasped for breath, and then she started crawling toward the exit, dragging along a fragment of the hood like a ball and chain. Henry grabbed her arm and tried to help her up.

"What the hell?" Henry jerked away the moment he touched her.

Her flesh was vibrating. That was the only way Henry could have explained it. Like a belt sander, all granular and tacky and shivering like mad.

Henry froze, gaping down at her. Moles and blemishes were effervescing along her arms, abruptly fading, then reappearing. All in the space of an instant. Henry tried to comment, his mouth moving but no words coming out. He was watching her skin, the pale flesh inside her elbows spontaneously puckering and scarring, but worse than that, he was watching something impossible sprouting from beneath her collar.

Her tattoos were growing.

"Sss-sarah?" Henry backed away, dumbstruck.

Struggling to her feet, woozy, Sarah was shaking her head like an animal shrugging off moisture. "Wait a minute," she murmured, slowly turning. "Wait just one minute!"

Two-dimensional roses were appearing beneath her collar, tiny, delicate stems spreading like cracks in fine china, climbing up her neck, leaves and thorns spiraling to a point beneath her ear. Other tattoos expanded in time lapse. The snakes slithered up the inside of her arm. The scorpions swam down her legs, their tails wiggling, sprouting new carapaces.

Henry reached for her again.

V

"God—no!"

Sarah spun away from Henry, tearing electrodes from her skull. She was panicking now, shivering, breathing hard and fast with the horrid crawling sensations all over her now, like insects, like millipedes on her flesh, billions of them. And with each prickling sensation, bursts of feverish yellow light splattered the dark terrain behind her eyes.

She headed for the exit, images spackling the canvas of her mind.

The storm clouds shrivel and pucker and turn into spindly, batwinged monkeys—flying monkeys—millions of them, making the sky turn black as pitch—

"Henry—the equipment—goddamnit!" Dave was across the room, wrenching a fire extinguisher from its mount. He ripped away the safety wire and sprayed the sparks and the flames. White clouds burst from the nozzle, fogging the room, swallowing the equipment and the furniture.

An alarm sounded, piercing the gloomy little lab like a machete.

"Sarah—wait!"

But Sarah was already through the door, staggering out across the boiler room. The darkness was closing around her, the kerosene odors and the aluminum octopus, the shadows and the fear and the sound of her heart. She ran toward the steps, trying to stop the images in her head.

The black-winged marauders are raining down upon Sarah and her friends, and before Sarah can run for cover, the spindly razor wings are in her face, ripping, tearing, spattering blood on the poppies, blood everywhere, BLOOD!

Sarah clamored up the steps.

VI

Henry rushed after her, but the moment he reached the

base of the stairs, he slipped on something wet. His shin slammed against the bottom step. He toppled to the floor, holding his leg, pain shooting up his tendons. Shaking it off, he gazed up through the steps into the shadows overhead. He could see Sarah up there, approaching the ground floor and trying to open the door. The door seemed to be jammed. She couldn't get out.

"Sarah—wait—please!"

The air was filling with smoke and chemical fog. Henry blinked. Something was dripping in his face, and he wiped it away, blinked some more, and tried to see better. Sarah was going berserk on the door up there. The backs of her arms were crawling with tattoos. In the haze, it looked as though her skin were spun glass shattering into a million pieces.

Another drop landed in Henry's eye.

It burned something awful, and Henry grunted, wiping it away. He looked at his finger. A pearl of blood clung to it. He snapped his gaze back up at Sarah, and he noticed it was coming from her leotards, the dark wet spot spreading between her legs. She was bleeding, bleeding in the crotch, bleeding so profusely that the drops were beading up and dripping in thick gouts down through the slats of the stairs.

"Oh-my-God-Sarah—you're—please-wait-wait-wait-please-you're-bleeding—" Henry climbed to his feet, got back on the stairs, and started upward.

The loud clang of the lab door's hinges echoed through the smoke.

Henry looked up and saw that Sarah was gone.

He cobbled up the rest of the steps, limping, favoring his shin. He reached ground level, and he staggered through the doorway. The corridor was empty, but the sound of footsteps were echoing nearby. Henry spun toward the side exit.

The door hung wide open, a shadow vanishing around the corner.

"SSSSARRAHH!"

He limped over to the exit and peered outside.

Night had fallen, and Sarah had vanished into it.

VII

Police work.

Since the dawn of Western civilization, police investigators had primarily been doing just that—work. In drafty offices with ancient coffee machines. In claustrophobic interrogation rooms with filthy cork walls and fluorescent tubes flickering overhead. In precinct houses with three divisions vying for a single broken-down copy machine and a couple of old IBM Selectrics that dropped more letters than a rerun of *Sesame Street*. In poorly ventilated courthouse parlors where restless assistant DAs sat chain-smoking behind metal folding tables stacked with crime reports. And mostly in cars, city-issue cars with no air-conditioning, faulty AM radios, and ironic names like Cavalier and Taurus, which blended into the gray stream of traffic like faceless drones.

It was within one of these spartan vehicles that Detective Becky Jones and Surveillance Technician Gary Levit currently sat, drinking stale coffee out of Long John Silvers cups, bored to tears outside Henry Decker's Evanston digs.

"Tell me again," Levit muttered over his fish sandwich, "just exactly what the concept with this guy is."

"Guy's the shrink." Becky took another sip of coffee and grimaced at the bitter gravel on her tongue.

The car was cloaked in darkness a half a block away from Henry's monolithic old Victorian. Gaslights dotted the parkway, and a dank, fishy smell hung in the air. Across the street, beyond the massive iron gates of Edgemere Beach, the autumn tides of Lake Michigan swirled and eddied. The weather was changing, and the encroaching cold had brewed up a thick stew of fog. Every now and then, a whitecap would peak out in that vast blackness like a skull's grin. It gave Becky Jones the creeps; as a kid growing up in Peoria, she had always hated the water.

"Whose shrink?" Levit asked, finishing his fried grease sandwich and wadding the paper.

"The suspect's shrink—chrissake, Levit, don't you read the twenty-four-hour reports?"

"I glance at 'em."

"That's wonderful," Becky Jones shook her head and tossed her empty cup into the abyss of the rear seats. God only knew what was back there. Old newspapers, titty mags, racing forms, crumpled crossword puzzles, spent shells. In the Criminal Investigation Division, these surveillance wheels got zero respect. They were disposable, like spent shaving cartridges.

"What's your beef, Jones?" Levit rooted a Camel straight out of his sport coat and lit it up. The orange dot crackled as he took a luxurious drag. "Moon orders us to stake this guy's place out tonight, write it up on the 151-form in the morning, biddy-bing—biddy-boom—it's Miller time."

Becky turned and shot a sour glance at the man. "You think just because this is ass-time you can—"

"Wait a minute!" Levit raised his hand and cut off her words, the orange glow of his smoke hanging in midair.

"What?"

He was staring out the front. "Maybe it's me, but it sure as hell looks like something's happening up there on Sigmund Freud's roof."

Becky gazed through the windshield. "That a possum? Raccoon—something like that?"

"That's a big fucking possum," Levit said.

In the distance, the upper stories of Henry's building rose up over the maple trees. The enormous attic garret stood out in harsh relief against the milky night sky. To the left, a circular turret vaulted above the naked limbs like a lonely church steeple. To the right, embedded in the heart of the sloping slate, was the baleful glare of the eyebrow window. A large cornice and parapet wrapped the entire third floor, providing more than enough space for a nosy squirrel or raccoon.

At the moment, however, there was something up there belonging to a higher genus and species.

"Show time," Becky Jones murmured, as she threw open her door and got out. She quickly slipped out of her wool blazer and tossed the coat back in the car. Underneath, she wore a sweater vest, turtleneck, jeans, and black Adidas. She reached around behind her and straightened her shoulder holster. The leather had been digging into her back all night. Then she did something that she had only been forced to do a couple of times in all of her eighteen years as the proud owner of a CPD detective shield.

She drew her gun.

They took the back way, along the beach, and they said nothing to each other. Merely a twitch of the head or a nudge of shoulder served as communication. Becky took the lead and crept along the weathered pier, service revolver gripped in both hands, barrel pointed downward. She didn't want to fire the .38 if she didn't have to; she didn't even want to point it at anyone. But she would do what she had to do. She kept her gaze riveted to Henry's roof, and the dark figure moving along the parapet.

Becky flipped her safety toggle off.

They were coming up the backyard, approaching the greenhouse, when the glass shattered. It echoed overhead like a dissonant chime, swallowed up in the dense fog. Becky raised her weapon at the roof. "Chicago Police Department!" she hollered at the shadows above the trees. "Come out to the edge of the roof with your hands on your head!"

Up on the parapet, the figure was trying to squeeze through the broken eyebrow window, his head and shoulders already immersed in the jagged maw of broken glass. At first glimpse, it looked absurd, dreamlike: a shadowy figure ferreting into the lidded window like a parasite. Becky focused on the intruder through a veil of mist, and she saw by the stoutness of the waist and the arms and legs that it was a man. Medium height, stocky build, dressed in black, some kind of cape flowing off his back. Then, in the blink of an eyelid, almost panther-quick—in fact, faster than anything

either Becky or Levit had ever seen—the figure pulled himself out of the window, spun toward the front of the house,
and vanished around the garret.

"Hold it, goddamnit!"

The porch light exploded in Becky's face.

"What's going on?" Henry Decker's voice cut through the
glare.

"Back inside, Dr. Decker—please," Becky was saying,
even as she was skipping around the side of the house, gun
raised and readied, heart hammering. "Please!"

She reached the front yard and saw the hedgerow quivering out by the street, heard the sound of a body shuffling
through the undergrowth and starting west.

"There he is!" Levit pointed his semiautomatic at the
shrubbery and cocked the hammer.

"No—Levit, no!" Becky shoved his gun hand aside. "This
isn't *Hard Target*!"

The figure was already sprinting across the street.

"C'mon!" Becky took off after the intruder, with Levit hot
on her heels.

Thank God Becky had worn her sneakers, because this
perp was fast. He led them across Sheridan, through the
backyards of a couple of mansions, and down toward Main
Street. And although the air was pea soup and Becky was
many pounds and many years and many Bloody Marys beyond her once-lithe high-school-tennis-team body, she could
see this guy in the distance, arms churning, body square and
graceful. Could have been fucking-Nuryev, he was so fast
and nimble, vaulting piles of leaves, Halloween pumpkins,
and chaise longues.

Main Street was a busy thoroughfare, especially on a Saturday. Light spilled out the window of a Starbucks, and college kids congregated on the corner of Main and Chicago
Avenue, waiting for the El into the city. Rap music thumped
from a passing low-boy, its purple neon undertrim sweeping
the pavement. Most heads turned when the shadowy figure
dashed by in all his caped and mysterious glory.

"Chicago Police!" Becky Jones hollered, digging her shield out of her jeans and waving it at the throngs while she ran. Pedestrians parted like a curtain.

The caped intruder turned left at Chicago and headed south, weaving behind buildings. Jones and Levit were starting to flag, slowing down, breathing ragged breaths. This guy had monster legs, this caped motherfucker. Becky's side was splitting open now, daggers of pain stitching up her torso with every stride. Up ahead, she saw the intruder vault the gate of a closed car lot, hop up on the roofs of identical Nissan Maximas, and tear across the cars like a kid playing a game.

This guy just didn't give up.

They approached a roadblock which separated Evanston and Chicago. The intruder jumped the sawhorses like an Olympic vaulter and headed for a narrow alley fifty yards away. The orange warning lights were blinking at odd intervals, painting the fog, and Jones and Levit limbed over the cordons and proceeded with caution, guns raised and lungs heaving.

The intruder vanished down the alley.

"Warning shot first, Levit," Becky said breathlessly approaching the mouth of the alley. The chances were good that they had the caped asshole cornered. "You hear me?"

"Yeah, whatever," Levit said, cocking his 9mm tactical gun, cheek twitching.

"You hear what I said?"

"Yeah, yeah, yeah."

They reached the mouth of the alley just as a crash echoed from its depths.

Then the strange, garbled cry.

Both cops dove for cover, landing near the stone ramparts on either side of the alley entrance. Guns readied. Hearts racing. Eyes shifting from each other to the darkness of the alley and back to each other. Finally, Becky caught enough breath to peer around the corner.

The intruder was lying on the ground at the end of the alley, motionless.

"Nice and easy," Becky told Levit, slowly rising to her feet and taking deep breaths. Across from her, Levit stood up, pressing his back against the rampart.

"Chicago Police! Stay on the ground with your hands behind your head! Fingers interlaced!"

No response.

Becky raised her .38 and moved into the mouth of the alley.

She stood there for quite some time, staring into the gloomy depths of the alley at the dead-end brick wall, the body of the intruder lying amid the overturned garbage cans and stacks of newspapers. He was stone still. Out cold. But Becky Jones didn't take any chances. She took a step toward him, gun aimed for a direct head shot.

"Stay on the ground! Fingers interlaced behind your head!"

She took another tentative step toward the body. Levit appeared behind her, gun raised and readied. Another step, another, and still another. No movement yet. Becky's sneaker crunched in the broken glass and offal. It smelled like sour milk and cat food back here. Becky walked the rest of the way to the body, her gun aimed right at its head.

When she reached the body and saw the intruder was face-down and passed out, the cape pooled like a black oil spill across his back, Becky's muscles relaxed. "Cuff him and turn him over," she said, holstering her .38 and taking a deep breath.

Levit went over, pulled a pair of stainless steel handcuffs from his belt, and shackled the figure's limp wrists. Then, with the toe of his Stacy Adams, Levit shoved the body right-side up.

Becky Jones blinked.

Levit backed away instinctively, his gun hanging at his side, his mouth working on words that just wouldn't come. It didn't make sense. Not one fucking bit of sense. He finally murmured, "What the fuck is this—fucking *Candid Camera*?"

Becky kept blinking and shaking her head and staring at the suspect.

It felt as though they had just wandered into a carnival funhouse, with all the wacky mirrors and that obnoxious laughing voice. Becky knelt down close to the intruder and felt for a pulse. It was faint but steady. "Go get an EMT unit on the horn," Becky said, "and call Frank Moon, and tell him Christmas is coming early this year."

Levit whirled and hurried back toward the streetlights.

"And make it snappy," Becky added, unable to tear her gaze from the slack, unconscious face of Sarah Brandis.

VIII

Cook County jail was a real anachronism.

Located in the heart of Chicago's financial district, the jail was an ugly, triangular, Euro-block skyrise with countless levels of mute multipanes. It sat rooted among the bustling law firms and brokerage houses like a granite Golem, its stony silence masking the agony and excruciating tedium of its inhabitants. On many summer days, when the weather was decent, the prisoners would stand on tiptoe and gaze down through wire mesh at the clusters of secretaries gathered around the fountain fifteen stories below, dressed in their silk dresses, feeding the pigeons, and gossiping about who's having affairs with whom at the ol' insurance company.

On the first floor, just beyond the central lobby and processing desk, there was a long narrow wing which housed a series of meeting rooms. Pegboard walls, two-way mirrors, wooden tables and benches, ashtrays and lamps bolted to the floor, the rooms were used primarily for meetings between prisoners and attorneys, detectives hunting down information, and DAs looking to talk deal with some wise guy.

Sarah Brandis sat alone in one of these rooms, shivering, her mind reeling.

She had awakened less than two hours ago in Cook County hospital, gasping for breath on a cot shoved against the wall in Central Receiving. Under heavy guard, a Pakistani doctor named Udri had examined her, given her a sedative, and released her into the custody of the Chicago Police Department. At that point, they had arrested her for breaking and entering, not to mention suspicion of murder. Both charges were completely baffling to Sarah. The cops had taken her directly to the jail, sat her down at a table in this stark, windowless room, and told her to wait. She was still dressed in the black, torn Danskins in which she had awakened—although she had no idea how they had gotten mangled. Thankfully, one of the jail's female guards had given Sarah a blanket, which was now wrapped around her.

Across the room came a click.

The door was opening, and Frank Moon was peering into the room. Dressed in his Italian weave, black turtleneck, and styled hair, he reminded Sarah of an aging child movie star. "We meet again," Frank said, and came sauntering in, shutting the door behind him. "Mind if I sit down?"

Sarah nodded and pulled the blanket tighter.

Frank took a seat across from her and offered her a cigarette. She told him that she didn't smoke. Frank stared at her neck and asked her about the strange markings. Sarah made up some story about getting new tattoos. Frank lit a cigarette and took a deep drag.

Finally Sarah sat forward and said, "What in God's name is going on? They're telling me I'm a prime suspect in a multiple murder case?"

Frank looked at her. "I understand you were given notice down at the dance hall." He spoke calmly, as though conducting a simple poll.

"What? Why is that—yeah—I was fired."

"Daniel Sellars was your boss?"

"Yes."

"Fellow dancer named Maxine Morrisey?"

"That's right." Sarah's heart began to thump, the panic returning like cool water in her veins.

"And the last time you saw them—" Frank took another puff, "was when?"

"Last week, I guess."

Frank nodded. "Well, unfortunately, both parties were found dead behind Dante's Inferno Thursday morning."

"What?" Sarah swallowed hard. "Found . . . dead?"

"In a very strange way," Frank added. Then he paused to let it sink in. "You know, you work in this business for any length of time and you see some pretty ugly things." He paused again and stared at her another moment. Then he reached into his coat pocket for something, and even in the throes of her shock, Sarah got the distinct impression that she was undergoing some kind of test.

"They were . . . killed—but . . ." Sarah started to say something else, then stopped.

Frank Moon had pulled two sheets of paper from his pocket. Folded lengthwise, they were Xeroxes of photographs. Black-and-white crime scene shots. Dead bodies. "I'd like you to take a look at these," Frank said, and shoved the photos at her.

"OhmyGod—" Sarah slammed her hand to her mouth, her stomach twisting.

The shot of Duff was a close-up, his face the color of egg whites. Shiny ropes of tendons showed through the horizontal gash in his neck. His eyes were gray marbles. The photo of Maxine was worse, although blurry and distant. A hogtied mess of a woman, her livid face and gaping eye peeking out of the plastic. Sarah felt the red-hot agony rising up her gorge. She turned away, and she nearly choked on her bile. Bile mixing with tears, saliva mixing with acid.

Detective Moon dropped his cigarette on the floor and ground it out with the toe of his designer shoe. "Not a pretty picture, I know—kinda hard to look at."

Sarah gagged for another moment, and then she gazed back at the photos. Tears filled her eyes, and she blinked them away, wiping her cheek. There was something about the way the bodies were wrapped and dressed like Christmas turkeys that was ripping at Sarah's gut. Something familiar about the bondage, something horribly familiar. Then she saw the grainy image of Maxine's eye, and Sarah started softly crying, thinking of her buddy dying like that, and poor, sweet old Duff. Sarah shoved the photos away, wiping her face in her blanket. "I don't understand—you're telling me . . . *you think I did this*?"

"Just trying to get a few things straight," Frank said evenly, putting the photos back in the envelope.

Another surge of pain rocked Sarah, and she let the tears track down her face. She wiped her cheeks, and she looked up at the cop. "I don't know what's happening anymore."

"Why would you want to break into Henry Decker's house?"

"I didn't."

"Okay, then tell me where you were last night."

"I don't— I'm not sure." She looked down at her hands and swallowed back the terror.

"Brain tumor messing with the old recall?"

She looked up at him, her teeth clenched. She refused to let this rude son of a bitch beat her. "You ever have one?"

"Any chance you remember Wednesday night?"

"I was . . ." Sarah paused and searched the scorched, wasted terrain of her memory. "I was with Henry; I was with Dr. Decker in the park."

"All night? You two camp out in your little pup tent?"

Sarah looked away, trying to breathe. "I don't— I can't remember."

"This is getting us nowhere," Frank said, and the venom was seeping into his voice.

Sarah looked at him. "Give me a lie detector test. I'm telling you the truth."

"Goddamnit—I don't have to put electrodes on you." Frank stood up, jabbing his finger at her. "I know you're lying. I got you at the warehouse killing, and I got a partial print at the scene behind Dante's, and it's just a matter of time. And I don't give two rats' asses if some shrink is trying to lawyer you outta here—I got your number."

He grabbed the Xeroxes and went over to the door. "Tell you what—I'm gonna go get some lunch, and you can sit here and think about being a sport and telling the truth, or you can go down in flames. Doesn't matter to me. It's your choice." Then the door slammed shut.

Sarah sat alone in the cruel silence.

IX

An hour later, Sarah found herself in another one of the myriad cells in the vast honeycomb of the fifteenth-floor processing wing. She was dressed in the blue dungarees of the female unit, her hands shackled with stainless steel cuffs and a short length of chain. Her ankles were shackled as well, bolted through a loop of iron mounted on the floor. Her head was down. Long, graying hair covered her face. She had been crying for most of the morning, crying for Duff and Maxine, crying for her friends whom she would never see again, crying for their senseless deaths. And now it was almost noon, and her tears had drained her like a rag wrung dry.

She was thinking of her late mother.

Jessie Brandis would have appreciated seeing her daughter in this particular kind of hell. The old lady had always been big on incarceration. Sarah couldn't remember much about the woman—or her childhood in general, for that matter—but for some unknown reason, she remembered the punishments.

They had started around the time Sarah was about to enter kindergarten. Her father had flown the coop four years earlier, less than a month after Sarah was born, and Jessie Brandis had gone sour soon after that. The woman withdrew into the Bible, falling in with a cultish Pentecostal group and becoming increasingly bitter and judgmental toward her only daughter. In

Jessie's eyes, Sarah couldn't do anything right. By the time Sarah was four years old, Jessie had started meting out the punishments, usually involving some sort of imprisonment.

The first major incident had taken place on a Sunday morning, during church service. Sarah had asked to be excused to go to the bathroom, but Jessie had insisted that the girl hold it until the interminable fire-and-brimstone rant had ended. The moment the final organ music chimed, little Sarah had made a mad dash for the ladies' room, but it was too late. She had tinkled all over her little cornflower sundress right there in the foyer. Jessie had gone ballistic, dragging Sarah home by the ear, whopping her hide, and then locking her in the kitchen pantry for the rest of the day. Sarah had thought she was going to go crazy, locked in that hot little pantry with the ants and the mice.

Other incidents followed with increasing frequency. For saying her first curse word, Sarah had been sentenced to a night in the coat closet. For breaking a tea pitcher, she had gotten an entire day in the root cellar. And there had always been the banishments to her room.

Her bedroom was the one thing Sarah remembered most about her childhood home in Arkham, Wisconsin. It was tiny, just like the rest of the little bungalow that her mother had purchased with the last of their savings in 1960. The bedroom had one window and a little trundle bed squeezed into the corner. The window overlooked the south edge of a landfill and a natural gully that bordered the home. It seemed as though Sarah had spent an eternity gazing out that window, locked away for some trumped-up crime, staring down at the abandoned cars-on-blocks, mounds of petrified rubbish, and stray dogs fighting over some festering morsel. That was where the real pain had started.

But mostly what Sarah remembered about her childhood was a big black void. It was Jessie's doing, more than anything else. The woman had refused to share anything with her daughter. No frank discussions about the facts of life (*too vulgar and sinful*). No words of advice about boys (*dirty little heathens*). Not even a little encouragement to do well in school (*no daughter of mine's going to be filling her head with junk*). It got so bad that Sarah had started sneaking books home and keeping them under her mattress, pulling them out after Jessie had gone to sleep. But more than anything else, Sarah's memories were like shadows, like faint stains on cave walls, traces of conflicts long ago faded into obscurity and covered up by a patina of time. And whenever Sarah tried to remember—be it during therapy with Henry or some three A.M. panic attack—she could only see the shapeless shadows, a glint of violence like the flash of a mad dog's fang, a pale face in a window late at night, a face without features—

A sound clanged across the cell.

"Wha—?" Sarah looked up.

The cell was one of the few single-occupancy holding cells on the fifteenth floor. Its walls were made of chalky white stucco, the floor scarred and worn tile. A ceiling vent rattled overhead, and a Madonna sticker was partially peeling off the corner of Sarah's bench. Sarah stared at the door, which was moving like a grimy iron clockwork, the reinforced bolts sighing open and disengaging with a clank.

A craggy-faced Amazon in a guard's uniform and oversized glasses appeared in the doorway, her keys jangling, a large nightstick propped under her arm. "Brandis, Sarah?" the guard mumbled as she approached.

"Yeah—yes, that's right." Sarah's voice sounded as if someone had taken a cheese grater to her throat.

"Sit up straight with your back against the wall," the guard instructed.

Sarah sat up.

"Hold your arms straight out."

Sarah held her arms out.

The guard slammed her nightstick down on Sarah's hand shackles and pinned them to the metal table in front of her, driving Sarah forward with the force of the blow. Sarah froze, hunched over the table, her heart racing. "What's going on?" Sarah asked, trying to keep the panic out of her voice. "I still haven't been allowed to make that phone call."

"Hold still and keep your legs together," the guard said tersely. Then she stomped her foot down on Sarah's leg shackles, holding Sarah's feet in place.

"What's the problem?" Sarah said.

The guard didn't answer, but instead knelt down and fished for a key. She found the appropriate key and fitted it into the floor bolt. There was another click, and Sarah felt the shackles fall away from her ankles.

The guard rose back to her feet and lifted Sarah off the bench.

"Would you please tell me what's going on?" Sarah said. The guard was dragging Sarah across the room by the hand shackles, urging her toward the door.

"You're leaving," the guard said flatly.

They passed through the doorway and entered the corridor. The sounds of other prisoners squawking at their lawyers, muffled interrogations in progress, typewriters clacking, and metal bolts rattling, all drifted through the air. The place smelled like a gymnasium. All the stress-sweat and bad breath and cigarettes. The guard was dragging Sarah toward a series of reinforced glass doors at the end of the hallway when Sarah stopped. She stopped cold, turned, and shot a look at the guard that could have melted an iron railroad spike. "I'm not moving," Sarah told her, "until you tell me what's going on."

The guard looked at her and said, "You're getting released."

"Excuse me?"

"Somebody put up bail."

Sarah stared at the guard for another long moment before following her the rest of the way down the hall.

X

"Easy does it," Henry warned, glancing over his shoulder, a large, tattered Samsonite under his arm. "Those leaves are slick as hell."

Sarah was following Henry up the front steps of the institute, carrying her makeup case and blanket roll. The sun had set an hour ago, and the wind was picking up. Now the black sky was threatening to spit freezing rain. Sarah felt the cold radiating through her, and not just from the weather, either. Cold from the fear. Gelid dread burrowing deep down in her marrow. Dread that she was not only losing her body, but her sanity as well. The cop named Moon was after her as a prime suspect in more than one murder. The prostitute in the abandoned building, and even Duff and Maxine. But Sarah knew beyond a shadow of a doubt that no matter how fucked up she was, she could never have taken the lives of her friends.

Thank God for Henry. He was proving to be Sarah's guardian angel, and for the first time in Sarah's life, she trusted a man unequivocally. Never mind all the strings that Henry had to pull to get her out of jail. Never mind that Henry had refused to press charges. Never mind that he had scraped up half his savings to hire a hotshot lawyer to get Sarah out on bail. Never mind that Henry had canceled all his other sessions for the next two weeks and was concentrating his every waking moment on helping Sarah. Henry also just happened to be the kindest, gentlest man Sarah had ever known, and even amid all the horrors of the past few weeks, Sarah was falling deeply in love with him.

On the drive home from the jail, Henry had convinced Sarah to move into the institute for a while. It made sense. It would give her time to address her deteriorating condition, her grotesque imaginings and the inexplicable blackouts. More important, it would allow her to work on her condition in relative privacy, without the risk of another sleepwalk. Henry could chain her to the bed at night, if that's what it took. There were also practical reasons. Without a steady income, Sarah would be hard-pressed to support herself. She had no health insurance, and the unemployment checks were hardly enough to keep her in instant coffee. Henry's services would have to be gratis. Of course, above and beyond all these practicalities, the fact was, Sarah needed Henry's love now more than ever. She needed his quiet strength, his big broad shoulders, and the sound of his rich baritone in the morning.

Still . . . something that happened back at the jail had rattled Sarah deep down at her core. The photos. The crime scene pictures that Frank Moon had showed her. The way Maxine and Duff had been wrapped and dressed was resonating in Sarah's midbrain. In fact, it had been eating at her from the very moment she had seen the hideous photographs. Although Sarah had no idea why, she was getting a terrible feeling that there was a connection between herself and the bondage. And if there was a connection, then maybe it wasn't such a good idea to be locked up with Henry right now. Maybe she was putting Henry in some kind of danger.

"Home sweet home," Henry said, unlocking the front door and ushering Sarah across the threshold.

Sarah sat her case down on the hardwood and glanced across the foyer. "I feel like Rumpelstiltskin all of a sudden, like I've been out cold for seven years."

Through the archway, Sarah could see into the living room, a spacious area defined by plants and sturdy wicker furniture. One corner featured a large comfy array of pillows. Tiffany lamps and antique photographs added to the homey feel. The odors of oiled wood and incense hung in the air, and a thin strip of moonlight was filtering through the stained-glass lintel, falling on the wall like spun candy. Only a metal flip chart and stack of brochures in one corner betrayed the therapeutic mission of the place. Henry was a good housekeeper, and he purposely kept the place cozy and informal to provide a mellow atmosphere for the clients.

"Let's unpack later," Henry said, setting the suitcase by the bottom of the stairs. "Right now, we need to sit down and talk some things over."

"You're the boss," Sarah said. She took off her coat and hung it on the rack. She was dressed in a pink sweatshirt and faded jeans—Henry had brought the clothes for her after he had picked her up—but she still smelled the jail on her skin. The stale smoke and old floors were clinging to her like a film. She needed a shower desperately.

She went into the living room and collapsed on the sofa.

"I'll be right back," Henry said, and walked out.

Five minutes later, he returned with a pot of orange pekoe. He served it in antique Courier and Ives china. The tea warmed Sarah's bones and helped her to relax, and soon she was talking about the death of her friends, the morbid way her imagery had mutated in the sleep lab, and her fears, her devouring fears. Henry listened closely.

When Sarah finally reached a lull in her confessional, Henry pulled a plastic vial of pills from his shirt pocket and said, "Here, take these." He shook two tiny white pills onto Sarah's saucer.

"And these are?"

"Oxydess; it's a form of Dexedrine—for the blackouts. Dr. Udri prescribed them at Cook County. I picked them up on the way to the jail."

"Oh," Sarah said, and looked at the tablets. She put them on her tongue and washed them down with a sip of luke-warm tea, the bitter aftertaste coaxing a pucker.

"There's something I want to talk about, Sarah," Henry said, his expression darkening. He wore a bright red flannel shirt, but the design belied his grim demeanor. His eyes were drawn and haunted.

"Go ahead."

"Detective Moon chewed my ear off this morning."

"Lovely fellow," Sarah said, rubbing her temples. Her skull felt like shattered glass.

"Sarah, they caught you trying to break into the attic window last night."

"I know, I know—the blackouts, the sleepwalking—I have

this horrible feeling that we made it worse in the lab yesterday."

"You have absolutely *no* memory of climbing up there?
Breaking the window and everything?"

"None whatsoever."

"What was the last thing you remember?"

"Before waking up at Cook County—I was running out of
the lab, and I, I, I guess I blacked out somewhere between
Northwestern and God knows where. . . ." Sarah paused for a
moment, remembering glimpses of the previous day. The
psych building door bursting open in her blood-slick hands.
The feeling of bugs crawling all over her. Rushing across
campus, blood on her legs. "I remember the blood," she
added after another moment's thought, "after running out of
the lab—I was bleeding."

"I saw it." Henry nodded. "It was almost as though you
had stigmatas on your body."

"What?"

"The admitting nurse at Cook County said she couldn't
find anything that would have caused the bleeding. The
blood was spontaneous, Sarah. The Catholics have a word
for that—*stigmatas*, sympathetic wounds, wounds that re-
semble those of Jesus on the cross, marks on the hands, the
feet, maybe even punctures around the head from the crown
of thorns, whatever."

Sarah set her teacup down. "Don't tell me you buy all that
crap."

"No, no way, that's not why I bring it up. I bring it up
because I want you to understand there's a source for every
behavior."

"Where are you heading with all this?"

"First, tell me anything else you remember—right before
blacking out."

"That's it," Sarah said, and then remembered something
else. The pain. A vague memory of pain. Pain that would always occur right before a blackout. And although her memory of it was usually sketchy, like a remnant of a dream that

fades by morning, Sarah could usually recall snippets of this
sudden and excruciating pain shooting up her spine just before an episode.

She told him about it.

"That's strange," Henry said. He rubbed his face for a moment, the weariness creasing lines around his pale blue eyes
like wrinkled parchment. His face was laden with regret, and
something deeper, perhaps shame. In the dim light of the living room he looked old. Older than his nearly fifty years. "I
might as well tell you," he finally said, "I have a theory and
it's going to be a little difficult to swallow."

"I'm all ears, Henry."

He looked her square in the eye. "I think it's very possible
you have a dissociative disorder."

Sarah stared at him. The word meant nothing to her. Still,
she was getting nervous. It seemed as though the room were
starting to change ever so slightly, as though the floor were
tilting just a fraction.

Sarah swallowed dryly and said, "I'm listening."

Henry took a deep breath. "Dissociative disorders are
often seen in people who've endured some kind of trauma—
some sort of horrible, traumatic event at a sensitive stage.
And they usually manifest it years later, in all kinds of nasty
symptoms—headaches, amnesia, trancing, even mild fugue
states—which, God knows, you've seen enough of."

"For Godsakes, Henry—we went through all this years
ago!" Sarah's heart was beating faster now. "Didn't we come
to the conclusion there was no single event in my life that
caused all this crap?"

"We never concluded anything, Sarah."

"What are you saying, Henry?"

"I'm saying . . . I think you may very well be suffering
from a multiple personality disorder."

Sarah stared at him and thought it over and laughed nervously. "Get outta here." The room seemed to be vibrating
now, and Sarah was sweating up a storm, her heart racing,
her mouth as dry as cow hide. "No way." She laughed some

more, and suddenly she couldn't sit still. She rolled up her sleeves and fidgeted out to the edge of the sofa, glancing around the soft light of the living room. She was dizzy and a fist was inside her, tightening around her guts. It was an awful yet familiar feeling.

A blackout was coming on.

"I'm serious, Sarah," Henry said, his voice fading, distorting, warbling as though underwater. "It explains a lot, if you think about it, the auto-hypnotic phenomena, the sleep disorders, the time loss."

Sarah wiped pearls of sweat from her brow. "What were these pills that I just took? Dexedrine?"

"Just a mild stimulant," Henry assured her. "Don't worry about it."

She tried to take a deep breath. "*Jesus, Henry—*"

"Sarah, listen to me—MPD is nothing to be ashamed of. It's a survival tool, and a very effective one at that. It's a defense against pain."

"What in God's name are you talking about?"

"I'm saying the origin of your MPD must go all the way back to your childhood. You probably weathered some kind of terrible abuse, something you've completely repressed, and the dissociation started in earnest. Your psyche split into two halves—*you* and *The Other*—and The Other is the child of that pain. A depository of all that rage. And as you grew, with all those gifted brain cells stewing around in your head, the switching just kept getting more and more discrete."

Sarah tried to rise off the sofa, but the dizziness was overwhelming. Instead, she collapsed back into the couch and dug her fingernails into the tufts of fabric. Her body was covered with a sheen of sweat now, and the centipedes were on her again. But now there was a new feeling. Amid the rising panic, amid the prickling sensations up and down her arms and legs, her eyes were pinned wide open.

Awake.

"What is it? What's happening?" Henry sprang to his feet.

"The *Dexedrine*," Sarah uttered, slamming her palms

against her temples to keep her head from exploding. "What effect does it have?"

"What do you mean?"

"*What is the purpose of the drug?*" Sarah blurted, squeezing her eyes shut.

The pain was returning. The familiar twinge at the base of her spine, the twinge that always preceded a blackout, and now Sarah started to remember the way it usually started, like a spring tightening around her kidneys, and then— TWANG! A hundred thousand volts surging up her vertebra, until the black curtain came slamming down.

Except now there was no curtain.

"The purpose of the drug," Henry said, reaching out and grabbing her by the shoulders, "is to keep you from blacking out, to keep you awake."

"*Awake?*"

Sarah lurched across the coffee table, sending teacups and spoons scattering. Henry tried to grab her, but she tumbled out of his arms and flopped to the floor like an epileptic. She began to convulse.

"*Sarah!*"

She couldn't see clearly anymore. The room had tilted on its axis, curling into a pipeline of light and sound. Sarah couldn't breathe. She crawled along the rug, gasping, flailing at the invisible lightning flashing in her face. The pain crashed through her in waves. Shooting up her spine, and striking her skull like a hammer hitting a gong. Tears filled her eyes, then streamed down her cheeks. The pain gripped her pelvis in a vice, and it squeezed, and it twisted, and it tore through her, and Sarah opened her mouth to scream, but only a silent string of saliva looped out across the carpet. Another spell was coming on; Sarah could feel it worming through her marrow.

And this time she would be awake to see it happen.

6

Metamorphosis

I

More than anything else, it was the sound, the horrible shifting sound like dry kindling twisting and snapping inside a leather sheath. It held Henry Decker riveted, as though someone had driven stakes through his boots.

Sarah's face was the first thing to go.

Twisting toward the window, grimacing, Sarah's expression went slack for a moment and then warped as if passing behind a pane of dimpled glass. Her brow bulged, and the bones cracked and solidified. Her jaw widened. Her lips thinned, and her hair seemed to shrivel back into her skull like delicate anemones. Soon there was a new male visage where Sarah's face had once been, glowering up at Henry with dark eyes blazing.

"S-ss-sarah—is that—what's going—" Henry was gibbering now, staring down at the incarnate.

There wasn't much left of Sarah's body. Her bosom had deflated and hardened under the sweatshirt, shoulders broadening, tattoos fading like watermarks. The incarnate rose to his knees. Inside the baggy clothing, he stretched his new limbs like a colt being born. His skin was pale, the consistency of new wood. He raised his hand and regarded it. His fingertips were candle wax drying in time lapse.

"Who are you, goddamnit?" Henry took a step toward the incarnate.

The incarnate rose to his feet, turned, and started toward the door.

"Wait!" Henry grabbed at the sweatshirt, but all of a sudden it was too late, the incarnate was spinning out of his grasp, moving with panther grace across the living room, over the ottoman, around an old Tiffany floor lamp. The lamp toppled. Colored glass shattered and sent shards of prismatic light across the room, painting the scene with slashes of gold and streamers of blue, and all at once the incarnate was heading toward the archway which led into the foyer, but Henry lunged across the east wall and blocked its path.

The incarnate froze, inches away from Henry.

"I don't want to hurt you," Henry said, breathing hard, looking into the stranger's eyes.

He was a young man, with cunning eyes and a face that reminded Henry of old sepia-toned Matthew Brady tintypes in Civil War books. Roughly the same height and weight as Sarah, but stocky as a fireplug, and handsome. Handsome in a rough-hewn, wily sort of way. Almost feral. And in that brief tableaux, with his heart racing and his mind swimming in terror, Henry saw something else about the incarnate that didn't add up. His skin—as pale and diaphanous as wrinkled chiffon stretched over muscle and bone—seemed almost artificial. *Unfinished.*

"Who are you?" Henry uttered.

"I'm the godforsaken one—the Escape Artist," the stranger said, and his voice was gravelly velvet, and he was grimacing, and the broken light from the floor shone up and reflected off his milky pearl teeth.

"Where's Sarah?"

"She's gone."

"What did you do with Sarah?"

"I sent her to the dark place."

"What dark place?"

The incarnate didn't answer, but instead gazed around the living room, sizing the place up, his pain-grin lingering. He started toward the opposite door.

"Wait!" Henry blocked his path again. "What dark place? Is Sarah inside you? Is that the dark place?"

"The dark place is the void from whence I came," the incarnate said.

"Where is that?"

The incarnate didn't answer.

"What is the void?" Henry clenched his fists, heart racing, waiting for the answer.

Henry was dizzy with fear. All he could think of was the standard line of questioning for an alter personality, but he knew deep down that he had stumbled upon something way beyond a multiple personality. Way beyond anything in the known literature. He had stumbled upon a nightmare, a fire-breathing dragon, something that would either change the course of psychometric science as we know it or kill Henry with flick of its wrist. But all Henry could think about was Sarah, poor sweet Sarah, and the pain that must lie at the heart of it all, and the threat of losing her forever inside this monstrous, unformed boy with the pale skin.

"What are you?" Henry finally said, taking another step toward the stranger.

The incarnate was backing toward the front picture window, muscles coiled. "Alive," he whispered, then turned and dove toward the glass.

Henry lunged.

They collided at the base of the window, Henry's bear hug pulling the stranger to the floor. They landed hard. Henry gasped, and saw stars, and the incarnate wriggled out of his grasp with the ease of a ferret squirming from a burrow. Henry grabbed at the sweatshirt, ripping a handful of fabric, but the incarnate was too strong, too fast.

The incarnate hopped up on the couch.

"No—wait!" Henry rose to his knees, hands up in surrender, but the incarnate was already leaping toward the opposite wall. "Please—*wait!*" Henry clawed at the air, watching in horror as the incarnate rushed at the French windows, the ones with the stained-glass lintel and brass fittings, the ones that Henry had installed himself the week after he bought the place, the same windows that opened out onto the side lawn adjacent to Edgemere Boulevard.

The incarnate crashed through the glass.

There was bullwhip crack as the windows gave way, splinters and stardust exploding outward. The incarnate's form tumbled into darkness. Shafts of halogen light invaded the living room, and the smell of chilled mist and smoke gathered in the gaping breech. Henry struggled to his feet and quickly staggered over to the opening.

The incarnate was sprinting across the lawn, heading toward the webbing of wrought iron.

"Jesus—*wait!*"

Henry started across the lawn.

Back in his glory days at the University of Illinois, Henry had been quite swift for an offensive center, swifter than he had to be. After all, the center's job, simply put, was to hike the ball and form a human roadblock. Period. Nothing more, nothing less. And if the center happened to draw continuous pummelings from the defensive line—*mazeltov!* All the better. But Henry had been an exceptionally athletic center. At the peak of his playing weight, he had run the forty-yard dash in just over six seconds. Midway through his career, however, something went wrong with his knees. The downward slide started with minor problems like bruised kneecaps, constant fluid accumulation, and pulled rectus tendons every other game. Then the problems worsened. Soon he was missing huge chunks of the season due to fractured patellas or serious dislocations. By the time he was a senior, he had suffered through five major surgeries.

After graduation, Henry had been forced to walk with

crutches for nearly a year, and it wasn't until he was halfway through his doctoral work that he could even jog around the block without intense pain. Unfortunately, the passage of time had not been kind to Henry's knees. Calcium spurs, scar tissue, and ripped cartilages made cold mornings almost unbearable. Jogging was out of the question, and even extended periods of kneeling in the garden brought on that horrible feeling in his joints, the feeling that rusty iron railroad spikes were being driven through his knees.

At the moment, as a matter of fact, Henry was getting that very same feeling as he approached the corner of Lee Street and Chicago Avenue.

In the darkness ahead, Henry could see the man who was once Sarah Brandis barreling south, passing through pools of vapor light on the sidewalk, heading toward the South Boulevard El station. This guy ran like an elk. Arms pumping, legs churning gracefully. And the little son of a bitch could move like a halfback. Henry poured it on, knees popping, bright surges of pain bolting up his legs and pelvis. It felt as though his joints had been dipped in kerosene and set ablaze.

Thankfully, the streets were fairly deserted.

Henry hobbled along as fast as he could, huffing and puffing, chasing the incarnate under a viaduct, down a narrow alley, and across a parking lot. Henry's vision was bursting with spark-flashes of pain, and his heart was beating so fast he thought it might erupt through his sternum. A moment later, the incarnate skidded to a halt and started climbing the weathered concrete slab beneath the South elevated station.

"Don't do this," Henry gasped as he limped to a stop under the trestle. "Goddamnit, don't *do* this to me—" he was muttering now, rubbing the cramps out of his knees, gazing up at the weathered beams.

The South station was one of the oldest in the area. Running parallel to the Northwestern commercial line, the CTA platform was a half-block-long span of ancient concrete, raised above the surrounding alleys by two mammoth pairs of tower legs. Henry squinted up at the silhouette of the incarnate. The young man was shimmying up one of these soot-covered legs toward the center span. Harsh yellow vapor strips filtered down through the platform, through the slatted railroad ties, throwing a halo around the incarnate. Off in the distance, the sound of rumbling rose.

A train was coming.

"Hey, kid—listen to me!" Henry called up at the young man. "You're gonna get yourself killed!"

The incarnate had reached the center span and was lifting himself up. Henry groaned and started up the leg, keeping his eyes on the young man. The train loomed closer. The sounds of its engine mingled with the swirling night winds, the vibrations building in the ancient timbers of the trestle. Henry bit into his tongue, trying to drown the pain in his legs, his thundering heart. He could see the silhouette of the incarnate. The kid was frozen up there on the lower span.

Something was wrong.

The incarnate shuddered, then shook his head as though shaking off a swarm of bees. The train was less than a block away now, and the roar of its engines flooded the air. The trestle shivered. Henry swallowed hard and climbed the rest of the way up, his hands tearing and splintering against the creosote-covered wood. He kept his gaze skyward. The kid was up there on the edge of the tracks, hunched over, heaving. Henry scaled the remaining rivets and swung his big leg over the edge of the piling.

"What's the matter, kid?" Henry yelled over the roar of the train as he climbed onto the apron.

The incarnate was struggling to his feet, silhouetted by the glare of vapor light. His face was obscured by darkness, but it was clear he was in severe pain. "No—*not yet!*" he cried as the train arrived. The steel wind blew past him. It was an express train, and express trains didn't stop at this station. The cars thundered by, the light from the windows like a strobe.

Purple sparks erupted from the wheels.

In the magnesium flash, the young man's face was visible

for just an instant. His flesh rippling, shifting and roiling from the inside. His eyes melting from gray to dark brown, his hair seeming to sprout and bristle with static electricity. He collapsed to the planks and vomited. Sheer agony knitted his face and gripped his shoulders.

The flash died away.

"What is it?" Henry was crawling along the edge of the span now, trying to get closer. He could only see the incarnate's silhouette, the outline of a person convulsing in agony, holding on with candle-wax fingers.

Another geyser spewed from the tracks.

In the sudden glare, the incarnate was visible again, rising to his knees, arms reaching up to the sky as though he were cursing the heavens. Another being was emerging, birthing herself crysalislike from deep within. The incarnate's torso shrank. Graying hair cascaded down around the shoulders, bosom swelling. Feminine curves undulating and setting like a delicate soufflé.

The flash faded to darkness.

Henry crossed the remaining few planks and reached the figure just in time for the final explosion of sparks. The light bloomed in their faces, drenching the span in silver daylight for just a split second.

Sarah Brandis was squatting before him, blinking, terrified and confused.

Henry embraced her as the train roared past the station. The tail car thundered away, pulling a gust of noxious wind and dead leaves and litter after it. Henry could feel Sarah's body trembling in his arms, Sarah's sobs drowned by the noise. And as the train shrank into the night, frantic footsteps loomed. Several sets of footsteps.

A wave of angry voices splashed across the platform. Two transit cops, guns drawn, and a cluster of onlookers were approaching, hollering at the lunatics who had climbed up on the tracks. Henry held Sarah tightly in his arms and whispered, "I'm here, and I'm not going anywhere, and I'm not gonna let go, not ever, ever, ever, ever. . . ."

II

In the wake of the movement toward political correctness, the world of psychiatric medicine had been renewed and jargonized and whitewashed like no other discipline. Head shrinkers had become *psychotherapists*. Madness had become *emotional disorder*. Shock treatments and lobotomies had been relegated to the era of witch doctors and leeches. The *DSM-IV-R* (*Diagnostic and Statistical Manual of Mental Disorders: Fourth Edition—Revised*) had become the practitioner's bible. And the grim old insane asylum had become the friendly neighborhood *mental health center*.

Even the atmosphere inside a psychiatric facility had changed from the old days. No longer were patients subjected to the crumbling catacombs of Bedlam or the banal sadism of *One Flew Over the Cuckoo's Nest*. The New Age mental health center was often a clean and well-lit place, a place of art therapy rooms and sprawling lawns and well equipped gymnasiums.

Not South Park.

The South Park Facility for the Criminally Insane was the asylum that time forgot. Located on Chicago's far north side, the facility was a half-mile-long reach of dilapidated, weatherbeaten brick buildings crouched along the banks of the Des Plaines River, walled off from the rest of the world by tall chain-link and concertina wire. Originally built in 1935 as low-rent "Negro housing" through the old post-fire *Plan of Chicago* renewal program, South Park consisted mostly of three-story barracks and two-story office buildings connected underground by narrow passageways. The bare dirt yards were heavily guarded. At night, if the wind was still, the anguished moans of inmates could be heard drifting across the far banks of the river.

Inside South Park, the air smelled of suffering, ripe and black and putrid.

Sarah Brandis was taking a big whiff of this odor as she lay on a cot in one of the empty interview rooms in which the authorities were warehousing her at the moment. The walls were brick. Whitewashed brick. No padded cells here. If an inmate wanted to bang her frontal lobe against the walls, by jingo, she was welcome to it. The floor was ancient tile, as cold as a salt mine. And all the mesh-reinforced windows were painted flat Rustoleum black. Two long fluorescent tubes shone down from the ceiling, flickering restlessly. And the smell, that mildew and vomit smell, permeated everything.

Shifting against the confines of her wrist straps, Sarah tried to calm the shooting pains in her lower back.

A few minutes ago, she'd been stricken with the urge to kill herself. Not in a messy way. She would do it in style, dressing up in some gorgeous evening gown, with a plunging neckline, wasp waist, and tons of pearls. Maybe even a pair of long white gloves and a fur stole. She would wear a deep red lipstick and fabulous blush and eye shadow. And she would do a *Madam Butterfly* number with a split of champagne and a bottle of Nembutal, pirouetting off the end of some tropic-bound ocean liner to the swells of Vaughn Williams. It would be tragically beautiful, and Sarah would make a lovely corpse as they dragged her from the water in her sodden chinchilla.

But, of course, it was not meant to be, not in this world, not while she was dressed in this gray matron's dress in this tight little white-brick room with the dried vomit smell and the flickering fluorescent and the nylon wrist straps holding her to the shit-stained cot.

Sarah swallowed back the flinty taste in her mouth and tried not to look in the mirror. The mirror was her nemesis. A three-by-six slab of silvered one-way mounted on the opposing wall, it was a constant reminder that she was being watched. Watched by the facility doctors who had questioned her that morning, prodding her for information about the *alter*, Sarah's other personality. Watched by Frank Moon and his people, the homicide detectives and the police psychologists. And most distressing of all, watched by her own reflection. Sarah could feel *his* gaze in the mirror, staring back at her through her own eyes.

The motherfucker lurking inside her body.

She closed her eyes and breathed steadily and tried to imagine that she wasn't sick anymore.

She lies on the grass in a tranquil little meadow in the Emerald Forest. The meadow is next to a lake. Sarah's gingham dress is covered with a soft blanket. And all the sweet little Munchkins are gathering over her. The little ballerinas. The boys from the Lollypop Guild. Even Glenda, the Good Witch.

"We'll heal you, Sarah," coos the Good Witch, and she waves her magic wand. And Sarah feels the warmth passing through her. And the Munchkin doctors arrive with buckets of cool water from the lake, and they rub the water over Sarah's arms and legs, soothing her.

Sarah gazes up and sees the deep blue sky overhead, and lemon-yellow sun, and the crows flying up there, their black wings fluttering, fluttering angrily—

"No!"

Sarah blinked, and she swallowed back the bile, and she concentrated on the healing images, and Henry's sweet touch, and all the good deep down inside her; and she tried not to think of the blackness.

She closed her eyes.

The sky fills with crows, and soon a thin contrail of smoke forms behind them, and the smoke forms letters, skywriting, automatic writing, ALIVE!, over and over, ALIVE! ALIVE! Then more words: SEE THE ESCAPE ARTIST FLEE THE RED PRISON!

"Fuck!"

Sarah jerked forward, shaking her head, shaking off the bad images.

Her body was filled with chaos again.

It was like a shortwave radio under her skin, drifting from the primary station and seeking another, the signals vying for attention. And Sarah couldn't make it stop. Like the hiccups. Only these hiccups were powerful surges of pain bolting up her spine, electric pain, and sudden disorientation. The alter was trying to turn her inside out. And every time she fought it, a stream of ghostly reverberations would waft through her mind, the after-echoes of words, his words, clamoring at her, hissing phrases like *I'm alive* and *cannot chain the master* and *demon of the red prison*, and at one point Sarah had bitten her tongue so hard it had bled for a half an hour.

Worse than all the pain and disorientation was the nagging familiarity of the words. *The needle trick* and *Escape Artist* and *the red prison* were phrases burned into her subconscious memory like droplets of acid on her brain. There was something terrible and dark and secret about those phrases, something buried in her past.

Sarah turned away from the mirror.

"Leave me alone, leave me alone, leave me alone," she kept repeating like a holy litany.

Henry had warned her about the struggle. With the detection of the disorder, the MPD, there was often a critical time immediately following diagnosis where the personalities learn of each other and try to dominate. Of course, in Sarah's case, there was no telling how her supercharged brain cells were going to react. Henry had stayed with Sarah through most of the previous night, through the arrest, through the initial observation period, gently explaining things to her. Explaining how she was probably the "host" personality, the alter which had the most frequent control over the body. How the "switch" usually happened during times of stress. And how Sarah shouldn't feel responsible for the actions of her "other" since she very well may be one of the most exceptional cases in the history of psychiatric medicine. But mostly Henry had stayed by her side as a comforting presence, as a friend, a loved one. Of course, that was before Frank Moon had separated them, before Moon had told

Henry that he couldn't interfere with the legal process anymore.

Sarah turned back to the mirror and regarded her reflection. Long strands of graying curls fell across her drawn face, her eyes wracked and shadowed with dark circles. She was a mess. Her skin was raw and blotched. And although many of the new tattoos had faded, there were still dark slash marks along her neck where her body had reconstituted.

She stared at herself for another moment and started to realize that she had a decision to make. She could fight this thing; she could fight it with all her heart and soul, fight it for Henry, fight it for Duff and Maxine, fight for her life. Or she could give up, surrender to the madness, and rot in this painted brick hell, a footnote in the annals of tabloid crime lore: *The Strange Case of Sarah the Shape-shifting Stripper*.

It wasn't going to be an easy decision.

III

Inside the airless little viewing cubicle, Detective Becky Jones was as nervous as a bug on a skillet.

First off, the ventilation in the room was piss-poor. The odor of cigarettes and stale coffee was so thick you could cut it up and knit socks with it. Second, the cubicle was hardly big enough for two people. A hundred square feet, a hundred fifty tops, of scarred parquet and acoustic tile, a single red light bulb glowing above the door, providing the only illumination safe enough to keep the room invisible behind the mirror. Third, the sight of the stripper gave Becky the willies. Becky didn't care that this broad was a frigging medical miracle, or that nobody had ever encountered anything like her before, or that any cop who was actively working the case would probably get a six-figure advance to write a book about it. Becky wanted out of this one. This chick was a nut case, and nut cases were unpredictable. They often got cops hurt or killed.

All this anxiety had already pitted out the underarms of Becky's navy blue blazer.

And then there was Frank Moon to contend with. Dressed in his sharkskin jacket and designer shirt, the detective-sergeant was leaning against the ledge in front of the mirror. Had a Walkman headset on, which hissed jazz very softly under the whirr of the steam heat. Practically had his nose pressed against the glass. Staring at the girl as though he were waiting for her to light up like a Christmas tree.

"So nobody's actually seen it," Becky said, crossing her arms in front of her, trying not to breath the air. "The change, I mean."

Frank lifted an earphone. "The shrink saw it, along with three witnesses on the El platform."

"I saw the statements, but nobody was real definitive."

"They saw what they saw," Frank murmured, staring at the girl in the room.

Becky Jones sighed. "I hate these damn press cases."

"It's not a press case yet."

"It'll get out."

"Maybe," Frank said, "but right now South Park is keeping it very low key. At least until the arraignment. DA wants to build a nice case and then get his name in the paper every morning when the tabloids start calling."

Becky thought about it for a moment, then said, "You know we'll never get a conviction. Even if we place her at Dante's, she'll cop a loony plea, get hospitalized, three squares a day, maybe a little basket weaving."

"Perhaps," Frank said, staring, half listening.

"What do we have on her?"

"Not much. Crime lab's still working on it. Word is they got a pretty good shot on that partial print. They're real close on the enhancements."

"A print off the bodies?"

"Off the tape."

Becky Jones nodded and rubbed her eyes. Then she gazed across the cubicle, through the mirror. The stripper was closing her eyes as though praying. "Nut cases," Becky said, "they're all alike."

"Yeah, maybe," Frank said, staring at the stripper.

"What is it, Frank?"

"What do you mean?"

"The wheels are turning up there in that noggin of yours."

Frank didn't take his eyes off Sarah as he murmured, "Puzzle pieces all over the place. The word *alive* scrawled everywhere. Maybe it's the other personality, maybe not. Then there's the locks, the chains, the bondage trip. Then there's the costume shop break-in. Witnesses in the Laundromat describe this guy in 1920s garb. Then there's the shrink, Decker, describing the other personality like its some kind of fucking vampire. Puzzle pieces rattling loose all over the place. I hate that."

"It's just fruitcake stuff, Frank. The lady's a goof. None of it means anything."

Frank turned and looked into Becky's eyes. "You ever have something on the tip of your tongue? Like it's right there in your head and you can almost see it, like a strip of light shining under a door?"

"Yeah," Becky said, "all the time."

Frank nodded. "I hate it when that happens."

Then Frank put his headphone back over his ear and gazed back at the stripper.

IV

"—if you'll just back me up on this."

"This woman is a suspected serial killer."

"I understand that, but she also may be the biggest psychiatric event since Freud bought his first settee. This lady's got symptoms we don't even have names for yet."

"You're moving too fast for me, Henry."

"Look, John, it's not that remarkable if you look at the microbiology."

"Enlighten me."

"It's like this: We've got a patient here—a classic multiple personality—whose alter personality is taking *physical* shape."

"Henry, I don't—"

"Wait. John, *please*. Think about it for a second. You know as well as I do that most MPD patients show discretely different physical traits among their alters. Different electrical activity in the brain. Different allergic reactions. One alter is left-handed, the other is right. One's nearsighted, the other's farsighted. In a way, Sarah's the logical extreme."

Henry swallowed thickly, his throat dry with nerves. The silence seemed to hang in midair like a glass web. Henry's hand was welded to the phone, the earpiece hot against his ear. He was standing next to the institute's greenhouse, and the purple rays of twilight filtered in and painted his face as he waited for Dr. Jonathon Hicks—chairman of the University of Chicago's Department of Clinical Psychology and frequent expert witness—to reply. Hicks was Henry's mentor, a father figure who had served as Henry's doctoral adviser back in the early seventies. The two men had drifted apart over the years, but Henry still called on Hicks's wisdom in difficult times.

Through the archway into the living room, Henry could see the busted French windows, a large sheet of plywood nailed across the jagged gap where the incarnate had broken through. A constant reminder of the very dangerous, very palpable side of Sarah's condition.

"And all this talk of supercharged neurochemistry?" the voice on the other end finally said. "You're telling me *that's* just another extrapolation you made from the PET scans and whatnot?"

Henry nodded fervently, as though Hicks could see him. "Yeah, exactly; as a matter of fact, I found out earlier today that Doug Callaway, the neurologist at Northwestern, did a blood sample during the final stages of one of Sarah's metamorphoses. He found that her red blood cells had become contractible—*contractible,* John—as though they're transforming into pigment-bearing cells, cells that are collecting right in the subcutaneous layers of her skin. Do you see what I'm saying? Her tissue's literally reacting to her neuropeptides."

"Contractible?" the voice chided. "What are you telling me—she's a bloody chameleon?"

"I know how it sounds, John, but there it is. She's incredible. She's been a patient of mine off and on now for over ten years, and I think she's always had this potential; it was brewing there, and it was touched off by the cancer and the imagery. But no matter how unprecedented her disorder, the core person underneath all this stuff is a lucid, intelligent woman. She would open up incredible research opportunities."

"Research opportunities. Is that what this is about? Is that *really* what this is about?"

"Okay. I admit it goes deeper than that. She's a very close friend, John, very close, and I want to help her. *I do.* I want to learn from her, and I want to study her, but mostly I just want to help her."

Another silence.

"What *exactly* do you want from me, Henry?"

"I know it sounds ridiculous, but in order to convince the district attorney to let me work with her, I need the imprimatur of a major forensic authority."

There was a long pained sigh on the other end of the line.

"C'mon, John, whattya say?"

More silence.

Henry started to wonder whether his motivations were indeed as pure as he claimed. He felt an incredible desperation to help his star patient, certainly. But there were so many other emotions and agendas stewing around inside him. There was an almost palpable lust for proprietary control over Sarah's case; he wanted so badly to write the book on this one. And as sleazy as it sounded, he saw Sarah as a route to legitimacy in the clinical field, ultimately leading to that

elusive acceptance by the scientific community. And maybe
Henry even saw this case as a way to gain the love and respect of a father figure such as Jonathon Hicks; the kind of
love and respect that Henry had never known. His real father
had died when Henry was three, and there was still a longing
deep inside Henry for that kind of connection. But beyond all
these aspects, worming around inside Henry like a sickness,
was a deeper motivation, a strange kind of possessiveness,
possessiveness toward Sarah's terrible miracles.

Possessiveness toward the woman he so thoroughly and
madly loved.

"I'll talk to Ray Prescott," the voice on the phone finally
replied.

Henry smiled. Dr. Raymond Prescott was the chief of
forensic medicine for Cook County College and a good
friend of Jonathon Hicks. Prescott held major sway not only
with the boys at CPD but City Hall as well. "That would be
fantastic," Henry said into the phone. "I owe you one,
John—big-time."

"Just do me a favor."

"Anything."

"Keep my name out of it," Hicks said, and then the line
went dead.

Henry hung up the phone, his gaze still playing across the
plywood-reinforced windows, his smile gradually fading.

                              V

Shortly after dinner they told her she had a visitor and prepared to move her to the first floor.

They gave her a thousand milligrams of Lithium and
dressed her in a restraint device known as the "evening
dress." The evening dress—which got its ironic nickname not
only because it was used at night to restrain manics and dangerous psychotics, but also because it resembled a grotesque
parody of a formal gown—was actually an updated version of

the old-fashioned straitjacket. Made of heavy beige canvas, the device had two heavy straps around each leg at the ankle, a center strip that ran up the torso, and a shoulder halter that bound the upper arms.

The minute they got Sarah into it, she started trembling.

"Please try to hold still," the matron said flatly, adjusting the straps in the back. Dressed in a gray South Park uniform, her hair puckered in a black net, the matron was a pear-shaped woman with a stoic face who treated Sarah like a rabid animal. The matron finished securing the restraints and then ushered Sarah out of the private room and into the corridor.

Sarah held her breath as she toddled along, taking baby steps in the taut material.

Something about the evening dress was sending an electric current through her bones and tendons. Like chemicals reacting. She tried to block it out, tried to ignore it, but the current was incredibly strong. Her flesh felt like metal shavings aligning under the canvas, and she started to hear the voice of The Other, faint blips in her mind, muffled after-echoes, as though underwater, and she knew it was the straitjacket. The straitjacket was drawing him out, summoning him.

Sarah was taken to one of the holding cells adjacent to the administrative offices. Two ratty upholstered chairs sat on a plastic mat in the center of the stark, unforgiving room. A squalid little floor lamp flanked one of the chairs. And an imitation wood-grain side table was filled with forms and magazines. Frayed nylon straps were affixed to the bottoms of the chairs. Waist-level safety bars lined the walls. And security cameras were mounted in each corner.

The matron led Sarah over to one of the chairs and clipped the bottom strap of the restraint garb to a U-bolt in the floor.

South Park was very big on security.

"Your visitor will be here shortly," the matron told Sarah. "Please try and relax, or the straps will dig into your ribs and be very uncomfortable."

This last comment was as close as the matron would come to kindness.

The matron walked out, and the door clanged shut behind her, bolting itself securely from the outside. Sarah held her breath. The silence descended like a funeral shroud, suffocating, palpable on her face. She felt the bonds, tight across her tummy, around her ankles and wrists. And the reverberating voice of The Other, a virus in her bloodstream, the half-formed phrases echoing, building in her

the sky is black

"No!" she hissed.

She began concentrating on NOT thinking, NOT imagining, NOT seeing the visuals in her mind, because her imagination had gone sour now, and a parasite was in her, making her see horrible things in her mind

the sky is pitch-black. The trees are blood-red, their cinnabar trunks like the bars of a prison. Sarah runs through the red forest, weaving through the trees. Bats flittering above her, squealing, SQUEALING—!

No! she thought frantically.

The voice was shrieking in her head now, after-echoes, muffled underwater sounds, ALIVE, snippets of buried memories, *see the mysterious escape,* NO, concentrate, concentrate, do NOT visualize it, do NOT imagine it!

Sarah runs, the tree trunks scraping her sides, slashing her with scarlet sap. Bats and crows and winged monkeys are clamoring overhead, debauching the treetops. Black spoor rains down on her. Acid hot on her skin. She slips and falls.

Sarah blinked, NO, and she concentrated on thinking

about something else, PLEASE DON'T, anything else, anything but the awful movie in her head.

Flickering

she crawls along the blood-slick path, her body wet with gore. She sees a clearing, an opening in the foliage up ahead, and finally, she reaches the clearing and discovers:

The tranquil little meadow and the secret lake. Something is wrong. The ground is moving, shivering beneath her. An earthquake. And suddenly . . .

An object bursts through the ground, birthing itself like a monolith.

The box!

Sarah gasped and blinked it away.

She swallowed back the panic, NO, the panic burning in her chest, and she felt the surface of her skin like molten metal lava flowing under the canvas, and she heard the voice, *I'M ALIVE!,* and she tried NOT to see it, but she was seeing it now, big as life in her mind—

more boxes bursting up through the ground, bobbing to the surface of the lake, forcing their way into the world, boxes, countless boxes, boxes everywhere.

Most of the boxes are broken open and smoking, their secrets wafting out like poisonous vapor.

Sarah screams. Her skin is burning from the acid rain, blistering from the poisonous spoor.

Something stirs within her, and her flesh bubbles like wallpaper buckling.

Something's breaking through, another body birthing it-self from deep inside her, forcing its way out of her skin like a snake, epidural layers cracking, fissuring like the quaking ground, a new set of fingers breaking through

and now she felt the pain twisting inside her, the cattle prod up her spine, and she felt herself shrinking, shrinking in the canvas dress, shriveling, disappearing into a tiny little seed inside her own body.

A tiny cold seed.

VI

An armed guard was waiting for Henry Decker in the main lobby; the guard had been notified by phone that the psychologist was coming.

"Evening, Doc," the guard said, tipping his headful of gray hair in greeting. The guard was in his late sixties, at least, and moved slowly in his gray uniform. Henry nodded a greeting and then followed the guard toward the far corner of the lobby. "She's waiting for you in E-Wing," the guard said as he approached the metal detector. Henry emptied his pockets, put his briefcase under the X-ray, and went through the metal detector.

"This way," the guard said, and started down a long, narrow breezeway bordered on either side by mesh windows.

Henry followed.

Outside the windows, the fences rose up into the black sky. Strands of concertina wire gleamed in the moonlight, and steam billowed out of neighboring smokestacks. October was crawling to a close, and Henry could smell the rot of harvest and the smoke of burning leaves through the windows.

"The patient will be in restraints," the guard recited as he led Henry over a threshold and into an inner lobby of scattered folding chairs. "Do not attempt to pass her anything or move her during the interview."

They reached another checkpoint and Henry waited patiently while the guard signed their names onto a clipboard and grabbed a laminated visitor's pass for Henry. Henry clipped the pass onto the pocket of his corduroy jacket and took a deep breath. He was nervous. Something about this place was making his scalp crawl, stiffening the tiny hairs on the back of his neck.

"You will be allowed twenty minutes," the guard continued, "at which time a buzzer will sound."

Henry nodded, half listening as he walked along behind the old geezer.

"There will be guards stationed at either end of the E-Wing corridor."

Henry felt helpless now that Sarah was incarcerated in this brick monolith, and he was prepared to do anything to get her out of here. He wanted to see her so badly, his chest ached. He didn't care what Frank Moon said, the threats meant nothing to Henry. He would gladly go to jail for Sarah. Sarah was the most important thing in his life now.

He was going to help her even if it killed him.

"You will be recorded by video cameras," the guard droned as he led Henry down a corridor of offices, numbered doors closed for the night, bulletin boards with schedules and memos and recipes for Halloween cupcakes. Henry felt his pulse quicken slightly as they approached a door marked E-WING—PERSONNEL ONLY, and the voice of the guard broke the stillness.

"If you have any problems," the old man said, pausing in front of the door, snapping a magnetic card through a motor lock, "there's an emergency call button on the wall near the door. The minute you lift it, you'll get security."

The bolt clicked open.

"Room twenty-three," the old man said and opened the door.

"Thanks," Henry said, and started down the E-Wing corridor.

The sound of the door bolt clicked behind him, and now Henry realized it wasn't just his angst over Sarah's safety that was bugging him. It was the air. The very air had pain woven through it, pain stitched into the shadows, pain sewn through the mildew odors and the grimy texture of the floor. The place was a tapestry of pain, and Henry could feel it against the stubble of his beard like a poison veil.

People had seen the fabric of hell in this place.

Henry found room 23. It had a metal door with a small, rectangular mesh window embedded at eye level. Henry peered through the glass but could only see amorphous blurry shapes through the layers of grime. He took a deep breath, knocked once, then opened the door and walked into room 23.

"Sarah?"

At first Henry didn't know what he was looking at. She was slumped in a chair in the center of the room. Head down, shivering, back hunching. Was she vomiting? Dry heaving? It looked as though her hair was levitating on a surge of static electricity. "Sarah—it's Henry—*stay with me*," he urged, and took a step closer and watched her hair fade to dishwater brown and shrivel back into her skull.

Then the face popped up, revealing itself to be the face of the mysterious young man.

Henry carefully set his briefcase on the floor and took another step toward the incarnate. "I came to see Sarah," Henry said sharply.

"Sarah's gone," the young man told him. The incarnate looked almost comfortable in the floor-length straitjacket. His eyes glowed with mischief, and his head was cocked at an odd angle.

Henry's flesh crawled. "Tell her to come back!"

"She can't come back."

"What do you mean, she can't come back?" Another step

closer, Henry could see the young man's gelatinous skin, his embryonic features.

"She can't," the Escape Artist said, and paused for effect, his eyes blazing, his words coming out like knives stabbing at Henry's heart. "Because. I. Made. Her. *Disappear*."

7

Vertical Red Lines

Henry Decker stood for several long moments in that stifling little cell, the words sinking in, the scalding rage flowing through his veins.

Henry had a long fuse, longer than most men's. Even during his football days, up against the meanest defensive tackles who were hopped up on Benzedrine and steroids and dead-set on poking Henry's eyes out, Henry was still the personification of restraint and self-control. He had even developed a system of channeling his own anger, a system he called the Furnace. The Furnace was a simple visualization that never failed. Henry would imagine an old blast furnace inside him, the old brick and mortar kind that was usually found in turn-of-the-century steel mills. Whatever happened to be bothering him at any given moment would be tossed into the cauldron like bits of kindling. Some asshole lineman trying to tear Henry's head off—POOF! Into the Furnace. Some maniac driver trying to cut Henry off on the Kennedy Expressway—WHOOSH! Into the Furnace. And the flames would swell and rise, and Henry would simply imagine all the rage billowing out an invisible stack on the top of his head, harmlessly, into the atmosphere like snowflakes of ash.

At the moment, however, the Furnace didn't seem to be working.

"Listen to me," Henry said evenly, fists clenching. He was moving toward the incarnate, the room distorting around him. The painted brick walls and the sputtering steam radiators and the faulty fluorescents all seemed to warp and contract inward as though exposed to great levels of heat. "You cannot *make* Sarah go away," Henry hissed, "because you are simply part of her psyche. Do you understand?"

"You're wrong, pilgrim," the incarnate said. And then he smiled, and the smile was the yellow gleam of evil and the twisted logic of madness. "She's merely a portal, a doorway."

"You're talking nonsense now."

The yellow grin lingered. "I've already walked through her and closed her behind me as tight as a drum."

"That's nonsense," Henry said, approaching the young man. "You cannot get rid of Sarah, because Sarah is the source of everything you are, and I can prove it."

The young man in Sarah's body did not respond. Instead, he closed his eyes and kept smiling faintly, as though remembering some lilting melody or pleasant experience from many years ago. His shoulders were working under the straitjacket, working gently like the hands of a lover.

"Do you want me to prove it?" Henry stopped a couple of feet away from the alter. Still no response. Just the tender movements beneath the canvas coverall. A slight twisting of the torso, a subtle stiffening of the upper lip.

Henry watched, a whirlwind of contrary emotions coursing through his mind. He hated this little man—this imposter—for taking Sarah away. But the truth of it was, the mysterious young man was indeed a part of her, a shard, a jagged fragment of her shattered psyche, and the sooner Henry dealt with that fact, the sooner he would be able to integrate Sarah back into her self. Of course, on top of all this, there was the undeniable freakishness of the phenomenon.

The young man had his own smell. Staring down at him, standing at this close proximity, Henry could detect the odors of pomade, cigar smoke, and dried sweat wafting upward, but it wasn't Sarah's sweat. Henry had savored that sweet perspiration the night they had made love, and this was something else altogether. It was a sharp, alkaline sweat. And there was something else about the sandy-haired young man's scent, something that Henry couldn't really put his finger on. A musty dank smell, like the pages of old books kept in a wet cellar for years and years. Was this a ghost? Was this a shadow of a real person? Henry felt a rash of goose bumps frost the back of his legs.

"Do you want me to prove it to you?" Henry repeated.

No response.

"All right, I'll prove it to you by asking you a series of simple questions," Henry said. "Who are you? What's your name? Where were you born? Where did you come from?"

The incarnate looked up, smile widening, and all at once the smile was no longer a smile, but a grimace. A grimace of intense concentration, as though his hands were shuffling a deck of cards under the straitjacket. Still no response, just that lopsided torture-grin.

"Please," Henry said, his heart cantering. "I'm not trying to trick you."

The incarnate closed his eyes and continued wriggling softly under the canvas.

Henry took a deep breath. "If you just answer these simple questions, I can help you. I promise I will help you. If you just answer the question: *Who are you?*"

No answer.

"WHO ARE YOU?"

The incarnate snapped his gaze up at Henry. "You want to know my secrets? My identity? My true identity?" The words poured out of the incarnate like steam escaping a pipe. "I will tell you; I am the devil's son, the master of escape, and no locks can hold me, no chains bind my supple limbs, I am the great and mysterious artist of evasion, and I am *ALIVE*!"

A spindly arm popped out of the straitjacket.

"What?"

Henry reacted instinctively, jerking backward, flinching as though confronted by the glint of a fang or the lurch of a wild animal. At first it just didn't make sense, this wiry arm jutting out the top of the canvas. Then there was another arm joining it, rising out of the collar like an errant chicken bone thrust out the top of a grocer's sack.

"All right, take it easy," Henry muttered, raising his hands awkwardly. He glanced over his shoulder. The door was still locked up tight, the emergency toggle mounted next to it. Henry turned back to the incarnate and started to say, "You can't get out of heh—"

A pair of sinewy hands shot out and grabbed Henry by the throat.

Henry reared backward, his momentum wrenching the incarnate off the chair, ripping the last restraint strap like a strip of paper. Some of the straps had already been worked loose, and the bolts on the floor were dangling free, and in the pandemonium of the moment, Henry realized with horrible clarity that he was dealing with a freakish prodigy here, an incarnate with the very skills of which he had boasted, and this was bad, very bad, because the Escape Artist was now free, and he was strangling Henry with fingers like iron bands.

The two men tumbled to the floor.

Henry gasped and tried to wriggle free, but the young man was gripping him like a vise. Henry couldn't breathe. The young man's face was only inches away now, his lips curling away from baby turtle teeth, his eyes gleaming brightly, his handsome features curdling. He was a wild animal. Henry made a fist and slammed it into the young man's belly. Again and again, and finally the young man yelped and released his grip.

Henry spun away.

The incarnate slithered the rest of the canvas off his feet and made a mad dash for the door. Henry lunged at him. They collided and slammed into the wall. Henry clawed at the emergency call button, but the young man had his hands on Henry's face now, digging for his eye sockets. It felt like ice picks on Henry's skin, cold nails sharpened over years of obsessive gnawing. Henry tripped over his own feet and went down.

The young man was on top of him now, with one of the torn canvas straps around Henry's throat. "*No prison can hold me,*" the young man hissed like a cat with its ears pinned, its back arched, a fine spray of spittle on Henry's neck. "*No locks, no cells, no bonds—*"

Something suddenly went haywire inside Henry.

Perhaps it was lack of oxygen to his brain, the way the room started swimming in and out of focus all of a sudden, the tears of panic filling his eyes. Or maybe it was the fact that he could easily die in the next few moments, his lungs seething for air, his upper body caught in the muscled arms of this lunatic. Or perhaps it was merely because, at that moment, Henry suddenly realized he could lose Sarah forever if this incarnate was allowed to win. But whatever the reason, Henry's body responded at once. His chest expanded. He clenched his teeth, and his legs suddenly pistoned the way they used to when he was cornered on the gridiron by some motherfucking defensive lineman pumped too full of anabolics and attitude.

He threw the incarnate off his back as though tossing a bean bag.

The young man landed against the wall by the radiator, momentarily dazed. Henry sprang to his feet and lumbered over to the wall. He reached down and grabbed the young man by the tunic, hauling him to his feet. "*Bring Sarah back!*" Henry howled, and swung a ham-fisted right to the incarnate's jaw.

The incarnate hurled across the room as if stricken by a large mobile home, bouncing off the wall and toppling.

Henry went over to the young man, scooped him up, and lifted him against the wall. Squeezing handfuls of the tunic, Henry slammed the dazed incarnate into the brick with all his might. *"BRING HER BACK!"* Henry bellowed, and then slammed the incarnate again, hard enough to elicit a resounding thud against the brick, then again, and again, and again.

Outside the meshed glass window, the sounds of frantic voices and footsteps were looming.

"Bring her back, goddamnit!" Henry moaned now as though gut-shot, wrapping his hands around the incarnate's neck, squeezing desperately, his big bare hands closing around the pale neck, and tears streaming down Henry's big ruddy cheeks, and the Furnace in his head spewing sparks and flames and smoke, overheating, as he stared into the eyes of madness, and strangled, and stared.

The incarnate was grinning.

"Bring her back," Henry uttered one final time, and suddenly all his blood ran cold.

The incarnate was changing. His handsome features went all milky in Henry's hands, runny, like a sculpture made of cream. It was like strangling an eel. The face rippled and shivered and the eyes narrowed, grew almond-shaped, and the hair teemed down the sides of the skull, peppering with gray, and all at once the face belonged to someone else. And just for an instant, Henry's heart seemed to stop.

He was strangling Sarah.

"OhmyGod!" Henry jerked backward as though shocked, releasing Sarah just as the door burst open behind him. Sarah folded to the floor.

"Get away from the patient, please!" A voice called out from the doorway.

Henry whirled. "Wait a minute—you don't under—"

"Get back!"

The matron was coming through the door, her tight

cropped hair net flopping and beady eyes flashing angrily. She was flanked by two armed orderlies dressed in white togs. One of the orderlies, an older man with frosty blue eyes and thin strands of hair combed across his bald pate, rushed over to Sarah. Kneeling down by her, he pulled a nightstick from his belt and pressed it hard against her collarbone, pinning her to the floor. Then he reached for his shackles.

"Wait a minute," Henry protested, taking a step toward Sarah. "You don't need to—"

The younger orderly blocked Henry's path, and then started urging Henry back toward the door. "Gonna have to leave now, Dr. Decker."

"This woman is my patient!" Henry said, struggling to get back to Sarah.

"Get him out of here!" the matron shouted.

Across the room, the balding orderly shackled Sarah to the radiator, then sprang to his feet and rushed back over to join his partner.

"She's my patient!" Henry cried, and tried to disentangle himself. The younger orderly had a strong grip on Henry's left arm, and the balding man took Henry's other arm, ushering him back toward the door. Henry started to struggle more fiercely. "Goddamnit—I told you she's my patient!"

The balding man murmured a southern accent in Henry's ear, "Don't make this tough on yourself, old sport."

"Sarah!" Henry had tears burning his eyes now, and a metal claw was closing around his heart. He had fucked things up very badly this time. The orderlies shoved him through the doorway, but Henry latched on to the jamb with one of his hands and held on for dear life. "SARAH!"

Sarah's voice came flitting across the room. "Henry? What's happening?"

"*Get him out of here this instant!*" The matron was so angry, she was shivering, preparing a hypodermic of thiopental with trembling fingers. Sarah's face was already starting to redden and swell, her left eye puffing from Henry's blow, revealing the terrible symbiosis between the two alters, as though two distinct human beings were time-sharing the same molecules. Her gaze shifted around the room, eyes blinking.

"Henry—where are you?"

"Sarah!" Henry was losing the battle. The orderlies had most of his body out the door. His hand slipped from the jam and they shoved him into the corridor. "SSSSSARRRAH!"

The door clanged in his face.

Henry slammed a meaty fist against the door and wailed, "SSARRRRRRRAAAAHHHHH!"

There was no answer, and Henry put his face against the cool metal of the door. Closed his eyes. Fought back the tears and silently cursed his pride, his idiotic pride, and his inability to deal with Sarah's unearthly state. Worse than that, Henry felt a powerful new wave of dread pouring over him, dread for the future, dread for the direction in which this insane monster was taking Sarah. Henry could hear the muffled movements of the orderlies inside the holding cell, sedating Sarah, moving her back over to the chair, getting the straitjacket back on her.

Henry stood there for quite some time, getting his bearings, taking long, deep breaths. There were more footsteps coming down the corridor. Sharp, regimented, businesslike footsteps. Probably guards. Henry knew they were coming for him. Coming to kick him the hell out of there.

Pulling a bandanna from his pocket, Henry dried his eyes and took a series of deep breaths.

He wasn't going to let them see him like this.

A mountain of a man crying like a baby.

II

That night, a small red EXIT sign burned above the barred door at one end of the infirmary. A row of bloody gashes in the blackness.

The ward was empty, as cold and still as a tomb, and

Sarah found herself staring trancelike at that EXIT sign, its letters blurring into awful red slash marks. She was strapped to a gurney a few feet away, shoved against one wall, her arms damp with sweat. They had given her something about an hour ago, maybe Haldol, maybe Thorazine, and it had formed a thin film of egg white over her face and her flesh, filling her mouth with cotton and making her lips go numb. But even through the narcotic gauze, she just couldn't tear her gaze away from those crimson letters, or stop thinking about the shapes

red vertical lines

Swallowing dryly, lifting her head from the pillow, she gazed around the infirmary.

It was a long, narrow ward with rows of hospital gurneys along either wall. The air had a chalky smell, like powdered disinfectant, and moonlight filtered down through the high meshed windows, crisscrossing everything with a dull silver sheen. Sarah craned her neck slightly to see around the nurse's cart that was sitting at one end of the aisle. Near the opposite exit, there was a metal guard's desk. The desk was situated next to a floor vent, probably some kind of cold air return. And directly above it, the guard's personal items hung on a pegboard panel. Hat, empty holster, key ring laden with color-coded keys

keys, keys, KEYS

Sarah slammed her head back on the pillow and closed her eyes, blocking out the voice of The Other, the after-echoes, the ghostly muffled sounds in her head. Even the drugs couldn't fully erase The Other from her head. But if she concentrated on neutral things, neutral thoughts, she was able to keep him at bay. Turning her gaze back toward the EXIT sign, she wetted her chapped lips and tried to remember what it was about the vertical *lines, red lines, red prison bars!*

She blinked.

It came to her faintly at first, like the lament of a foghorn, distant, wavering on the wind, but rising, rising, the letters of the EXIT sign mutating into something new, becoming dark vermillion verticals across the blackness, metamorphosing hardening into bark, the trunks of red pines, native jack pines, endless rows of them in some black primordial forest where the cold air never sees the light of day, and the sound of the foghorn rose, keening, becoming a piercing clarion call in Sarah's skull, like Morse code, blocking out everything but the rhythmic gong, the signal, the semaphore spelling out a single word

ARKHAM!

Sarah's scream rended the darkness, tearing the moonlight to shreds; and she was still screaming when the fluorescents started flickering to life.

III

In the haze of Legacy Lager, Halcion, and medicated half-sleep, the sound of a telephone is like the chirp of a seagull over endless hissing waves. It came to Henry this way, at some point in the wee hours.

He jerked away from the pillow, sitting up with a start.

The room was in deep shadows except for the tiny amber spot of a crystal night-light by the door. Henry scooted out to the edge of the bed and rubbed the cobwebs off his face. He'd been dreaming feverish vignettes, one after another; reaching out for Sarah's face and feeling it melt like candle wax; falling into the mysterious box, plunging into the endless black void; and the face of the Escape Artist, materializing behind a frosted pane of glass in some forgotten asylum, vengeful eyes gleaming insanely. Henry had awakened to the sound of the telephone with a poem on the tip of his tongue. Something he remembered from grad school lit class many years ago, some old German tome by Heinrich Heine, echoing in Henry's mind like an incessant melody.

Nothing can scare us more/ Than chancing to see our face in a glass/ By moonlight.

The phone rang again.

Henry leaned over and flipped on the side-table lamp, illuminating a modest bedroom cluttered with file boxes, forgotten manuscripts, and old research notes. The back of Henry's neck and his big belly were still clammy with sweat, and he shivered slightly in the dim room as he rose and stepped into his slippers. The telephone rang again, and Henry went over to the side table, his heart racing, and picked up the receiver.

"Hello?"

Nothing but a muffled strangling noise, like a wounded animal, or person choking on a bone.

"Who is this?"

"H-h-henry?"

"Yes, this is Henry Decker. Who's this?"

More panting, labored breathing. "H-hh-henry—I'm in— ss-something's happened—"

"Sarah?" Henry's heart started to gallop in his chest, his hand tightening around the receiver.

A choked whisper: "I'm on a pay phone in the infirmary, and I don't have much time—I'm not supposed to be talking, but I pulled the receiver into the bathroom, so I only have a—*Oh, Jesus Henry I'm scared.*"

"Take your time, Sarah, it's okay, I'm here, I'm listening. How do you feel?"

"I dunno, it's like, he's getting stronger—the magician."

"You're talking about the Escape Artist?"

There was an agonized moment of silence on the other end, a ragged breathing and a sniffing back of tears. "It's like . . . he's a broken radio in my head, and he's, he's—Oh, my

God, Henry, I'm losing my mind, I can't handle this anymore."

"Easy does it, kiddo, keep talking."

"I don't want to hurt anybody—I just—I just want him out of me."

"I understand; you just gotta keep talking. That's how we're going to beat this thing. Tell me—who's the Escape Artist? Who is he? What's he escaping from?"

"I don't know—some of the words in my head, his voice, some of the things he says are familiar."

"Tell me about it."

"Something's happened, Henry."

"Tell me."

"Maybe a clue, maybe nothing, I dunno, maybe it's all just insane. . . ."

"What is it, Sarah? What's happened?"

"Okay, here's the thing—the imagery. The imagery started getting twisted, ugly, I dunno. But tonight, some of the images started looked familiar, some of the things in my head, they started reminding me of something."

"What?"

After a long, wheezing silence: "Arkham."

Henry bit his lip. "Arkham? Why does that sound familiar?"

"It's my old home town, Henry. Arkham, Wisconsin. I keep seeing shapes, shapes that remind me of the red pines that thrived in the woods around there."

"Red pines?"

"They weren't really red. But there was this one spot, way up in the hills above Arkham, deep in the forest—it was like a corridor of red pines and maples. In the fall, when the leaves changed color, it got so red, it was like, like a filter over the sun. I keep seeing that red light, and hearing that bastard voice in my head."

"What's he saying about Arkham?"

"The red pines, Henry—folks used to say that part of the

forest had gone bad, like it was haunted or something, you know how small towns are."

Henry thought about it for a moment. "What happened back there in Arkham, Sarah?"

No response; only the sound of stifled breathing and teary panic.

"C'mon, kiddo—*think*. Was it your mother? We've talked about this many times before. Was it something that your mother did to you in the forest?"

"No, no, she was . . . she was cruel, and she would punish me—but that was all. She didn't touch me."

"What's all the Escape Artist phenomena? Who is this guy, Sarah?"

"*I don't know!* When Moon showed me the bodies—Maxine and Duff—the horrible way they were locked up, the rope and the tape, it all seemed familiar, but I just couldn't—I couldn't place it."

Henry swallowed hard. "Okay, we're going to figure this thing out."

Another hissing silence. "Henry, I miss you."

Henry felt a sharp twinge of emotion in his chest, bringing water to his eyes. "I miss you, too, honey."

Sarah's voice seemed to steady itself then, lowering its pitch slightly. "I've been thinking about what you said, about repressing memories, traumas, you know."

"You didn't buy that for a second."

"Well, people change," the voice said wearily, belying the painful irony. "I'm starting to think there may be something to it, something about Arkham."

Henry pondered the notion for a moment, staring at the wee-hour shadows outside the window. There was a coating of frost on the glass, the first of the season. It was October 28, Henry realized absently, three days until Halloween. "How would you feel about undergoing hypnosis?"

"No. Forget it. Besides, after tonight, they wouldn't let you set foot within a mile of this place."

"Sarah, listen, what happened tonight—I'm so sorry; when

I hurt you, I didn't mean to do it, it's just—it's just so difficult for me to see you melt away like that."

"You think it's hard for *you*—you oughta try it sometime."

Henry smiled sadly.

"Henry, listen"—Sarah's voice lowered even further—"there may be only one way to figure this stuff out."

"And that is?"

"I've got to go back there myself."

Henry's stomach knotted suddenly. *"What—?"*

"I've got to go back to Arkham."

"Sarah, you know they'll never agree to take you back there with Moon building his case against you, with the arraignment coming up tomorrow—they'll never allow it."

"Doesn't matter. I've got to go back there on my own, figure this thing out once and for all."

Henry's scalp tingled, and panic shot through his veins. "Wait a minute—what are you telling me?"

"I'm getting out of here."

"Breaking out?"

"Look, Henry, I'm not sure where these images will lead me, but it's something I have to do."

"Sarah, for God's sake, you're gonna get yourself killed."

"I have a choice, Henry. Really very simple. I can either dry up in some asylum, or I can follow my instincts and pursue this."

"If you get hurt, I'll die."

"Henry, stop it."

"Let me talk to Jonathon Hicks again. Maybe we can get them to postpone the arraignment."

There was a muffled sound on the other end, distant voices echoing. Then the rustle of fabric over the phone. Then Sarah's tense voice: "Gotta go, I love you."

"Sarah, wait—"

There was a click

Then a dial tone.

IV

If Sarah had been in any ward other than the infirmary, she never would have been able to get down the ancient wooden steps leading into the basement power plant. But several factors were working in her favor. First, security in the infirmary had always been relatively informal. Second, the graveyard shift had quite a few people out with the blue-flu tonight. As a matter of fact, word was going around that Local 2081 of the American Federation of Municipal Employees, along with the Independent Guards and Watchmen of America, were about to go on strike. And this was making nightly operations around South Park somewhat strained, to say the least. But it wasn't until approximately eleven, when the night nurse had shown up for one final dose of lithium, that Sarah encountered the ultimate opportunity.

A simple mistake.

"Damn it," the nurse whispered under her breath, looking down at the tip of her syringe. The tiny metal fastener joining the hypodermic needle to the plunger was loose. "I'll be right back," she said, and resecured the restraint strap behind Sarah, except that it had never been secured in the first place and was only partially buckled, probably because the nurse was doing her rounds alone tonight rather than with a guard at her side, which had been standard op before the impending walkout. The loose buckle had enabled Sarah to sneak into the bathroom a few moments ago and make her call to Henry, and now, as the nurse walked back across the ward and disappeared momentarily inside the supply closet, Sarah made another instant decision.

She quickly pulled her hands free, slipped off the edge of the gurney, and padded toward the exit.

The alarm buzzer didn't start until Sarah was halfway across the next ward. The sound was so shrill, so abrupt, that it seemed to have a color. Bright magnesium blue, streaking across the dim reaches of the corridor, spattering gooseflesh up and down Sarah's legs and arms. She started running. The slap of her bare feet against the tile sounded like raindrops, delicate raindrops in the middle of a war. She reached the metal door at the end of the corridor, the one with the barred window and the dents where past inmates had slammed bloody fists and foreheads and heels, and she tried the knob.

Locked.

She spun toward the opposite wall, her cotton hospital gown flapping open in back, and she frantically searched for another potential passageway. The sounds of bootsteps and jangling keys were approaching down an adjacent hallway, the angry voices of the overworked and underpaid. Sarah whirled and saw an unmarked door right behind her. She opened the door and saw mop handles, buckets, and drums of cleaner. She quickly slipped inside the maintenance closet and latched the door, shutting out all the light except for a thin thread at the bottom of the door, and then she was listening to the pounding of her heart, the pounding in her ears, and the sounds of heavy bootsteps approaching, sweeping the corridor with flashlights, flickering across the strip at the bottom of the closet door.

Now the fear started spreading through her, beading her upper lip with sweat, twisting her stomach in knots and rashing her flesh with more goose bumps, goose bumps on her goose bumps. She stood in the darkness of this horrible ammonia-smelling closet and watched the strip of light at the bottom of the door strobe with the passing movement of boots and beams, and the angry voices, and the sudden heat flashes in her mind like mortar shells

memories

cowering in the dark pantry, a scared little girl, a bad girl, the smells of stale crackers and rat poisoning choking her. She can see baskets of moldy potatoes and onions hanging off the ceiling like corpses.

Sarah slammed her palm over her mouth, backing deeper into the darkness as the guards shuffled past the door.

*Jessie's muffled voice was outside the door. "You stay
in there, and you think about the next time you feel like
pissing your sundress!"*

Sarah was blinking, blinking away the tears and the memories, her eyes adjusting to the dark.

She could see objects stacked along shelves and hanging
off pegboard on either side of her. Coils of electrical cable,
cans of paint, wrenches, paintbrushes. She kept backing
away from that thin yellow strip of light at the bottom of the
door, and soon the sounds of the guards were drifting beyond
the closet, shuffling toward the end of the corridor, and
Sarah took a long, deep breath, swallowing hard.

Then the floor disappeared.

She fell facefirst, hard, on a set of wooden steps, then she
started slipping downward, her knees scraping the sharp
edges, splinters biting into her flesh, her hands clutching at
the side rail, clutching instinctively, clutching for purchase
until she finally latched on to it and held firm. She realized
all at once, with her body screaming in pain, that it wasn't a
closet she had ducked into, but the mouth of a staircase leading down into the bowels of the building, probably left unlocked by some absentminded janitor. She struggled up to a
standing position, turned, and looked down the remaining
steps.

A sickly yellow emergency light glowed at the base of the
stairs, revealing a metal catwalk leading into a dark, noisy
power plant. The shadows of huge generator casings and aluminum conduits vibrated nearby. And the air stank of cordite
and cinders and filth. Sarah limped down the rest of the steps
and entered the power plant.

Another stroke of luck. Not only was the cellar deserted,
but the catwalk led straight between the hulking machinery
and into the farthest reaches of the underground.

Sarah started limping toward the darkness beyond the
power plant. She had no idea what she would find there, but
she had a hunch it would lead her out of this wretched place.

Her legs were shrieking with pain and fire. Lacerated and
bleeding. And worse, she felt the light-headed, buoyant nausea that always proceeded a blackout. But she refused to
buckle under to the sickness tonight; she was going to get the
hell out of this madhouse and find her answers if it was the
last thing she ever did, which it may very well be; but not before she fought this thing with every last ounce of piss and
vinegar she could muster. She passed the broken glass
gauges, the knots of pipe, the dripping, crusted joints, and
the humming generators, until she came upon another door.
It was a scarred metal hatch, like that of submarine, with a
small metal wheel for a knob. Sarah turned the knob, muscled the door open, and cautiously peered through it.

The tunnel snaked into the distance just as pretty as you
please.

Sarah felt her heart starting to race. Bare light bulbs hung
on frayed cord every ten feet or so, bathing the tunnel in a
kind of dirty incandescence. It was the underground passageway that linked the various South Park buildings, and it most
certainly contained a way out. Sarah leaned out the doorway
farther and gazed in either direction, finding the tunnel
empty. She started down the tunnel, then paused and turned
back to the hatch, pulling it closed to cover her tracks.

It was then that a voice called out above the hum of generators.

"Hey!" It was an elderly janitor, dressed in dirty blue togs,
coming through the steam and filthy shadows. "Git yer ass
back here, missy!"

Sarah turned and ran.

"She's down here, Carl!" The bark of the janitor's voice
echoed through the gloom. "Just took off like a bat outta hell
down the tunnel!"

Sarah ran for all she was worth. Cotton gown flapping,
heart jittering, bare feet stinging and sending bolts of pain up
her legs with every stride, she was madly searching for a
route of escape. The floor of the tunnel was smooth concrete,

ice cold, and she could hear the shuffling bootsteps of guards entering the passageway, calling after her.

"Sarah, sweetheart! Ain't no way out! Why don't you come on back—we're not gonna hurt you!"

Sarah recognized the voice of the balding orderly, the good ole boy with the frosty blue eyes. His shout was distorted by tension and the pounding of his strides. He and his cohorts were gaining; Sarah could hear them closing the distance in the narrow tunnel behind her. She ran as fast as she could, passing endless lengths of exposed plumbing and bare light bulbs and jagged rock-cut walls, but she saw no doorways, no traps in the ceiling, no ways out. Her heart was about to burst when all at once she came upon an intersection of two tunnels.

She slammed on the brakes and turned sharply to the right, entering a new tunnel.

That's when her luck ran out.

The dead end loomed less than twenty feet away, the tunnel terminating in fifty square feet of ancient concrete with a partially torn happy face sticker on it, a bare bulb flickering madly off the ceiling. Sarah instinctively tried to stop and reverse, and her momentum tangled her up and sent her sprawling to the cool cement.

She skidded up against the concrete and red splashed her field of vision

red slash marks across the darkness, blood red, wet like incisions, becoming prison bars

"No! No-no-no—NO!"

Sarah tried to stand, but her body was convulsing now, her stomach turning inside out, her flesh tingling as though two chemicals were reacting. She rose to her knees. Then she vomited air, heaving stringy loops of bile. She could hear the sounds of the guards approaching. *"NOT NOW!"* Sarah shrieked, and clutched handfuls of her hair

*and the prison bars warp, bowing outward, rending,
breaking in two*

"Please—"

The sound of her own voice was changing, its timbre
plunging into baritone. Her skin tightened and the pain
shocked through her, a cattle prod up her ass, twisting her
pelvis and tossing her to the floor.

The guards were nearing the intersection, and Sarah felt
herself shrinking again, contracting like a time-lapse film of
a seedling in reverse, the stem and leaves shriveling inward,
cells coalescing, molecules aligning in hard new little patterns. Her vision began to bifurcate, splitting into fragments
like a shattered prism. The glare of the light bulb dwindled,
and she saw a kaleidoscope closing around the grim little
passageway, synchronized with her pain, twinges of bright
cadmium orange, pangs of intense chromium yellow,
swirling tighter and tighter and tighter into a pinprick of cataclysmic agony.

Then the dot faded like an old-fashioned television screen
going cold and black, and a new voice was coming out of
her, soft and confident.

"I'll take it from here."

V

The balding orderly was the first to round the corner at the
intersection, the first to see the blur of motion, and the first
to realize that maybe this particular patient retrieval wasn't
going to be as easy as he had thought. The orderly reared
back, throwing his hands up in front of his face. There was a
figure vaulting at him, all gray cotton and flailing limbs, and
by God it sure as hell was *not* the lady they had chased into
this corner.

"Good *night*!" The orderly ducked, and the other two

guards ducked behind him, and the shape soared over their heads, skimming their scalps.

The Escape Artist was swinging from one overhead pipe to another, his legs tucked like a Thoroughbred arching over an oxer gate. One of the guards pulled a .38, aimed it, and pulled the trigger, and the muzzle blast lit up the tunnel. The bullet tore a chink of insulation out of the ceiling, but the near-miss didn't even faze the Escape Artist, because he was concentrating now, he was making it a performance, perhaps his greatest ever, to escape a high-security insane asylum with nothing but a cotton gown and his wits.

He landed in the main tunnel, rolled a revolution, and sprang to his feet. Before the guards and orderly could even gather their bearings, the Escape Artist was halfway down the same tunnel from which Sarah had come.

It took him less than a minute to get back to the power plant. He slipped inside, moving stealthily through the dimness, and started searching for the objects he had noted through Sarah's eyes a few minutes earlier, the objects that were going to aid his escape; for he knew the tools of a truly great escape artist were those of nature itself, common household items, or the natural processes of the body. A moment later, he came upon the loudspeaker. It was mounted in a small wood-grain enclosure above the doorway near the stairs, an eight-inch job probably used for emergency announcements or interdepartmental communication. Invented in the late 1920s, the modern loudspeaker required an extremely strong magnet, at least ten to twelve ounces for the proper amplification to occur.

The Escape Artist reached up, ripped the speaker out of its housing, and tore the donut-shaped magnet off the backside of the horn.

Footsteps were coming down the tunnel now, the sounds of weapons, speed loaders, chambers being clanged and cocked. The Escape Artist moved quickly across the power plant to the far corner, where rows of wooden joists were sandwiched with insulation, rising up into the ceiling. He gauged his position under the first floor, quickly moving along the joists until he reached the air duct leading up into the infirmary. Remembering the location of the guard's desk, he pulled himself up by a ceiling joist, flipped upside down, and slammed his heels against the top of the wall, rattling the ancient supports. Again, and again, and again he kicked the wall . . . until the fifth kick coaxed the sound he was awaiting. The jangle of the guard's keys slipping off the pegboard hook and falling to the duct below.

The guards were just outside the doorway now, he could hear them entering the plant, and he worked quickly.

Pressing the magnet up against the rotting planks of the ceiling, he guided the key ring along the floor, down through the grating, into the duct, and clattering down into the plant works. He drew the keys out with the magnet, drew them through a vent in the duct. Then he tossed the magnet. Clamped the keys in his mouth. And lowered himself to the floor. The guards were moving through the filthy shadows now, their guns raised. The Escape Artist shimmied snake-like across the floor, reached the stairs, and silently ascended the steps on his hands and knees.

The rest was relatively simple.

He made it to the top of the stairs and down the main hall-way in a matter of seconds. The alarms were clamoring everywhere, footsteps and pandemonium echoing. But all the chaos only helped mask his movements, drown out the sounds of his efforts. He reached the barred archway leading out into the barracks. Twisting sideways, he puffed up his chest like a steel-belted balloon, all sinew and muscle and tendon, then edged between two bars and squeezed, then re-laxed, squeezed again, then relaxed, again and again, until he was through.

Striding swiftly across the barracks, he came to the outer door. Always locked. Always from the outside. The Escape Artist filled his lungs with a deep breath as he searched for the appropriate key. He found it on the third try.

The door opened easily.

And then he was out, out in the crisp air, out in the dark and the skittering leaves and the moonlight, and he kept low, and he crept along the brick rampart that bordered the service entrance and the loading dock. Beyond the litter-strewn loading dock was a large vacant lot. The Escape Artist bounded across it, moving east toward the city, the sounds of alarm buzzers fading into the breezes behind him.

He reached Irving Park Road and paused to catch his breath and savor the feelings.

Freedom coursed through his veins like heroin. He turned north and gazed at the glow of the suburbs and the highways and the dark pasture lands beyond it. The lights were like a magic carpet of tiny twinkling fires. He could see for miles, and the feelings raged in his guts, spreading like a brushfire through his arteries, the rage and the anger and the hate feeding the flames in his heart. He was free.

He started north.

Much work to do, many plans. He was going to bring such mayhem to this world, no one would ever be the same. He was going to transform the night. He was going to rule the shadows. But first, he was going to destroy, once and for all, that pathetic alter ego inside him, the bitch with the bosoms, the woman who lived in his skin. He was going to eliminate her in the most inventive way. The idea had occurred to him only a couple of days ago, and it was brilliant. And now he had it all planned out, every last detail, like a fine performance, like a great trick.

The end of Sarah Brandis.

He picked up his pace, head down, hugging the storefronts and shadows. As soon as the opportunity presented itself, he needed to find some new clothing. Get out of this ridiculous hospital gown and into some finery. Then he would end his lifelong symbiosis for good, rid himself of the albatross around his neck.

Forever and ever.

Amen.

PART III

Arkham

The old folk have gone away, and foreigners do not like to live there. French-Canadians have tried it, Italians have tried it, and the Poles have come and departed. It is not because of anything that can be seen or heard or handled, but because of something that is imagined. The place is not good for imagination, and does not bring restful dreams at night.

—H. P. Lovecraft
The Colour Out of Space

But strange that I was not told
That the brain can hold
In a tiny ivory cell
God's heaven and hell.

—Oscar Wilde

The Prodigy Ascending

The speaker took another long, deliberate pause in order to gather her bearings. Another sip of lukewarm tea. She had been reading from the volume for several minutes now, and her throat had gone slightly raspy. She took a deep breath.

Then she continued.

"*The prodigy's early years were spent performing in beer halls and show taverns, with Jacob, his friend from the necktie factory, as a partner. These venues were vulgar, little out-of-the-way places for men only, thick with cigar smoke and stale body odors.*

"*It was a tough apprenticeship, the noise was usually deafening; and most of the time, the audiences cared more for the blue comedians or burlesque dancers than the two young magicians. But our prodigy refused to let the poor conditions stop him. He began developing his skills, as well as inventing new and exciting routines. One of his early successes was a trick he dubbed 'Metamorphosis.'*

"*The Metamorphosis routine was a variation on the classic substitution trick. The young prodigy acquired and cus-*

tomized a special wooden trunk with a secret panel that opened inward. The trunk could be locked and tied with rope, and a person inside it could escape without disturbing the restraints. The trick itself had been invented twenty-five years earlier, but our young prodigy made the trick his own. He invited people from the audience to come up and tie his hands behind his back before sealing him in the box. And the crowning touch: After a few seconds of melodramatic music or smoke, our prodigy would appear outside the trunk, free from his bonds. And with a flourish, he would open the trunk and reveal poor Jacob, lying hogtied inside."

Another pause.

The reader glanced up, gazed across the room and out the window. It was clear that the prodigy's tale held untold secret meanings for the reader. Hidden undercurrents. But there was also something dangerous unraveling with the mere telling of it. Something inchoate.

She gazed back down at the yellowed pages.

"Word began to spread about the young prodigy's talents. The venues began to improve. And eventually, Jacob left the act, only to be replaced temporarily by the young prodigy's brother, Theo. But Theo eventually left as well. It seemed the world of the traveling magician was simply too rough for the timid soul.

"But the prodigy kept refining his act, becoming obsessed with the minute details and the perfection of his craft. He started integrating more and more escape routines into the performances. Handcuff gags, roped tricks, more and more kinds of trunks and cells and boxes from which to escape. He played the World's Columbian Exposition in Chicago, he played Coney Island, and Kohl and Middleton's Dime Museum, and Tony Pastor's Vaudeville Theater, and even the Welsh Brothers' Circus. The prodigy became known as the Handcuff King and Escape Artist; and the legend began to spread.

"Throughout his life, the young man had always harbored a morbid curiosity abut the insane. And one day, while on

tour in the Great White North, he visited a lunatic asylum in St. John, New Brunswick. He was shown the facility by the director, a Dr. Steeves. And toward the end of the tour, the two men paused outside a heavy door in the violent ward. The prodigy peered in through the barred window and saw a deeply disturbed man trying to wriggle out of a strange outfit of canvas and leather. The garb was a long tailed shirt, with oversized sleeves that wrapped around behind the man and buckled securely; according to Dr. Steeves, it was known as a straitjacket.

"The prodigy convinced Steeves to sell him one of the straitjackets, and the prodigy spent the ensuing weeks teaching himself how to escape from the thing. His newlywed, Bess, must have thought him mad. He would spend hours in their hotel room, tensing and flexing and wriggling inside the straitjacket, and soon he had figured out a way to escape. The prodigy's secret was, and always would be, his incredible physique, his muscle control, and his ability to concentrate. In fact, he had always made it clear to audiences and interviewers alike that there was really nothing magical about his magic. Only the application of God-given skills and abilities.

"The straitjacket became his trademark.

"And the prodigy became an institution, appearing on the world's greatest stages, in films and command performances. He became a household word, like Babe Ruth, Valentino, or Lucky Lindy. His very name became synonymous with escape. And mostly, he became the personification of the shadow side, the dark regions of humankind, and the secret world beneath the bright surface. But in many ways, his fortunes came too late. His beloved mother Cecilia had left him at such a young age, much too young to see the greatest fame; and in his success, the prodigy had become the living embodiment of the man in his performances. Lonely, driven, naked, bound and chained, alone against all odds, alone against the world.

"And yet again, he escapes. . . ."

8

Finger Painting

I

There is a place that the cops go; it's a little off the beaten path, just a few miles south of Elgin. Blink, and you'd miss it. Zoom past it on Randall Road, and you'd never even know it was there. It's set back in the soybeans at the end of a winding dirt road, buried between an auto wrecker's lot and a vast concrete waste-treatment plant. Somebody at some point had dubbed the place the "Shop," although you'd be hard-pressed to find a sign anywhere, or business hours, or a lease, or even an official owner. It was once a gas station. But the two islands out front had long ago been torn off their moorings, leaving jagged cement bases like a pair of unmarked graves in the gravel.

The building itself was a rusted-out 1950s Quonset, the single garage boarded over with moldy plywood, the office windows blackened out. There was a temporary door in front, and if you looked closely, you'd see the video security camera canted off the top of a gutter. This was the place to go if you were looking for heavy artillery, unmarked and clean as a whistle. The Shop was an urban arms dealership, and the place served everyone, not just cops, everyone from the Bloods and the Crips to judges and John Q. Public.

At approximately noon, two days before Halloween, Frank Moon arrived in front of the Shop, his tires raising dust and debris in the powdered gravel. He parked, got out, and went up to the door. He knocked three times and told them who it was.

"Whatchoo want, Captain?" said a voice, as the door gapped a few centimeters.

"Let me in, Thel, it's Moon."

"You ain't got no warrant, right?"

"Chill, Junior—if I had a warrant, I'd have my foot up your ass right now."

"Whatchoo want?"

"Iron."

"Hold up a second," the voice said, and the door clicked shut in Frank's face.

"Be quick about it," Frank muttered, his hands in his pockets making tight hard fists, so tight and hard that his meticulously trimmed fingernails were breaking the skin of his palms, making little stinging crescents of blood. Frank was a lone wolf now in every sense of the word.

Less than an hour ago, he had told the shift commander to take his Form 95 and shove it up his ass. Now that the Sarah Brandis case had gone Red Ball—a term the county used for a strict priority track-down—they wanted Frank to work with the South Park people, the federal marshal, the tactical folks, the state boys, and worst of all, the press. They wanted Frank to liaison the fucking press, for God's sake. Frank told them to get somebody else to quarterback all those jerk-offs. Frank was working alone on this one. As a matter of fact, Frank was making this one a personal crusade. There was something about this Brandis lady that was keeping Frank up at night, like a moth flitting around his face, and he wanted to squash that bug ASAP.

At first, the shift commander had threatened to remove

Frank as primary. But Frank had leverage now. The puzzle pieces were starting to fit in his mind like blood cells coagulating. The crime lab was close to identifying a partial match on the prints at the Dante's scene. And the notes from the shrink and the staff at South Park had gleaned useful information about the lady's background, her former jobs, stuff like that. Most important, the significance of the padlocks and the bondage and the wrapping tape was starting to come into focus for Frank, and that meant he was finally working in sync, in rhythm, right on the downbeat with the motherfucker, and by God, this was turning into the noisiest case he had ever worked. And for the first time in his career, he wanted the music to go away.

BADDA-BADDA-BOOOOMMM!

"C'mon in, Chief," the voice said, and the door swung the rest of the way open.

Frank entered the converted filling station office and gazed around the room, eyes adjusting to the dimness. Smelled like cancer in there. Kool cigarettes and Courvoisier and gun oil. There was a long, scarred laminated counter down the middle of the room drenched in a single overhead billiard light. In the shadows beyond it, an obese black woman sat rocking in a bent-wood rocker with a luxurious Siamese cat on her lap. A plastic jack-o'-lantern glowed in twenty-five watt splendor on top of a file cabinet.

"Whatchoo gonna be wantin' today, Chief?" the young man behind the counter inquired, placing wiry brown hands on the counter top. The overhead gleam pooled across his face and torso. Young Thel—short for Thelonius—was a sharp-eyed black kid with a gangster fade haircut, Oakland Raiders silk jacket, and plenty of gold. He gazed up at Frank like a greengrocer waiting for the next order of beefsteaks.

"Gonna need some iron," Frank told him.

"What kinda iron?"

"Clean. Clean and serious."

Thel looked at him sideways for a moment. "You want serious iron, all you gotta do is go down to that precinct arsenal of yours; I hear they give out free car washes with every round of nine-mil."

Frank bored a cold stare into the young black man. "I'm planning to augment the company-issue stuff."

"Why the hell waste the money, brother?"

Frank ignored the question. "Need a pair of Smith ten-mils, maybe a pump-action, 243-caliber maybe."

Thel smirked, popped a toothpick into his mouth, and started picking his teeth. "Watchoo doin? Huntin for mother-fuckin' bigfoot?"

Frank reached out, grabbed the young man by the collar, and yanked him across the counter. Nearly jerked him out of his hightops. Looked him square in the eyeballs, nose to nose, squeezing the sass out of him. The room went cold then, and the lady in the rocker stopped rocking.

"Correct me if I'm wrong," Frank hissed, "but I seem to remember a certain détente between customer and supplier in this industry."

The toothpick slipped from Thel's mouth and fell to the counter. "Whatever you say, Captain."

"You don't ask me questions about my business and I don't pop your ass for about three dozen felonies."

"Yes, sir."

Frank released the young man.

Thelonius straightened, licked his lips, smoothed down his jacket, and looked around. There was a dark figure filling a doorway behind him, staring out suspiciously, the glint of a shotgun in the darkness, and Frank slipped his hand into his side pocket until he felt the reassuring beavertail grip of his service revolver, but then Thel raised his hands and said, "It's cool, it's cool, cool, no problem."

The figure receded back into shadows.

"My fault, Captain," Thel said, leaning down and sliding open a cabinet door. "I think I can help you out today."

Then the guns came out.

Frank bought them all, and Thel even threw in a couple of free holsters and three extra clips of 10mm hollow points to make up for the little misunderstanding, and Thel kept saying how Frank should stay and try some of Mama's pumpkin pie, but Frank just kept shaking his head, checking the slide on the shotgun, clicking the autofeeds on the pistols, and shoving the weapons into a canvas duffel bag. After another couple of minutes, Frank paid the man with cash, scooped up the duffel bag, turned, and walked out without another word.

He returned to the Lexus.

Tossing the duffel in the backseat, Frank got in and started up the car.

He was reaching for a Krupa CD when he noticed his hand was shaking. He looked at it for a moment, pondering the way his fingertips were vibrating, nerve endings sizzling, jittery as hell. He knew it wasn't because of the little encounter he had just had in the shop. He knew it wasn't even because of the real possibility that he would soon be drawing a weapon and actually firing it at another human being for the first time in nearly ten years of duty. No, it wasn't any of that.

It was because of Houdini.

Frank had been thinking about the famous magician for the past twenty-four hours, ever since the game had gone down in the squad room last night. The game was Frank's secret weapon, a system of mnemonics or little cognitive devices designed to help him loosen up the logjam of a stubborn mystery. Sometimes it was an incessant string of rhymes in his head springing from circumstantial evidence: *Moe Green got shot in the eye/ Not that he was a very nice guy/ But who would want to see Moe Green go bye?/ Who would give such a bold thing a try?/ Who would be so bold and then lie?/ Who would lie straight to Moe's eye?/ Mob guys would lie/ Mob guys are bold and they lie/ Michael Corleone's mob—he's the guy!* Other times it was a sequence of mental crutches stemming from the root facts of a case: Some dealer gets popped on a school playground, no witnesses, just a couple of 9mm casings in the dirt, and Frank starts screwing around with the first few letters of key words, as if he were about to take a test. *The DIRTbag on the PLAYground was PLAYing in the DIRT with the DRugs and we look in the DIRT for DRag marks from DIRTy tires, tires, tires of DRIVE-BY shooters.* But with this psycho stripper, this freak on the run who was making Frank's life miserable, an entirely new process had yielded interesting results.

It started in the deserted squad room late last night, after the four-to-twelve guys had taken off and before the next shift had planted their fat asses in their desk chairs. Frank had been sitting at his desk for over two hours, rifling through photos of bound bodies. He started thinking in similes—as in, *this victim is like a sausage with its casing wound too tight*—and suddenly his mind kicked into gear. *The stiff behind Dante's was like a UPS package from hell . . . like a leftover . . . like a doggie bag . . . like a poorly wrapped Valentine . . . like a magic trick gone awry . . . like a magic trick . . . like Houdini on a bad day . . . like a fucking Houdini . . . Houdini . . .* YES. Frank started putting it all together, the padlocks, the victims sealed in drums, the exaggerated wrapping and bondage, it was like the fucking Ed Sullivan show; and all at once Frank had the key, the MO, the psychology; however twisted and arbitrary, it was clear.

Frank snapped out of his rumination, shoving a Krupa CD into the dash.

"Hippdeebip" poured out of the speakers, recorded in 1954, with Johnny drew on bass, Bobby Scott on piano, and Eddie Shu on tenor sax. Frank put the car in gear and pulled away from the Shop, weaving down the serpentine drive and roaring back out onto Randall. The music calmed him some, steadied his nerves, and he opened the side vent to let a little air in the car. He was still shaking.

BOOM-DIDDAP-DIDDAP-BADADDA-BOOMMMM!

Frank had no idea why this Houdini thing was bugging him so much, why it was gnawing at him like a rat in his belly. He'd seen his share of pathologies. The sicker the killer, the more detailed the MO. And the really sick ones had the simplest sorts of logic behind their behavior. *I was killing all those prostitutes in order to stop my mother's spirit from taking over the world.* Or: *I was severing their heads to keep their thoughts from corrupting me.* Or: *I was cutting out their hearts to prove my everlasting love for Whitney Houston.* With this Sarah Brandis creature, this Dr.-Jekyll-and-Mrs.-Hyde, the Houdini connection made a sick kind of sense. The bodies, the MO, the way she did the stunts with her other personality, and the ease with which she had escaped from South Park—it all added up.

She was on a major Houdini trip, and Frank was going to track her down and put a stop to it.

Still, there was a kernel of doubt festering in Frank's belly; perhaps there was more going on here than smoke and mirrors. Although he hadn't seen the woman's body change with his own eyes, he had heard all kinds of cockamamie crap from the shrink Decker and the other hospital personnel. It sounded intriguing, though Frank had trouble swallowing a bite that big. He was a homicide detective, for God's sake, a thinking cop. There had to be another explanation. Everything was explainable, no matter how ugly or pathetic. And Frank was going to solve this one just like he had solved all the others, and he didn't care about procedure anymore, or the fucking politics of the homicide unit, or the fact that he was putting his job on the line. He was going to track this creature down and stop her.

Close this fucking case for good.

BIP-BIP-BIP-BADDA-BIP—BADDA-BIP!

Frank reached the tollway and took the entrance ramp going about thirty-five miles an hour over the speed limit.

He planned to cross the Wisconsin state line by lunchtime. All he had to go on were the notes from the woman's files. No living relatives. She had grown up in a small town somewhere in central Wisconsin, a place called Arkham, and Frank figured he would start there. He had already alerted the Arkham sheriff's department. And the rest of Frank's team was working Chicago and points south, setting up roadblock inspections and searching for the mystery woman. But for some reason, Frank didn't think she—or *he*, or maybe *it* was a better term—would head south. He pegged her for northbound.

Frank reached the bottom of the ramp and merged into traffic, which was pretty heavy for a Sunday afternoon. And he kept his eyes glued to the horizon, and he listened to the rumble of Krupa's tom-toms, and he thought about solving the world's mysteries, and he kept on driving.

Heading north.

II

She was backstage, and the world was in Technicolor, and she was naked.

How could this be? Completely naked, and they're about to shoot her big number, and she doesn't even know her lines or the steps or any of the lyrics. For some reason—and she just knew this intuitively—she was about to step through the wings and join Donald O'Conner and Debbie Reynolds and Gene Kelly for the legendary "Make 'Em Laugh" number from Singin' in the Rain, *the show-stopper, the one with all the clowning and the gags and the somersaulting furniture. It was a complicated dance routine, full of little bits of business, strenuous movements, lots of dialogue and singing.*

She covered her breasts with her right forearm, and she noted with embarrassment how her boobies spilled out the sides of her arm like great lumpy pillows. They were enormous stretch-marked monstrosities, and she was ashamed of herself. How could she hope to be a great song-and-dance gal with tits like these? She cupped her left hand over her pubis and frantically scanned the backstage area for Wardrobe. She was standing on a wooden platform, cordoned off on three sides by a navy blue curtain. The rear wall was brick, covered with ropes and cables and lighting gear, and the area was bustling with activity, technicians scurrying back and forth, voices and hammering and drills buzzing chaotically. She looked down and saw her body was an odd color.

Her flesh was bright beige, three-strip Technicolor beige, and her bare toes were painted ruby red. She could feel a wetness between her legs. And all at once she realized it was blood, the blood was seeping out of her, languid and sticky, running down her inner thighs, and it stood out garishly against her pale tattooed skin. Sarah screamed. But her scream was silent.

She glanced up.

The entire wooden platform on which she stood was now beginning to move. It was a great turntable, and it was rotating out toward the studio. She could see the glare rising under the curtain, the glare of the stage lights, and the sounds of technicians and dancers rising now. She shivered, and she tried to move, but her feet were glued to the platform. The curtain was parting. She looked down and saw the blood spattered across her thighs, pooling around her feet. The curtains fell away, and the cheers rose up, and she realized where she was.

A freak show.

She was standing in a sawdust pen, in the center of some stinking, tawdry little freak show in some godforsaken county fair. There were bleachers rising up in front and along either side of her, and she recognized the faces. The big fat Twins were up there on the left, howling, their identical bellies jiggling. The Straw-Sucker was down in front on the right, his young lips puckered around his rum-and-Coke. And even Mister Peepers was there, front row center, his thick glasses glimmering. The little boys from Dante's, all present and accounted for, stomping their feet, pounding their fists on the table, and gawking at the freak show girl.

She tried to twist away from them, tried to wrench herself from this hideous shame, but something was riveting her to the sawdust platform, something warm and moist constricting around her legs. She looked down and saw that her toes

*were growing. Both big toes had darkened and elongated
like thick vines, curling back on themselves. The others
started sprouting. She shrieked a silent shriek, and the crowd
jeered, and her toes seemed to feed off the attention. Like
blackened grape vines her digits grew and teemed around
her feet. Snaked up her ankles. Twisted around her legs.
Until she was covered with dense ivy.*

The platform began to tilt.

*At first she thought it was simply the terror and disorien-
tation of being covered with the sproutlings of her own extremities. But the entire flooring was continuing to lean. And
she was tilting right along with it, as though she were a passenger on this macabre* Titanic. *She gazed out into the crowd
and saw they were melting like figures made of molten
pewter, melting into silvery, watery ripples. And she
screamed, and she screamed some more, and the entire room
turned upside down.*

*The blood started rushing to her head as she hung sus-
pended over this hellish place, and the vines were growing
over her face, smothering her, and she couldn't even muster
a silent scream anymore, she was choking, choking on the
smell, the musty alkaline smell of the vines, and the shit, and
the ammonia decay radiating down from the ceiling, which
was the floor, which was impossible, but it was happening, it
was happening, and the world had gone completely bug-
house crazy, and there was the sound of rushing water all
around her*

rushing water
rushing

III

Her eyes snapped open, myriad impressions assaulting her
all at once.

There was whiteness all around her, gleaming, and bright
white light shining up from below. There was a mist above

her head, and a rumbling sound, as though the sky were about to cut loose with a hard rain. And she had the foggy impression that someone was embracing her, maybe holding a hand over her mouth. She blinked some more. And she tried to focus. And with a jolt of terror she realized it wasn't a hand over her mouth at all. Those weren't arms around her.

She was bound and gagged, and hanging upside down.

Wriggling, twisting, testing the strength of her bondage, she tried to see. Her eyes were still blurry and crusted with sleep, and she was still having a hard time identifying her surroundings. Thick rope or straps or something like cable was binding her wrists together behind her back. And she smelled the rubbery mucilage odor of duct tape over her mouth. But where was she? Where the hell was she? She felt the weight in her chest, the G-forces against her spine, against her shoulder blades, against her face. It was pressing down on her eye sockets. Making her dizzy. And she blinked and shook her head, and she finally saw, through gradually gaping eyes, just exactly where she was.

Her heart started thumping.

The shower stall was barely three feet by three feet square. Through the dimpled glass door, she could see the rest of the meager little bathroom. The porcelain commode, the single sink, the mirrored medicine cabinet. All of it, upside down. She glanced down at the floor of the stall, and she saw that the water was running full blast, both spigots wide open. Nearly twelve inches of water had gathered already, and it was rising quickly. Finally, she strained to get a glimpse of her feet, to see how in the hell she could be hanging upside down in this little shower stall; and when she finally saw the answer, her throat nearly closed up with panic.

Her feet were shackled and mounted to a thick iron U-bolt that had been driven into the ceiling.

Impressions started flooding her brain, awful inchoate impressions, a fissure in the earth, human flesh splitting open, a faceless devil peering out, peering out of the wound and gazing at her predicament, giggling at her, giggling, his face melting into the face of death, skeletal, raising a killing scythe and wending out over fields of human limbs, the blood raining up from the earth, raining upward! The red tide rising! RED! And then she screamed, and her scream filled the little tile cell like a mortar blast.

And then Sarah went berserk.

The struggle lasted a solid minute. She strained, and she twisted, and she squirmed inside the little stall like a fish still fighting on the stringer. She scissored her hands against the rope until her wrists blazed with pain. She contorted and writhed until her pelvis exploded, white-hot agony slicing down her vertebrae. Finally she let out a muffled growl and shook frantically for several more frenzied moments, until she eventually went limp, sucking in desperate breaths through her nose. She realized then, her heart sinking, that it was futile to fight; that fighting would only use up her oxygen and kill her a lot quicker than the water.

The water was six inches away now.

Hanging there, helpless, the sound of faucets spewing beneath her, Sarah began to see little details through the hurricane of her panic. She saw the long rubbery beads of caulk freshly applied to the seams of the stall door. Through frosted glass she saw the toilet, and the strip of paper—SANITIZED FOR YOUR PROTECTION—stretched across the horseshoe seat. And beyond that, through the threshold of the bathroom door, she glimpsed the corner of a twin bed, an empty closet, the hideous orange carpet. The telltale signs of a cheap roadside motel. She glanced at the rest of her body, and she saw the plastic wrapped around her torso, the chains wrapped tightly around the plastic, crisscrossing her breasts, digging into her soft flesh. And the padlocks. They hung like fishing lures from ends of the chains.

And all at once it made terrible sense to her. The other personality had done this to her. A trick only a skilled gymnast or magician could do. The correct order must have been essential. Installing the hook, binding his feet, and hanging himself by the ankles. Then came the locking of the chains, and wrapping the plastic, and turning the faucets on. The hands must have come last, sealing Sarah's fate—to die like a game fish in a sleazy motel bathroom. But how the hell was The Other going to use her body once it had expired? Did he have the power to resurrect himself? Could he empower the dead cells of a corpse? Was this some sort of double suicide?

Sarah had no time to ponder the big questions.

The water was three inches away.

She started panicking again, her arms and legs tensing underneath the bondage. Then she caught herself, and she told herself to relax, and she took deep breaths through her nostrils, and she closed her eyes and saw soothing images, and she imagined her body was a cloud, a cloud floating over the Emerald Forest, and nothing could catch her way up here in the sky, nothing could hurt her.

Then the water touched her scalp.

It felt like a tongue lapping at her, a lukewarm tongue, and her pulse began to quicken, and she tensed again, and she began repeating in her mind, a single word, like a mantra, *relax, relax, relax, relax,* and then the water was starting to gently envelop her skull, rising over her face, and she started tossing her head, splashing the tile and the glass, and frantically thinking, *relax, relax and think, think, think of a plan,* but she didn't have a plan, she didn't have one fucking iota of how to get out of this mess, *THINK!,* and the water was bobbing over her eyes, *THINK!,* and she realized with a bolt of panic that she was about to take her last breath, *THINK GODDAMNIT!,* and she was about to drown, and this was one horrible way to die.

The water rose over her face.

The world changed. All the sound and light and smell and texture seemed to suddenly turn to pea soup, and Sarah's fear seemed to surge and then flash out like a fuse overloading. She froze, dangling there, her head underwater, her ankles screaming, because all of a sudden she realized her only chance was to be as still and calm as possible, in order to conserve oxygen, in order to think, and that's exactly what she did. She became limp. Limp as a side of beef. Her body felt as though it weighed a thousand pounds. The straps were digging deep into her ankles, the ropes around her wrists like branding irons. But she calmed herself, and she dangled motionlessly, and she realized with a sudden surge of warmth in her chest: a revelation.

She was going to fight this fucker.

The first thing she tried was wrestling an ankle free of the ceiling. She did it quickly. It didn't take much energy, and she tried finessing it out rather than forcing it out. But alas, all her weight kept her ankles firmly in check. She tried the same with her hands, with similar results. The stall was half full of water now. Or was it, Sarah thought deliriously, *half empty*? Half full or half empty? Her lungs were beginning to burn, her pulse rising to a gallop. She gazed through the watery haze at the upside down world outside the glass. The floor mat had the MOTEL 7 legend embossed across its cheap cotton terrycloth, and Sarah wondered if that was the last thing she would see on this earth. The banal contents of a cheap motel bathroom viewed through the dimpled glass of a shower stall.

Glass . . . GLASS . . . *wait a minute,* she though suddenly, *I could break the glass.*

She was at the end of her oxygen reserves, and her body was starting to shut down, and the effort that she would have to expend in her attempt to crack the glass would surely use up the rest of her energy. But she had to try. She had one last chance. Twisting her shoulder around toward the glass, she closed her eyes and she rocked backward and lurched at the panel with all her might.

The impact was a dull thud.

God no, no, no no, *NO!* Now that the stall was almost completely filled to the brim, and her body had become buoyant, she was as weightless as an astronaut, and she could get no leverage, and she could generate no impact, and her lungs were exploding, and she was dead, dead, DEAD, and there wasn't a goddamned thing she could do about it.

Not a goddamned thing.

IV

"Hello? Anybody home?"

The state trooper's name was Fitzgerald, Armand Fitzgerald, and he was a soft-spoken freckled man with a nose like the beak of a meadowlark. He held his hat politely under his arm as he rang the counter bell out in the lobby of the Motel 7, which was just a stone's throw over the state line from Harvard. The motel's manager, a gruff Polish woman named Margaret Pavic, had called the local sheriff's office about twenty minutes ago, complaining about "a strange character" who had checked into the motel earlier that evening.

Armand was simply following a hunch. He had received an all-points bulletin from the local FBI when he had shown up for work that night. Female, Caucasian, large frame, early forties—escaped from South Park Mental Hospital down in Chicago on the previous night. Considered dangerous. Wisconsin connections had convinced local feds to set up a series of roadblocks, one at Highway 51 leading into Beloit, and another one at the junction of 41 and 94 into Kenosha. But Armand had wondered about the less traveled inlets. And when he got word of a homicide near the border on Highway 14—a trucker found strangled and slashed all to hell in the cab of his Kenworth—Armand started paying attention to any unusual calls coming across the scanner.

" 'Bout time somebody showed up," the woman in curlers said as she emerged from the inner office and strode up to the counter. She wore a floral print house dress that had seen better days, and her breath smelled like the inside of the motel's closets, musty, stained with smoke and liquor. A Camel straight dangled off her lip as she spoke, bobbing in tempo with her angry words. "I called the sheriff over a half an hour ago," she huffed. "They said they'd send a car, but chrissakes, you sure took your sweet time about it."

"Actually, ma'am, I'm not from the sheriff's department," Armand said softly. "My name's Fitzgerald and I'm in the investigative unit of the Wisconsin State Police. But I'm real sorry you had to wait so long."

"Whattya gonna do about it?" Helen Pavic stood behind the counter with her hands on her wide, boxy hips.

"You said someone suspicious checked into the motel tonight?"

"That's right."

"Man or woman?"

"Man. A young one, at that. Real strange-lookin' character, looked like he had his hair greased back with motor oil. Wore some kinda raggedy old coat over his shoulders like a cape." The woman took a big puff and smoke billowed from her mouth as she spoke. "Wouldn't have thought anything of it, but when I was checking him in, I noticed he was paying with somebody else's wallet."

"Somebody else's wallet?"

"Yeah." Helen nodded, cigarette bobbing. "Caught a flash of the license and it sure as hell wasn't him. Then I saw his hands, and I pretty near barfed right there on the guest register."

"You saw blood on his hands?"

"No, I didn't see no blood." She puffed on the butt and shuddered slightly. "It was his damn fingernails."

"His fingernails?"

Helen lifted her hand and fluttered her imitation nails. "The kid had no fingernails—damnedest thing I ever saw."

"He had no fingernails?" Armand fingered the grip of his .357 and regarded the woman for a moment.

"Nothing but fleshy little pads," she said.

"Pardon me?"

"Instead of fingernails," Helen told him. "He had these soft little fleshy pads at the end of each finger."

Armand thought about it for a minute. "Did he sign in?"

"Take a look," the woman said, rolling her eyes, opening her register and swinging it around so Armand could see it. She traced her fingertip down a column of names to the last one on the page. The words were scratched in childish scrawl.

Saru Brandiz

Armand looked up at the manager. "What room is he in?"

V

There are several ways that the condition known as shock can set into a person on the verge of dying. Cardiogenic shock, which is the most dangerous variety—deadly in about eighty percent of the cases—is caused when the heart fails to supply enough blood to the body. The result is a gradual shutting down of sensory functions, an overall numbness, and eventual myocardial infarction: heart attack. Hypovolemic shock, another common variety, is caused by massive blood loss due to a severe injury or internal disorders. It is swiftly progressive and can result in extreme low blood pressure, brain damage, and ultimately death. But the trickiest form of shock is neurogenic shock, a state brought on by extreme trauma or damage to the nervous system, accompanied by a widening of the blood vessels in the arms and legs.

Sarah was flirting with the edges of neurogenic shock when the flailing started.

Cocooned in plastic, spinning on the meat hook of her shackles, she slammed the glass door again and again, slammed it with her elbow, her shoulder, her head, the muffled thuds rippling around her, feeding her panic, feeding the fire in her lungs, her throat shrieking with fire, fire coursing down her capillaries, fire spreading through her, body convulsing now, convulsing for air, air, AIR, and the realization that she was going to die, and it was going to be ugly and chaotic and messy and, please God, the fire in her lungs was consuming her now, sending shock through her body.

At some point, the water had started overflowing at the top of the stall, creating a sudden buoyancy and loosening her feet from the bolt. And now she was floating freely in the stall, completely drained of oxygen, the shock pouring over her.

Shock.

A funny word, shock; an absurd description for such a syrupy, languid condition, as though God had thrown in a reprieve at the last minute to the violent throes of death. Sarah felt it like a virus spreading through her limbs, arteries widening, blood pressure plummeting, her vision going all runny. The water became milk. And the sweet angelic light gelled around her, bringing warmth. Then cold. Then absolute paralysis, as though she had melted into the very water itself. Her vision began to fade. And the last thing she saw clearly was the halo of light at her feet, the ceiling light, glowing diffuse and silvery in the bathwater.

I give up, God, take me, take me now and at least stop the burning in my lungs.

Then came the twitch.

Ordinarily it would have signaled Sarah's demise, an involuntary jerk of the torso, an automatic zap of neurons arcing across her dying synapses. Her body jackknifed violently one last time, and her elbow punched the glass. Sarah barely heard the noise, the crackling sound reverberating through the milk, faintly at first, but rising in her ears. A shifting sound. She turned and looked through lazy eyes at the spider web growing across the glass.

A crack.

The next few moments unraveled in a swirl of movement and sensory flash, much too fast for her dying gaze. The water seemed to grab hold of her, slamming her against the glass, and then the spider webs were spreading furiously, and then the sudden surge of collapsing glass, collapsing outward, and her body was sucked through a jagged opening, and Sarah was blinking, and the cold sharp sensations were filling her nostrils again, like air, *by God it's air,* and she landed hard on the cold tile, shoulders first, the rest of her somersaulting and landing prostrate, pain rocketing up her spine, gasping, coughing into the tape, trying to see through the milky diffuse light.

She was floating.

The water gushed over her, tossing her across the tile. It came from the jagged hole in the stall door and billowed across the floor for several moments. Sarah landed in the corner, bent into a sitting position between the door and the stool, nostrils flaring, sucking up that sweet wonderful air. She breathed deeply and painfully for several moments, clenching her bound wrists, flexing her limbs, trying to get the feeling back into her marrow.

Moments later she found the strength to shimmy back toward the tub.

She was soaking wet through and through, her plastic shroud pregnant with water, her hair matted to her face, but she managed to get herself back up against the tub. Her head was spinning, her throat as dry and prickly as desert saguaro. She saw the razor jags of glass sticking up like fangs along the base of the busted stall door, and she shoved her backside against them. Rubbing, tearing through the outer layers, tearing through the ropes around her waist and around her wrists.

When her ropes tore free, she collapsed to the tile and lay there for several moments, taking deep breaths and staring at the ceiling.

It took a while for her senses to come back and her pulse to settle. She tried to steady herself on the watery floor by thinking things through. Asking herself the obvious questions. How long had she been out? How long had she been metamorphosed into the other body? And where the hell was she? Lying there in three inches of water, gathering her bearings, she started to feel the glowing embers of rage in her belly. More than ever before, she felt the incarnate inside her like a germ. A deadly parasite. And she wanted to cut him out so badly she could feel it in the roots of her teeth. But there was something else brewing inside her, something so subtle and imperceptive, it was hard to label. It was a sense that her other personality was doing more than merely trying to kill her. He was toying with her, playing a game with her. *Leading her somewhere.* And then it occurred to Sarah that Henry Decker might be right after all, that maybe the real fact of the matter was that *she was leading herself somewhere.* That this monstrous Other was simply a deeply rooted part of her own psyche—a part that she had repressed for so many years, it had simply exploded like a box-shaped tumor bursting open. But from what part of her past? What was she repressing? From what dark corner had this nightmare child been born?

She ripped the remaining ribbons of plastic from around her torso and legs. Underneath, she was dressed in her black leotards. The leotards had been through a war, torn and frayed in places, and painted with strange horizontal stripes of off-white. Her tummy and breasts were bulging sorely beneath the bondage. Wrapping a towel around her hand, she scooped up a long shard of broken glass and started sawing through the remaining ropes and loops of cable. A moment later, she was free.

Standing up on her own power was another matter altogether. She rose slowly, head throbbing, and she nearly vomited. The wooziness rocked her. She grabbed the edge of the sink and steadied herself for several moments. Then she took a deep breath, walked out of the bathroom, and went into the main room, her bare feet squishing the sodden carpet.

At first, she simply froze. The room was so cluttered it was hard to absorb it all in one glance. She took a tentative step toward the bed, and she gazed around the walls, the mirror, the television screen, the headboard, the heating unit, the drapes, and even the front door.

Messages were everywhere.

VI

Trooper Armand Fitzgerald felt an odd compulsion as he headed toward the shadows of the bungalows. It started along the back of his neck, a slight stiffening of his short hairs, and then shot down his arm and into his fingers. The urge to draw his gun. But as he approached the first bungalow, he controlled the compulsion.

He unsnapped the leather safety strap and loosened the grip instead.

In over ten years of patrolling the Wisconsin border, nailing speeders, hauling teenagers in for drunken joyriding, ferreting out contraband truckers, and investigating various and sundry roadside mayhem, Fitzgerald had learned the simple wisdom of keeping his .357 in its holster. Everybody knew it was there, sure; and in case of an emergency, Armand would drop a bead with that thing faster than you could say *Put 'em up!* But Armand also knew the psychology of the gun. He knew that drawing a gun on a criminal was not always the best way to get him to mind his manners. He knew that a convict staring down the barrel of a gun gets a little bolder, almost as if a switch goes off in his head. As if the stakes get raised so high, the convict just figures he doesn't have anything else to lose. And he might as well do something crazy, he's going to eat lead anyway.

"Nice and easy does it," Armand whispered to himself as he walked along the row of bungalows.

The Motel 7—named thusly because of the simple fact that it had seven little ramshackle cabins lined up along the gravel parking lot—was a modest affair. Yellow bug lights, hectic with moths, glowed above every bungalow door. And a natural gas smell hung thick in the air. The bungalows themselves were wood-frame single bedroom jobs in varying degrees of disrepair. Mrs. Pavic had said that the man with no fingernails had checked into number seven, lucky seven, the last cabin in the row, and Armand approached it cautiously, his right palm resting gently on the grip of the gun.

For some reason, the trooper wanted to play this one strictly by the book.

VIII

She was shivering, her eyes playing across the clutter of the motel room, taking it all in.

The bloodstains looked like fingerpaints, like the delusional ravings of a mad child. The words *Alive—ALIVE!* were mingled and melted into odd phrases from her nightmares, phrases that had echoed in her mind, voices solidifying, *Nothing can hold him—nothing—NOTHING!* Across the bedspread: *BOOK NOW!* Along the wall above the headboard: *The Handcuff King!* And across the mirror in blurred hash marks: *You thought I was dead—but I am alive! ALIVE!* And Sarah felt the tears of rage welling in her eyes as she scanned the room, clenching her fists.

"No, goddammit!" She blurted, her deep, raspy voice stretched to the breaking point. "*I'm* the one who's alive, you shit head!"

She glanced across the room to the bedside table. A Gideon Bible was lying on the floor below it, open and face-down like a dead bird. Wadded Kleenex, scattered clothes, personal items stolen from a dead trucker, and a metallic puddle of chains lay near the Bible. On the tabletop articles were strewn in disarray, rolls of tape, an empty bottle of Cognac, a paintbrush, a small tin of paint, a hunting knife tacky with blood, frayed pieces of rope, and a Polaroid camera. There was a snapshot taped to the wall above the bedside table.

The moment Sarah saw it, her heart started pounding.

She walked over to it, took a closer look, touched it, traced her fingertips around its edges where *he* must have touched it, her stomach tightening with dread. There he was, The Other, the parasite, in all his glory, and Sarah stared for several horrible frozen moments. He was in the leotards, leaning forward in a determined crouch, staring intensely into the camera lens, one hand vanishing off the border of the photo to hold the button. Bandoleer chains crossed his chest, and his striped leotards resembled an old 1920s bathing suit, and all at once the revelation hit Sarah like a crystalline bullet dead-center between her eyes.

Houdini.

She had successfully blocked out her strange aversion to the legendary magician for years, but now, in a sudden jolt of terror, Sarah felt the old frisson returning like a ghostly dirge, the haunting images bombarding her mind, Houdini, the tortured soul in chains, tied and locked into a milk can, suspended off a bridge, returning each time from the brink of destruction, Houdini, his brooding eyes staring into the fuzzy newsreel camera, the mysterious Houdini, the master of escape, returning from the dead. And Sarah realized then, standing in that lonely motel room, the autumn winds rattling the cheap panes, just exactly who the Escape Artist was trying to be. If only she knew why the old images of Houdini were tearing her apart inside.

The sudden knocking wrenched her attention to the window.

"Wisconsin State Police," said a muffled voice. "Need to ask you a few questions."

Sarah went into hyperdrive.

She ripped the photo from the wall, scooped up the pile of clothing, the wallet and the knife, and whirled toward the opposite wall. She wiped as much of the blood off the mirror and the walls and the television as she could manage with the wad of clothes. Then she scanned the rear for an alternate way out. Her heart was racing frantically again, and her forty-one-year-old joints were creaking under the strain. Across the room came more knocking, louder and more forceful this time.

"Sir, I just need to ask you a couple of questions," the voice said. "Be a lot easier on both of us if you just let me in."

There was a narrow window in the back of the bungalow. An ancient air conditioner was caulked into the lower half, the upper half spanning a space barely two and a half feet high. There was a hinged window in the upper pane. It was her only chance. She rushed over to it, pulled the metal hook, and discovered it was welded shut with congealed paint. She yanked it, and she punched it, and she finally loosened it enough to creak the window halfway open.

More knocking, sharper, angrier.

"Sir, I'd hate to have to use the master key—now, I'm gonna give you one more chance to open the door."

Sarah lifted herself up and over the air conditioner and then squeezed through the opening. The cool mist of the evening kissed her fevered brow, and the breeze was icy on her wet skin. She got her shoulders through, and she was halfway out when the flare of her hips got wedged between the window and the top of the air conditioner.

Behind her, the sound of a key fiddling into a deadbolt.

"C'mon-c'mon—c'mon, dammit!" Sarah's frantic whisper came out on a grunt as she crammed herself farther and farther into the opening. She had most of her hips through, but was stuck at the widest, fleshiest, curviest part, and she started silently cursing her genetics, her saddlebag hips, and those goddamn peanut-butter milkshakes down at Ennui's, those fucking shakes that Sarah would suck down every time she got depressed, and the way the last five years had settled around these fucking saddlebag hips, and she kept cursing, and stuffing, and grunting, and the sudden sound of the door bursting open behind her—

"Hey!" The trooper's voice was cold water on the back of her neck.

One last grunt, and she was through. Sliding down a wet, leaf-matted plastic awning, clutching the wad of bloody clothing and crumpled Polaroid.

She landed hard on her hands and knees, the sudden pain jolting up her tendons, her palms stinging, needles of light bursting in her eyes. She quickly scrabbled to her feet. Tak-

ing ragged breaths, she scanned the shadows and saw that
she had landed on a concrete garbage slab. The stink was
thick, a pair of rusty Dumpsters to her right filled with rot
and compost. She shook off the disorientation and started
across the leaf-matted gravel.

The rear of the motel was an empty parking lot, pitch-
black, bordered by a row of birch trees lined up like skeletal
sentries in the misty darkness. Sarah lurched across the lot
toward the darkness behind the trees. She could hear the cop
yelling something behind her, sticking his head out the window, calling after her.

She kept on running.

Her mind was a circus now, all pandemonium and racing
heartbeat, pulsing with her strides, flashing images out of
control in her midbrain. The wind was a razor on her wet
skin, the ground icy hot on her bare feet. But amid all the
noise in her head—the need to get into some dry clothes, the
need to find a safe place to think, to hide out, to get her bearings, to find a map, maybe some food and some first aid and
some peace—there was a stronger current flowing like a low
dissonant counterpoint to the shrilling symphony of panic.

Half-formed memories of Houdini were coming back to
devour her.

She reached the tree line just as the trooper's searchlight
landed on her back.

The darkness engulfed her.

9

Old Haunts

I

Henry Decker found the old postcard in Sarah's bedroom, folded in half and shimmed between the back of her nightstand and the wall behind her bed. It had either fallen out the back of her nightstand drawer or she had used it to steady a squeak in her bed.

Most of Sarah's furniture, Henry had noted sadly while searching her room, was of the cheap, particle-board variety. The kind they sold at Venture or Wal-Mart, which came unassembled in long rectangular boxes. Not that Henry was a snob about interior decor, it was just that Henry had always thought Sarah deserved better. She deserved better than the meager living "house dancers" at middling strip clubs were able to eke out nowadays. She deserved better than the generic macaroni-and-cheese and two-dollar wine she had most nights of the week. She deserved better than the bleak agony that had infected her life after decades of walking the edge of clinical depression. But then, Henry had mused, maybe it didn't matter what kind of cards a person was dealt.

Deep down, Sarah was simply a good soul, despite the particle board and the macaroni—perhaps *because* of it.

"How you doing in there, Doc?" The voice drifted in from the living room, and it was edgy as hell. It belonged to Detective Becky Jones.

"Not finding much of anything," Henry lied, unfolding the postcard and taking a closer look.

The glossy side was a cartoonish rendering of a cow, a big smiling guernsey with sunglasses, jovially waving. The legend underneath it said, *Say Cheese! Greetings from America's Dairyland.* Henry turned it over and saw that the card was addressed to Sarah Brandis. The space at the left had a brief note and was signed by somebody who called herself Aunt Ludy. But the part that grabbed Henry's eye, the part that got him thinking, was an address at the bottom of the note. *Please write me at my new digs,* it said, and then it gave an address for a nursing home in Arkham, Wisconsin.

Henry folded the card and put it in the pocket of his jeans jacket.

"Hey, Doc," the detective called impatiently from the living room, "let's wrap it up."

"Coming," Henry said.

He walked out into the living room.

Becky Jones was standing near the window, arms folded across her navy blue Dona Karan jacket. The late morning light came through the blinds and made her ashen face look older, furrowed with worry. The sharp corner of her .38 automatic bulged under her jacket. "You know," she said softly, speculatively, "I could get my ass busted down to traffic guard for doing this. I only let you back in here because Dr. Prescott called my squad supervisor this morning, got him all juiced about your insights into this Brandis woman."

"I know, and I really appreciate all you've done for me, Detective," Henry said, walking up to her, wringing his hands. His tone was measured, barely concealing his nerves.

The truth was, Henry Decker was a desperate man. He felt responsible for this entire nightmare, for Sarah's deteriorating psyche, for her flight. And he had called Detective Jones the previous night, spending nearly an hour on the phone with her, trying to convince her to let him take another look at Sarah's things, take another sweep of her apartment. Henry had no idea what he was looking for, but he was hell-bent on gathering as much information as possible before he went up north looking for Sarah. He needed more to go on than simply the town of Arkham or the red pine forest. By now, the cops were probably closing in on her, but Henry needed more insight, needed background that perhaps even Sarah herself might not be able to give him. And for some reason, he thought it might be contained in a smudged return address on an old postcard.

"Can we get out of here now?" Jones asked him, tension rising in her voice.

"Absolutely," Henry said, and he followed the woman out the door, under the ribbon of yellow crime scene tape, and down the stairs.

They were crossing the foyer when Jones added in a sour tone, "Gotta get back for a conference call with Frank Moon. He's up in Wisconsin, annoying the local constables, looking for your girl."

Henry stopped abruptly. "He's in Wisconsin?"

"Yeah, I understand the Brandis woman's hometown is up there somewhere."

"She hasn't been back there since she was fourteen."

Jones shrugged. "Moon's got his theories."

Henry stared down at the scarred hardwood planks of the foyer for a moment, wondering how much Frank Moon knew about Arkham, about the Escape Artist, about the red pines. Up to now, Henry had been banking on the fact that Sarah would elude the authorities for at least a day or two, giving Henry time to figure out how to help her; but now, a stone of doubt was burrowing in Henry's stomach. What if the authorities caught up with her, and Sarah did something stupid, and the cops got a little itchy?

"That's absurd," Henry finally said, wanting to throw

Moon and his bloodhounds off the scent. "Sarah would never ever go back to Arkham."

"Why not?"

Henry thought about it for a moment. "Too many painful memories."

Jones shrugged again and sighed. "Try to tell Frank Moon he's wrong about something."

"They'll never find her up there," Henry said.

"C'mon, Doc," Jones said, ushering Henry toward the exit, mumbling under her breath. "I got work to do, and if I'm late tonight, my kids won't have their Halloween costumes ready in time, and if they don't have their costumes ready, it's my ass."

Henry followed her out into the rainy autumn morning, thinking about Wisconsin, Frank Moon, the red pines, and the significance of Halloween.

II

The previous night had been hell.

After wandering for nearly an hour through a vast, unincorporated stretch of Rock County, her bare feet wrapped in bloody towels and sealed tight with duct tape, Sarah had stumbled upon Interstate 90. The four-lane slab was a major artery up the backbone of the state, and she had decided to follow it until she came upon a familiar town. It had taken her most of the night. For almost eleven miles she trudged along the gravel shoulder, brooding, ruminating on the parasite inside her, fighting the images, the virulent images in her head, images of Houdini, images of chains and trunks and milk cans and straitjackets, and the sounds in the chilled shadows behind her, and the shapes of deer and possum around her, and the deeper, unformed, shadowy memories just on the borders of her awareness. Memories of pain and terror so tremendous, they seemed to loom over her consciousness like a black cloud blocking out the sun. Thank

God she had a mission now, a mission to keep her from going completely insane, a mission to keep her moving north through the cold toward Arkham, toward the answers that she dreaded facing as much as she dreaded not facing. Of course, every now and then a car would pass, and she would slip back behind the tree line like a ghost, like a folk tale, like the spirit of some vanishing hitchhiker. But the demons of the outer world were the least of her problems. She kept waiting for The Other to come calling, to come bubbling up from within her, taking over again right there on the open highway, this time killing her in some exceedingly hideous way.

But he had never emerged.

By the time the lights of Madison flickered on the horizon, it was nearing dawn, and Sarah was flirting with hypothermia. Though the night was relatively mild for late October in Wisconsin, and she had covered herself in the flannel shirt from the motel room floor, the dampness of her leotards and the prolonged exposure to the wind had taken their toll. In the faint glow of distant city streets, and the hazy moonlight shining down through low-slung clouds, Sarah's flesh was looking like a fish belly. Her pulse was starting to falter and weaken, and she felt the heat shivers feathering up her spine. She was very sick. Nevertheless, somewhere deep down at her core was a tiny spot of nuclear fusion that was keeping her going. *Anger.* Red-hot anger. Anger for what this parasitic being, this changeling, this alter ego, this whatever-the-hell-you-want-to-call-the-little-fucker, was doing to her. She was coming to think of The Other as a petulant child, a spoiled, tantrum-throwing, bad seed buried inside her. And she was starting to feel powerful surges of maternal rage. And maternal rage—real, honest-to-goodness, Oedipal-flowing, Tennessee Williams, Freudian-nightmare rage—was the most powerful rage of them all. It could consume a woman like cancer. It could tear a woman's sanity to shreds. And it could keep a shivering, frightened, sick-as-hell woman marching alone at night on a desolate stretch of Wisconsin highway for miles.

The truth was, over the years Sarah had secretly dreamed of being a mother.

In her unspoken thoughts, she had imagined every phase of the experience. She had imagined what it would be like to feel her body change during pregnancy, to feel her breasts swell and her nipples darken and her belly grow with the gentle pulse of life. She had imagined the long march through the final trimester, the hormonal changes, the cravings, the shifting of gravity down into the haunch of her pelvis, the baby pressing against her bladder, and ultimately, the charge toward birth. The ritual blood of labor, the sweat and the fluid and the tears. She had imagined the first few months with the child, the inseparable time, the inextricable bond, the sensual draw of lactation, motherly secretions, and nursings in the middle of rainy nights when time seems to stop. She had imagined watching her child grow, comforting him or her when the world turned sour, holding him or her when the tears came, teaching, supporting, shaping, giving, mothering, mothering. She had imagined it again and again, and the more lonely and alienated she became as an adult, the more distant she grew from other men, the more she imagined motherhood as some karmic state, unattainable, impossible.

Approaching the outskirts of Madison, Sarah had decided to loop around the southern shank of Dane County, weaving through the Kegonsa Woods.

It was here, deep in the dark cathedral of hemlocks and yellow birch, that Sarah, shivering uncontrollably and refusing to give up, had started warming herself with imagery. She had visualized the yellow brick road baking in the sun. She had visualized a perfumed summer morning in the Emerald City. She had visualized the warm rays of the sun beating down upon her and the Tin Man and the Scarecrow and the Cowardly Lion, flowers growing all around them, little Munchkin ballerinas in their bathing suits, suntanning, lounging in the heat. And mostly she had imagined her own skin, bronze and toasty in the sultry morning heat, a fine glow of perspiration, healthy and luminous.

The technique had worked wonders.

Emerging from the forest an hour later, the morning light in her face, Sarah had stopped shivering. She felt a second wind now, and the fear was tempered with anger. And the anger was driving her northwest toward Arkham with renewed vigor. She scrabbled up a hill of crabgrass and deadfall logs to the shoulder of Highway 151, and then worked up enough nerve to hitchhike. She caught a ride on the third vehicle that passed her. It was a Chevy pickup, driven by an old man in a greasy denim jacket, caterpillar hat, and bad teeth. The cab had smelled like wet dog fur and Sarah had chosen not to speak until she was spoken to.

After about five miles of creaking silence, the old man had said, "Sauk City's 'bout as far as I go."

"That'd be fine," Sarah had told him.

"You ain't from around here," the old man had commented, tossing a look over at the duct-tape-wrapped feet.

"Was once."

"Sauk City?"

"Arkham."

The old man had grinned then, showing his green teeth. "Shit, nobody's from Arkham."

"You got that right," Sarah had said, gazing out at the rush of gravel and high-tension wires and patchworks of farm fields stretching out across the hills. Most of the acreage had been harvested, brown and fallow, and looked desolate under the overcast morning sky. Memories were flooding back to Sarah by the minute now. She remembered long brutal summers detasseling corn up near Waunakee, the scrapes and cuts inside her palms stinging for weeks afterward. She remembered the revival meetings her mother used to take her to up in Baraboo, the stinking, body-odor-thick tents, the little old ladies waving themselves with cardboard fans, and the faulty PA system squealing with fire and brimstone. And mostly she remembered the black hole in her mind, the horrible shadow in her past that was beginning to coalesce like a thunderstorm brewing, the dark clouds laced with lightning, the flash illuminating images of Houdini like an old flip-card animation. *What was it about Houdini? What kind of terrible, festering pain was radiating out from those old images?* Sarah knew she was close to finding out.

Although she had no idea *how close.*

The old man had pulled over just East of Roxbury, at the intersection of two blacktop access roads. A phalanx of ramshackle storefronts stood nearby, festooned by cardboard skeletons and plastic jack-o'-lanterns, and bordered by a small asphalt lot. Off the east edge of the lot rose a large wooden sign. Mounted on tall telephone poles, the sign was high enough to be visible to passing Highway 12 traffic. Its legend was spelled out in kitschy cowboy-rope letters.

It said TRADING POST.

III

Sarah went over to the window and gazed out at the midmorning sun. The day had turned bright, autumn bright, with a sky so blue it looked liquid, and maple leaves so fiery yellow they could burn your eyes. The air inside the little knotty pine room smelled of wood smoke and old linen. Sarah hated these places, these little tourist-trap lodges. Wisconsin had millions of them, one for every small lake town. Some retiree couple would prop up a few old cabins, bring in a couple of pumps of unleaded, stock a little general store, and all of a sudden . . . *boom.* Instant Visitors' Center.

She turned away from the window and continued pacing across the floor, the old timbers squeaking under her weight. She was wearing a University of Wisconsin sweatshirt, brand-new men's Levi's, and a pair of knee-high moccasins that she had purchased a few minutes ago in the Trading Post general store. She felt ridiculous, like an aging barfly trying to pass as a sorority girl. She also felt wired. God only knew how long it had been since she had slept; and she wasn't really sure if the blackouts counted as rest. She had taken a No Dōz tablet a few minutes ago, and it was just starting to kick in, just starting to bring on the hand sweats, the rapid heartbeat, and the paranoia.

The lady behind the desk had given Sarah the once-over during check-in. Sarah had used the first name that had popped into her mind—Frances Gumm, which happened to be Judy Garland's real name—and the woman with the bad dye job and cat's-eye glasses behind the desk had responded by giving Sarah a look that could have curdled milk. "Do you have any luggage, Miss *Gumm*?" the woman had asked, emphasizing her skepticism by overenunciating the word *Gummmmmm*. Sarah had told her no, and explained that she was traveling light, and that she was an archaeology professor doing fieldwork for the University of Wisconsin—another bit of vagary that was the first thing to pop into Sarah's mind—and that she just needed a home base to rest and make notes and collect her thoughts while she explored the surrounding environs.

Now it was going on eleven A.M. and Sarah was staring at a charred empty fireplace in a knotty pine prison, trying to think, trying to lay low, out of sight, long enough to make sure she hadn't been followed, and mostly just trying to figure out her next move.

She didn't want to just walk right into Arkham, which lay five miles to the north, like some kind of demented Johnny Appleseed looking for the next place to plant her magic seeds. The fact was, she had no idea exactly what she was looking for in the little backwoods hamlet. She merely hoped that revisiting the old haunts, the old schoolhouse, the main drag, the swimming hole, the trailer park in which she and her mother used to kill their miserable hours together, would somehow bring back memories, spark an insight, trigger some kind of catharsis, something, *anything*. Anything to exorcise the parasite. But the more she thought about it, the more she felt certain the whole Houdini mystery would be lurking outside of Arkham proper, lurking somewhere in the forest up in the hills beyond town, somewhere up in that shadowy place she'd been dreaming about, hearing in mind-echoes, seeing in blood slashes across her life.

The Red Prison.

Sarah glanced down at the meager little bed, the tattered western kitsch bedspread with its tufted lasso design looping around tiny little cowboy hats and Indian headdresses, the map of central Wisconsin tented across the fabric, the pile of empty pouchettes of aspirin, speed, Vitamin C, candy wrappers, and the spiral notebook open to a blank page. *That* was exactly how Sarah felt at the moment, like a blank page, like a stone, all empty but rotting away underneath the surface. Who was she kidding? Running around like some psychic detective, on the run from the law, trying to find some repressed memory like a needle in the haystack of her own past. Maybe the archaeologist story wasn't so far from the truth; she was trying to turn over a rock, dig something up, exhume some hideous trauma.

She stared down at the crumpled candy wrappers. Her stomach growling. Starved. Hadn't eaten much of anything since the plastic tray of gray Salisbury steak, applesauce, and Tater Tot torture of her last South Park dinner. She went over to the door, plucked the flannel shirt off the hook, and put it on, tying the tails in a neat bow beneath her bosom. Then she walked into the morning chill.

The parking lot was still rather deserted for Halloween Eve. A station wagon was parked near a pay phone, an obese man in a suit jabbering on the phone. A pickup was over by the store's service entrance, a farmer and his teenage son loading bags of dog food onto the bed. Sarah walked past them with her head down, trying to remain as anonymous as possible. On her way up the steps to the general store, she caught the farm kid out of the corner of her eye, looking her up and down, his hormonal gazing lingering on her bust.

Sarah was used to it. Matter of fact, it was oddly comforting in the midst of all the danger.

A tiny bell jangled as Sarah entered the general store.

The place smelled of scented candles and smoked meats. There was an antique hand-crank register mounted on an ancient butcher block near the front door, serving as the general reception area. From there, patrons could check into the lodge to the left, get seated in the small country restaurant to the right—where they could sample Phyllis's cheddar soup or Uncle Vergne's chicken-fried liver steak—or they could peruse the general store, which was straight ahead. The store was six narrow aisles of bricabrac, convenience foods, endless varieties of cheese and various smoked sausage products.

Sarah went straight over to the refrigerated section and started quickly selecting lunch items, ignoring Mrs. Cat's-Eye Glasses, who was keeping a sharp eye on Sarah from behind the register. Sarah gathered up a pint of milk, an orange, a tub of yogurt, some bread, and a tube of summer sausage. She cradled the items in her arms and started back toward the front of the store. She wanted to get out of there as swiftly as possible, avoiding any unnecessary conversation or delicate questions. But when Sarah came back around the comic book spinner and was approaching the register, she noticed Mrs. Cat's-Eye was on the phone, speaking in hushed tones and glancing nervously up at Sarah.

"Get here now," were the final words hissed by Mrs. Cat's-Eye before slamming down the receiver.

Pausing, swallowing hard, Sarah felt the tiny hairs along the backs of her arms prickling. Something was wrong. Very wrong. It had been wrong from the moment Sarah had arrived at the Trading Post earlier that morning. She had seen it in Mrs. Cat's-Eye's face during check-in, and again just now, a pinched sort of suspicion. And now Sarah was sure this woman had recognized something. Eyes scanning the store, mind racing, Sarah started weighing her options. She could drop the goods and just run out the back. But there didn't seem to be a back exit. She could calmly proceed as though blissfully unaware that anything was happening, buying her food and taking her sweet time about getting out of there. But that didn't seem wise, either. All at once, Sarah's gaze fell on a little wire dispenser of local newspapers near the base of the comic spinner. Today's edition of the *Sauk City News* was stacked up a dozen or so thick. The top one revealed a front-page black-and-white photo, sandwiched between headlines about school referenda and visiting senators, showing a woman smiling seductively into the camera, underneath which a subheading read FORMER ARKHAM WOMAN A FUGITIVE FROM JUSTICE.

The photo was a publicity head-shot of Sarah from her early ballet days.

The orange slipped from Sarah's arms and bounced off the hardwood, rolling past the register. The Cat's-Eye lady was shaking now, reaching under the register for something, and Sarah started backing away, and she dropped the remaining items, the milk, the bread, the yogurt. Her mind was buzzing now, a wasp of panic in her head, and she saw the Cat's-Eye lady pulling a dark object out from underneath the counter, a gun, or a pipe, and Sarah didn't see the postcard spinner-rack directly behind her, and her hip grazed the rack, and dozens of postcards fluttered to the floor. Sarah glanced down at the postcards, and her scalp crawled suddenly. Her breath caught in her throat, and her gaze contracted like the iris of a camera, shrinking inward, closing down around one single postcard on the floor amid the America's Dairyland and the Greetings from Devil's Lake State Park.

A glossy rectangular painting of the Houdini Museum in Appleton.

Sarah felt the world starting to spin, textures swirling around her in streaks of sound and color and meaningless violent movement as she knelt down and picked up the postcard. Her memories were strobe-blast lightning flashes in the pitch of her backbrain, spurting out of the postcard like electricity, zapping up her fingertips as she picked it up and looked at it, barely absorbing the words on the back of the card, the smarmy travelogue words

Located in the beautiful Medina Valley northwest of Wisconsin's famed Lake Winnebego, the Houdini Museum attracts visitors from all over the world.

Sarah jerked backward as though she'd been snakebit by images of teeth and fingernails, partially formed memories, long repressed, sparking in her mind, images of dark cinder eyes boring into her, big rough hands ripping fabric, the flash of eye-white in darkness

This modern facility was designed by local architect Daniel Bohm and features replicas of Houdini's boyhood home in Appleton, Wisconsin, as well as many of the magician's famous milestone performances.

lips curling away from teeth, jagged fingernails digging into flesh, making tiny little half moons

The museum also features a hundred-seat theater, a magic shop, and a fascinating hall of lifelike dioramas depicting the Escape Artist's ten great illusions.

"OhmyGod!" Sarah slammed her palm to her mouth, as though her sudden realization might escape on a scream so loud it would wake the dead.

Everything seemed to suddenly freeze in that little general store, as though time itself had suddenly clogged, as though sand had been thrown into the cosmic clockworks, until all that could be heard was the beating of Sarah's heart and the dripping of spilled yogurt and milk, leaking down through the floorboards. The revelation burned in Sarah's chest, drew scalding tears from her eyes, and made her mute as she crouched down there by the postcards and the milk and stared at the beautiful, world-renowned Houdini Museum.

No use crying over spilled milk, her mother would have said, and the sudden tsunami of pain was so consuming, so enormous, that Sarah barely noticed the figure rising up at the front of the store.

Mrs. Cat's-Eye was clutching a shotgun.

"Hold it right there!" the woman barked, coming around the counter and backing toward the front screen. She snapped the hammer back on her squirrel gun. The metal clicked menacingly.

Then there was a sound behind the lady, a rushing noise, and it sounded at first like a waterfall, but then it sounded like tires on gravel, a couple of cars roaring into the lot, skidding to a stop in front of the Trading Post, and Sarah heard the sound of doors opening, and the crackle of a radio dispatcher, and all at once Sarah realized it was the police, and she grabbed the postcard, sprang to her feet, whirled toward the rear, and slipped on the milk.

Sarah went down hard, pulling over a display of Hostess Fruit Pies and Twinkies.

Her cheek smacked the hardwood, raising a welt and flash-spark in her vision. Junk food rained down upon her, cellophane packages squashed open by the weight of the wire rack, spongy cream between her knees, her fingers, beneath her legs and her feet, and she tried to rise to her knees but her feet were slipping and sliding in the sugar gunk, and her joints were screaming in pain. Behind her, the door burst open, the little bell jangling madly and then the sudden bellowing.

"She's over there!"

"Brandis?" The voice was familiar, the dry wheeze baritone. "Chicago Homicide! Dane County Sheriff! Show yourself!"

Sarah managed to crawl across the center aisle and gaze up over a shelf of Pampers and Q-Tips, glimpsing two newcomers in the doorway.

Frank Moon was there, holding a large silver pistol with both hands, scanning the store with the tight hot look of a man about to parachute out of a plane. Behind him, an older, gray-haired gentleman in the olive-drab uniform and sheepish expression looked as though he would rather be fishing. Moon took a few measured steps toward the center aisle. The place got very still and quiet, horribly quiet, like the air in the eye of a hurricane. And Moon took another step.

Sarah lurched toward the restaurant.

At that point, several things happened at once, almost too quickly for the casual observer to absorb. Sarah managed to spring to her feet and stagger across the weathered floorboards to a decorative shelving unit that separated the general store from the restaurant, and she didn't even slow down or lower her head or hesitate, she simply put her forearms up and crashed through the imitation wood-grain, glass, and rows of Hummel figurines, and at the moment of her impact, Moon got off a warning shot that sounded like a cherry bomb exploding in a metal drum, the flash and plume of smoke and recoil filling the shop like a lion's roar.

Sarah landed in the restaurant, a place of fake country cupboards and wrought-iron skillets on the walls and gingham curtains along the far windows, and she slid across the top of a trucker's lunch table on a wave of broken glass and wood shards, the shrapnel gouging her arms and legs. Coffee and ketchup looped up through the air, and the trucker whiplashed back off his chair, eyes gaping open, hands waving dumbly in front of his face. He was a fat man in a greasy Hank Williams, Jr., T-shirt, and when he landed a few feet away, the floor trembled. Sarah felt the tremors as she scudded across the tile on a wave of blood and pain, slamming into the iron base of a booth.

Frank Moon was coming through the entrance now, his eyes blazing, silver gun raised and readied.

Sarah struggled to her feet, and oh my God how she hurt, everywhere, in her aging joints and her shrieking knees and her split and lacerated arms, and she frantically sucked breath and tried to figure a way out, a way out of this death game, a way to escape. She started lumbering toward the back, dog-paddling at the air, stringers of spit flagging, eyes locked on the rear windows, the shuttered windows, if she could only make the windows, the shuttered windows, the windows—

The voice splashed her back like chilled water.

IV

"Everybody down!" Frank hollered, his eyes wide and wet and stinging.

The place emptied on a wave of hysteria, like an ant farm flooding with gasoline. The busboy tossed his tub of dishes and scurried through the swinging door into the kitchen. The waitress followed. Three other patrons followed the staff into the kitchen, and then out the fire exit, and the trucker scooted along the floor and vanished behind the grill counter.

Across the room, Sarah was staggering toward the rear wall, and Frank saw the row of windows, and Frank saw the girl reaching for the fake pine slats, clawing at the cheap shutters, and Frank felt his chest seize up with rage, because he knew the girl was about to escape, and Frank made an instant leap into red-zone procedure.

"STOP, GODDAMNIT! LAST WARNING!"

Frank's verbal warning was strained thin and hoarse, and he knew that it was futile, he knew it was time for extreme prejudice, he knew it was the O.K.-fucking-Corral and it was time to drop a bead on the perp. All at once Frank dropped to his knee in the middle of the broken glass and ketchup slime, and he raised the Smith & Wesson Model 1006 semiautomatic 10-mm, and he lined up the staggering woman with the two white dots on the pistol's rear sight, and he drew in a quick breath, and he snicked the slide, and he bit his lips.

And he fired.

V

Tearing at the shutters, Sarah heard the blast before she actually felt it, a flat bass-profundo pop like a huge paper bag exploding.

Then the wasp sting in the center of her back.

Strange, strange sensations, all at once, the sharp dagger of pain in her spine, the smoke in front of her, the fabric and flesh seared, and the chink of glass out of the window. She was sliding downward when she realized that she'd been shot, and the bullet had passed through her, and the god-damned thing had probably ripped clean through her heart because the cold was spreading through her now, cold like never before, mercurial cold.

Sarah collapsed to the floor, holding the bloody exit wound in her chest, gasping.

Across the room, Frank Moon rose and approached cautiously, his feet crackling over broken glass.

The cold was washing over Sarah now like a blanket, and she curled into the fetal position, and she closed her eyes, and she bit down hard on her lip, drawing blood, salt-copper tang on the tip of her tongue, the rage roiling inside her. How could she die like this? The answers, like the taste of her own blood, on the tip of her tongue. And now she was dying like a gimp dog in a room full of fake skillets and gingham curtains.

She squeezed her eyes shut and felt the cold tighten around her neck.

And she saw images.

Gingham. Blue gingham. The gingham curtains are melting into the gingham dress.

She wears a bloody gingham dress and lies dying on the shore of the secret lake. And the Munchkins gather around her, fanning her with fronds and big whimsical leaves. "Don't die, fa-la-la," cry the little ballerinas,

rub this magic oil into the wound. "*Don't die, Sarah,
fa-la-la—fa-la-la!*"

Frank Moon was approaching, and Sarah's chest was itching fiercely.

The seething pain beneath her sternum had flashed out like a light bulb overloading, popping silver magnesium blue, and then melting into heat, white heat pouring through her arteries, pulsing with the rhythm of her rage.

Imagining . . .

The Munchkins gathering over her, massaging her, rubbing magic oil into her wound. The lollypop boys are giggling, "Look—you're healing, Sarah! Ta-da!"

Sarah looked down at the exit wound, the ragged, charred hole in her sweatshirt, and the thick, congealed blood underneath. Congealed? How could it be congealed? Sarah looked closer, and saw the scab forming like black wax drying, and felt the flesh puckering around the wound, and sensed the organs working like eels beneath her skin. It was the strangest feeling, this sudden recasting of tissue and bone.

"Oh—Jesus!" The words came out of her on a whisper, as she closed her eyes, realizing what was happening.

TA-DA!

VI

Frank stopped abruptly, about ten feet from the fallen stripper, and stared down at her, his 10mm still poised, his heart starting to thump, a whiff of cordite smoke still curling around his head and all sorts of strange processes working in his mind, a Chinese abacus reshifting its beads, now you see them, now you don't, now you do again.

She was getting up.

An ordinary person, when faced with something inexplica-

ble—a weeping Madonna, a UFO, the face of Jesus in the
melting snow—will usually react in a relatively predictable
manner. He or she will become paralyzed, and his or her ad-
dled brain will spontaneously cast back to childhood, back to
the primal memories of life's unaccountable horrors. The
slap of the doctor's hand, the crack of a thunderstorm, the
bark of an angry dog. And nine times out of ten, this person—the *ordinary* person—will be stricken dumb for a
stretch of time, trying to get a handle on what he or she is
witnessing, until he or she is better able to react rationally.

Not Frank Moon.

Watching Sarah rise slowly to her feet, her chest rising
and falling like the bellows of some freakish machine, Frank
was undergoing his own sort of metamorphosis. His blood
ran cold, and the very top of his spine began to vibrate, and
he felt the paradigm shift of a Galileo gazing at the orbits, a
John witnessing the seven-headed beast, a Neanderthal
touching fire. He felt every fiber of his being realigning, as
though some great magnet had burst up through the ground
and caused all his inner compasses and gyroscopes to go
haywire. And he tried to holler out some snippet of proce-
dural dogma, but all he could do was quickly and silently
come to a purely innate decision.

The decision was from the deepest core of Frank's personality, the deepest part of his psyche, the part that enabled him
to solve nine out of ten cases, the part that made him dress so
impeccably, the part that urged him to manicure his nails and
groom himself to perfection, the part that nobody else understood, the part that compelled him to keep all the stray nails
and screws and bolts in his apartment filed away in tiny little
baby food jars with plastic label-tape identifying their gauge
and manufacturer, the part that prevented him from dreaming
at night, the part that compelled him to think of human behavior, even his own, strictly as neurochemical impulses. He
drew on this deep-rooted part of himself, this unwavering belief in order, this devotion to unnatural symmetry, in order to
make his decision. And in his stricken state, it was the only

way to deal with this impossible creature rising up before him, this mutant of a woman, this modern Lazurus.

Destroy it.

Frank made a graceful move to his left, lurching behind a table and pulling his second 10mm from under the back of his belt. Now he held two enormous pistols, one in each hand, both stuffed to the gills with full magazines. Fourteen loads of expandable bullets a piece. Crouching behind the table, raising the guns, Frank remembered what the FBI had known for years, that "knockdown" power was a myth, that the only way to drop a human target was through penetration, that the bullets must pass through the large, blood-bearing organs and be of sufficient diameter to promote rapid bleeding.

Sarah had risen to her feet and was spinning toward the windows when Frank started promoting rapid bleeding.

The first shot was an M-80 in a wind tunnel, subsonic and deafening. It pierced Sarah's shoulder and sent her slamming into the wall, fragments of bone and matter splattering the rooster print wallpaper. Sarah whirled instinctively. Frank fired again. And again. And again. One shot went wide, exploding through the shuttered window above her, fountains of glass and wood shards engulfing Sarah. Another struck her in the ribs, chewing through her sweatshirt and soft tissue. The third landed just below her left ear, the impact whiplashing her backward like a rag doll and sending her careening.

She hit the floor in a spattering of blood and slid several inches before coming to rest beneath a booth.

Frank was breathing hard, as though he had just run a marathon. He wiped his brow with the back of his hand. The guns were warm in his hands like model train transformers. He started toward the booth, dropping one of the magazines, just to be sure. The metal sheath clattered to the floor. Frank pulled another clip from his back pocket and slammed it home, snicking the slide. The guns felt like living things in his hands.

He was about fifteen feet away from the booth when Sarah started moving again.

"No way—"

The words burbled out of Frank on instinct, so stricken they sounded like the yelp of a startled animal. Sarah was rising, gripping the edge of the booth, her gaze fixed on some distant image. Her ravaged shoulder was healing in time-lapse, the serum clotting, ragged tissue curling away, shedding itself, revealing new pink tissue underneath. The jagged phalanx of rib bone peaking through the gash in her side was turning to solder, reshaping itself. Frank watched it all in the bright light of the coffee shop fluorescents. He watched the new epidural layers forming like the skin of a soufflé. He watched the bloody pulp of her left earlobe pucker and dry. And he watched her suck in a quick breath and start toward the kitchen.

"No way!" Frank shouted it this time, raising the guns and starting after her.

Sarah dove for the kitchen doorway just as Frank fired again. The sound was gargantuan, a thunderstorm of smoke and spark and debris, and Frank turned into Jesse James, firing again and again and again, his shots going wide, puncturing the wall in spurts of dust, and going high, piercing fluorescent tubes in puffs and flashes and sparks. Sarah vanished inside the kitchen. Frank followed.

"NO WAY!"

Sarah was staggering toward the rear exit. The kitchen was a long aisle of greasy flooring, flanked on one side by an ancient range, a filthy aluminum pot rack on the other, and Frank emptied both magazines in her general direction. The firestorm erupted across metal counters, ricochet-flames pinging left and right, chewing through old aluminum, a 10mm monster gobbling up the air. Sarah was hit four times, once in the back of the neck, once in the left hamstring, and a couple of deep gouges in her lower back.

She crashed through the rear storm door, punching through the screen and tumbling out into the yard.

Frank was still firing behind her, hammers clacking, cartridges empty, engulfed in the blue stink of cordite and burning oil. He dropped both magazines, stumbled across the remaining length of flooring, fumbling for more clips in his back pocket, his heart crashing in his chest, his eyes stinging from the heat and the smoke and the stress. He reached the busted screen door, elbowed it open, and stumbled into the yard.

Onlookers were stumbling behind barricades of wrecked cars and patches of weeds, crouching and gawking, as Sarah limped furiously toward the tree line fifty yards away. The back of her neck was clotting sticky blackness, the gouges in her legs and arms puckering magically.

"NO FUCKING WAY!"

Frank Moon was trembling now, too juiced to chase her, slamming both clips into both guns, cursing inarticulately, aiming and firing, firing, sparks and thunder drowning his cries, shooting wildly at the figure vanishing into the woods, firing into the air around her, firing at the very *idea* of her, shot after shot after shot, until the sound and the fury were too much to bear, and the heat of the guns burned his hands, and he dropped them and sat down in the brown grass.

And he stared at his trembling, scorched hands.

No fucking way.

VII

Henry drove through the afternoon in his battered Nissan Sentra.

By the time he reached Madison, the sky had turned the color of dark cement, the kind of diffuse gray that only a late October sunset in the Upper Midwest can brew, and Henry found himself feeling bone-deep dread. He had already fucked over his practice, to the point that he doubted whether he would ever be able to get another license, even with the backing of a Jonathan Hicks. He had embarrassed himself in

front of the staff at South Park, and he had acted as a catalyst
in bringing about Sarah's deteriorating condition. The cops
had told Henry to stay home, stay by the phone, stay out of
their way; if they needed him, they would call. And now
Henry was heading north, loaded with clues that he was
keeping to himself. The stuff about the red pine forest. The
postcard. The nursing home. He was probably breaking
about a half a dozen laws, suppressing evidence, interfering
with an investigation. But none of that seemed to matter anymore to Henry. What mattered was Sarah. And the longer
she was out there, the more he dreaded what could be happening to her.

But before he found the red pine forest, he needed to know
what had happened to Sarah. What horrible seed had been
planted in her psyche only to be frozen over all these years
by the glacier of her own repression? Henry had a gut feeling
he might find out from dear old Aunt Ludy.

A sign loomed along the gravel shoulder that said 94 EAST
TO MILWAUKEE—51 NORTH TO PORTAGE.

Henry consulted a crumpled page of directions that was
clipped to his visor. Loosely drawn from investigative phone
calls to the Arkham Chamber of Commerce, the directions
said to take 51 North and be on the lookout for County Road
"V." Henry loathed the highway system in Wisconsin. All
the little access roads crisscrossing the dense dairy land.
Their alphabet soup names crowding the map. It was enough
to give Daniel Boone a migraine.

He took the exit ramp and turned west.

County Road "V" was a ribbon of two-lane asphalt that
took him through a series of quaint little farm towns. Dane.
Lodi. Roxberry. If it wasn't for the Amoco marquees at
every crossroads, these villages could easily be from the
nineteenth century, perhaps rustic little hamlets along the
English countryside. The changing colors of autumn carpeted their backyards. Great stone fences, tarnished with age
and moss, cordoned their fields. Wisconsin was an old terri-
tory. Stolen from the Chippewa and the Potawatomi, traded

back and forth over the ages, it was the country's attic. A cool and dank depository of old secrets and skeletons. And making matters worse—or exceedingly brooding, one might say—was the fact that Halloween was closing in, and its garish icons were perched on every fence corner, every newel post, every milestone and driveway gate.

The Nissan whizzed by rows of enormous, leering jack-o'-lanterns, rows of them lining the farmhouse parkways, passing in orange blurs. Tepees of cornstalks and Indian ears wrapped every other light pole. Some of the roadside homes were festooned with jaunty papier-mâché skeletons, frozen mid-dance, grinning Madison Avenue grins. Henry glanced at his watch and saw that the date was October thirtieth. *Of course.* The day before Halloween. Perfect. Not that Henry was a big fan of the holiday. Still, it seemed apropos somehow: an amalgam of modern and archaic rites. Ostensibly, a celebration preceding the Christian feast of All Saints' Day, the date actually possessed a much more spiritual and ancient origin. The Druids believe it was during this time that the god Saman, the lord of the dead, would call forth his hosts. Henry felt he was about to do the very same thing, calling forth the long-dead spirits of Sarah's psyche.

Moments later, Henry crossed an old rusted bridge that made marching band noises under his wheels.

Arkham, Wisconsin, lay just north of Sauk City, in a generous valley between the river and Highway 12. The center of town was a two-mile thoroughfare bordered by rows of boarded storefronts, strip mall merchants, and defunct warehouses. The place looked like Chernobyl on a slow day. The scars of changing economies and plant closings had ravaged the little town.

Henry arrived at ten minutes to seven and drove all the way to the end of the main drag.

The Danlee Nursing Center was located on the edge of town, near the woods. Nothing more than a warren of nondescript brick buildings nestled in a stand of poplars, the home had been the final pit stop for area geriatrics for nearly seven decades. Henry pulled up its circular gravel drive, parked in front of the visitors' sign, and went inside.

"Excuse me," Henry said, approaching the front desk of a modest little lobby. The air smelled of camphor and old furniture polish, and there were several well-thumbed *Saturday Evening Posts* on the coffee table.

"May I help you?" The blue-haired receptionist looked up from her IBM Selectric.

"Yes, uh, please," Henry said, measuring his words carefully, feeling like a bull in a china shop. "I'm a family counselor from Evanston, Illinois, and I'm trying to track down a relative of a client of mine. I'm told her aunt might be a resident here, or maybe was at one time."

"Could you give me the name?"

Henry told the woman that "Aunt Ludy" was all he knew, and then Henry waited for the receptionist to search through a phalanx of yellowed index cards pressed into a metal file box. So much for the nineties. Up here, folks still used rotary phones and put GONE FISHIN' signs in their windows. After a few moments, the receptionist looked up and said, "Nope, don't see no one named Ludy here. Not ever."

"How about Brandis? You ever have any Brandises in this facility?"

The receptionist started thumbing through more index cards.

"That'd be Lucille!" A voice cackled across the room, nearly making Henry jump.

Henry whirled. "Pardon me?"

The ancient cherub sat in the corner of the lobby, so tiny and withered that Henry hadn't even noticed him when he first came through the door. Dressed in a tattered seersucker jacket with a banlon golf shirt buttoned up to the top of his turkey neck, the old black man pushed himself out of his chair with the tip of his cane. "Woman who was an aunt to the child name of Sarah," he wheezed. "That'd be Lucille Harmon. Some folks called her Ludy—kids, I believe."

Henry was speechless for a moment.

"This here's Clyde McMasters," the receptionist said. "He's celebrating his fifteenth anniversary as a resident here at Danlee. Ain't that right, Clyde?"

The old man waved a gnarled brown hand at her. "Keep that shit to yo'self."

The receptionist grinned and shook her head. The old man started shuffling toward the inner hallway. Henry walked over to him and said, "Pleasure to meet you. My name's Henry Decker."

The old man just kept shuffling toward the inner hallway.

"Mr. McMasters?"

The old man paused on the threshold of the hallway and turned back to Henry. "You gonna jes' stand there?" he asked. "Or you gonna come meet the woman?"

Henry glanced at the receptionist for a moment, then shrugged and followed the old man down the hallway.

It took them several minutes to traverse the entire corridor; McMasters moved slowly, and he just had to pause at every other doorway to nod at a cronie or wave at one of his lady friends. Most of the residents of Danlee were in their eighties and still relatively alert, although several of the less fortunate souls lay in darkened rooms, hooked to machines, murmuring.

"This here's Lucille Harmon's room," McMasters said, pointing his palsied finger at the last closed door on the left. "Poor old gal don't get around much no more, but she's still sharp."

Henry nodded.

McMasters opened the door and let Henry inside.

"Oh, uh, I'm sorry." Henry froze just inside the door, his stomach tightening. He had made a huge mistake. He had to get out of that room immediately. He had to get out of there. "I didn't mean to bother you," Henry stammered, backing toward the door. "We were looking for someone else and—"

The door clicked shut.

Henry spun around and saw that McMasters had shut him into the room. Now it was just Henry, just Henry and the poor, pathetic creature known as Lucille Harmon, "Aunt Ludy" to her younger friends. Turning back to the bed, which was bolted to the center of the floor, Henry said, "I didn't mean to disturb you."

"Come closer," a voice crackled through a tiny speaker.

Henry took a few steps toward the bed and paused near the dressing table. "My name's Henry, and, uh, I'm a therapist, and I'm looking for, well, any information you might have about Sarah Brandis."

"A little closer, honey," said the electronic voice.

Henry moved to the edge of the bed and peered down into the oxygen tent.

Inside the womb of gauze, the woman with only half a face gazed up and, with what could only be described as a crooked smile, said, "How's my sweet sugar cube of a niece doing?"

"She's—" Henry thought about telling the old woman the truth, then changed his mind, "doing just fine."

"Not a day goes by that I don't think about that child."

Henry swallowed back the flinty taste in his mouth, a mixture of pity and revulsion. "Anything you can tell me about her, especially her childhood, will be very helpful."

"Fair enough," Ludy said through her tracheostomy tube. The old woman was barely more than a bag of brittle bones nestled in urine-stained bedding. Her liver-spotted face was carved out on one side, scorched like a crater from below her left brow to the edge of her jaw, evidently the results of past cancer surgery. Her left eye was completely blind. And her upper mandible was exposed, showing a fair amount of old decaying molars, giving her a perpetual rictus of a smile.

"Take your time," Henry said, suddenly wondering what to do with his big awkward hands.

The woman with half a face kept smiling, and then began to talk.

VIII

Only minutes after night had collapsed over the land like a cold shroud, Sarah did a little collapsing of her own—into the scabrous weeds and litter-strewn grass behind a billboard for Carnation evaporated milk.

She was buzzing with pain, the shiver of new flesh puckering, the sharp pang of bones mending and organs rearranging inside her. She could just barely make out the front of the billboard reflecting off water in the dark distance, about twenty yards to the right, where a little man-made pond sat on the edge of the two-lane. The ad on the billboard was a seasonal promotion, a glamorous star-filter rendering of God's bounty on a Thanksgiving table. Anchored by an enormous Butterball, carefully browned and nestled in a wreath of cherry tomatoes and parsley. Trimmed and laden with all the extras, boats of gravy, fluffy mashed potatoes and roasted chestnuts in gleaming sterling silver trays. And, of course, lots of creamy, thick Carnation evaporated milk to achieve the highest level of cholesterol possible. It looked like an alien landscape to Sarah, visions of comfort and coziness that were light-years away as she sank to the cool padding of the pine needles, her chest heavy with fatigue, her brain swimming.

"Goddamn you!" she uttered, addressing the voice inside her. He had returned during her flight from the Trading Post with a vengeance, sparking and barking and flickering in her head.

"The red prison water—the water—the water-the-water-the-water-thewaterwaterwaterwater!"

"Go to hell!" Sarah hissed, and crawled over to the base of the billboard, flopping down and resting her back against the weathered support pole.

She pulled the creased and crumpled items from her pants and looked at them. Pieces of a larger puzzle. The postcard was sticky, and one corner of the museum was torn away. And the Polaroid looked luminous in the shadow of night, the pale skin of the Escape Artist glowing a dim putty blue. He seemed to be staring balefully out of the photo at her, and Sarah thought about the connection between this pathetic alter ego and the man from the Houdini Museum, the man who had ruined her life, the man who had nearly killed her.

The pain surged in her again, a jolt of agony twisting the base of her spine.

And the sounds and images in her head.

The lake is visible across the imaginary meadow, the secret lake, and all the Munchkins are gone now, and it's only Sarah and the voice and the water. "Look at it," the voice whispers, "look at the water!"

"Shut up!" Sarah cringed, dropping the photos, bending over and clutching her belly.

The agony writhed in her, as hot as a branding iron pressing inward on either side of her pelvis. It wrung tears from her eyes, acrid tears, tears of rage. She wanted to peel her skin from her bones, flay herself alive with her own bare hands. It felt as though an umbrella were being opened up inside her cervix.

"The water!" The voice seems to hang over the tiny lake, its surface as smooth and still as black glass.

"NO!"
She gasped and grabbed handfuls of crabgrass and squeezed and prayed for death.

Something bursts through the water, a tiny hand, a tiny pale hand.

"NO—goddamnit!"
Sarah jerked back against the wood slats of the billboard,

her ears ringing, her verbetrae shuffling like dominoes inside her. The pain was wringing the life out of her now. And she held up her own hand, and she saw the change worming under her nails, tiny cocoons, tearing open creases in her flesh, splitting fissures, popping open moist seams, the unformed fingers wriggling out like pupae tasting the air.

"Please don't do this," she shivered, her voice corrupting in stringers of phlegm.

"Alive—alive-alive-alive—alivealive—ALIVE!"

"Stop it!" She was fading again, a test pattern shrinking down to a tiny nimbus of light.

"Feel it—"

"You're a goddamn parasite, and you can't keep this up, you can't!"

"I am you"

"No, no you're not—*I am me!*"

"You made me what I am."

"I'm not—nn-n-not a murderer," Sarah slurred. She saw the shadows fragmenting, shattering, her skull turning inside out and stealing her thoughts.

"You are me."

"Paruhhsssssite—" Sarah's final utterance was swallowed up by her new throat, her new vocal chords, new skin, new eyes scanning the darkness beyond the billboard.

The incarnate rose on sturdy bow legs, gazing across the weeds.

He felt the crisp night air on his skin, the distant snap of leaf smoke, and the silver back mist. And the new feeling surged in him. The poison rage. Sweeping into his empty soul like squid ink clouding a water cabinet, galvanizing him. The smells, the texture of the air, the constellations winking across the black void overhead, all so familiar. He was home, home, home sweet home, and the locusts were swarming in his head now, the need, the itch, the hunger, tingling from the base of his muscular neck down to his gifted fingertips.

He started toward the two-lane, creeping predator-silent, planning mayhem with every heartbeat, every breath, every stealthy footstep.

Time to destroy the world.

10

Through the Doorway

I

Sarah's seventh-grade English teacher had been an intense little man named Abner Weed. Wiry and rawboned, with a shock of unruly, bright red hair, Mr. Weed had always appeared younger than his actual age. Most parents reckoned him to be in his late forties, if not early fifties; but Abner always carried himself like a younger man. Perhaps it was his attire, his flannel shirts and Lee jeans with the plaid linings, always cuffed at the bottom, always rising a few inches above his Tom McCann loafers, always very eccentric for the mid-1960s. Or maybe it was his manner, the way he was always smirking, cracking Juicy Fruit and quoting Carl Sandburg at bemused schoolgirls, flitting about his classroom like Gene Kelly in *On the Town*. Of course, all the girls had mad crushes on the man, and all the boys wanted to *be* the man, unless they were the bullies or jocks who hated Abner Weed for being different, for being a sissy. But Abner never let the Goldwater conservatism of Arkham bother him. He taught in a kind of trance, reciting Shelley and Byron to eleven-year-olds as though their lives depended on it. And every once in a while he would inspire some giddy student to devote his or her free time to the classics. He was a good teacher, some might even say a great one; but alas, Abner had a fatal flaw that would ultimately ruin him, not to mention tear the quiet little hamlet of Arkham apart by the seams.

Abner Weed had secrets.

First, there was his obsession with Houdini. As obsessions go, it was a fairly harmless one. Abner knew Houdini's life story backward and forward. He collected souvenirs. His house, which was a modest little bungalow on the east side of town, was filled with memorabilia, posters, one-sheets, books, scale models of old theaters and trinkets. And Abner could even perform many of the tricks himself, usually alone in his cluttered back bedroom. Unfortunately, obsessions had never really played well in small-town America, and because of Abner's high-profile teaching job, he kept his obsession relatively low-key. Of course, over the years, it only worsened, occupying his mind more and more, bubbling up into his everyday routine.

Second, and perhaps more significantly to the folks of a small town, Abner had been treated for mental problems. It had started when he was still in graduate school in the late forties at the University of Missouri, dating freshman coeds who were swept off their feet by Abner's beat poetry and romantic soul. A few months into his final year, Abner was picked up one night for getting a little randy with his latest Lolita. He was subsequently charged and convicted for indecent exposure and sexual assault, and he did one month in a work farm and a year of community service. He got kicked out of grad school after that, and he started drifting. North, across Illinois, and up into Wisconsin. He eventually crash-landed in Appleton—boyhood home of Houdini, land of killer winters—where heavy depression set in, as well as the first stirrings of his obsession with the great Escape Artist.

The early years in Appleton were brutal for Abner. There were a series of odd jobs, chronic nightmares, and the constant temptation to pursue young girls, which was probably the origin of his obsession with Houdini. It was as though Abner wanted to escape his own tormented soul. But eventually, Abner started seeing a succession of psychiatrists, and regular doses of lithium and frequent therapy got him back on track. In 1960, he finally got his teaching certificate from Appleton Junior College. And two years later, he landed the job that he considered his last chance to make a life for himself.

He became an English teacher at Arkham Middle School.

Most of the aforementioned facts were public knowledge, and they had been for years. The facts had been gathered decades ago by local law enforcement authorities, private detectives, and reporters for the *Arkham Gazette*—all long ago retired. It all came out after Weed had been caught in the school infirmary, fondling a sixth-grade girl, after which he was arrested and booked on molestation charges, prompting six other girls to come forward and testify that he had fondled them as well. But what was not public knowledge was Abner's assault on a young, impressionable Sarah Brandis, and the untold havoc it would ultimately wreak.

"You think Weed assaulted Sarah, too?" Henry asked after a long stretch of silence. He was standing over a yellowed oxygen tent, staring down at the little delicate crone inside, listening to the story of Sarah's past crackle through the tiny loudspeaker like an intercom linked to hell.

"Ain't never found out for sure," Ludy wheezed, "and Jessie would never talk about it, but I'd bet the ranch and all the horses in the stable that Abner Weed attacked that poor girl."

Ludy Harmon paused then, and rested for a moment. Her breathing sounded like old wood being cut with a rusty saw. She could speak only for a few seconds before she had to stop and take a breath.

"Take your time, Mrs. Harmon," Henry said softly.

"My age, you pretty near don't have a choice but to take your time." Ludy grinned her damaged smile, wet her lip, and took another uneven breath. "Anyhow . . . I just knew deep down that Abner Weed had done the evil deed with little Sarah. Poor girl was so vulnerable, and she just worshiped that man, with his silver tongue and his worldly ways, spouting verse all the time. Sarah was ripe for the pickin'." The old woman paused, caught her breath, and added, "Matter fact, I believe that was why she run away from home."

Henry blinked. "She ran away?"

"Yessir, poor sweet thing just up and vanished, for near three months, couldn't have been more than twelve years old. 'Course it made Jessie madder than a hornet. Jessie started in to drinking, and by the time the girl was found, pretty near starved to death out by the highway, Jessie was outta her skull, crazy as a loon with sorrow."

The old woman paused again and turned her face away from Henry for a moment. At first, Henry thought the woman was laughing. Shoulders trembling softly, Ludy had her eyes closed and was either grinning or grimacing; it was hard to tell with her ravaged face. But soon, a big fat tear leaked out of her good eye and crept down her cheek.

"Listen, it's late—if you'd like me to come back"—Henry began to rise—"I'd be happy to—"

"It's okay, honey," Ludy wheezed. "Didn't mean to come unglued on ya."

"So what happened to Weed?"

"Heard tell he went back up to Appleton after he got outta jail, but I dunno for sure. Heard tell he became caretaker of that Houdini museum."

"Houdini museum?"

"Up to Appleton," Ludy said, "there's a Houdini museum up there. Old Abner Weed's probably still up there, shuffling around that place, mad as a hatter. Ask me, he shoulda got the 'lectric chair."

Another pause. Ragged breathing crackled through the voice box, along with the sterile hiss of oxygen. Henry waited. Looking around, he noticed the hideous paneling on the walls. Cheap imitation cedar, peeling at the corners. In

the corner, there was a little oak side table with a tensor lamp
and a gallery of family photos. Ludy's daughter, a bunch of
grandkids, a son in a Navy uniform, an old sepia wedding
picture from the 1920s. Henry went over to the pictures and
picked up the wedding photo, pondering the archaic, yellowed image. A fresh-faced woman in traditional white
dress, clutching an earnest young man in high tab collar and
spats.

"What can you tell me about the red pines?" Henry asked,
turning back to the oxygen tent.

Ludy looked away for a moment, an odd expression on her
face. "The red pines? You mean them woods up by the
lake?"

"I guess," Henry said. "Sarah talks about it often, and I get
the feeling there's a clue there."

"A clue?" Ludy's brow was furrowed all of a sudden.

"Yeah, you know, something that might help with Sarah's
therapy."

"She's having therapy now?"

"Yeah, you know, we've been working on some issues."

The old woman swallowed dryly. "The girl's in trouble,
isn't she?"

Henry rubbed his mouth, wondering how much he could
reveal, wondering how far to push this delicate old wreck of
a woman. "Yeah," Henry finally said, nodding, "you could
say that."

"Damn pine barrens," the old woman suddenly blurted,
the loudspeaker sputtering. "Place has brought this world so
much heartache."

"Excuse me?" Henry moved back to her bedside.

"I'll tell you about the red pine forest," Ludy cackled.
"Some folks say the woods is damned up there, they claim it
was a logging disaster, happened back in the 1800s. Other
folks claim it was an Injun battle between the Potawatomie
and Louis Jolliet. They say the spirits of the dead done
turned them woods sour as a compost heap. Red prison, they
call it. Even heard some of the older drunkards 'round town

say the place is like a—a—a doorway, something like that—
a doorway in ta Hell—some kinda purg'tory or some sss-ss-
such nosense like that. I say it's nothing but *nonsense!*" Ludy
looked away again and caught her breath and screwed her
face into that odd, brooding expression, like she was searching the past. "Sweet Sarah didn't have nothing to do with
them woods," she finally said softly. "Only time she ever got
near them woods was that time she ran away, and she must
have got turned around in there or lost or something, 'cause
they found her months later on the side of the two-lane over
to Leland."

Henry nodded. "And you don't think the red pines will tell
us anything?"

The old woman took a raspy breath. "Sarah is a sweet
woman, and she always has been, and, and, and the red pines
is all nnnn-nnnah-nuh—" Ludy closed her eyes then and
began to tremble again and cry.

"Listen, I'm sorry if I'm upsetting you," Henry said awkwardly, wringing his hands. "I just wanted to—"

"I have these l-ll-l-l-little spells sometimes," the old
woman interrupted.

Henry looked around the room. "Maybe we should—"

The sudden shrill of an electronic tone nipped off Henry's
words. One of the monitors behind the oxygen tent was
chiming loudly. Henry glanced back at the old woman.
Something was wrong. Ludy's face was shaking wildly now,
shaking with palsy, her lower lip curling downward.

Henry started toward the door.

Just then, the door burst inward and a nurse came bounding into the room. Middle-aged, portly, with big Olga fashion glasses, the nurse had a syringe in her mouth and a
stethoscope around her neck. She quickly waved Henry away
and rushed over to the bed. The monitors started clanging.

"I'm sorry, I didn't mean to—" Henry stammered, backing away.

Inside the plastic tent, the woman with half a face convulsed and flailed. Her hands were twisted talons, fingernails

blackened and infected. The nurse threw open the tent and administered the syringe. Ludy began hyperventilating. Her good eye was blazing urgently. Scanning the room. Seeking Henry. "It's—nnnuhh—nahhhhh—!"

"What did she say?" Henry was in the doorway.

"No more talking!" the nurse yammered. "It's nearly ten o'clock!"

Ludy's loudspeaker sizzled and popped. "—nnnnnnuh-hhh—!"

"What is she saying?" Henry gripped the doorknob, opened the door, but stood firm. "Is she going to be all right?"

"She'll be fine," the nurse snapped back, "if you would just leave."

Ludy groaned. "—nnnnnnah—!"

"I'm sorry, Mrs. Harmon, if I caused you any—"

"Out!" The nurse came over and shoved Henry out the door, slamming it in his face.

Henry stood in the hallway for a moment, heart thudding in his chest, head spinning. He had no idea what had just happened. Was it the strain of so much reminiscing? Was it the grief of discussing her sister who had passed away in a sanitarium? Or was it something about the red pines that the old woman wasn't revealing? Something that had touched off the spell?

"Nonsense."

The voice came from across the hall. Henry spun and saw Clyde McMasters leaning against a water fountain with his cane tucked under his arm. The withered little black man was rubbing his fingers together thoughtfully. "That's what Ludy was trying to say to ya there at the end—*nonsense*." The old geezer lifted a single crooked index finger and seemed to poke the air. "But I ain't so sure, myself. May be somethin' to what folks been sayin' 'bout that red piney forest. Matter o' fact, I believe I may have proof that them woods is special."

Henry licked his lips, a current of nervous dread traveling up his spine. "Proof?"

The old man cocked his head. "Follow me."

He led Henry down the hall, through a narrow doorway, and down a rickety staircase into the nursing home's cellar.

The old man pulled a light string and illuminated a dank, cavernous room. The air smelled of wet mortar and mildew. And every available square foot was crowded with generations of castaway heirlooms and family files. Forgotten legacies rotting away in the damp air. Henry followed the little man across the room to a metal shelf bending with the weight of countless file boxes. "Gotta be around here somewhere," the old man sniffed.

A moment later the geezer located the portfolio behind a crate full of plastic ferns.

It was enormous, a great leather file cracked with age and filmed with dust. At one time it had been a deep maroon, rich dimpled cowhide and gold leaf corners, but the patina of age and moisture had turned it to gray wax. McMasters unzipped the edges and opened it, the binding crackling delicately. He blew dust off the sheaf inside it and murmured, "Fella used to live here, Kettlekamp was his name, geologist by trade, and he had these top'graphical maps done."

McMasters found the map of Arkham and surrounding environs and pulled it out of the portfolio so that Henry could clearly see the dusty pale green paper.

"What are we looking at?"

The old black man pointed a jagged thumbnail at a dark blob of hash marks across the landscape north of town. "This here's the red pines area," he said. "One time, when Kettlekamp and me was in our cups, he took me down here and explained just what that dark area meant. Said it was a driftless region, one of the few on this continent."

"And that would mean?"

"That would mean you got one goddamn piece of history up there. See, accordin' to Kettlekamp, back when this continent was formed, eons ago, there was glaciers driftin' down from the north, formin' the land masses. But this here land

right here, right where the red pines is—it ain't made of glaciers. This here land's been here since before Jesus left
Chicago. I mean, you got one old goddamn piece of land
there. Older than the hills. Older than time, for chrissake."

Then the old man pulled out a scroungy handkerchief and
blew his nose.

Henry stared down at that faded topographical map for
quite some time before turning back to the old black man and
saying, "Mind telling me how to get out there?"

II

They went from room to room, hallway to hallway, working in the darkness, destroying all that had been erected in
their honor. They didn't know how late it was, and they
weren't aware of the noise they were making. All they knew
was that it felt delicious, this secret search-and-destroy mission.

"Trash that fucking shit!" Joey Marston growled, shoving
one of the boys away from the long table angled across the
library entrance.

The younger kid staggered backward, slamming against
the hall bulletin board. Some of the construction-paper
pumpkins fluttered to the tile floor.

Joey turned back to the display table of spooky books and
little plastic spiders and bats and bookmarks shaped like long
pointy witches' hats. He chose silver—Testors silver metal-
flake spray paint, to be exact—and started spraying big X's
across the display, slashing the books and novelties with a
thick mist of paint. The odor wafted up at him, smelling ex-
quisite, smelling like kick-ass fun in the dark, that acrid-
chemical odor of dime-store enamel.

"C'mon, dweeb patrol!" Joey chortled at them, stuffing
the can of spray paint back in his pocket. "We got work to
do!"

They started down the dark corridor toward the classrooms, whooping and hollering as they ran, their voices echoing off the tile and metal and glass. Some of them dragged nails and Swiss army knives along the rows of lockers, making horrible keening noises. Others carried BB guns and shot tiny holes in window after window. There were five boys in all. Joey Marston was the leader, a gangly eighth-grader in a black leather jacket and flattop haircut. Behind Joey ran two other eighth-graders: large, dim-witted boys named Kent Salinas and Larry Helfrich. Behind Salinas and Helfrich ran the younger ones, a hyperactive seventh-grader with a peroxide 'do nicknamed Roadrunner, and the quiet one, the one who had been coerced into coming tonight, the only one who regretted being along on this crazy ride, little Billy Barclay. They had gotten in through the windows in the front breezeway, and they had started with the front reception area and principal's office. They had overturned the coffee machine, slashed the chairs, made Xeroxes of their penises, scrawled FUCK MR ANTHONY and EAT SHIT AND DIE in spray paint all over the walls, pissed on the conference table, and for the piéce de résistance, Joey had even climbed up on Principal Anthony's large mahogany desk, opened the center drawer, dropped his pants, and defecated a great steaming log of shit into the stamp pads and Avery labels.

Thank God for Halloween.

"Let's start with Puss-Wad's room," Joey called out to his troops as he rounded a bend in the hallway, a reference to their beleaguered English teacher, Mr. Prudhomme.

The Arkham Middle School was a relatively well equipped facility for a small-town junior high. The beneficiary of 1960s tax reform, the building was laid out in a grand T-shape, with administrative offices, library, a huge gymnasium, an Olympic-sized pool, and a decent cafeteria spanning the front acreage. Down the center were rows of specialized classrooms, physics labs, workshops, and the like. Unfortunately, over recent years, the facility had fallen victim to Reaganomics and stingy town councils, to the point that the decor had not been changed since Nixon was in office. The same sixties aqua-blue tile still covered the hall floors, the same hideous orange chairs still filled the classrooms, and the same portrait of Bobby Kennedy still hung above the boy's room at the end of the corridor. The place felt stale, like a huge closet that hadn't been opened for two decades.

"Show time!" Joey blurted as he kicked open the door to Mr. Prudhomme's classroom.

The boys froze.

"What the fuck?"

The silent room clamored at them, all odd angles and garish stains. Words scrawled everywhere. A salty rancid smell in the air. Evidently some anonymous enemy of Mr. Prudhomme had beaten the boys to the punch; some secret vandal had already made his mark. In the gloom, the devastation looked almost organic, as though a great freakish storm had passed through, leaving furniture upturned, the walls impaled by shards of splintered wood and spatterings of paint. Joey entered cautiously, scanning the shadows for any sign of their unexpected competition. The other boys followed, expressions falling. This was not fair; this was going to be their greatest achievement, and now somebody else had come in and had all the fun.

"Bet you that faggot Tug Armstrong did this," Joey grumbled, as he knelt over a puddle of paint. The lights were off and the windows on the far wall were all closed up tight, webbed in shadows. In front, the blackboard glimmered, errant strokes of cursive gleaming across the slate. A single word, slashed again and again, some in big caps, others upside down, some backwards—*WEED, weed, weed, W-E-E-D!* Prudhomme's desk was canted off one corner of the board, its blotter obscured by strange piles of crumpled paper with ballpoint pens driven through them and threads of red paint everywhere.

"Fuckin'-A," Salinas uttered, backing into the room, scanning the destruction. The desks were scattered like leaves across the parquet. Nails were driven through some of the desktops. Every few feet, a rusty spike had been driven into a floor tile. In fact, there seemed to be an odd pattern to the disarray: *impalement.* Everything was either impaled or pierced. Violated.

"Motherfuckers messed this place up good," Helfrich commented, a trace of alarm in his voice.

"What the fuck is that smell?" Joey said, looking down at the paint spattered across the tile. The odor was like a two-day-old beef roast, thick and coppery. Joey ran a fingertip through the paint. It was sticky.

"What do we do now, Joey?" The query mewled out of Roadrunner, who was fidgeting next to Billy Barclay over by the door.

"Stick your thumbs up your asses, all I care," Joey replied, springing to his feet and hopping up on the teacher's desk. "I'm gonna add my own signature to this painting." He pulled a hunting knife from his belt, flung it down, and it thwacked into the wooden desktop. Then Joey unzipped his fly, wrestled out his uncircumcised penis, and started urinating on the mangled papers and wadded notes.

"Lookit!" Kent Salinas chortled nervously from across the room. "Joey's watering the faggot's desk!"

Helfrich whooped and kicked a desk.

Across the room, near the door, little Billy Barclay was paying little attention. The younger boy was too busy gazing around the darkened classroom, thinking about the words scrawled everywhere. *WEED,* upside down, *WEED,* in cursive across the windows, *WEED,* in block letters by the coat rack in that dark red sticky paint.

"Wait a minute!" Billy's voice was like a spray of cold mist on the other boys.

Joey stopped urinating, pivoting on his heel and shooting an annoyed glance back at Billy. "What the fuck is it?"

"You guys hear something?" Billy was scanning the shadows, licking his lips.

"Whattya talkin about, numb-nuts?" Larry Helfrich said, his eyes suddenly hot.

"Something's moving—"

"Shut up, chicken-shit!" Joey interrupted, brushing off Billy's concern with a paint-spattered hand. "You just don't have the balls for this kind of work."

Joey started kicking the crumbled papers off the desk. He hopped down and began slamming his bootheel against the desks, sending the furniture skidding like bumper cars into the walls. The other boys watched, still a bit reticent to join in, still a bit unnerved by the sticky words and messages and odd arrangements around the room.

"Hold it!" Joey suddenly froze and held up his hands. "Hold it a second," he murmured, and then listened closely to the sound of someone moving across the ceiling.

Footsteps creaking.

"What the fuck?" Kent Salinas whispered under his breath, his eyes widening.

All at once, in perfect unison, each boy's face clocked slowly upward, upward, upward until they were all staring at the old yellowed acoustic tile ceiling above them and listening to the creak of the crawlspace overhead. The sound was somewhat familiar to them. The building had undergone minor repairs last spring, which had required workmen to shuffle around up there during school hours. Each boy remembered that annoying sound, that creaking sound, moving back and forth up there during interminable forays into the world of Charles Dickens. But now, tonight, in the darkness, the sound was completely out of context. It raised gooseflesh and tightened sphincters and drew on each boy's latent fears of incarceration.

The footsteps seemed to move inward, from the far edge of the crawlspace, toward the center of the building, and then, without rhyme or reason, they ceased.

"Time to get the fuck outta here," Joey announced, and started toward the exit.

In that split instant before he reached the door, which was still standing a few inches ajar across the room, a wave of contrary emotions swirled through Joey Marston's mind. He

was angry for the interruption; there was so much left un-
done. He had planned on flooding the bathrooms, and
spreading rat poison throughout the cafeteria, and filling the
pool with gallons of ink, and rubbing shit into every seat
cover of every chair behind every teacher's desk. He had
planned on turning this fucking place upside down, and now
this. But beneath the current of anger, there was an undertow
of fear. Something just didn't add up here, something weird
about these footsteps. And when Joey finally reached the
door, he learned what it was.

The door slammed shut.

"Wha—" Joey's first reaction was to jerk backward, as
though rearing from a flame. The deadbolt clicked in his
face. Joey fumbled with the latch, but someone had jammed
it from the other side. Joey stepped back, and movement
loomed in the tiny window in the top half of the door. Something black and shiny slapped in place over the window.

Black plastic.

Joey wrestled with the deadbolt latch some more, but it
wouldn't budge.

"What the fuck is going on?" Joey uttered, and started
backing into the room, scanning the corners. The other boys
were dumbstruck, eyes blinking stupidly, still not compre-
hending, the events unfolding too quickly to be absorbed.
Billy Barclay started moaning softly, his back pressed
against the far corner, his eyes ablaze with terror. Joey
started toward the windows, preparing to slam a boot
through the glass.

An enormous object loomed outside.

"Jesus!" Joey flinched backward, again acting on instinct,
and skidded to a stop beneath the last window on the left. A
huge filthy roll of fabric had slammed against the glass and
was unfurling along the row of panes, a two-foot-wide strip
of ancient nylon, driven by some shadowy presence, obscured by the darkness outside. Joey couldn't manage to
react fast enough to do anything about it; he could only gawk
up at that huge soiled ribbon traveling across the windows.

"We gotta get outta here, man," Larry Helfrich said suddenly, his voice going all warbly.

The boys were backing into the center of the classroom now, their shoes crunching against broken glass, their fists clenching and teeth gnashing and eyes shifting around for an answer, a way out. Fight-or-flight current coursing through their veins. They didn't know exactly what was going on, but they knew it was not good.

"It's somebody else doing a prank, Joey, man, it's nothing," Kent Salinas was murmuring, watching the dark fabric close over the windows, blocking out the last of the vapor light. There was a sharp thud, and the sound of glass breaking, and then the horrible wrenching noise behind the wall to the right, a sound so strident and metallic that it snapped Joey out of his terrified daze.

"C'mon, motherfucker!" Joey bellowed, marching across the room toward the noise, holding his Swiss army blade aloft like a scepter. "Come and get us!"

At that moment, little Roadrunner decided to bail. He spun toward the shrouded windows, and he lowered his head, and he dove straight at the shattered glass. There was a dull crack, and the impact of his bony shoulder and tense little body barely made a ripple in the iron fabric. He bounced backward off it like a stone in a slingshot, careening across the floor into the splay of overturned desks.

"COME AND GET US, MOTHERFUCKER!"

Joey's rage had turned to madness, and now things were happening around him too quickly to comprehend. The creak of footsteps was moving across the ceiling again, closer, louder, and something was nudging the acoustic tiles, tiny spritzes of dust motes cascading down into the darkness, and all the boys were gazing up now, stunned, because the ceiling was caving in, and something was forcing its way down into the room, and it came like a great black bat, shimmying upside down into the room, and then unfolding its arms and legs.

"*Run!*" Larry Helfrich shrilled like a little girl, scurrying toward the windows, his gridiron toughness evaporating with every stride.

The dark intruder flipped gracefully upright and landed on his feet.

The boys scattered.

What happened next occurred in a great theatrical flurry, so violently graceful and quick that the untrained eye would think it some kind of macabre ballet. The intruder was whirling, whirling toward Joey and Salinas and Helfrich, and something long and ropy was looping out from the intruder's black garb, gleaming in the shadows like strands of silver chain or belt sash, and Joey was the first to feel one of the hooks, a sharp sting in the meat of his calf, jerking him off his feet, and then the others were falling, Helfrich, and Salinas, and the little one, Roadrunner, yanked off their feet by the trawling hook teeth, and little Billy Barclay watching from a far corner, whimpering, witnessing the assault unravel like a waking nightmare, a dance of screams and blood and gleaming silver linkage.

The intruder brought pain, sharp pain, flashing like teeth glinting in the darkness, cables twining flesh, hogtying their ankles to ankles, wrists to wrists, hands moving faster than the eye could see, and then there were more strange sounds, Joey could hear them as he flailed madly to escape, clawing at the litter-strewn floor, trying to see in the darkness, his leg screaming sharp pangs of agony, the clicking sounds, and the padlocks, and the hooks, tightening around Joey's ribs, his thighs, his feet, and the final sensation of being dragged backward across the tile like a fish on a stringer.

The boys were gathered in the center of the floor as though culminating some ancient ritual hunt.

Joey Marston was the last to be padlocked to the group, and he squirmed and wriggled around enough to gaze up into the face of his assailant.

The man was pale, pale and muscular and wild-eyed. Dressed in a ragged cape that looked cut from a bolt of black muslin, dark Levi's and knee-high moccasins, he gazed down at his prey with the absent disgust of a man about to wring a chicken's neck. And in that taut moment of terror, Joey's fevered mind began to cast about the darkness for explanations. Was this guy some deranged security guard? A rogue teacher? Prudhomme's personal henchman? Some kind of bizarre serial killer who preyed on vandals? Joey's vision was going in and out of focus, the vomit rising in his throat, the pain threatening to devour him.

The intruder spoke.

"I'm sorry," he said in a velvet-hoarse whisper, "but you have to die."

Then he pulled a small metal object from his belt. The object was a ratchet, Joey recognized it from his summer job as a lifeguard up in Green Bay, a small metal prawl designed to tighten cables on sailboats and large tents. The intruder knelt down by Joey and threaded a strand of cable, which was wrapped around Joey's wrist, into the ratchet. Then another around his crotch. Then another around his neck.

Then the intruder began tightening the prawl with a *tick-tick-tick-tick*—

"No, wait, mister, please—" Joey gibbered, suddenly realizing what the maniac was going to do to him. "Please, please, please-please-please!"

tick-tick-tick

The pressure grew, and grew, and became tremendous, like crescents of fire around Joey's wrists, across his anus, and around his collarbone. The fire turned to molten lava as the cables tightened, *tick-tick,* and the lava turned to lightning flashes in Joey's head, *tick-tick-tick,* and he couldn't breathe anymore, and he could barely see, and all he could do was form silent words with his lips: *please-please— PLEEE—*

Then his air was cut off, and the skin started to cleft.

Tick-tick-tick—

—snapping delicate tendons, pressing down on the sinew and bone, and everything was going gray and numb for Joey, the blood seeping now in rivulets down his arms and torso, the warmth pooling beneath him, and the pressure, the pressure, a demon's embrace, a hand inside him, gripping his bowels and his bladder, squeezing out fluids, blood, tears, and the last thing Joey saw was the face of the killer hovering over him like a scabrous, pale harvest moon.

And the face was changing.

"No!" The intruder roared, tossing his head back as though shaking off a fly. In fits and starts, the side of the intruder's face was bloating and shivering, his right eye turning liquid, the corner of his mouth curling downward as though another face were insinuating itself through his flesh.

tick-tick-tick

"Stop!" A new voice blurted out of him like a ventriloquist trick.

"Get back inside!" the intruder hissed.

tick-tick

"Murderer!" the voice cried.

"BACK INSIDE!" the intruder barked, bearing down furiously on the ratchet, faster and faster—*tick-tick-ticking*—until Joey Marston was no more, the last of his consciousness flickering out like a candle flame, a death rattle sputtering out of his throat, drowned by the terrified moans of the other boys, wriggling in the nearby shadows, listening to the horrible sounds, the wet sounds, as Joey's extremities gave way, collapsing and pinching off at their stumps like moist pieces of cordwood, opening up the bloodgates.

"GOD, NO!" the inner voice came out of the intruder like a phantom, the side of his face a liquid jigsaw, his jaw rippling, his right eye moving independently, gaping down in revulsion at the quivering mass on the floor.

"You can't stop me!" the intruder hissed petulantly to himself, giving the ratchet one last shove.

TICK

Joey's pelvis collapsed, fracturing like a wishbone, flooding the tiles with billows of fluid as black as India ink in the gloom. The intruder reached down and scooped up magnificent handfuls of spoor, baptizing himself, bathing himself, the thick rivulets of juice sluicing down his arms, spattering off in all directions. Joey's severed hands were carried away on the currents of blood and bile like dead, overturned crabs.

The intruder rose to his feet, triumphant and bloody as a newborn.

"YOU CAN'T STOP ME NOW!" he cried, his face undulating, the flesh of his jaw creasing on one side like melted plastic, the corner of his mouth forming an anguished divot. He raised his quivering arms to the heavens. In the darkness he looked like the tragicomic death mask of the theater made flesh. And all the pain and the terror and the repulsion seemed to settle on the right side of his face like a cancer, forming one half of a tormented, unmistakable condition.

A silent scream.

"I'm alive!" he sang out suddenly, all the rippling flesh vanishing suddenly, as though his alter ego were abruptly absorbed into the cauldron of his own brutality. He reached down and released the prawl. The boy's body sagged like a ruined rag doll, going slack in the sheets of blood, and the intruder wrestled the corpse from the tangles of cable and chains, lifting the body upright and swinging it out into the heart of the shadows. To the choruses of moans from the other young men, the intruder began to dance.

He danced with the wet and sagging shell once known as Joey Marston.

The intruder was a graceful, intuitive dancer, unschooled in the actual steps, but able to approximate an instinctive rendering of a classic ballroom waltz. Of course, his partner was a limp rag, and the floor was quite slippery and treacherous in all the blood, and yet, in the gleaming darkness, the air thick with fear and whimpering, there was a certain horrible grace to the intruder's dance, the strands of blood spinning off with each twirl, the wet threads shimmering.

"ALIVE!"

The intruder sang his hideous refrain to the silent opera music rising in his head.

Across the room, little Billy Barclay had scratched his fingertips bloody, trying to claw himself out the window. Finally realizing that he wasn't going anywhere, he turned and gazed one last time at the bloody room, his throat closing up, choking off the last of his moans. A dark veil was drooping over Billy's eyes. His back was pressing against the window now, and he slid downward until his butt struck the tile. His body seemed to sink inward, a tiny little sparrow in the jaws of the dragon, and he closed his eyes.

He didn't even notice the fact that the intruder was coming toward him now.

III

"I don't have time for foreplay, Taggert," Frank Moon shrilled into the phone, "so just lube yourself up and put it in."

It was almost three in the morning and Frank was standing in the doorway of the meager little cigar-choked cubicle that served as the Arkham sheriff's office, his hand welded to the telephone receiver, his stomach feeling like an active volcano. Sheriff Dillihuddy, the aging town constable, had planted his fat ass in a creaky swivel chair across the office and was doodling on a scratch pad as though he couldn't care less that Armageddon had come to his sleepy little village.

"All right, here's the skinny," the voice on the other end replied quickly, tersely. Brian Taggert was the chief print guy at the CPD crime lab, and he'd been working overtime on the Dante's murders. "The central database practically blew a gasket trying to match the prints we got from behind the strip club. Looked like we had a partial match for a while, but now I'm pretty doubtful we got anything real."

"What do you mean, a partial match?"

The sound of Taggert's sigh was like a hot needle in Frank's right eye. "What I mean is, I'm not sure we ever had enough matching ridge artifacts to light a fire under the DA."

"Who's the partial match?"

"Well, see, the thing is, I was going to call you earlier." Taggert was obfuscating all of a sudden. "But Detective Jones—she noticed where I was heading with the thing, and she did a little background on the guy—"

"Goddamnit, Taggert, stop circling the fucking landing strip already."

"It's not the stripper," Taggert said flatly.

"What?" Frank felt his gut burn.

"The thing is," Taggert continued, "we ID'd this guy named Weed. Abner James Weed."

"Weed?"

"Yeah," Taggert said, and spelled it, and then said, "The guy's prints were on file from a stretch he did down in Missouri back in the forties; morals charge. It wasn't a perfect match by any stretch; it was the same tented-arch ridge pattern, a couple of similar whorls, but it certainly wasn't definitive enough to get admitted."

"I don't care about that," Frank said, "I want Jones to run this guy down."

"But Frank—"

"I don't have time for this court TV crap, Taggert, I want Jones to nail this guy ten minutes ago."

After a pause: "That isn't possible, Frank."

"What the fuck are you talking about?" Frank said, raising his voice enough to startle Dillihuddy.

The reply came over the line like the voice of doom.

"The guy's dead, Frank."

There was another pause.

Frank tried to keep his calm, chewing his fingernail, staring across the dusty little office at the venetian blinds above the sheriff. The orderly world was unraveling in Frank's mind like a needlepoint sampler coming apart, seam by seam, the picture melting into a brightly colored mishmash of thread.

First, there was the scene at the Trading Post, the revelation of the freak. Then, only a few minutes ago, Frank and the sheriff had returned from the Ace Hardware Store on the corner of Third and Main. The store had been broken into, evidently while the owner, Wily Perkins, had been working late, doing inventory. Perkins had been brutally strangled to death, and several incongruous items had been stolen. A huge roll of nylon truckload-restraint material, black plastic, tire chains, and various tools. And now this cryptic bullshit from Taggert.

"What do you mean, the guy's dead?" Frank finally said, his chest tight and buzzing with nerves.

"Jones tracked the name down," Taggert explained. "Guy's been deceased for over twenty years. Used to teach in the stripper's hometown. Had a thing for little girls. Got run out of town. Offed himself in a mental hospital up in Appleton, Wisconsin, all the way back in 1974."

Frank felt a coppery wetness on his lip, looked down, and discovered his index finger was bleeding. Chewed down to the cuticle. Frank had always made a point to keep his fingernails meticulously manicured, and now they were jagged, bloody crescents, gnawed down to the nubs. Disgusting. The nerves were tearing him apart inside. "I don't know what you lab guys have been smoking," Frank said then, "but I've got better things to do than listen to this bullshit."

"Wait—Frank—don't hang up," the voice said.

"What is it, Taggert?"

"I'm not sure you're aware of this," Taggert said, speaking with a tautness in his voice that reminded Frank of a guitar string wound too tight, "but in the eighties, I got halfway through a residency at Rush Presbyterian before I transitioned into this crazy business. My specialty was obstetrics, and I learned a lot about—"

"Taggert," Frank interrupted, "I've got a body count going up here; if there's a point to all this, I wish you'd make it, and make it *now*."

"It's the print," the voice said. "The fingerprint partial we got at Dante's. The way the ridges are partially fused, blending together; the way the whorls fade across the pattern, the papery creases. It's goddamn prenatal, Frank."

"Pre—what?"

The sound of the dispatch radio crackled out in the receiving area. Frank could hear it like a blackbird cawing, goosing Dillihuddy out of his chair. The sheriff hauled his fat ass into the outer room and started yelling something at the girl behind the radio rig.

"Prenatal, Frank—*pre-fucking-natal*," Taggert's voice opined through the receiver. "Never seen anything like it, closest thing to a fetal pattern I've ever run across; but *big*, adult-sized, like fucking Baby Huey—"

Frank slammed the receiver back into its cradle.

The sheriff had just returned, his big hound-dog eyes popping wide and hot. He threw open the metal cabinet behind his desk and pulled out a pump-action shotgun.

"What's wrong?" Frank asked.

"Plenty," Dillihuddy murmured. "Got three calls, one after another. Noises coming from the middle school, glass breaking and kids hollering."

"Tomorrow's Halloween," Frank said. "Maybe it's just kids being kids."

The sheriff cocked his shotgun, came over to Frank, and spoke in a low, strained baritone. "One of the neighbor ladies got close enough to see something spattering the insides of the windows. Might have been red paint. Might have been something else."

Frank nodded. "You drive."

IV

Sheriff Sterling "Bud" Dillihuddy was one of the few elected officials in greater Sauk County who didn't give a flying fuck about staying in office. A large, pear-shaped man with great doughy jowls and a belly like a feed bag, he was less than a year away from retirement. Eleven months away from daily rounds of golf at the Stinson Country Club, nightly tenderloin dinners at the Moose Lodge, and endless hours sitting in his backyard, drinking Pabst Blue Ribbons and doing bad oil paintings of Margie's begonias. Dillihuddy didn't want to be a hero. And be sure as hellfire didn't want to be first through the door of that dark middle school. But as long as he was sheriff of the greater township of Arkham, Wisconsin, he was bound to serve, and to protect, and to make sure no hopped-up psycho city homicide dick screwed things up.

"Hold your horses, Moon!" Dillihuddy yelled at the detective, who was throwing open his door and lurching out of the cruiser into the darkness of the schoolyard, semiautomatic drawn and cocked like he was some kind of goddamn special agent. They had just come to a skidding halt in a cloud of carbon monoxide and grass debris in front of the classroom windows bordering the east courtyard. Frank had seen the big two-foot ribbon of nylon stretched across the windows, along with the broken glass glimmering in the yard, and he had immediately thrown open his door.

"Call for backup," Moon said over his shoulder as he crept toward the building. He reached the corner rampart and slammed into the brick, his gun gripped in tight sweaty hands, his breath coming out in puffs of vapor.

"Goddamnit," Dillihuddy grumbled, climbing out of the cruiser, clutching his twenty-gauge with one hand, fumbling for his radio with the other. He wore a small two-way with a hand mike clipped to his pocket protector. He grabbed the mike as he rushed after Moon. "Moon! I told you to stand down for a second!"

Dillihuddy reached the brick wall, staying as low as his creaky knees would allow. Sounds were leaking out the edges of the nylon, whimpering sounds, shuffling. Dillihuddy grabbed Moon by the arm. "I told you to cool your pits," the sheriff whispered angrily. "You said yourself this might just be a couple of kids out soaping windows."

"I smell my gal," Moon whispered, snicking the slide mechanism on his cannon and trying to peer over the top of the filthy nylon which covered the windows. Muffled noises were seeping out the windows, terrible noises.

Dillihuddy wasn't letting go of Frank's arm. "Long as I'm sheriff in this town, you go my way. You got that?"

"Let go of my arm."

"Stand down, Moon."

"I told you to call for backup," Moon hissed.

Dillihuddy squeezed. "You're cruisin' to get shipped back to Chicago, boy. Your shift commander begged us to cooperate with you boys, and we agreed to let you come up here and advise us on this escapee thing. But this is still Arkham, and I'm the friggin' law in Arkham, so you're gonna stand down now or I'm gonna lock your ass up faster than you can say internal affairs."

Frank started to say something, then stopped, took a breath, and looked down at the ground. "Okay, all right, listen—"

The butt of Frank's pistol suddenly swung upward, the unexpected flash of movement, the silver blur of metal, catching the sheriff completely off guard. The beavertail grip struck Dillihuddy hard in the jaw. Star-sparks leaped into his eyes, the teeth-jarring impact sending the big man lurching backward, dropping the hog leg.

Dillihuddy landed in the grass with a thud, as dazed and harmless as a spring grizzly.

"Never mind the backup," Frank added, and then pulled a long retractable switchblade from his belt. He turned back to the windows. Reaching up to the top edge of the nylon restraints, his heart thumping, his mouth dry with adrenaline panic, he flashed a two-foot incision into the thick fabric.

The restraints fell away, revealing, through the broken glass, a dark room swimming in black blood.

"EVERYBODY DOWN ON THE FLOOR—NOW!" Frank yelled suddenly, working on instinct, cop instinct, gun raised and readied, moving sideways along the jagged window line, gazing into the dark classroom. He saw the bodies on the floor, some of them squirming in their own blood, some of them silent and still, the familiar bondage wrapping their limbs, and the figure in the middle of the room, the suspect, the perpetrator, dancing with a terrified little boy, lording over all the death and the pain, moving with preternatural grace, drawing Frank's rage like a lightning rod.

"ON THE FLOOR!"

Frank fired a warning shot.

The cherry-bomb muzzle flash lit up the sky, and the subsonic boom seemed to galvanize the darkness inside the classroom. The shadowy figure froze in the lightning burst, then tossed the little boy aside. The child dropped to the floor like a parachute deflating. Then the figure crouched suddenly, as though gathering some kind of unearthly store of strength, trembling, perhaps in pain; and Frank froze in the moonlight, staring in through the broken glass at the perpetrator's face. It wasn't the stripper after all, Or was it? In that brief, stunning instant, Frank's breath seemed to abruptly freeze-dry in his throat, as the figure's upturned face passed through a slice of vapor light. One side was male, and the other side was female, and Frank somehow recognized instantly the corner of Sarah's Brandis's anguished, downturned mouth, crying out for some hideous deliverance. Then the female side seemed to ripple away like an echo in the surface of a pond. And then the figure leaped. Straight upward. Latching onto a beam in the broken ceiling.

Frank snapped out of his daze and starting firing madly through the jagged breaches of broken glass.

The first shot ripped a crater in the window ledge, sending dust and debris imploding into the room. The second shot peeled a chunk out of the center window. The third, fourth, and fifth opened a portal wide enough for Frank to see through the smoke and silver moonlit motes, and he glimpsed the figure lifting itself up into the ceiling-works, and Frank Moon roared inarticulately, a garbled cry, an airrending curse directed at this freak of nature, this creature that was bringing death and disorder to Frank's ordered world, and as the thing vanished up into the darkness within the ceiling, Frank made another split-second decision.

Taking three steps back, sucking in a breath, he lunged at the windows, vaulting over the ledge.

He landed in the battlefield of broken glass, sliding across the blood-slick tiles, the finely double-stitched seams of his Pierre Cardin wool blazer ripping open, slamming hard into the far wall. He shook off the shock, caught his breath, and struggled back to his feet. He was in a world of death now, death as black as ink. A world of twisted bundles of flesh, and whimpering sounds of traumatized little boys, and a shadowy figure shrinking up into the ceiling. A world where cops forgot they were cops, and bad guys were magic, and the whole damn thing unravels in explosions of blood-red thread.

The figure was above him now, moving along in creaking, jerky footsteps across the crawlspace, and in that instant of madness, Frank followed the last logical impulse of his shattered cop psyche.

Chase the bad guy.

11

Halloween

I

Less than four feet high, framed in ancient timbers and sheets of recently installed insulation, the crawlspace had no floor. Only splintered joists crisscrossing the fiberglass. The air was dense and inert, thick with odors of old cedar and varnish. The Escape Artist leaped from joist to joist like a nimble lumberjack, heading toward a phalanx of heating ducts in the distant shadows. He could hear the footsteps of the cop below him, the *snick-snick* of his pistols, and the ragged, heavy breathing like the panting of a hellhound.

Relax and concentrate.

Bounding through the darkness, shoulders hunched, legs pumping like pistons, the Escape Artist kept playing these basic principles of escape over and over in his mind. Relaxation and concentration. They were his mantra. They calmed him in the black void of the magic cabinet, in the watery depths, in the heart of the impossible prison. Together, relaxation and concentration could melt steel, loosen the tightest bonds, break the stoutest cable, snap the thickest chains as if they were so much frayed hemp. They were the holy duo, the

yin and yang of escape, and at the moment they were helping
the Escape Artist see that he couldn't climb out of the
Arkham Middle School the way he had climbed in, because
the lawmen were out there now, waiting for him in the east
yard, and the best escape lay to the west.

There was a sharp pop, and the first shot burst like a poison flower through the pink insulation.

The Escape Artist jerked away from the shaft of flickering
light, then he dove across the joists. He landed on his hands
and knees, flesh lacerated by the rough-hewn planks. The
corridor lights were coming on below him. Sharp silver
threads of luminance flickered up through the cracks and
gaps in the ceiling. The Escape Artist kept moving, crawling
along the pathway, hand over hand, breathing evenly, moving steadily toward the heating ducts, concentrating.

More shots came up through the fiberglass, shafts of magnesium brightness like deadly spears piercing the dark
around him. One barely missed his right arm, another zinged
past his left ear like a wasp. The air filled with soup. He kept
scrabbling toward the ducts, mind focused, ignoring the
noise and the light and the sudden blips in his head.

*Curtains made of blood, curtains made of human flesh,
beginning to split, fissuring apart, revealing—*

He froze.

The image flashed in his mind like a photographer's
strobe, and he knew who was responsible, and for a brief
moment it threw off his steely concentration. He lowered
himself to the wood, sucked in a breath and held it, pressing
his forehead to the joist, concentrating, focusing all his powers to rid himself of this assault

*The face, the face behind the curtains, her face, hover-
ing, looming in midair like a massive nightmare effigy,
the great and powerful mother-Oz. Her features stretch-*

ing, distorting with agony. "Monster!" *she shrieks at him.*

"No!"

"Give it up!"

"No—NO!"

The Escape Artist suddenly lurched across the planks, on hands and knees, knowing that he had just made a fatal mistake, that the sound of his voice would draw the cop's fire. And sure enough, the cop fired immediately, emptying both magazines of bad news up into the crawlspace.

The air erupted.

Bullets hailed up through the pink stuffing in rapid succession, strafing shadows with brilliant white blades of light. The Escape Artist tried one last desperate attempt to reach the warren of air ducts, clawing at the greasy iron apron a few inches away. Then one of the bullets struck his knees. Pain exploded, a bone-fragment cymbal crash, then waves of agony bolting up his femur.

Giant lips. Filling his vision. The lips of the bitch-mother goddess—Sarah—shrieking at him, wailing, "You stop this—stop it now—stop it this minute!

"NO!"

"We're gonna die! Both of us! We deserve to die!"

"I SAID NO!"

More bullets made contact. One shattered his rotator cuff, sending up a geyser of bone fragments, leaving his arm dangling useless. Another one blasted through his jugular, arterial spray spuming up through shafts of light. Then an entire series. Puncturing his abdomen, his lung, his arms and wrists and fingers and cheekbones, and the Escape Artist crawled the rest of the way to the ductwork on screaming bloody limbs, his vision curling into kaleidoscopic fractures, prism fragments turning amber, then red, then black.

Die!

"Shut your MOUTH!" he bellowed in pain and rage, a prison guard addressing his rebellious prisoner, and all at once he realized that the line between the two personalities was blurring, that he no longer was the possessor, he was becoming possessed himself, a parasite being devoured by its host, and he closed his eyes and wished for great storms of fire, and rivers of blood, and endless pain.

Sudden silence fell in the crawlspace.

The Escape Artist heard the clatter of ammo magazines hitting tile somewhere beneath him. The cop was reloading. One last chance. One last chance for the Escape Artist to win the game. With his last gasp of life, he crawled the remaining distance and grabbed the edge of the air duct with his good hand and pulled himself up, up to the edge of the metal chimney chute, and the pain was like acid in his veins, his bad arm dragging along like a dead fish, his neck gushing hotly, his ruined lungs wheezing, blood oozing everywhere, dribbling across his collarbone, percolating down his pants legs, and he just kept thinking *Relax, relax, relax and concentrate.*

He managed to shove the chimney conduit apart at the seam, and he climbed inside the chimney just as the gunfire resumed behind him.

Thunder and lightning filled the crawlspace as the Escape Artist lifted himself upward, upward, toward the top of the chimney, his bloody limbs wedged in the conduit, the two-foot slice of night sky above him, beckoning, the pings and sparks of gunfire raining on the metal below, and the pain, the pain like a hideous lover caressing him now, whispering DIE in his ear DIE DIE DIE, but he was almost there, almost had his face out the top, and the cool air was swirling around him now, and he strained and he groaned and all at once . . .

He was out.

Swinging his leg over the mouth of the chimney, he top-

pled out onto the cold and pebbly tar of the roof. The night
wind was bracing against his face, and he found enough
strength to rise to his feet, and keep the bitch-mother quiet,
and tear off pieces of his cape, wrapping them around his
neck and his wrists to squelch the bleeding. Then he hobbled
across the sandpaper surface to the edge of the west wing, his
vision fragmenting, darkening, his body shutting down. He
could feel his heart beating furiously inside him, the blood
trickling down his chest and the wicked wind buffeting him
as he leaned out over the edge.

A twenty-five-foot drop.

He started taking quick breaths, realizing it was too far to
jump, but refusing to give up, refusing to give in to the
mother-voice. He scanned the edge of the roof for any possible mode of escape, and his gaze fell on the huge drainpipe
off the opposite corner, and the idea struck him, and he
started creeping toward it, holding his ruined arm, breathing
hard, and reaching out for the top of the downpipe assembly,
swinging his body around and mounting it like a hobbyhorse,
and then sliding downward, downward on a rush of black
wind and shrieking pain and blood-slick flesh-on-metal.

He landed in a bloody heap.

Rising to his feet, breath sputtering, lungs drowning in
their own fluids, he gazed across the barren stretch of playing field and chain-link backstops, and he saw his last chance
in the distance like a dream viewed backward through a
cracked telescope, and he started toward it, limping fiercely,
holding his lifestream against his chest like a boy with his
finger in a dike.

Concentrating . . .

II

Burdette Steagall just happened to be driving his whiskey-
bumped, rust-spotted Chevy S-10 pickup along McCallister
Street around the time all the ruckus was taking place up at

the middle school. A withered little brown man with long black hair pulled back in a Willie Nelson braid, Burdette was half Pottawattomi Indian, half Irish, and all character. He could tell a story that would hold a barroom rapt or keep a group of kindergarteners in stitches. He could turn his eyelids inside out, pull his wrinkled bottom lip over his top, and shake his ears like a mad elephant. He also just happened to be circulation manager for the *Arkham Gazette,* which would explain why he just happened to be out in his pickup at this hour of the morning.

McCallister Street was not much more than a lane and a half of scarred concrete snaking around the back of the school grounds and heading down Cranberry Hill into town. There was a little greasy spoon at the bottom of the hill where McCallister emptied into Main, a place called Leslie's. Burdette usually stopped there, unloaded a stack of papers for the machine, tossed a couple of witticisms at the waitress, and got a cup of mud to go.

But before Burdette made it to Leslie's, extraordinary things started happening.

The first to catch his eye was a flash of movement in his right-side mirror. A blur of shadows out in the darkness of the soccer field behind the school. It was there one second, and then gone the next, and Burdette did a double-take, almost as if he wasn't even sure he had seen it in the first place. Then, gazing back at the road ahead, he saw the flashing blue and red lights of a deputy's cruiser hauling ass down Main Street toward the entrance gates of the middle school, and Burdette started to get the idea that something was up, but before he could come to any conclusions a sharp tremor nudged the back of his pickup.

Somebody had hopped on board.

Burdette saw a figure crawling toward him in his side mirror, struggling across bundles of morning editions, bleeding all over the *Gazettes,* the son of a bitch. Burdette snapped his gaze around and looked through the rear window. Just as the figure pounced across the remaining newspapers, rocketing at the window like some kind of rabid mountain lion.

The window imploded.

A wiry little arm burst through the shattered glass. Burdette swerved, and the truck jumped the curb. The bloody hand clutched at Burdette's shoulder, then latched onto his deltoid, squeezing through Burdette's flannel shirt like a vice. The front of the truck kissed a fire hydrant, then bounded back over the sidewalk. Burdette slammed on the brakes, and the truck started spinning, newspapers sliding off the back into oblivion, the hand squeezing tighter and tighter, the desperate, mangled voice bleating in Burdette's ear.

"Keep moving!" Then a ragged breath, and blood spattering the vinyl seats. A long shard of glass was pressed against Burdette's neck. Then a wheezing death rattle: *"Keep moving! Or you die! You die right where you sit!"*

Burdette followed orders. Shoulder blazing with pain, his hands riveted to the wheel, the razor edge of the broken glass digging into his Adam's apple, Burdette pulled the truck back onto the road and headed north, back up Cranberry Hill, back up the way he had come. He kept the pedal pinned to the floor, trying to catch his breath, his heart racing, his mind swimming in fear and shock, shock that something like this would happen to anybody in this sleepy little two-bit town. And then Burdette saw the reflection in the rearview mirror, the face of the young man lying belly-down on the newspapers behind him, and Burdette felt his bones go cold.

The face was sculpted out of pain. Covered in spatterings of blood like a newborn calf, the guy must have been on drugs or something. The right side of his face was drooping in fits and jerks, like a stroke victim, only changing rapidly in the green glow of the truck's dashboard. And his body, wrapped in blood-soaked clothes, mangled and gouged by some inconceivable assault, was undulating like an eel.

"HEAL ME!" the highjacker cried.

"I'm sorry—I ain't—I don't know what—" Burdette stammered for a moment, then the glass pressed tighter around his neck, cutting off his words.

"Not you!" the highjacker barked.

"Sorry, fella," Burdette murmured, trying to keep the truck steady with the glass pressing against his throat, moving around the hairpins of Cranberry Hill.

The road was rounding the top of the rise, where the pavement ended and gravel began. The truck roared over the rocks, shimmying slightly, going about forty-five miles an hour, plummeting down into a gentle valley, then heading toward another rise. In the distance, the ancient bluffs and hills of the pine forest were becoming visible. The horizon was just beginning to lighten, and the tops of trees stood out in harsh relief against the predawn glow, like the spires of haunted castles.

"Just keep driving," the highjacker hissed, gasping for breath, coughing wetly, and then cocking his head as though hearing inner voices. "No!" he snapped, coughing up a spattering of blood. "No—damn you! *Heal* me! Heal me now!"

A stretch of agonizing silence followed, and Burdette kept driving.

The highjacker was shivering now, coughing up gouts of oily black blood and bile, the fluids streaming down the vinyl bench seat. This guy was dying, Burdette could see that, any idiot could see that. But then again, the way the highjacker's flesh was rippling, the way his eyes were melding from one color to the next like some insane, rotating Christmas light, Burdette's fevered mind raced back to the stuff he used to read in the *Weekly World News* or the *Enquirer*, the stuff about aliens from other worlds, babies born with devil horns, bigfoot, or even the tall tales that he used to yammer around town about the Vanishing Highhiker, Kentucky Fried Rats, or the Choking Doberman, urban folklore. Burdette had always loved that stuff, but now he was silently cursing the very thought of it, silently asking God why *he*—Burdette Steagall, harmless lover of children, spinner of tales—was chosen to be attacked by this bloody, dying, mythic creature leaning over the seatback behind him.

"HEAL ME!" the highjacker bellowed, tossing his head as though shaking off flies, looking like a spoiled little boy throwing a tantrum.

Burdette turned his gaze back to the road ahead. They were rumbling up a steep grade, climbing up into the thicker pines. Rows of birch trees flickered past them in the half-light, stoic sentries standing guard at the gates to the distant past, the primordial past. The road was narrowing. Burdette couldn't remember the last time he had come all the way up here. Used to be a pleasant getaway spot. But at the present moment Burdette Steagall sure as hell wished he was anywhere else.

"I cannot do it myself, and you know it!" The highjacker was yelling at himself again, gasping desperately for air, and Burdette had had just about enough of this shit.

"Hey, son?" Burdette said sharply all of a sudden.

"HEAL ME NOW!"

"Hey!" Burdette hollered over the roar of the engine, which was groaning to lift them up the hairpins.

The highjacker flinched at a sudden jolt of pain, and Burdette saw the shard of glass fall away from his neck. Just for an instant. And in that brief moment, Burdette made a decision, a split-second decision that he wasn't going to stand for any more of this psycho tantrum-throwing bullshit. Burdette decided to do something about it, right then while the bastard's guard was down. And all at once Burdette reached up with his right hand—the same hand that had won the Lake Geneva Junior Golden Gloves championship in his weight class almost four decades ago—and slammed a jaw-crunching, tooth-shattering uppercut right to the guy's kisser.

The glass shard slipped from the highjacker's hand and tumbled across the seat, skittering to the floor on the passenger side, shattering on impact.

"Fool!"

The highjacker became a wild animal, lurching suddenly

at Burdette, before the older man even had time to twist around and grab his door handle. Iron-belted fingers latched around Burdette's throat, cutting off his air, sending fireworks of pain and panic across his field of vision.

The truck went out of control.

And then things were happening quickly again, Burdette's legs kicking involuntarily against the pedals, the heavy press of his boot on the accelerator goosing the engine, his hands clutching at the vise grip around his throat, choking him, tighter, tighter, the steering wheel spinning free, the front wheels going haywire, the truck swerving right, swerving left, and then the limbs of trees sweeping down and clawing at the windows like talons, and the G-forces throwing the men against the far door as the truck was skirting the edge of the path, and then tipping.

They were falling then, the sky spinning under them, the black earth turning to sky, and Burdette felt fingers crushing his windpipe, squeezing the life out of him, as the Chevy became, for one dreamlike moment, completely weightless.

And the forest turned black as pitch.

III

Henry Decker was in no shape to run, but *run* he did, joints screaming and popping like champagne corks, heart slamming under his denim jacket.

The first rays of morning sun were just beginning to peek out from behind the treetops, and the light strobed in Henry's face as he motored along the narrow footpath bordering a rim of jack pines and hemlocks. Through the foliage, he could see the parallel dirt road down below, about fifty yards away. A sheriff's cruiser was tooling along the dirt, bubble lights flashing, a thunderhead of dust and carbon monoxide trailing after it in the chilled morning air. Henry was trying desperately to keep up; but he knew it was futile.

Henry had a terrible feeling that he was too late, that these bastards were going to find Sarah before he did, or worse, that Sarah was already either dead or driven completely out of her mind by the alter. Or maybe it was simply the immensity of these woods that was making Henry so terrified. Old Clyde McMasters had been right, the forest above Arkham was prehistoric. You could smell it, especially at night. The trees smelled petrified, like black decay long iced over, like the bottom of a vast, very old, very filthy well. And there were other odors, too, like counterpoints to the dark dirge. A hint of spoor, the alkaline spice of animal droppings and nests of pine needles turning to humus, and something else beneath the mélange, something unidentifiable. Henry had been smelling it ever since he entered the forest in the wee hours last night.

The smell of secrets.

"Goddamnit!" Henry uttered breathlessly, stumbling over a log and coming to a painful stop, grabbing his knee. His joint was trumpeting in pain. He looked through the foliage and saw the cop car being swallowed by the trees, vanishing into the deeper woods. "Dammit—dammit—dammit!"

The footpath ahead of him curved to the left through a cluster of hemlocks and then corrupted into a series of natural steps formed by exposed tendons of roots and jagged shelves of limestone. The steps led up a limestone rise. Henry limped over to the base of the steps, and then paused to catch his breath. "Jesus, what am I doing out here?" he muttered softly, and could not, for the life of him, find a satisfactory answer.

He had been creeping around the forest since three A.M., searching for Sarah, or a sign that she had been here, or any clue that might help Henry understand her past. The battery in his flashlight had sapped out around four, and by the time predawn had begun to burn off the darkness, Henry's arthritis had burst into full flame. To make matters worse, he still wasn't sure if he had located the red pine forest or not; oh, sure, there were pine trees aplenty, but they all looked alike to Henry. And even though Mr. McMasters had given Henry explicit directions, Henry had gotten lost the moment he had entered the deep woods. The problem was the denseness of the forest. The trees and foliage scraped the sky, tall and thick and opaque, and even in the glow of morning light, it was as dark as a coal mine.

But then, only a few minutes ago, Henry had come upon a faint cloud of mist hanging in the branches by a dry creek bed. As he cautiously approached, it became clear that the mist was coming from an overturned vehicle, still idling softly in the fog of its own vapors. A pickup truck, crumpled and shattered. The driver had been lying halfway out the window, dead, his spine twisted and his face livid. Several sets of footsteps had been clearly visible, snaking off through the mud. And somehow Henry had just known it had something to do with Sarah.

"What now, Kimosabe?" he muttered to himself, gazing up the shelf of limestone. *Might as well climb,* he thought. *You've come this far, and you might find a better view of the surrounding landscape up there in the scrub.*

He started up the root-steps, his sore knees complaining all the way. Despite the damp chill, he was sweating like a hog beneath the layers of his denim jacket, sweater, and chambray shirt. He hadn't had anything to eat in almost eighteen hours, and he was getting dizzy as hell; but he kept climbing steadily upward. He told himself it was guilt. Guilt was making him continue obsessively onward, guilt for making such a mess of Sarah's situation, guilt for acting so unprofessionally. But deep down, he knew his motivation was much simpler, much more primal. He loved this woman. And he was dying inside, dying in tiny increments, dying a little bit more with each passing moment Sarah was out there, alone with the monster inside her, alone in the void of her past, alone in the red prison.

It took Henry nearly five minutes to make it to the top of the limestone rise. When he reached the plateau, he lifted himself up on weak knees and gazed across an overgrown thicket of juneberry and bluestem grass, and he started feeling a tide of emotion rising in him.

The meadow was like a natural entrance to a thick corridor of pines, their trunks choked with undergrowth and vines, rioting with color. Deep scarlet creepers twined around the bark, maroon and gold maple leaves festooning every limb. And the giant primeval pines, their geometrically spaced trunks like the masts of great ships, were docked all in a row, their branches feathered with wine-dark needles, spreading off into the distance as far as Henry could see.

The red prison.

Henry walked into the mouth of the forest, tears in his eyes.

"Sarah?" he called into the void, unable to come up with any other response to the vastness of the woods. His voice rang for a moment, the strangest sort of echo Henry had ever heard. A ghostly reverberance, as though the forest were one great cosmic schizophrenic, and Henry's voice was just another vocalization in its wild, feral brain. Something to be ignored, like the endless birth-sex-death-decay cycle of its denizens. The echo died. And the silence that followed was the worst silence Henry had ever experienced. It was glacial, and it made Henry reel at the gigantic emptiness of it.

"SSAARRRRRRAAHH!"

All at once Henry's voice had been reduced to the terror-song of a child, a frightened child, alone in the darkness, lost, calling out for his mommy. He dropped to his ass then, drained of his last reserves of rational thought. All bets were off. Henry had tasted the cruelty of the red pines, the unblinking, stoic gaze of those dark trees, and now he could never go back to his safe, professional world; he could never return to his objective practice. He'd just become an inmate in the red prison, and he was going to break Sarah out of this hellish place if it was the last thing he ever did.

He wailed her name one final time, and now there was more than a little madness in his voice.

IV

"—Sarah—?"

A voice long ago forgotten, yet horribly familiar.

Eyes popping open, the first sensations coalescing around her like a funeral shroud. *(What was that voice?)* The damp ground was on her back, the smell of pine decay in her crusted nostrils, skin shivering, crawling, maybe with insects, maybe tattoos *(that voice)*, sharp pains in her lower back and shoulders, breasts extremely tender, mouth as dry and cold as cement (that damned gravelly voice), and the shapes above her, the steeples of red pines rising up into the overcast morning.

She tried to sit up, but her back was wrenched. She turned her head and saw that she was lying in the weeds smack-dab in the heart of the red pine forest. *Okay, we're here,* she thought groggily, *home at last, where's the revelation? Where's the burning bush?* The Escape Artist was silent, dormant inside her, maybe injured, maybe biding his time until he could kill her properly.

Whose voice was that?

She looked down at her belly, her ripped and scorched clothing, the scars on her hands, the holes in her sleeves still sticky with her own blood. The wounds underneath the fabric were puckered and dried, and she remembered the horrors of the previous night, the struggle for her body, the struggle to emerge and stop the killing. The sensation had been a lot like drowning, like wrestling herself out from under a powerful wave and nearly coming up for air, and then getting engulfed again. But the worst had been the flash-frame glimpses she had gotten of the killing, her own hands like the wooden limbs of a puppet, strangling people, torturing those young boys.

"You bastard!" Sarah blurted, and grabbed handfuls of her peppery gray hair, as though she would be able to literally tear the incarnate from her head. "Get out of me!" She rolled across the weeds and smashed her face against the ground until she was eating crabgrass and smelling the rich stench of earth and shrieking, "GET OUT!"

She climbed to her feet and stood on wobbly legs, the rage coursing through her. "Bastard!" she swung at the air, as if fighting a ghost. She kicked divots in the ground and tore wisps of hair from her scalp. "Get out—you fucking bastard—get-out-of-me-NOW—NOW!"

Tripping on a log, she fell facefirst into a clump of ironweed.

The tears came on a hot surge of pain, and she curled into a fetal position, the sobs rocking through her. Tears streamed down the side of her face, dripping into the weeds, irrigating the scrub with agony. And she convulsed for several minutes like that, helpless and quivering in the dirt, until something struck her, an odd sensation, a mingling of strong odors and textures and sounds and feelings, a nexus of sensory overload.

She caught her breath, and she rose to a sitting position. Her chest was still hitching with after-sobs, but she was feeling something much worse now; it was pouring over her on a wave of earthen smells and cool air and rough spindly weeds.

A memory long repressed, blossoming now like a horrible black flower bursting up through the weeds . . . *weeds.*

Weed.

(that voice—)

V

"Sarah?"

The voice came from the depths of the bungalow, soft yet gravelly, like a man who was perpetually wakening from a long troubled sleep.

"Mr. Weed?" Sarah was moving cautiously through the dining room, hugging her schoolbooks to her chest. She had turned twelve only last month and was still a bit nervous

about being alone in a grown bachelor's home. But then again, Mr. Weed was not your ordinary adult. He was, without a doubt, the dreamiest teacher at Arkham Middle, with his deep green eyes and wavy red hair and muscular arms. And the way he recited poetry with the dramatic gestures and the graceful movements, and that thing he had about Harry Houdini. It was mysterious and it was neat and it made Sarah feel all quivery whenever she was around him. And besides, Mr. Weed had personally invited her over here after class yesterday in order to be tutored on iambic trimeter.

"In here, Sarah," the voice called, drifting out from within an arched passageway.

Sarah started toward the sound of the voice, still a bit reticent and tingling with nervous tension. She passed a series of framed artifacts on the wall. Yellowed photos of Houdini at various ages, their creases ironed out and mounted in ornate old frames. NO PRISON CAN HOLD HIM! Antique padlocks and ropes encased in glass. BURIED ALIVE! Publicity sheets and show bills. DEATH-DEFYING FEATS! Posters and lobby cards and news clippings. SEE THE MASTER MYSTIFIER CHEAT DEATH! Each detail seared itself into Sarah's brain as she crossed the threshold of the archway and headed down the narrow corridor to the bedroom.

The bedroom? It didn't seem right somehow. Why would Mr. Weed be meeting Sarah in the bedroom? She wondered about it as she strode along the worn carpet runner which covered the scarred hardwood of the hallway. Maybe he was making some kind of point, the way he always did in class. He would do some outrageous act, like sticking his tongue out and making farting noises to demonstrate onomatopoeia, or he'd break one of the windows with the corner of his Emily Dickinson Reader to demonstrate free form. That must be why he was calling her into his bedroom right now, making her skin rash with goose bumps.

She reached the door at the end of the hallway, which was half ajar, and peered inside the bedroom.

"C'mon in, sweetheart," a voice said, and Sarah gazed around the room for a moment. There was no sign of the teacher. Only an enormous burlap sack levitating over an unmade bed. The sack seemed to be connected to a bolt in the ceiling. There were other bolts, and thin chains hanging from the ceiling like spindly lengths of Spanish moss.

"Oh—" Sarah put her hand to her mouth, finally recognizing the purpose of the sack.

Weed was inside the burlap. Hanging upright. Hands behind his back, chains wrapping his midsection, he peered through a hole in the top of the sack and stared at Sarah with wet eyes. The burlap was secured to the ceiling through a worn leather girdle around Weed's shoulders, and Weed swayed slightly with each breath. He looked like a giant baby. "C'mere, sweetheart," he murmured, and smiled enigmatically.

Sarah didn't even notice how his speech was slurred and his movements were strangely lethargic, or the fact that there were pill bottles and an empty fifth of Jim Beam on his bedside table. She didn't notice any of that stuff. All she heard was the word "sweetheart." The great and powerful Mr. Weed had called Sarah "sweetheart." It put a flutter in her stomach and made her blood feel as though it were vibrating.

"Closer," he said.

Sarah moved closer.

"Closer still."

"Are you doing a trick?" Sarah asked, pressing her knees against the edge of the bed, her face only inches away from his dangling torso.

He told her he was doing one of Houdini's classic escapes.

"I brought all the poetry books you asked for," Sarah said. "All five of them."

"That's lovely," he said, pronouncing the word "lovely" in a way that only Mr. Weed was able. Other men never said the word "lovely" like that. It made Sarah's fingertips tingle as though they had been asleep and were waking up.

"You going to show me an escape?" Sarah asked, smiling nervously down at the floor. She had heard rumors that Mr. Weed did tricks for students, but she had never really believed it. Now she was trembling with excitement. If only Linda and Wendy and the gang down at the Dixie Café could see Sarah now! Thank God she had worn her best corduroy skirt today, and her new saddle shoes, and a thick sweater. Sarah's mom didn't like her wearing sweaters. Sweaters always made Sarah's breasts look more grown-up, especially since they had already swollen into D-cups. But Sarah wanted to appear as sophisticated as possible around Mr. Weed, so she had smuggled the sweater into her book bag that morning.

" 'O fan of white silk,' " Weed recited down at her, swaying beatifically. "You are a vision today, my darling."

Sarah frowned. Something wasn't right. Something about the way he was talking to her, the way he was gazing down at her with his thickly lidded eyes. It was making her feel kind of ooky inside. "Why don't you come down from there?" she said finally, trying to get him out of this strange state. "And we can, you know, read some poetry or something."

Weed looked at her another moment.

"Wha—?" Sarah felt a stinging sensation on her hands. She glanced down and saw something tightening around her wrists. Dark nylon straps. "What are you doing?" Sarah asked, still dazed and somewhat giggly.

Somehow, Weed's hands had worked themselves through holes in the sides of the burlap and were now doing strange things to Sarah. Binding her. Sarah's heart started to race. Her mouth went dry. Weed was pulling Sarah's wrists upward, lacing them through a chain connected to the ceiling. This wasn't right. This wasn't right at all.

"Wait," Sarah uttered, the giggle evaporating. "What are you doing?"

"*Relax, honey,*" Weed murmured, working Sarah's arms over her head, pulling another length of strap from inside the bag and binding Sarah's shoulders, binding her waist, binding her arms, binding her spirit.

"*What . . . are you . . .*" Sarah was having trouble breathing, the straps were so tight all of a sudden, digging into her wrists and her shoulder blades, yanking her up like a side of beef in a packing plant. It felt as though her ribs were about to collapse, her breasts straining the front of her sweater.

Weed's hand came up and cradled her neck, gently, tenderly, and it made her shiver. "*It's okay, sweetheart,*" he said. "*Look at me.*"

She looked at him.

"*We're going to perform the levitation trick together,*" he explained softly, caressing her neck. "*But in order for it to work, you must concentrate.*"

Sarah's eyes welled with tears, and she nodded, and she swallowed a gulp of icy cold terror. Then she closed her eyes and began to pray.

"*That's good,*" Weed murmured, "*concentrate . . . concentrate and relax . . . the elemental components of every escape . . . concentration and relaxation . . . very good, good.*"

Sarah opened her eyes.

Her mouth fell open, the shock flooding her system. She tried to rear back, but his hand was rock-steady around her neck, holding her in place, urging her to look at the enormous erection which was sprouting through a rip in the burlap. It hung weightless at about the level of her collarbone; and it was hideous that such a thing could belong to Mr. Weed. Sarah had never seen a penis before, let alone an angry one. It was like a splash of turpentine in her face. "*Why?*" she blurted, trying to wriggle out of his grasp.

He tightened his grip and started urging her face toward the erection. "*Relax, sweetheart, and taste all that life has to offer.*"

Sarah started to struggle, but her bonds were steel-tight, and the chain kept her moored to the ceiling, and Weed's *hand was like an iron pincer around her neck, forcing her face forward, forward, toward his fleshy purple knob, this man-object, and soon she was close enough to smell the salty, Elmer's glue smell, the tip of its head glistening, and Sarah started to whimper, tears scalding her eyes, and the hand was tightening, and finally it shoved her mouth down upon the glans.*

She gagged.

"Relaxation!" he barked at her.

Now Sarah was in the arms of a monster. He shoved her mouth up and down on his thing, and it tasted like a warm bloated finger, gagging her, lubricated by the salt of her own tears and his presemen, and everything seemed to go all screwy then, like a Keystone comedy nightmare, all the film running too fast through the projector, until all at once, the pressure sagged, and her mouth was empty again.

There was a ripping sound.

Sarah opened her eyes just in time to see Weed emerging from the burlap like a moth from a chrysalis. He was pink and glistening with sweat, completely nude, and he reached up with a wild clawing motion, releasing a cable snap, freeing the two of them from the ceiling hooks.

Sarah plummeted.

They bounced onto the bedsprings as though they were on a trampoline, as though they were playing a game, a horrible game, and Sarah tried to call out, call for help, but Weed's salty wet fingers were pressing over her mouth. She felt his free hand clawing off her sweater, tugging her bra up and over her breasts. He got himself wedged between her legs, and he tore away her underwear as though it were paper tissue. Sarah went a little crazy then, wriggling and kicking and screaming. And Weed suddenly made a fist, reared back, and struck her. Just once in the mouth. Hard.

The blow knocked her silly for a moment.

Then she surrendered.

More than anything else, it was the symbolism that made her submit. The menacing familiarity, the promise of more

pain if she kept fighting, and the bracing, ugly lesson that
Sarah had learned from her biological father, as well as a
succession of stepfathers. That it doesn't pay to fight; that
fighting only prolongs the horror.

Weed took immediate advantage. He entered her with
moderate difficulty, forcing his peg into her dry cleft, and he
thrust once, twice, three times, and Sarah felt things snapping inside her, tearing apart and seeping out of her, the tissue of her hymen, the tissue of her sanity, the tissue of her
entire world. Weed kept thrusting, and thrusting, and thrusting, until he spasmed, and Sarah felt the hot throb of his seed
in her.

A moment later, Weed threw her off the bed.

Sarah landed in a heap of tears and blood, her lip
swelling, her legs slick with fluids, the shock washing
through her like a cold acid bath. But Mr. Weed wasn't finished yet, dear God, he wasn't finished by a long shot, because Sarah felt his hands on her shoulders again, yanking
her up into a sitting position, Sarah's bare, sore breasts
pressing against the bed, her lungs heaving for air, the
straps digging into her flesh. Weed gripped her head in a
death vise, his fingers pressing inward on either jaw, forcing
her mouth open, forcing his moist, bloody erection into her
mouth, thrusting again, and again, and again, so hard now
that Sarah thought he was going to ram his member through
the roof of her mouth, gagging her, strangling the life out of
her.

"Gonna fuck your skull, sweetheart," he hissed in that
satiny strained voice, and Sarah barely heard it above the
loud, watery choking-strokes. But she started thinking about
it, she started thinking about what he was saying between the
violent groaning thrusts.

"Gonna fuck your brain—gonna fuck that little gifted
brain of yours—fuck that sweet little gifted brain of yours—
fuck it good and hard—FUCK IT GOOD!—"

He popped off a second time, and Sarah felt the scalding
spurt of his sperm on her tonsils.

*Then he let her slip away, and Sarah collapsed to the floor
again.*

*Sarah lay there for several moments, sobbing into the nap
of the throw rug, trying to breathe through her mouth, but
her throat was clogged with the bloody paste of Weed's
semen, and the dank stench of the rug and the incense smells
were overpowering, and Sarah started coughing fitfully. Her
hands were still over her head, her shoulders and wrists
going numb. And then, all at once, Weed's hands were on
her again, yanking her upward, and she flinched.*

*She gaped up at him. He was sitting on the edge of the bed
now, naked as a hairless ape, and he had his benevolent
teacher's expression on his face, that paternal smile, and
Sarah felt her heart racing in her chest, because she knew
beyond a shadow of a doubt that the worst was yet to come.*

He began to softly speak.

The worst part.

VI

"The worst part," Sarah blurted out suddenly, breaking the
stillness. She was on her hands and knees in the shadows of
the red pines, her tears dripping on the leaves. She sprang to
her feet, heart thundering in her chest.

The long-repressed memory had leaped into her mind like
a demon dog breaking its leash, and now it was rampaging
inside her mind, all growls and flashing fangs, and Sarah
started stumbling back the way she had come. Sun strobing
in her face, feet sucking through mud in which no human
foot had stepped in decades, she was lost. Lost. Lost in every
conceivable way. She was remembering most of the secret
horror now, the worst part of rape, the way Weed had looked
down at her from the edge of the bed and had calmly explained the situation to her, how he would kill her if she ever
told anybody about their little tryst, how he would come after

her and find her and kill her, how he would track her to the ends of the earth if he had to.

If she ever told anybody.

Get outta here!

Sarah sidestepped a deadfall and stumbled through the undergrowth, brambles clawing at her ripped pants legs, thorns clinging to her moccasins. She had to get out of this horrible place, this place of dead memories. She was rubbing the imaginary stink from her hands, rubbing the wetness from her mouth, as though the memories had seeped out of her flesh. But she couldn't get it off, she couldn't rub off the smell of Weed's semen, the smell of her own blood, she couldn't rub off the memory. It clung to her hands like tree sap.

Weed's attack and subsequent threat had changed Sarah's destiny. From the moment she had stumbled home from that hideous little bungalow on that fateful afternoon, quickly taking a shower to eradicate all the evidence before Jessie got home, Sarah had become a different soft of girl. She had turned inward, developed neurotic habits, experienced chronic nightmares and flights of dark fancy. She had started believing that Weed had indeed planted some kind of virus in her skull, some kind of cancer. And the rest of her life became a string of denials, fear, and disgust. But there was still a dark place inside her, a place stirred by the recollection of the rape, a black hole, something that happened in the months after the rape, a memory so deeply repressed that its very possibility felt like a dark wind swirling through Sarah's soul.

If she could only get out of these woods . . .

"Jesus Christ, please!" She realized she was moving in circles now, flailing at the low-hanging branches in her face, gasping at the overwhelming odors. Nothing looked familiar and everything looked familiar. She was on a hopeless loop, stumbling through the deep woods of her childhood, and the panic was just making it worse, as though the memories were seeping out of her now in blips and flashes of sounds and odors and sensations.

(the box)

She tripped on a root and stumbled to the ground, landing on her hands and knees and gasping for breath. She could feel the woods changing around her, the tall masts of pine bark rising and curling over her like the ribs of a great black beast, a monstrous entity closing down on her. The sun was draining away, a dark gray canopy lowering over her. And waves of dread poured over her, so powerful they stole her breath away. Was she changing again? Was she changing for the final time, doomed to starve out here, a monstrous killer forever wandering this medieval forest? She winced at the pain in her belly, and then, all at once, she opened her eyes, and she froze.

A smell.

It was very faint, and was drifting in and out of detectability on the breeze, but it was there nonetheless. A pungent fishy aroma. Sarah picked it up, latched on to it, and felt the tiny hairs on her arms stiffen. A carousel of half-formed impressions and memories swirled through that odor, that rotting swamp smell. Sarah rose to her feet and took a deep breath, feeling her flesh crawl with memories. The door to the black hole was opening in her mind; and she could feel the pressure giving way inside her like a leak in the hull of a boat. *This is it,* she thought gravely, finding a certain strength all of a sudden, a strength she never knew that she even had. *This is why I came here, goddamnit—to face these fucking demons.*

Wiping the tears from her cheek, she started toward the source of the smell.

It took her several minutes to negotiate the thick underbrush. The trees seemed to be thinning. Sarah could see the timbers clearing through a delicate lattice of juneberries and vines, almost as if the land simply dropped out from under the world. And the scent of fish and decay rose, and Sarah started breathing quickly, her breath pulsing now in puffs of white vapor, her flesh rashing with gooseflesh, her tattoos tingling, sensing that this was ground zero for her, that this was her deadly Rosetta stone. She swam through the foliage, flailing at the shriveled huckleberries and tendrils of brown-shrub, finally emerging through a break in the forest.

Onto the banks of a pristine little lake.

"Oh, Jesus." She whimpered softly to herself as she gazed across the smooth emerald-brown surface of the lake, her voice seeming to rise several octaves in her throat, tightening like a quivering string. It was the sound of her own voice as a child, the regression spreading from cell to cell, tissue to tissue, like wildfire. Memories were flooding her. *"The secret place,"* she muttered, remembering the aftermath of the rape.

The secret . . .

This little spring-fed lake had been the end of the line for Sarah, the farthest point from her life of pain and agony in the months following the rape. And standing before it once again, seeing the way the afternoon sun glinted off its rippling surface, she suddenly remembered the real reason she had run away into the woods, the real reason she had come here, the real reason she had buried the rape in the deepest soil of her brain.

It all came back to her like a corpse bursting up through the grave dirt on a Halloween afternoon, an unstoppable corpse, the way the first month after the rape had passed in an agonizing blur of numbness, with no feelings, no hope, and *no period.* Sarah had been menstruating for over a year at that point and was still keeping close track, and when the second month passed and still no period, she had started worrying and reading books on the subject and silently praying that it was just something called "hysterical reaction," but when the third month passed and still no period, and waves of nausea were gripping her every few days, and an odd heavy feeling was building down around her pelvis, she real-

ized the nightmare was real. She was pregnant. good God in
heaven she was pregnant, and she was so scared that Mr.
Weed would find out and kill her and kill her baby, or that
Jessie would find out and make her have an abortion, that
she couldn't tell anyone. So she had packed a rucksack full
of supplies, full of tins of corned beef and cans of peaches
and bags of rice and a hunting knife and a hammer and
matches and things that would help her survive, and she ran
away, vanished into the woods.

To the secret place, to the banks of this secret mountain
lake, to quietly watch her life shrivel and bleed away, her
baby disintegrating inside her, her body hemorrhaging out
every hope and dream in dark gouts of fluid between her legs
like some kind of horrible cataclysmic Catholic guilt ritual.

"Jesus . . ." Sarah uttered, the last dead leaves of autumn
swirling around her as she gazed across the shoreline. She
wasn't even consciously aware that she had fallen to her
knees.

A solitary supplicant at the darkest of masses.

VII

Gene Krupa was playing a number in Frank Moon's head
that he had never heard before as he prowled through the deep
woods, a thunderstorm of chaos, metallic, violent, scattershot
drumbeats fighting each other, and it was driving Frank fucking insane. BIDDIP-BUP-DAP-BADOOOMMMM—and this
time, there were no Walkman headphones, only the sound of
Frank's angry march through the sticks, his Lagerfeld shoes
spackled with mud, and the pandemonium in his brain.

He approached an abandoned campsite.

What the fuck is this mess? he wondered as he scanned his
sawed-off twenty-gauge across the mound of black earth, the
still-smoldering fire, and all the Halloween googaws that
some doped-up platoon of high-school kids must have put up
for fun and games. Where the hell were the kids? Off soap-

ing windows somewhere? Making out in the bush? Getting
some bush in the bush? Frank flinched at the plastic skeletons hanging above him, their nooses hooked to tree limbs,
the rubber spiders and bats dangling nearby, the jack-o'-
lanterns lying strewn about the ground, caved in on their
sides like victims of cancer surgery, and Frank started superimposing in his mind all the carnage he had seen over the
years, the homicide victims hanging up there in the trees,
their livid tongues lolling out, their bulging bloodied eyes
winking at him, the severed body parts lying about the dirt,
the ghosts of an entire career of grieving family members
gathered around the dying embers, wailing, their accusatory
gazes leaping up at Frank.

BIDDIP-DAP-BOOM-DUP-DUP-BIDIP-BOOOOOOM-
MMMMM!

Frank cocked the gun and stormed through the fire, kicking sparks and marching toward the denser section of woods
on the far side of the camp. He entered the woods like an
avenger, like Father Death, swinging his pump-action killing
scythe and pummeling his way through the undergrowth.

After Frank had been swimming through the forest for an
undetermined length of time, something caught his attention
in the distance, filtering through the webbing of undergrowth, which was now turning cobalt-blue in the cool dying
light of the afternoon. It was a sparkling diamond-dot, several hundred yards away, wavering in and out of focus like a
ghost. At first Frank thought it might be another campfire, or
a light, but the closer he got, cutting through the foliage with
the barrel of the shotgun like a snubnosed machete, the more
certain he became it was water.

A lake.

BAMMMMM-BOOOOMMMMMM-BIDDIP-BIP-
BOOOOMMMMMM—the cacophony rose in Frank's mind
as he approached a natural clearing, and he smelled the fish-
belly odor, and he saw a figure kneeling less than forty feet
away on the sandy leaf-carpeted shoreline. KA-
BOOOOOOOMMMMMM! His heart started beating its own

tattoo, adding to the din, his blood pumping syncopation in his temples, fingers tingling with the killing-ache.

It was *her*. The object of Frank's obsession, the source of all his scattered, disorganized, chaotic feelings. The fucking *perp*. There she was, just sitting there, as though she were waiting for Christ to return from the black waters of the little hidden lake. And Frank swallowed back the urge to cry out, to shriek obscenities at her, to charge her. Instead, he cautiously moved to the mouth of the foliage and stood on the threshold of the clearing, slowly cocking the pump mechanism so that she wouldn't hear the clang, and judging the distance to be about thirty-five feet, he was close enough to smell her sweat, and Good God, he had a great bead on her now.

Frank lifted the shotgun. Aimed it. Gazed down the sighting grooves at the target. *(What the fuck was she doing—quivering there by the lake, looking as though she were about to puke?)* Procedure told Frank to holler a warning, get her on the ground quickly, get the cuffs on her quickly and get her under control. *(What the fuck was she doing?)* Procedure told him to treat the suspect with respectful caution, shouting out firm demands, acting quickly before the complexion of power had a chance to shift. Procedure told Frank a lot of things, but the drumming was thundering in his head now, and the suspect was vulnerable, and he was all alone with the monster, and he was holding the death-ray that would destroy this freak, this bringer of chaos, this shambler from hell.

A sound, off in the foliage to Frank's right, like static in the transmission between Frank's brain and his tingling trigger finger.

Frank sucked in a breath and held it, staring down the flat grooves directly at the woman named Sarah, his hand sweating on the hardwood grip, his shoulder aching from the press of the stock. He was thinking about procedure, how procedure called for a simple disabling shot to take down a potentially dangerous suspect, a shot in the leg or the knee or the hamstring. But the free-form music was thundering in Frank's head, BIDDAPADDIDAP, and he was dying from the chaos, the inexplicable, the pandemonium, BADOOOM-MMM, and he had to stop the disorder, the confusion, the jumble in his head, BADDABADDABOOOOMMMM, and he was flashing back to the FBI workshop he had taken, the talk of head shots, the absolute knockdown power of a head shot, BIDDIP, the certainty of head shots, BUDDABAP, the only way to put a stop to this monster.

The sound was approaching off Frank's right flank, footsteps, coming at him.

Frank aimed at Sarah's skull.

"NO!"

The voice burst from the forest, barely penetrating Frank's veil of concentration, as Frank held his breath for one last instant, aiming directly at Sarah's brain, and finally snapping the trigger.

BOOMMMM-BOOOMMM—KABOOOOOOMMMM-MMM

The sound was colossal, an immense muzzle-flash blast that seemed to shatter the air. Frank jerked at the recoil, his eyebrows singed, his gaze fixed on Sarah long enough to see the side of her head erupt, flashing red, as if someone had instantly peeled away her scalp. Bloody bone and brain matter ejaculated through the air, and her body lurched furiously forward as though blown by a violent gust across the shoreline.

Sarah careened at the edge of the bank, hit the water, and sank like a stone.

"NNNNOO!"

Frank spun toward the footsteps at the precise moment the enormous body arrived.

It was like being struck by a freight train, and Frank whiplashed backward so hard he was jerked right out of his Lagerfelds. His shotgun pinwheeled through the air, and Frank landed hard on his lower spine, biting his tongue and expelling bloody spittle. The grizzly bear of a man landed directly on Frank, squeezing the breath out of him like toothpaste from a tube. Frank yelped, and he gasped, and he writhed, and he struggled in vain to see through his watery vision.

Henry Decker was hovering over him, straddling him and blocking out the sun with ham-hock fists and a mottled, grass-stained, teary face. "No!" Henry uttered once, his mouth contorted by blind rage and shock, before bringing his fists down on Frank, the barrage of a wrecking ball.

"No—NO—NO—NO—NO!"

Frank felt the first few blows of the battering ram, rattling his molars, cracking facial bones, raising sparks and pangs in Frank's darkening field of vision, and Frank screamed and flailed, and tried to wriggle free, but Henry was out of control now, and Henry was former All Big Ten, and Henry was insane, and soon Frank Moon went numb, and the blows became like mallet strikes, driving Frank farther and farther into the ground, until all that was left was the black earth, and the soothing silence, and the end of the chaos in his head.

And that was okay with Frank Moon.

VIII

Henry released his grip on Moon, letting the unconscious cop collapse into the dirt.

Then he rose to his feet, head swimming with noise, and whirled toward the water. He saw Sarah's body out there in the shallows of the lake, facedown in a cloud of dark red matter, sinking, gently twitching. And the razor panic slashed through Henry's insides and held him paralyzed for a moment, watching his future hopes and dreams and love sinking into the black oblivion. Then he found his voice, and he wailed her name one last time, as though the sheer force of his pain would bring her drifting back.

The echo that bounced off the far hills and returned to Henry was the cry of a madman.

Henry stumbled across the shoreline.

By the time he reached the water's edge and lumbered into the shallows, Sarah's body had vanished, leaving only a trace of thin bubbles where she originally submerged. "No-GOD-no!" Henry clamored through the water, his gaze riveted to the bubbles, his arms pumping wildly, his boots bogging down in the soft silt beneath him.

Soon he was flailing impotently, getting nowhere, wailing garbled, inarticulate cries at the silence, splashing useless armfuls of water clouded by Sarah's blood.

As the delicate little bubbles dwindled away to nothing.

12

Magic and Blood

I

A needlepoint of light in the cold blackness.

At first, it's so infinitesimal, so inert, that it barely seems perceived by any consciousness, a distant star whose light has already flashed out billions of years ago, but whose existence is still measured by its image reaching earth. Then things start happening to the pinpoint, a chain of events so intricate that they first appear to transpire over a great length of time, but in reality they occur in the blink of an eye. The dot grows luminous, bloated and swollen, expanding into a tiny chip of matter, a diamond chip glimmering in the cosmos, which in turn grows into a large hunk of brilliant white, which in turn reveals other chunks of jagged broken white around it, the jagged pieces of a little ornate head, the head of a china doll, its little ruby pout, long-lashed eyes, and tiny ears lying scattered across the blackness.

Something begins tugging at the pieces, a magnetic force, drawing the fragments closer, tugging at the jagged puzzled pieces, pulling them together, mending the ragged shards and rough edges of bone-white, sucking all the splintered glass together, until the doll head begins reconstituting itself, the lips turning upright, the eyes leaping back into place, the glossy black hair flipping into position, and the very fabric of the china stitching itself back together, stronger than ever.

The face begins to animate, like bone-white milk glass turning liquid, transforming into flesh, pink flesh, pink Technicolor cheeks and sapphire eyes and scarlet lips, and the face becomes familiar, the face becomes Esther Williams in the classic 1944 musical Bathing Beauty, *and Esther is underwater, and it's the big finale, the spectacular water ballet sequence, the one choreographed to the music of "The Blue Danube Waltz," and all the aquatic chorus girls are circling her now, and the lights are turning blue, and Esther does her spectacular spins, and the water fountains and curls sensually overhead in rhythm with her spins, in rhythm with the music, in rhythm with the bones mending and the tissue rehydrating and the tendons reconstituting, and each time she spins, her body gets stronger, and stronger, and soon she is one with the underwater blue, the color of space, the color of grief, the color of endless depths, the color of secrets, and she smiles for the final money shot, the final shot of the picture.*

She opens her eyes.

Underwater.

II

"Aahhhhhhhhhhhhvvmmmmmph—!"

The instant she opened her mouth to cry out, to gasp, to breathe, she gulped a mouthful of cold swamp water, and she slammed her lips shut.

Blinking fitfully, she struggled to hold her breath in this dark green rheum. Up was down, and down was up, and the world had gone icy dark, blue-green, and soupy, and she had no idea how she had gotten down here in this underwater nightmare, she only knew that she had been sitting on the shore when there had been a loud pop in her ears, and the feeling that someone had slapped the back of her head, and the next thing she knew, she was in the lake, flailing weight-less, sinking fast, arms and legs akimbo, the cool fingers working in her skull, sealing up the icy leak in her head, caulking the cracks and fissures even as she frantically pad-dled. And in these early panicky moments, she could feel her bone-cap melding back together, itching underneath, itching deep in her brain, itching to get out of this water torture cell.

Then she hit bottom.

At first it felt as though she had landed on a membrane of very old, wrinkled flesh, so soft and yielding and moist that she nearly broke through it. Then she started panicking, jerk-ing about, stirring up the silt, realizing that she was at least thirty or forty feet below the surface, and the rays of sun were barely penetrating the gray haze, and she was out of air, and she was out of time.

Panic seized her then, starting a surge of helpless flailing and silent gurgling cries for help. She had experienced this kind of panic before in the motel shower stall, hog-tied to the ceiling, bound and gagged and left for dead. But this time, there was only one way out, and that was *up*, and Sarah had completely lost any sense of direction, and her lungs felt as though they were bursting into flames, and her recently healed brain reeled and pitched, and she was dying, and she knew it, and she still couldn't find her way back to light. And she started visualizing the Munchkins pumping air into her lungs, her bloodstream, her brain, tiny little pumps in the darkness all around her, keeping her alive, and the visualiza-tion began to work, an invisible bellows infusing her blood-stream with oxygen.

She began to calm.

That was when her toe scraped the smooth, sandy surface of the chest.

It was as though electric current had bolted up her leg, and she suddenly went limp, the shock washing through her. The last thought to cross her oxygen-starved mind was, *What in*

God's name is that? And she fell slowly to the silt, twisting around with her last ounce of strength and awareness, and she tried to see through the pea soup.

The object sat about six inches from her face, buried in the watery sediment. Man-made, covered with moss and rust and a patina of age, it was a rectangular wooden chest. The cracks and holes had widened, and the wood had softened to mulch over the years of being underwater, but even in the gloomy fog it was obvious that it was an old tackle box, probably abandoned by some lone fisherman eons ago, forgotten, forgotten by everyone in the world, everyone except the parasite inside Sarah.

The box.

The tackle box.

Something snapped inside Sarah then. Might have been the psychosis of oxygen deprivation, or some kind of purified hallucinatory state. Might have even been the final twitch of a death throe, the same kind of twitch that paramedics often whisper about at accident scenes, the kind of energy surge that enables mothers to lift cars off of children or schoolteachers to walk through fire unharmed to rescue kids from a burning building. But regardless of the physics, Sarah lurched through the soup, and clawed at the wooden chest, and tried her damnedest to wrench it from the clay.

The box was like a moist saltine; it came apart in her hands, collapsing into a cloud of wood strew. But something bubbled out of its dark center, something pale, worn smooth from the years of water seepage, curious fish, and hungry parasites. It rose out of the soup like a miniature little flock of doves. And Sarah saw it, and her heart leaped into her mouth.

(IN THE BOX!)

She reared away from the madness.

Had she spun in any other direction, she most certainly would have drowned then, going to her watery grave with her secrets intact, her legend unresolved. But she got lucky. She happened to spin in the direction of the shallows, and the sheer horror of what she had seen rising out of that box drove her far enough forward that she was able to grab a handful of the stony sandbar before succumbing to the water in her legs.

(INSIDE THE BOX! *THE BOX!*)

the box the box the-box-the-box-the-box-the-box-the-box-theboxtheboxthebox

Everything went gray.

Something was moving through the water behind her, a shadow, a fish, the muffled sounds of a voice spewing bubbles, something grabbing at her, big fingers clutching at her sodden top, and then tugging. Tugging. Tugging. She began to slide backward, up the sandbar shelf, toward the surface, toward the green light, and then—

Sound and light erupted in her face, and she tried to gasp, but her throat was paralyzed, her lungs full of lake water, and she felt her last blips of consciousness draining away. But wait, wait, somebody was dragging her toward the shallows, big hands and long strands of gray-brown hair, sopping wet, dragging her to safety, and Sarah's vision was already fading away when she finally identified the big man dragging her out of the mire.

It was Henry, big sweet old Henry.

She tried to pronounce his name with mute blue lips, but she couldn't make a sound. Didn't matter. Henry was too busy anyway, turning her over on her distended tummy, lifting her midsection with a jerk, and another jerk, forcing her to vomit, vomit out the water, heave it all out in pink foamy spumes, and the coughing, the watery coughing and gasping, and then everything was getting all syrupy and blurry. Sound and light seemed to evaporate away. Time seemed to bog down. And Sarah felt herself flipping onto her back, and Henry's powerful hands pressing down on her sternum in rhythmic thrusts, and his sweet lips on hers, shoving the breath of life into her lungs.

A moment later, Sarah was coughing air.

Henry cradled her head in his trembling hands. "You're—ohmyGod—you're okay," he muttered, dumbstruck. "It was Moon, Frank Moon, he shot you in the head—I saw it. Jesus, Sarah, Jesus, I saw it."

Sarah tried to speak again, but couldn't.

"Easy, easy, easy does it." Henry lifted her into a cold, damp embrace.

Sarah clung to him for several agonizing moments, sucking air, trying to get her voice back. The distant sounds of sirens could be heard drifting across the opposite banks of the lake. The clamor of four-wheel-drives blazing trails through the thickets. The sheriff's deputies were on their way, probably responding to the sound of Moon's shotgun blasts.

"Henry—I saw something—down there—I saw the—" She still couldn't make the words come out right. She took his face in her icy fingers, and she brought her lips to his. Their kiss was desperate and wounded, and Sarah could feel the grit of sand mingling with her mucus and tears. Henry's cheek felt warm against hers.

"I'm here," Henry said, and held her tight. "I'm never going to let this happen again."

"Henry—I saw—"

"It's okay," he said. "Take your time, Sarah. I'm here, I love you, and I'm never going to lea—"

His words seemed to freeze and crystallize in the air like delicate icicles.

Henry had noticed the objects out on the surface of the water, the pale and delicate objects floating there above the depths from which Sarah had come, the spot in which she had disrupted the ancient tackle box. And Sarah buried her face in Henry's damp shoulder, closing her eyes, not wanting to look. The sudden realization was a million centipedes shivering up Sarah's spine. And before Henry said a word, Sarah knew she hadn't hallucinated; the box was real. And the contents that had issued forth in the gloom were real.

And all the buried trauma that had festered in Sarah's subconscious over the last thirty years of her life was real as
well.

"My God," Henry uttered.

Sarah looked up.

The bones were scattered and floating on the ripples like
tiny gossamer tusks. Pale as alabaster, and delicate as whispers, they were perfectly smooth. Stripped clean by the algae
and the microbes. Sarah swallowed the fear, stood up, and
started walking across the shallows to take a closer look, her
feet sinking into the mire.

"Sarah? What's going on?" Henry was standing behind
her, wringing his hands, searching the woods for inevitable
flashing bubble lights. The sirens were rising, and the sound
of footsteps could be heard in the near distance, crunching
through undergrowth, approaching fast.

"My baby," Sarah whispered in a quivering voice, the
emotions welling in her, a strange feeling turning in her
belly, as though her womb were turning inside out.

"What did you say?" Henry asked.

Sarah didn't answer, but instead gazed out across the dark
ripples shimmering in the Halloween dawn. The tiny bones
were tossing on the gentle currents. Sarah saw the little
pelvis, so fragile it looked like a ball of brittle white thread.
She saw a leg. An arm. Another arm, and a miniature little
hand like a milky water spider. Sarah trudged closer, sinking
deeper into the mush, close enough to reach out and touch
the bones.

When she saw the tiny skull, she flinched.

A surge of memory shooting up her spinal cord to her
brain.

III

"AAAAAHHHHGG—!"
She bit down hard on the bitter bark, her legs splayed

*across the blanket of leaves beneath the makeshift lean-to.
She was close now, so close she could feel the red-hot poker
inside her, the contractions surging closer and closer. The
baby was coming, dear God, it was coming and Sarah was
only twelve and a half years old and she was alone in the
woods having a baby, and she was going to die from the
pain. It was too early, Sarah knew this much, only six
months, and the cramps were so unbearable she thought she
was going to rupture in half.*

*Another cramp seized her, squeezing another shriek from
her lungs.*

*"Please God make it come," she murmured, hyperventi-
lating, "make the baby come, make it come, make it come
and be alive, alive, alive!"*

*She reached down and rubbed more grease on her vagina,
feeling the fiery dilation. Still too damn small, too small for
the baby to crown. She frantically massaged in the grease,
the grease from a rabbit that she had killed and cooked the
night before. And she tried to breathe through the pain,
breathe just like she had read she was supposed to do. Sarah
was a resourceful girl. She had taken along a book on mid-
wifery and was trying her best to survive this secret hell on
her own. She had been living in the lean-to for nearly a
month, starving, living off the scrawny bluegills from the
lake and the wild huckleberries, but the baby had dropped
much too soon, and the nightmare had started late last night,
and now it was all happening too fast, and she was certain
that she was going to die and there was nothing she could do
about it.*

Then the hemorrhaging started.

*Blood seemed to gush out of her on a quickening of pain,
and Sarah screamed as she gazed down between her legs,
because the dark rich serum was pulsing out, blood-tainted
amniotic fluid, soaking the leaves, and the baby wouldn't
come, and Sarah knew this was the worst possible news, and
she reached down and shoved her fingers into her blazing
uterus, and her pelvis convulsed, and she wailed as she*

*rooted the baby's head from her perineum like a tuber from
the dark seeping earth.*

*Sarah didn't know how she got the baby out, because she
passed out then.*

*She awoke moments or minutes or hours later; Sarah
wasn't too sure how long. She was in a kind of catatonic
trance. The woods had changed color, turned inside out, like
a photographic negative glowing sickly shades of gray. The
baby lay dead in a brittle patch of dried blood and leaves, its
tiny premature face calmly set, its skin an ashy blue, the
color of cornflowers. A stillborn. Somehow Sarah had been
able to tear the umbilical off and get the infant covered in
rags, but the baby never had a chance.*

It was a boy.

*Madness swirled through Sarah's brain at the realization
that it was a boy. A boy. A lovely little boy. That knowledge
made her brain snap like a rubber band drawn too tight, and
she struggled to her feet, and she scooped the baby up, and
she held it against her bosom. It was cold, like a tiny rubber
doll, and Sarah sang to it, and carried it back and forth
along the shoreline for nearly an hour until the sun began to
droop on the horizon and Sarah's legs grew so weak she collapsed.*

Now Sarah became a robot.

*She worked in silence, as the sun set and the magic light of
dusk turned golden and soft. She found an ancient boat half
buried in the loam, its bow sticking out like a driftwood fos-
sil. An old empty wooden tackle box sat nearby, covered in
age. Sarah went over to the box, and she lay the tiny corpse
on the ground, and she wrapped it in rags. Then she
wrapped the rags in leaves. Then she wrapped the leaves in
strands of twine and old rope that she had found in the boat,
tighter and tighter. And she must have gone a little crazy, because she wrapped that dead child like a mummy.*

Mommy's little mummy.

*Sarah began to softly sing as she worked, her mind an
empty shell of pain. Tighter and tighter, she twisted the knots*

like the ends of a sausage. Then she put the package inside the box, nestling the tiny cocoon in a bed of rags and leaves. Then she gently closed the lid. The box had an old weathered buckle, and Sarah secured it tightly. Then she wrapped vines around it, vines and old hanks of twine, singing lullaby after lullaby. Vine after vine. Sealing the secret inside forever, the secret born of violence and magic and blood and chains, sealing it so tightly that nobody would ever know.

Sarah's little boy.

Then she went down to the water's edge and cast the box out into the lake.

The box floated and swirled buoyantly for endless moments, then slowly sank into the murk. And Sarah watched the little bubbles gathering on the oily surface, then fading away, the acid tears filling Sarah's eyes, the buzzing in her head throbbing sympathetically with the sounds of the forest, the unforgiving rhythms, the ancient locust-pulse mingling with the tremors of rage inside Sarah's soul, and soon something unexpected was happening.

On her knees, clutching handfuls of hair, sobbing silent cries of horror, Sarah felt the forest changing behind her. Opening. A vast carnivorous flower, blooming suddenly, its prehistoric poison-power erupting, sending brilliant black light into Sarah, into her back brain. Into her soul. And the sudden surge of energy, the ancient energy, was so abrupt, so galvanizing, that Sarah's breath was knocked cleanly from her lungs.

And her vision sputtered out like the flickering bubbles.

IV

"Oh, Jesus God," Sarah moaned, reaching out into the ripples strewn with the bones of her stillborn, the memory melting her veins and arteries until all the agony flowed through her as one great wave of pain.

In that one hideous instant of recognition, Sarah remem-

bered the whole ordeal as though it were a single long nightmare narrative buried by the light of day. She remembered
waking up a full twenty-four hours later, nearly dead from exposure, not even sure what she had done, or what had entered
her from the depths of that ancient forest. The gears of repression were already shutting down her memory. She remembered finding her way back through the woods to Jessie's
tawdry little bungalow, Jessie going berserk with anger at the
sight of her daughter, slapping Sarah silly for running away
and then seeing all the old blood caked all over Sarah's legs
and belly, and telling Sarah that she was probably experienc-
ing her first period and she should just shut up and go wash
herself. And Sarah had never consciously thought about what
had happened in those red pines ever again. She had buried
the box deep in the soil of her back brain, buried it in an unmarked grave.

"Sarah?" Henry's voice was breathless and taut. He stood in
the shallows behind her, fists clenching, the crackle of sheriffs'
walkie-talkies approaching from the deep woods to the south.

"It was *him*—Henry, it was—oh-*God!*" Sarah scooped up
a handful of the bones and brought them to her face,
smelling the coppery alkaline stench. Some of them were so
fragile they crumbled in her grasp, little white granules sift-
ing through her fingers and falling into the water. Sarah
buried her face in the bones and began to weep.

She wept convulsively, her snot and her tears and saliva
seeping down through the bones and her fingers, dripping onto
the water, the salt tears of grief mingling with the ancient lake.
Sarah wept for the wasted life she had spent secretly imagining how her son would have grown, what kind of little boy he
would have been, what kind of handsome, dashing young man
he would have grown into; she wept for the secret yearnings
that had been stitched through the fabric of her dreams her entire adult life, the codes and the cryptic symbols festering in
her brain; and most of all, she wept for the secret life that had
grown inside her, her brain the incubator, her pain the nourish-
ment; the monster child who lived in her flesh.

Something was happening.

Sarah looked up at the surface of the water and blinked. Her face felt cool all of a sudden, as though a great black film were peeling away from her flesh, as though a caul of voices and impressions and images were being stripped away. It wasn't painful exactly, although it carried a current of gnawing discomfort, like a nosebleed or a sunburn or a scab tearing off fresh pink epidural. Sarah took a deep, pained breath, her blood thinning.

"Good-bye," she murmured, not really knowing why, merely because she felt an incredible wave of loss flowing through her like an old, dirty river. And all at once she realized that this was the first time she had ever really said *good-bye* in her life. She had always detested the very *word*, and she never accepted those who said good-bye to her. But now, standing waist-deep in the terrible stew of her past, she felt it was time, it was time to say the dreaded word.

"Good-bye," she whispered again, and the noise in her heart finally died away.

V

"Sarah, your arms—look at your arms!" Henry took a step closer, his heart racing, his big boots sinking into the mire behind Sarah.

At first he couldn't believe what he was seeing. In the green half-light of the dying afternoon, Sarah was murmuring good-byes, letting the tiny bones slip through her fingers and tumble into the water. Her flesh had gone milky. Like frosted glass. A thin layer shedding snakelike into the water. Henry swallowed hard and gawked at the phenomenon. It was nearly indescribable, a white, gelatinous substance, a substance neither liquid nor solid, flowing off Sarah's fingertips.

Across the lake, a Range Rover burst through the foliage and skidded to a stop in the sandy clay. Doors springing open, and shotguns swinging out and cocking. Sheriff Dillihuddy emerged from the backseat, his head hastily bandaged, his expression sour and urgent. The sheriff raised a bullhorn to his face. "HOW 'BOUT YOU TWO KIDS PUTTING YOUR HANDS UP WHERE WE CAN SEE THEM!"

The amplified voice sent chills up Henry's spine.

He turned back to Sarah, and he saw the bones, the delicate little bones floating on the surface of the water around her like an icy wreath. "Sarah? You okay?" Henry took a watery step closer and reached out for her, but the moment he touched her shoulder, a spark of static electricity arced across his fingertips and sent him jerking backward with a start.

She was shedding an outer layer of flesh, flesh that wasn't really flesh at all, but a thin membrane of ectoplasm, like pale egg white, peeling off her in great reptilian strips, from across her face, down her arms, over her fingers, and even under her clothes as though she were molting. Henry gazed at it with rapt fascination. It locked as though a husk of a ghost were dripping off her fingertips.

"GODDAMNIT, I'M NOT GONNA TELL YA AGAIN!" The amplified voice was getting angry.

Henry raised his hands. "We're unarmed!" he shouted. "Don't shoot!"

But Henry couldn't tear his gaze from the ghost-flesh dripping off Sarah and flowing into the water. Henry was transfixed by the odd way it was flowing, not like an ordinary liquid at all. It seemed to drip *into* the bones, as though the ectoplasm were absorbing directly into the tiny infant skeleton. As though the bones were a poultice, drawing all the pain and poison of the past out of Sarah and into the forgotten world of the lake.

"Sarah, please," Henry whispered as gently as possible, "put your hands up before we both get cut in half."

The last of the ghostly substance dripped away.

"Good-bye," Sarah whispered one final time, and then raised her hands in surrender.

13

A Silence Eternal

Sheriff Dillihuddy ran the show, his left eye still throbbing under the bandage from his bout with Frank.

The cleanup took only a few minutes. Two deputies cuffed and shackled both the woman and the psychologist, and then put each of them in separate Rovers. The sheriff wasn't sure what role the shrink had played in all this, but the sheriff wasn't taking any chances. The calls had been flooding his switchboard all day, FBI, Chicago Homicide, the press, even some lady from the National Institute of Mental Health. Seemed like everybody and their brother wanted to know about this lady named Sarah Brandis.

They found Frank Moon barely alive, in the weeds over by a deadfall. Looked like he got hit by a bus. Major concussion. Fractured collarbone, jaw out of whack, teeth missing. Didn't bother Dillihuddy in the least; matter of fact, the old sheriff kind of wished he had been around to see that son of a bitch get decked by the shrink. What a sight that must have been. They took the detective out on a makeshift stretcher made of two logs and a length of fire blanket.

Dillihuddy secretly hoped it was painful.

"That's about it, Sheriff," the young deputy named Adams said as he strode up with his evidence bag tucked under his arm. He'd been gathering and dusting for the last ten minutes or so, and he hadn't found much.

"You get the shell casings from the detective's shotgun?" the sheriff asked.

"Yessir."

"Anything else?"

The deputy sighed and glanced across the water. "Thought I saw something when we first pulled up, floatin' on top of the water by the lady. Turned out to be nothing."

"Whattya mean?"

"Thought it was something, musta just been the sun glintin' off the surface."

The sheriff nodded, hiked up his trousers, winced at the pain in his eye, and started back toward his Range Rover. The deputy walked alongside him. A crow was cawing off in the woods somewhere, the sun setting on another Halloween. The sheriff raised the collar of his brown leather coat, and he pointed at the squad car slowly pulling away, descending the dirt grade back toward town. "You know somethin', I recognize that gal."

"The woman from Chicago?"

"Yeah, years ago, working guard out at the brewery, used to see her playing hopscotch all alone in the parking lot. Good kid, always seemed kinda sad."

They walked in silence for another moment, and then the sheriff paused by the door of the Rover. "Just goes to show," he mused, "you never can tell what's in a person's head."

The deputy agreed.

A moment later, they were gone, and other than a few tracks and a couple of chewing gum wrappers, it was as though they were never there.

And the forest fell silent once again.

And the silence was deep, and the silence was eternal.

EPILOGUE

Last Chance

The strange and buried men will come again, in flower and leaf the strange and buried men will come again, and death and the dust will never come again, for death and the dust will die.

—Thomas Wolfe
Look Homeward Angel

She finished the tea, set the cup on the windowsill, and turned to the final passage.

" 'Late in his career, after all the escapes, all the incredible feats of magic, the prodigy became obsessed with the paranormal. He became a psychic investigator, debunking séances and disproving psychic charlatans. But deep inside, the prodigy had always wished it were indeed possible to contact the dead. He wished to speak with his beloved late mother, and he eventually worked out an intricate code with his wife, Bess, so that in the event of his own death, he would be able to communicate with her from beyond the grave.' "

Sarah paused and looked up.

Henry was staring out the window, thinking. He hadn't said a word for what seemed like hours, ever since Sarah had started reading from the little antique book on Houdini. It was titled *Spirit in Chains* by Mortimer Longly, and was a thin little leather chapbook for young readers published by McFarland back in the late thirties. Once upon a time, the book had been in the Arkham Middle School library, but was pulled long ago by some irate parent wanting to banish all ugly reminders of the Abner Weed legacy. Last week, Sarah had stumbled upon the book in the Research Hospital's library, and was overcome by memories, as well as a strange sort of longing for vindication. She felt if she could share the biography with Henry, she would somehow be able to make better sense of the strange intersections that had ruined her life. Granted, Henry had already heard more than enough Houdini lore; but Sarah still felt compelled to share the very words she had read as a girl.

"You okay, Henry?" she asked finally.

"Absolutely," he said, turning back to her. "Question is, how are you doing?"

"I'm fine."

"You sure? You sure there's nothing I can get you?"

"I'm just fine, Henry."

"Then keep going."

Sarah gazed back down at the book. " 'Late in 1926,' " Sarah continued, " 'the prodigy was in his dressing room, chatting with some students. One of the students asked the prodigy if he would be able to take a hard punch in the stomach without being injured. The prodigy answered affirmatively, if he was allowed time to brace himself properly. The student asked for a demonstration, and the prodigy agreed. But before the prodigy had had a chance to prepare, the student walloped him in the belly. Again and again. The student had gone berserk, and several other students had to drag him away. The prodigy was seriously injured by the attack.' "

There was another long pause.

Sarah was sitting next to a bank of meshed windows at one end of an innocuous little lounge in the Knox County Mental Health Center. The sun was streaming through the mesh, stippling the floor. The room's institutional checkerboard tiles and fluorescent light fixtures and white stucco walls were counterpointed by Sarah's homey touches. A throw pillow here, a Tiffany lamp there, and of course, a framed lobby card of the Emerald City.

"Amazing," Henry said, getting up and stretching his sore knees. "Absolutely amazing." He strolled over to the window and gazed out at the rolling landscape, the scabrous crabapple trees, and the modest little town that lay beyond the high chain-link fences.

Galesburg, Illinois, was never going to be the Mecca of the Midwest that its city planners had once envisioned. A tiny sun-baked oasis peeking out of the vast sea of corn in west-central Illinois, Galesburg boasted no world-renowned international airports, no Big Ten universities, and no enormous, monolithic industries other than a network of small manufacturers and grain elevators. The economy had flattened out decades ago, and the citizens—mostly white-ethnic, middle-class—went about their banal businesses in their meager little four-wheel-drives, rust-pocked station wagons, and postwar brick bungalows. And yet, the little town had something special going for it that few others could claim: Call it *character*. The palette of the town was golden, golden fields of corn, golden sun hammering down on the golden clapboard barns and puffs of golden dust from the grain buildings.

Galesburg was a Brueghel painting come to life.

Situated on the north side of town, nestled in the rolling plains dotted with oaks and hickories, was a large innocuous brick building that most folks around town called the Research Hospital. Built shortly after World War II on state grants, the facility was one of the oldest state mental hospitals still in operation in this part of the country. It had several wings equipped for high-security, high-profile *guests,* which were mostly empty. Richard Speck once spent time here. As well as Kyle Hunting, the infamous nylon stocking killer. Ironically, over the last few years, the place had softened its procedures slightly. Spruced up its residence areas. Brought in family specialists and opened up new, somewhat politically correct wards. Drug rehabilitation programs, day-care centers, Gulf War veteran counseling, that sort of thing. As a matter of fact, at the moment, Sarah Brandis was the last guest left in the high-security ward, and she was practically a mascot for the men and women who worked the quiet shifts.

"One last section," Sarah said softly.

Henry turned and gazed into her eyes. "Go for it."

" 'The prodigy never recovered from the internal injuries of that attack. Eight days later, while on tour, he became incapacitated and was admitted to Grace Hospital in Detroit, Michigan. That night, with Bess at his bedside, and peritonitis spreading through his bloodstream, the prodigy sank toward his final hours. And with his last ounces of strength, he made Bess repeat the code words that he had worked out as a signal to authenticate that he was contacting her from beyond the grave.

" 'He passed away minutes later.

" 'In the years following the prodigy's tragic death, many attempts were made to contact his spirit, many of which were believed to be successful. But the prodigy's closest friends were always a bit skeptical. For they knew the single code word that the prodigy had worked out with both his mother and his wife, a single word that would be evidence of his authentic communication, a word that seemed to sum up the best of all human gestures and capture the prodigy's inner goodness.

" 'The word was FORGIVE, and the prodigy's name was Harry Houdini. The date of his death was October 31, 1926.' "

Sarah looked up at Henry for a moment, letting the words sink in.

"Halloween," Henry uttered, gazing at the dust motes floating in the afternoon sun.

Sarah smiled sadly. "Exactly."

A pause.

Henry turned to her. "Incredible. . . ."

"Yeah."

"Your psyche absorbed the Houdini legend like a virus, like an invisible scar." Henry thrust his hands in the pockets of his corduroy sport coat and shot a sad look at Sarah. The five years since the trial had not been kind to Henry Decker's face. His craggy eyes had sunken and now looked perpetually sad, like an old hound gazing out at the world from a front porch. His bulk had settled, his hair had gone completely gray, and his new goatee, which was the color of slate, only served to accentuate his sullen, academic demeanor. Nevertheless, his love for Sarah still flourished. It seemed impossible, but he felt as though he loved her more than ever.

The trial had taken its toll on both of them. Henry had to beg his old friend Jonathon Hicks to serve as an expert witness at the sanity hearings; and only after weeks and weeks of grueling testimony, including endless viewings of the macabre security-camera footage from South Park, did the judge agree that Sarah was not in control of her faculties during the killing sprees. The Other seemed to hang over the proceedings like a phantom, constantly being referred to in the third person, past tense, as though he were a real human being who had died in the revelation at the secret lake. And maybe he *was* a real person; the jury was still out on that one. But through it all, Sarah seemed at peace, quietly steadfast in her belief that she was innocent of the murders, and that the killer was gone forever. After the trial, she had been sent back to South Park for an indefinite period of warehousing; but Henry was relentless in his pursuit of her well-being. Although he had lost his license, he still held sway with some of the more powerful state medical administrators; which was precisely how he managed to get Sarah transferred to Galesburg.

Henry had chosen the little town for numerous reasons. It was far from the beaten path of Sarah's past. It was safe, and it was clean, and it was just right for starting new lives. And the hospital itself was more, shall we say, *hospitable*. Henry had worked there for about six months back in the late seventies as an admissions counselor, and the facility's director, an aging farm boy named Ebby Belden, had been a big fan of the Fighting Illini in the sixties when Henry was playing center for the team. Henry got Sarah admitted into the long-term high-security wing.

And then Henry convinced the state to allow him one last privilege.

On a rainy October night, almost exactly one year from the final showdown at the lake, Henry Decker asked Sarah Brandis to marry him. Sarah had said yes; in fact, she had said *yes-yes-yes-God-YES* through her tears, and they had embraced like children, and they had made love that night in the rainy darkness of Sarah's room, the shadows of security mesh striping their bodies. The staff had passed the word to leave them alone that night; and the next morning, practically everyone in the building, from the doctors down to the orderlies down to the janitors, had gone about their business with sheepish little smiles on their faces. A week later, Henry and Sarah were married in the facility's chapel. Dr. Jonathon Hicks was best man; one of the nurses was maid of honor; and the local Unitarian minister performed the service. It was the beginning of a new life for both of them, as well as a harbinger of extraordinary things to come.

"It's over now, Henry," Sarah finally said from her perch by the window, "he's gone."

Sarah's eyes were shimmering with emotion, her face still radiant in spite of the added lines and wrinkles she had picked up over the last few years. Her hair was longer now, longer than it had ever been, almost down to her lower back, full of heavy curls, shot with iron-gray streaks. She wore a long, loose-fitting muumuu, an African print, and sandals. In the last couple of months her weight had ballooned to almost a hundred and ninety, and it all seemed to swell around her matronly breasts, thick chin, and plump cheeks. In the diffuse light of the window, though, her beauty was luminous, baroque, as though she had just stepped out of a Rubens still life.

She closed the book.

"Ouch!"

"What is it?"

"Nothing, it's nothing," Sarah said, gazing down at her finger. The book's ancient binding was jagged at the top, and upon closing it, Sarah had punctured her index finger on the sharp corner. Now a scarlet spot of blood appeared in the center of her finger. Sarah gazed down at it intently, thinking healing thoughts, sending warmth through the digit.

The blood dried immediately, and the tiny wound puckered away to nothing.

Henry walked over to her, knelt down by her chair, and gently brushed a curl of gray from her eye. "You're not still nauseous, are you?" he asked softly.

"No, no, not at all—he's quiet today," Sarah said, softly smoothing the wrinkled cotton fabric over her swollen belly. She was in her second trimester, and the morning sickness was almost completely gone.

Henry put his cheek against her tummy. "The strong silent type, huh?"

"That's right."

"I talked to Dr. Bennaham last night," Henry said, straightening back up, touching her cheek. He was referring to Galesburg's favorite obstetrician. "He says all systems are still go."

"You still nervous about me being so old?"

Henry regarded her hair. "I would die if anything happened to you."

"Stop worrying, pops—I'm a natural-born mommy," Sarah said, and grinned a little wider, gently rubbing her tummy.

Henry lifted her hand from her belly and softly kissed each finger, one after another. "I love you, mommy," he whispered, "love you something fierce."

"Same back at ya, daddio."

Henry gently took the book from her and walked over to the door. "I'm going to return this to Margaret's book cart," he said, "and then I'm going to go down to the cafeteria and get you a big fat vanilla milkshake. What do you think of that?"

Sarah grinned. "I think you're pretty goddamned incorrigible."

Henry smiled, turned, and walked out, leaving Sarah alone in the sun-strafed silence, her hands cradling the curve of her belly.

She sat there for quite some time, thinking, feeling the warmth of another being inside her. For the first time in her entire miserable life, she was actually happy. She knew that this aging hospital was no place to raise a kid, and she wondered if the state was ever going to release their most notorious female serial killer back into society. But none of that mattered anymore, because Sarah had Henry, and Sarah had her sanity, and Sarah had the promise of her pregnancy, the promise of a child. She saw this pregnancy as a chance to finally get it right, a chance to be the kind of mother she had always dreamed of being. And what of this little life inside her? Into what kind of man would her son ultimately grow? She gazed out the window and regarded the gently rolling hills in the distance, the sun drooping low on the horizon, the long purple shadows of oak trees falling across the grounds, and she thought of Halloween, and she thought of the secret lake, and she thought of all that pain. It was already late September, and there was a hint of a chill in the air.

Sarah turned back to her easel.

An idea.

Such an obvious notion, such a simple idea, so perfect; Sarah was stunned it hadn't occurred to her before now. But then again, maybe it had been brewing deep inside her since last week, from the moment she had laid eyes on that fetal ultrasound, that strange little black-and-white image, that sweet little alien drawn in fuzzy X-ray squiggles. The fetus in the X ray looked like a little lump of clay. And all at once, it had dawned on Sarah—a way to help this little boy be great. A way to mold him, strengthen him, give him a thick skin that a child needs nowadays. A way to toughen him so that the cruelty of the world would slough off him like water off a duck.

A way to make him perfect.

Sarah shoved the easel aside and positioned her chair in front of the window.

The warm setting sun was on her face now, and she took a deep breath, calming herself, slowing her heart rate, steadying her nerves. Sarah began to breathe, slowly and steadily, a quick breath inward and a long breath outward, and she began to imagine the delicate little bones of her fetus, the texture of its rubbery, pellucid skin, the salty smell of its mucus, and the soft springiness of its unformed fingers and palms.

Then Sarah closed her eyes and started reshaping the little creature inside her.

ABOUT THE AUTHOR

Jay Bonansinga is an incorrigible vidiot who collects Chinese martial arts movies and resides with his film editor wife and three antisocial cats in Evanston, Illinois. The holder of a master's degree in film, he has made numerous award-winning short films and music videos. His short fiction has appeared in such magazines as *Grue*, *Cemetery Dance*, and *Outré*. His first novel, *The Black Mariah*, is being developed into a movie, and he is currently hard at work on a new novel, as well as a kung fu script that has been in development since before Christ left Chicago.